BROKEN BLADE

Kelly McCullough

ACE BOOKS, NEW YORK

THE BERKLEY PUBLISHING GROUP
Published by the Penguin Group
Penguin Group (USA) Inc.
375 Hudson Street, New York, New York 10014, USA
Penguin Group (Canada), 90 Eglinton Avenue East, Suite 700, Toronto, Ontario M4P 2Y3, Canada
(a division of Pearson Penguin Canada Inc.)
Penguin Books Ltd., 80 Strand, London WC2R 0RL, England
Penguin Group Ireland, 25 St. Stephen's Green, Dublin 2, Ireland (a division of Penguin Books Ltd.)
Penguin Group (Australia), 250 Camberwell Road, Camberwell, Victoria 3124, Australia
(a division of Pearson Australia Group Pty. Ltd.)
Penguin Books India Pvt. Ltd., 11 Community Centre, Panchsheel Park, New Delhi—110 017, India
Penguin Group (NZ), 67 Apollo Drive, Rosedale, Auckland 0632, New Zealand
(a division of Pearson New Zealand Ltd.)
Penguin Books (South Africa) (Pty.) Ltd., 24 Sturdee Avenue, Rosebank, Johannesburg 2196,
South Africa

Penguin Books Ltd., Registered Offices: 80 Strand, London WC2R 0RL, England

This is a work of fiction. Names, characters, places, and incidents either are the product of the author's imagination or are used fictitiously, and any resemblance to actual persons, living or dead, business establishments, events, or locales is entirely coincidental. The publisher does not have any control over and does not assume any responsibility for author or third-party websites or their content.

BROKEN BLADE

An Ace Book / published by arrangement with the author

PRINTING HISTORY
Ace mass-market edition / December 2011

Copyright © 2011 by Kelly McCullough.
Maps by Matthew A. Kuchta.
Cover art by John Jude Palencar.
Cover design by Judith Lagerman.
Interior text design by Laura K. Corless.

ISBN: 978-1-937007-08-9

ACE
Ace Books are published by The Berkley Publishing Group,
a division of Penguin Group (USA) Inc.,
375 Hudson Street, New York, New York 10014.
ACE and the "A" design are trademarks of Penguin Group (USA) Inc.

PRINTED IN THE UNITED STATES OF AMERICA

10 9 8 7 6 5 4 3 2 1

For Laura,
forever and always

Acknowledgments

Extra-special thanks are owed to Laura McCullough; Jack Byrne; Anne Sowards; my mapmaker, Matt Kuchta; Neil Gaiman for the loan of the dogs; and artist John Jude Palencar and cover designer Judith Lagerman for a truly amazing cover.

Many thanks also to the active Wyrdsmiths: Lyda, Doug, Naomi, Bill, Eleanor, and Sean. My Web guru, Ben. Beta readers: Steph, Dave, Sari, Karl, Angie, Sean, Laura R., Matt, Mandy, April, Becky, Mike, and Benjamin. My family: Carol, Paul and Jane, Lockwood and Darlene, Judy, Lee C., Kat, Jean, Lee P., and all the rest. My extended support structure: Bill and Nancy, Sara, James, Tom, Ann, Mike, Sandy, and so many more. Lorraine, because she's fabulous. Also, a hearty woof for Cabal and Lola.

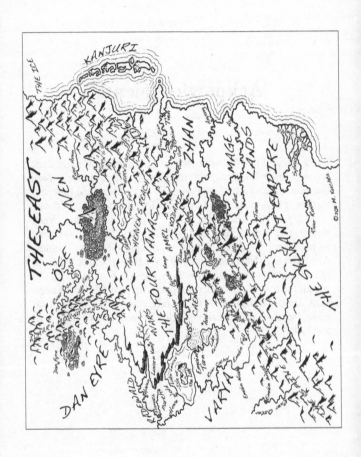

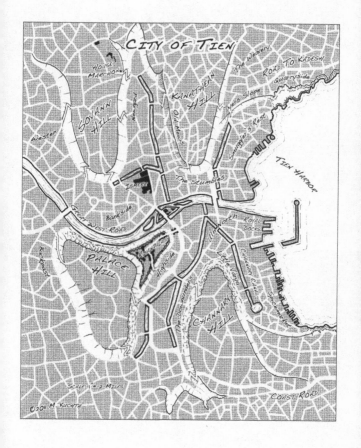

1

Trouble wore a red dress. That was my first thought when the girl walked into the Gryphon's Head. My second was that the dress didn't fit as well as it should for a lady's maid. It was cut for someone both bustier and broader across the hip than the current occupant. Not that she looked bad. The wrapping didn't fit right, but the contents of the package more than made up for any lack in presentation.

The poor fit of the dress was a definite puzzler. Red was the coming fashion for servants in the great houses of Tien, and while your average duchess might not give a cracked cup whether her servants' clothes fit comfortably, she cared enormously whether their looks reflected poorly on her. The fashion was too new for hand-me-downs, which meant the dress had to belong to someone other than the girl wearing it.

She turned my way and marched across the room without so much as a glance at the filthy straw covering the floor of the Gryphon's common room. Jerik, the tavern's owner, changed it out once a year whether it needed it or not, much to the annoyance of the rats and their more exotic magical playmates, the slinks and nipperkins. When I added her indifference to the awful things in the straw to the length of her stride and the set of her features, I had to revise that "girl" to woman though she was quite young.

"Are you the jack?" she asked when she reached my table. She leaned down toward me as she spoke, silhouetting herself against the only light in the room—a dim and badly scarred magelight chandelier.

"I'm *a* jack, and open to hire if you're looking for one." A jack of shadows, the underworld's all-purpose freelancer—how very far I'd fallen from the old days.

"I was told to look for Aral . . ."

She drew the word out almost into a question, as if hoping I might supply something more than my first name. It was a tactic I recognized from long, personal use and one I didn't much like having turned back on me. But if I wanted to keep paying my bar tab, I needed to work, so I nodded.

"Aral's a name I'll answer to, among others. Why do you need a jack?"

"First, let's find out whether you're the right sort for the job I have in mind."

Out of the corner of my eye I saw my shadow shifting slowly leftward as if seeking a better view of the young woman. I leaned that way as well, to cover the shadow's movements, and accidentally elbowed my whiskey bottle off the table. It thudded into the straw but didn't break. Not that it mattered. I'd finished the last of the contents twenty minutes ago. Which, in all honesty, might have had something to do with my knocking it over.

"Hang on a tick," I said, and bent to pick the bottle out of the moldering straw.

I took the opportunity offered by the cover of the table to make a sharp "no" signal to Triss with my left hand. I couldn't afford to let anyone notice my shadow moving of its own accord, not with the price on our heads—prices, really, as there was more than one interested party. And even this darkest corner of a seedy tavern had light enough for a trained eye to make a potentially fatal connection.

I swore silently at my shadow familiar while I returned the bottle to the table. *Cut it the hell out, Triss!* That was just frustration. If I didn't say it out loud, Triss couldn't hear me, and if I did, I might as well just cut my own throat and get it over with. The Shade did stop moving, but whether that was because of my hand signal or simply because he'd gotten an adequate eyeful, I didn't know.

I did give the woman a more thorough looking over myself at that point. Triss never pulled anything *that* obvious without a damned good reason. He owned the cautious half of our partnership. Besides, as noted earlier, the lady merited plenty of eye time on her own account.

Tall for a woman, perhaps matching my own five feet and eleven, and built and muscled more like a Zhani warrior-noble than the lady's maid her dress proclaimed as her station. Hair a few shades darker than my own middling brown and nearly twice as long, with a luxurious braid that reached just shy of her waist. Her eyes were dark though I couldn't tell the exact shade in the dimness that had originally drawn me to the Gryphon. More telling still, she had sword calluses on the inside of her left thumb.

That made the dress a lie for sure. It more likely belonged to her girl than to her. Which left me with an interesting question: Why, if she really was a minor noble of some sort herself, hadn't she simply had her seamstress do her up one that fit properly? But that was more a matter for idle curiosity than any real concern. I didn't much care where my jobs came from. Not anymore. Not if they paid enough to cover my bills. Besides, in the jack business, the client *always* lies.

The whole point of coming to a jack is that we don't belong to anyone and so don't answer to anyone. A sunside jack might find your stolen necklace for you without asking any of the inconvenient questions that the watch would be obliged to because of their allegiance to the law and the Duke of Tien. Questions like: *Where* did you get the necklace in the first place? Or *why* does it look so much like a necklace that was reported stolen by someone else last year?

On the shadowside, the questions we don't ask have even

sketchier answers. Why do you want me to steal that? What's in this box that needs to be delivered to a dockside location at four in the morning? How come Taurik Longknife isn't getting his cut of this little deal of yours? What did they do that you need them roughed up? Or, for a black jack, *why* do you want him dead? Sometimes the client supplied an answer anyway, but it was rarely an honest one. Not that it mattered. Mostly, I just don't want to know. That's part of why I became a jack in the first place. A jack doesn't have to care.

I *did* wonder about a couple of interesting little scars showing where my potential new client's neck met her right shoulder—but it was an idle sort of wondering. While I was studying her, she was doing the same with me. Judging by the slight crease between her eyebrows, she didn't think much of what she saw. She wasn't the first to make that judgment. She wouldn't be the last.

"Well," she said, after a moment, "what sort of jack *are* you?"

"Me? I'm a shadow jack, of course, but never a black one. I'll take risks if the money looks right and I'm not fussed about the law, but I won't ghost anyone for you. Not for anyone else either, for that matter."

I was done with the blood trade. Triss and I had long since sent our share of souls to the lords of judgment and their great wheel of rebirth. More than our share.

It was her turn to nod though the frown stayed. "I'm not looking for contract murder, just a bit of sensitive delivery service."

That was good and, if true, probably why she'd chosen me from among Tien's many shadow jacks. Courier work and its close cousin, smuggling, provided the bulk of my income these days. Shadowside, but not the deep dark. Few jacks anywhere could boast a better reputation for quiet deliveries, but then, I had Triss. And that was the sort of advantage that not more than a score of people in the whole wide world could boast.

"How much are you offering?" I asked.

"Don't you want to know the where and the what?" For the first time since she'd come through the door, my lady of the red dress looked knocked off her stride.

"Not really, or at least not until I find out whether it's worth hearing any secrets. Those always come with their own risks."

She pulled a small but full silk pouch from the depths of her bodice and dropped it on the table with a clank, tipping its mouth toward me. I picked it up and flicked it open. It was full of silver Zhani riels still warm from her skin and smelling faintly of lavender perfume. A thefty bit of cash, but not ridiculously so for the right job.

I set the bag back on the table. "Is this the whole payoff in advance, or the first bit of a half-now, half-later sort of arrangement? Or is it simply by way of showing me what's to be paid on proof of delivery?"

"This is a third down, with the rest on proof of delivery."

"It's dangerous, then?" I asked.

It had to be if she was willing to go so high before the haggling had even opened. Danger worked just fine for me. The longer the odds, the better you got paid and the less you had to work. And if someone ghosted you along the way, well, then you got out of working entirely. Nobody expects anything of the dead.

She shrugged at my question, then flipped her braid back over her shoulder when it fell forward. "It's only dangerous if things go wrong." Her eyes narrowed. "Do you object to *all* killing or just when it's the point of a job?"

"I try to avoid ghosting anyone when I can avoid it, but I'm no renunciate." My shadow moved again, and so, perforce, did I, leaning back this time, though mercifully without knocking anything over.

Dammit Triss, stop dancing around! It wasn't a big move, but even half an inch was half an inch too much. Too many people wanted to see my head nailed up over the traitor's gate or sent off to the Son of Heaven in a jar of rice wine. To distract from my little shadow two-step, I gestured for the woman to take the other seat.

"I'd offer you a drink, but . . ." I sadly flicked the empty bottle—Kyle's fifteen-year, the rather expensive Aveni whiskey I favored when I could afford it. It rang emptily and rocked, giving off a tantalizing little whiff of peat and honey. "So unless you're buying the round you'll just have to settle for going dry while you tell me what you want done, Lady . . . ?"

I gave her the courtesy title that might belong to a duchess's first maid in hopes of getting her to give up more information. She ignored the bait and shook her head impatiently.

"Call me Maylien." But she did not yet sit. "You *will* take my commission then?" She smiled a smug little smile.

That made me want to turn her down flat. Unfortunately, sending her away would leave my purse even flatter. If I wanted to keep drinking the good stuff, I had to work. And I wanted to keep drinking the good stuff. It was one of the few things left in my life that gave me any pleasure.

"Let's just say that I'm open to the idea," I said. "The fee looks adequate for some things, less so for others."

"I can't tell you more without some surety . . . of silence at the very least."

I raised an eyebrow at her. "If you've learned enough of my reputation to find me here, you've learned enough to know I don't discuss my clients. Not even my offers."

"May I presume that constitutes your word?"

"If you want to; though why you'd accept the oath of a jack of the shadow trades, I don't know."

She smiled like a woman holding a secret. "Most jacks I would not, but I've reason to believe I can trust yours. Have you ever heard of the Baroness Marchon?"

It took an effort not to start at that name, though perhaps a wasted one, since my shadow jerked a good inch on his own. I had, of course, heard of the Marchon, but I rather doubted that the person I'd chosen to become would have. Thinking daggers at Triss and his sudden tendency to jerk and start, I pasted a confused look on my face and shook my head. The gesture made the world bob and twist—a not wholly unpleasant side effect of the empty bottle.

"Is this Marchon a city noble? Or country?" I asked.

"More the latter than the former, but she does maintain a city house—a big estate right on the north edge of town, just off the royal preserve. That's where I need the delivery made."

I knew it well. The Marchon place had once housed the old king's last mistress, the younger sister of the then Baron Marchon. I had slipped into the house on no less than three occasions while trying to catch a quiet moment alone with the king.

"That's a neighborhood with an ugly reputation for the shadow trades, heavy security on all the estates plus the occasional royal patrol in the streets," I said.

Not to mention the fact that the Elite had a clandestine chapter house near there and watchers in the park most nights, but I certainly wasn't supposed to know that, nor how to slip past them.

I pushed the purse back toward her. "I think you'll have to find another jack."

She bit her lip in a quite convincing and quite fetching imitation of worry. I wondered how often she practiced.

"How about a bigger fee?" she asked. "I think I could come up with half again more if I had to."

I had just opened my mouth to tell her no, when I felt a tugging all along my back, sort of like peeling away a sweat-soaked shirt. Triss again, letting me know he wanted me to take the job for some reason. I didn't like the smell of the thing, or Triss's pressuring me on it, but I really did need money. I decided to push Maylien a bit and see how she responded.

"Half again *might* do," I told her. "But indulge me for a moment by biding here, won't you? I have an urgent matter that I need to attend to." I flicked my eyes in the direction of the back door and the sign marking the privies beyond and gave her a what-can-you-do sort of look.

It was a rude request under the circumstance, and she had every right to take offense, but I actually did have something that needed my private attention. Also, if she chose to see it as an insult and walk away, I would have solved my dilemma over whether to take the job.

Before she could answer, or do much more than blush angrily, I pulled myself to my feet and tipped her a ragged tradesman's bow—it wouldn't do at all to deliver the proper Zhani high-court version. Besides, I'd put enough whiskey away over the past two or three hours that I might not have been able to manage the more formal one if I'd tried.

"Back as soon as ever I am able, my lady."

A couple of lanterns filled with the cheapest oil money could buy guttered and sputtered in the yard. There was no risk of fire out on the cobbles, so no need for a magelight, which meant it was as dark out there as old King Ashvik's heart had been. Some of the noble neighborhoods could afford to use magelight to illuminate the main streets, but the Stumbles was about as far away from being a noble neighborhood as it got. On nights like this, with the moon near her nadir, even night-trained eyes like mine had trouble, and Jerik's lamps provided just enough illumination to find the privies.

I slipped inside, trading the stink of one sort of shit for the stink of another. Given a choice, I preferred the yard and the horse; but I needed the privacy. I closed the door behind me and wedged it shut with a thin knife pulled from the sheath on my left wrist. The light inside was better than the yard's, provided by a fading magelight nailed firmly to the ceiling— night-market certainly, but still costly. I presume the more expensive choice had been made because Jerik didn't like what happened when the drunks couldn't find the holes, and so he wanted to give them as much help as possible.

I turned a stern eye on my now much-clearer shadow, and demanded, "What are you trying to pull?"

Though my arms remained tight to my sides, the shadow's arms lifted and broadened into wings at the same time its legs fused themselves together into something much longer and narrower. Combine that with the way the head and neck respectively flattened and lengthened, and you no longer had a shape that looked even remotely human. In fact, were you to go by the form and movement of my shadow alone, you could be forgiven for making the assumption that I had become a rather small and agitated dragon.

My shadow, or rather the Shade that inhabited it, tilted his head to one side and shot out a long slender shadow of a forked tongue to touch my cheek. And that was Triss.

"I want you to take the job," he said.

I say "his" and "he," because Triss lives in *my* shadow, and I'm a man, though "its" and "it" would probably be more accurate, for what is sex to a shadow? His smoke-and-syrup voice reinforces the ambiguity, lying as it does midway between tenor and contralto.

"Why?" I asked him.

"Because you're broke and you're bored, and when you're working, you drink less."

I shook my head. "I'm not buying it, Triss. That's been true of the last dozen job offers, none of which made you break cover like you did with this one. That's dangerous. What if someone had seen you?"

Triss reared up. "Since when did you care if something was dangerous? I can't even count the number of times your frankly reckless attitude about the kinds of work we take has nearly gotten us killed in the last five years!"

"That's different. Killed in action on a job is a risk I've *always* been willing to take. Getting tumbled in a tavern and nailed to the traitor's gate or sent off to provide amusement for the Son of Heaven is a fucking amateur's death! Do you want that to be our legacy?"

"As opposed to what?" demanded Triss, his wings vibrating with agitation. "Killed while delivering a stolen painting to its buyer? You're not seriously comparing the risks of the last five years to dying on a mission from the goddess. At least if someone sells us to the King of Zhan or the so-called Son of Heaven, we'll be dying for what we used to be. Back before the fall of the temple, what we did mattered. We worked for a cause bigger than just getting paid."

"In case you hadn't noticed, Triss, the goddess is dead, murdered by her heavenly peers, and most of her servants followed her into the grave. The Son of Heaven pronounced the ban on our entire order. *Nothing* we do matters anymore and it never will again. The fucking gods themselves have decreed it through their official human mouthpiece."

"May he rot from within," snapped Triss.

I threw up my hands. "There is no *cause* anymore, just you and me and the work and getting paid. So we might as well hold on to our professionalism because we sure as hell don't have anything else left. Which is why I'd really rather not get taken down for the kind of mistake a rank amateur would make."

Triss's wings sagged. "Dead is dead, Aral. *How* doesn't really matter." Before I could answer, Triss contracted briefly—his version of an embarrassed shrug. "But I am sorry about moving around like that. I hadn't intended to be so obvious. It's just that this Maylien is more than she seems, possibly much more. It made me curious."

I sighed and accepted the peace offering. "I'm sorry, too, Triss. I know it's harder for you, always hiding in my shadow, having to pretend you don't even exist." I hated fighting with Triss. Far more than the work, he was what I had left. His friendship and love were what made me keep getting up and going on even when I no longer saw much point. "If you want me to take this job, I'll do it."

"Thank you."

"I'll go tell Maylien now." I reached for the dagger I'd used to wedge the door.

"It's wrong," said Triss, his voice barely above a whisper, "what the gods did to us, to the whole order. Their ban is wrong, and so is the Son of Heaven, even if he is the head of the high church of the eleven kingdoms. We should be free to return to the duties laid upon us by the goddess. I will never concede otherwise. Why have you?"

I looked away from a certainty I could no longer bear. "Because the unblinking eye of justice has closed, Triss. The goddess has gone into the grave, and the rest of heaven and all its priests are against us."

"If the gods truly approve of the actions of the Son of

Heaven, they're wrong, too. You've done nothing to earn such a ban. I've done nothing to earn such a ban. None of the Blades or the Shades who companioned them did anything beyond what was needful and just."

"That doesn't change the fact that every last one of us is under religious sentence of death and meat for any man's hand. Nor that the Emperor of Heaven himself struck down our goddess."

Triss closed his wings sadly. "If you cared so very much about living, I do not think you would have started to drink as you do."

I wanted to argue with him, but nothing I could say would make him any less right. Just then, something banged into the door from the outside.

A moment later, the handle began to rattle. "What the hell's wrong with the door?" asked a slurred voice.

"Nothing," I replied, "just finishing up."

Triss sank back into a reasonable semblance of my shape, and, a moment later, I stepped out into the night, pretending to fumble with the buttons of my pants as I went. I was actually glad of the interruption and glad of an excuse to return to the common room as well. If Maylien hadn't walked out yet, she'd certainly be getting suspicious about what was taking so very long.

"Well?" she asked when I got back to the table. Her lips were tightly compressed, and her tone was freezing. "Did your business go as it ought?"

"Near as needs be," I replied. "I am sorry about that, but it was a most urgent transaction."

She snorted, then, much to my surprise, smiled. "I suppose that we've all had to face such a need for haste on occasion. Now that it's passed, though, what do you say to the job?"

"Is the package small?" I intended to take the job but not before I'd gotten all the information I needed.

"Two sheets of folded parchment."

"Where does it have to be delivered?"

"There's a large balcony on the third floor of the Marchon

great house, around the back of the main building. You'll need to wait beside one of the windows—I'll tell you which. You'll meet the person the message is intended for there. And that's all you need to know until you accept the commission."

I still wanted to turn her down, but I had promised Triss. Besides, the money was very good, and Triss had it right—I was bored and I was broke.

"Two conditions." I tapped the pouch, which lay right where I'd left it. "Double the fee, and tell me where you got that dress."

"For the first, done." She reached into her bodice and pulled forth a second identical pouch along with two sheets of tightly folded and sealed parchment. It made me wonder what other treasures she might have tucked away in there. "The delivery has to happen tomorrow night, five minutes past the tenth hour bell. Wait by the fifth window from the right on the back balcony. The recipient will be there."

"At the Marchon city house?" I wanted us clear on terms.

She nodded and rose from her chair with a smile.

"And the dress?"

"Why, I stole it, of course." Then she turned and walked away.

2

Maylien had barely made it through the front door when Jerik slid out from behind the bar and came my way. He was a big man with a thick patch of scar tissue where his left eye and about half his scalp used be. When asked about it, he always pointed to the gryphon's skull hanging behind the bar, and said, "The other guy got it worse. I nailed his sorry ass to the wall."

"Work?" he asked me.

"Looks like."

"Pay up."

I tossed him one of the pouches. "Put half on my room tab and the other half toward the bar bill. That ought to pay both forward a bit."

Jerik glanced into the small bag and smiled. "That it will. Shall I get you a fresh bottle of the Kyle's?" He snagged the empty as he asked.

I really, really wanted to say yes, and I might have if not for the gentle pressure I felt rippling all along my back, where my shadow lay against my flesh, like dozens of disapproving centipedes marching angrily from my hips to my shoulders and back again. I shook my head regretfully.

"Not tonight, I'm afraid. The job."

Jerik shrugged casually and turned away. I might be done drinking for tonight, but he knew I'd come back whenever the work ran out. For the second time in an hour, I ducked out the back door into the dark of the yard. This time I went into the stables and up the ladder that led to the loft and the tiny room I'd been renting for the last two years.

There was no light above, just the musty-dusty scent of last summer's hay and near-perfect darkness. The hay made an unattended lantern too risky, and Jerik wasn't going to waste the cost of a magelight on the likes of me. Not that it mattered. I'd been trained by the temple priests to operate in the dark from the age of four, when they first took me for the order.

I made a show of fumbling with my key when I got to the door though I was alone and there was no light to see me by even if I weren't. The priests had taught me to *live the role*, a lesson quite as useful for my jack work as in my old trade.

While I scraped at the door with my key, Triss did the real work. Effectively invisible in the darkness, he climbed and enfolded my body, sheathing me in a nearly transparent layer of shadow, like a smoky second skin. It felt a bit like being wrapped in icy silk. Then he extended the portion of himself that covered my right hand, sliding a tendril of hardened shadow into the keyhole. Through our temporarily shared senses I could feel/taste the tumblers and the spell binding them as he twisted the extension of himself to release both.

The door opened with a barely audible click, and I slipped into the even darker room beyond, closing and locking the door behind me. It was a far better lock than the room demanded, Durkoth work and damned expensive. But I valued my privacy.

Reaching up, I touched a shadow-gloved hand to the

small stone globe I'd mounted above the door—its magic visible in magesight as a dim green spark. That released the spell of darkness binding a tiny but very bright magelight and illuminated my room. It was more the habit of a life-time's training that had made sure of the door before I exer-cised my power than any real worry about being discovered there and then.

Stretched thin as he was now, Triss did little more than darken my skin by the same degree a few hours in the noon sun might achieve. Of course, those who had been trained to observe might also have noticed that when I went clothed in shadow, I cast none, not even in the brightest of light. Fortunately for me, individuals with such training were exceedingly rare.

The small magelight revealed a narrow room tucked under the slope of the eaves, with my pallet wedged into the corner where steeply slanted ceiling met rough plank floor-ing. The only other furniture was a low table and, beside that, a small trunk that doubled as a bench. A tattered and much-stained rug prevented any glimmers of my magelight from leaking through the cracks between the planks to the stalls below.

Except for its shape, the room wasn't all that different from the cubicle the priests had given me at the temple complex all those years ago. Well, that and the fact that my old cubicle now lay under several hundred tons of rubble surrounded by acres of barren fields sown with salt by the forces of the Son of Heaven. I pushed the thought aside, but not without a sharp pang of regret at turning down Jerik's offer to bring me another bottle.

Triss squeezed me in a sort of whole-body hug, then relaxed onto the floor, taking his otherworldly senses with him and returning me the semblance of a shadow. If said shadow belonged to a small dragon, of course.

"Thank you for taking the job," said Triss.

I shrugged and knelt to rub a finger along his jawline—as always fascinated by feeling scales and warm, living flesh where my eyes showed nothing but shadow lying on a threadbare rug. Even in that shape, he had some substance to him. "You're all I have left, and you wanted me to. How could I deny you?"

The shadow of a dragon ducked his head abashedly. "I worried that the way she lied to you and concealed her magery might drive you to turn her away."

"Magery?" I closed my eyes and rubbed the lids for a long moment. "You didn't mention *that* part earlier, only that Maylien was more than she seemed. Perhaps you'd better elaborate now."

"I know she wasn't showing any visible spells, and I couldn't spot her familiar. But when she first leaned over you, her shadow fell across me and it tasted of mage gift— very recently used, or I wouldn't have been able to detect it." He cocked his head to the side thoughtfully. "She probably had her familiar wait for her outside, though it's possible she's allied with a lesser spirit of some sort, and it was simply invisible."

I suppressed a desire to growl at Triss. But we'd done more than enough fighting for one night. "Well, if she is a mage and a noble, it's no wonder she's hiding her familiar, whatever it is." Perhaps something that left scars on your shoulder when it perched there? A hawk maybe, or an eagle? But it really wasn't important. "The Zhani take a dim view of their peers using magic. They claim it distorts the whole challenge system of succession." Which it did, and that might explain why she had to come to me in disguise.

I sat down on my trunk and wished I had a drink handy. The last thing in the world I wanted was to get mixed up in Zhani high-court politics . . . again. I still had the scars on my leg and the price on my head from the last time, a decade ago. I massaged my temples.

"Triss . . ."

"I know. I should have told you. You're not going to back out of the job, are you?"

"No, I took her money, and it's not like I really expect clients to tell me the truth. You, on the other hand . . ." I sighed. "Next time you taste magic on someone's shadow, signal me secretly, and we'll go talk about it." We both knew he ought to have done so this time, but I let it slide—he's a willful sort of creature when he wants to be and quite possibly smarter than I am. "No more of this jerking around like someone poured a cupful of shadow ants into your shadow pants, all right? It makes you look like a twitchy tyro."

"I . . . You . . . I never . . . Hmmph."

Triss relaxed back into my shape, raised shadow hands to shadow ears like a set of antlers, then rudely wiggled his fingers at me, effectively terminating the conversation. *Gotcha.* I grinned and went to reshade the light. I'd need a solid ten or twelve hours of sleep if I was going to refill the wells of magic and be at my best for tomorrow's delivery.

I got up late in the afternoon and killed time while I waited for the sun to go down by alternating shadow-fencing with Triss and pretending to read a book I had "borrowed" from the Ismere, a wealthy merchant's lending library. It was a ridiculous adventure story set in the long-destroyed realm of the Necromancer, which used to lie on the northern edge of the mage wastes. I was so distracted by thoughts of Maylien as mage and wondering what her real game was that the words just flowed through my head without leaving any real imprint. I vaguely gathered there was something in this most recent chapter about methods for strengthening various breeds of the restless dead, but that was about all I got out of it.

When the sun finally fell within a handsbreadth of the horizon, I snapped the book closed with real relief and hurried back up to my little room. There Triss wrapped himself around me, and we opened the spelled lock I kept on my trunk—another bit of Durkoth work. The Other smiths were the best in the world though I couldn't afford any but their cheapest pieces.

From the inside I pulled a matched pair of battered short swords, straight-bladed and double-edged, with simple cross hilts and the blades darkened for night work. Decent smithwork, but not fancy and nothing like as good as the pair of curved temple blades they'd replaced. I checked their fit in the hip-draw double back sheath I'd had made to replace my old temple-supplied shoulder-draw rig. Then I set the whole on the pallet.

Working clothes came out next, and I put them on as I went. Shirt first, then loose trousers cut very full in the leg and tucked into soft knee boots, all in nondescript shades of gray—the sorts of things any Zhani peasant might wear. Crushing the oris plant made for an easy dye and a cheap one as long as you didn't want to concentrate it enough to make a true black.

A heavy belt with a short, plain knife went on next, followed by my broad, flat trick bag. Then my sword rig, with its straps and darkened steel rings for attaching other gear— left empty for the moment. Finally, I pulled on a dark green and much-stained poncho. It smelled of old wool and fleabane and came down far enough to cover the hilts of my swords. Over that I added a traveler's hood to complete the picture.

Triss watched quietly from the wall opposite the open window, content to sit where the westering sun put him though he did retain his dragon shape. After I finished dressing, I had only one task left before we could leave—reading the letter. I didn't trust Maylien, and even if I did, I wasn't about to walk into a job any more blind than I absolutely had to be. I set the folded parchment on my little table and pulled a six-inch strip of flexible copper from my trick bag.

"Triss, could you give me a hand?"

The little dragon flowed down off the wall and back along the fall of my shadow to puddle around my feet before slithering up my body and pressing himself tight to my skin. For work of this sort I needed very fine control, so Triss subordinated his will to my own, putting his mind into a sort of waking dream that tracked but could not direct our joint actions. His physical self—inasmuch as a shadow can be said to have such a thing—now moved to my commands, a necessary condition for most higher-order magic, which needed to be guided by a single will.

The mage and his familiar are like the swordsman and his sword. The swordsman makes the swing, but the sword delivers the killing blow. The raw stuff of magic, the nima, comes from the mage, power drawn from the well of his soul, but without a familiar to provide a way to focus and deliver that power, nothing happens.

I directed that part of me that was temporarily a thing of animate darkness outward, enclosing the thin metal tool in shadow and charging it with magic. In my magesight, the strip of copper took on a bright blue glow. Then I slipped it under the edge of the seal on the letter. Through Triss's senses, I could taste dye and bees and turpentine in the wax of the seal but no concealed magic, which made things simpler. With a tiny flash of power, I separated it from the parchment without hurting either.

Unfortunately, Maylien, or whoever had prepared the letter, had anticipated the possibility of seal lifting—one of the easiest of the gray magics. The exposed pages appeared as blank as if they'd come fresh from the stationer. That made exposing any message significantly harder. There were easily a dozen magical means of blanking the pages, ranging from a fairly simple charm of concealment up to a destruction-primed soul key, though most of those would leave some visible light of magic on the page. The wrong sort of spell could as easily wipe away what I wanted as reveal it, and I couldn't tell enough about this one to decide on the right approach. Time for a second opinion.

I released my hold on my familiar's will and tapped the parchment sheets. "Triss, what do you make of it?"

He slid off my shoulders and onto the table, shrinking into the shadow of a dragon perhaps ten inches from nose to tail. As I passed my hand back and forth between the sheet and the light, he spread his wings and flew across the surface in tandem with my motions. Then he settled beside the paper and extended a shadow tongue again and again until he'd tasted every inch. Finally, he shook his head.

"Not only can I not tell you *how* any words might be bound away from prying eyes, I'm not at all certain there's a real letter here to be read. The spell is either too clever, too strong, or too absent to unravel."

"That's what I thought, and I don't like it. Not even a little bit. It's magic out of proportion to the scope of the job, and more expensive by far than my courier fee. Though, if our Maylien's a mage, it's possible she managed it herself."

Triss shrugged. "Possible but unlikely. This is specialist's work, and I don't see a noble devoting herself to the necessary study. I wish I could show this to Serass or Malthiss or one of the other old Shades. They might have done better, and Serass in particular would have enjoyed the challenge. But they all faded into the great black when the temple fell." His wings slumped.

I ran a fingertip along the shadow of a spinal ridge from Triss's neck to his tail, but I had no soothing words for my familiar. Only shared pain at the loss of so many of our friends and fellows. Names slipped through my mind. Master Kelos, Devin, Sharl . . . beloved teachers, close friends, lovers, all gone, and with them their Shades, Malthiss, Zass, Liess. Triss and I were virtually the last of our kind. A four-hundred-year tradition would end with us.

I pushed anger and grief aside for perhaps the ten-thousandth time and resealed the letter, tucking it into my trick bag along with the copper strip. We had a job to do, and the prospect of action offered distraction if not comfort.

"Triss," I said.

"Yes." He didn't look up.

"We ought to go."

"You're right."

He relaxed into my shadow, his dragon shape fading into a dark mirror of mine. But only briefly. A moment later, he was flowing silkily up my body, covering me from toes to top in a soft skin of darkness. No sooner had he finished that transformation than he began another. This time he extended himself outward in every direction. As he grew in size, he became ever more diffuse, like cream stirred into a fine froth. By the time he reached maximum size, I could no longer feel him as a physical presence at all.

The blackness that enclosed me was absolute. I could see nothing and no one, and no one and nothing could see me. Not even with magesight, because the effect wasn't a spell. It was a part of Triss's nature.

From the outside we would appear as a sort of dark moving hole in the vision, a lacuna, like the blind spot some headaches bring. As long as I stayed away from bright lights and places where no shadow had any right to go, we could move about virtually unnoticed by normal eyes. And as long as I kept from using magic, magesight couldn't see us either. That was why we Blades so rarely made use of actual preset spells. The glow negated our biggest advantage.

It wasn't quite invisibility, but it was the nearest thing available and vastly superior to what any other order of mages could achieve. The powers of the familiar defined and shaped the powers of the master. A barely gifted hedge witch with a snake for a companion might be able to do a lot with poisons and potions, things that even a master sorcerer would find nearly impossible if he happened to be bound to a fire elemental.

I stood in the dark until Triss again subsumed his will to my own, giving me control over our joint actions and allowing me to take in the world through his senses. Though I had given up my eyes to the darkness, Triss now provided me with a sort of unvision tuned far more to textures and the interplay between light and darkness than the shapes and colors so central to human sight.

Through Triss's senses, I could feel the level of light in the room as almost a physical presence, a painful sort of pressure against the skin that faded away as the sun slid below the horizon and left Tien to the night and to those whose work required darkness. The housebreakers, the smugglers, the night watch, and me.

I opened the shutters over my window and slipped through onto the narrow ledge. Once I'd closed and set the spell-lock on the shutters, I leaped and caught the edge of the stable's tiled roof, pulling myself up on top. A spring breeze coming in off the sea made me shiver and briefly long for a warming drink in the tavern below, but I pushed the thought aside. Exercise would heat my blood faster than any whiskey and leave me feeling better the next morning to boot.

Standing astraddle the roof's peak, I ran through a series of quick stretches while I reset my expectations of the world around me to accommodate my enshrouded state. With the very different range of Triss's unvision distorting my visual picture of the city, I had to rely more on my other senses, and I wanted them operating at their peak.

The sounds of the streets below gave me clues about the immediate vicinity. A boot scuff could speak about cobblestones or packed dirt. The way it echoed and traveled said things about alleys versus wider streets or even open squares. The sudden flutter of a bird's wing might warn me of the arrival of another traveler in the chimney forest—a thatch cutter or burglar perhaps. Or, more dangerous, a hunting ghoul or some other strain of the restless dead. Though they mostly stayed out of the open, this moon-dark night would allow them more freedom to haunt the streets.

Smell provided a broader sort of map of the city. Here in the heart of the Stumbles, the odor of badly maintained sewers blocked out most other scents. Farther along, I would find spicy sauces designed to cover the flavor of elderly meat, which would in turn give way to the perfumes favored by the better-off merchants. And that would shift to the floral aromas of the ornamental gardens only the truly wealthy could afford.

Touch didn't matter as much up on the rooftops, but it might become critical if I had to move inside later, so I made sure to attune myself to the messages sent by skin and bones. I let myself really pay attention to the way the rounded ceramic tiles of the roof felt through my soft-soled boots, the roughness of my woolen poncho as it rubbed against the backs of my hands, the sharp cold touch of the sea breeze on my cheeks and neck.

Only after I felt fully settled within Triss's enshrouding darkness did I begin my run through the city's chimney

forest. Tien was ancient and had accreted rather than growing to any real plan. In most places, the roofs stood so close
together that I could actually pass more easily from place
to place on the chimney road than in the twisting and often
crowded mess of the streets below. Even when I hit the broad
canyon of Market Street, which separated the decrepit maze
of the Stumbles from the saner Dyers Slope neighborhood,
it didn't slow me much.

I simply spread my arms and had Triss spin himself into
great wings of shadow like sails. Then I took a run and
launched myself into space to glide across the open area.
Sail-jumping was more than a jump, if less than true flight,
and could be extended by magic if necessary or if you
weren't worried about being spotted. The one real drawback
of the technique was that there wasn't enough of Triss to
both enshroud me and make wings. For the brief seconds
of flight, I was exposed to watching eyes.

But that seemed a small price to pay for the joy of the
experience. It always made me feel fifteen again, when Triss
and I used to sneak out onto the temple roof at night just so
we could leap off the edge and make the long, giddy glide
down into the lake. When I landed on the far side of Market
Street, I felt a brief stab of jealousy for the birds. They got
to feel that way every day of their lives.

Racing across the rooftops with Triss made for a weird
dichotomy of experience, at once dual and singular, familiar
and alien, Shade and human. In moments like this, with my
familiar surrounding and overlapping me, we were more
one being than two, living within each other's skin if not
actually mixing our minds in the way some familiars did
with their companions.

The powers Triss wielded became an extension of my
will, his senses mine to use, and yet there was still a funda-
mental separation. It wasn't just that Triss floated in dream
while I controlled our conjoined bodies. The Shades inter-
acted with reality in a manner wholly alien to human experience. Even if Triss could have approached the melding of
our beings fully awake and aware, we had no common frame

of understanding. If we wanted to share thoughts or even the sort of simple abstract ideas that a human familiar-bound to a cat might have easily managed, we would always have to resort to speech.

Twice more as we moved across the city, we had to cross a too-broad gap, and I got to be a bird for a few shining seconds—both times for canals coming off the Zien River. The nearly three-mile run took us from the ugliness of the Stumbles to the skirts of the Sovann Hill and up along the western edge of the carefully crafted faux wilderness of the royal preserves. There we had to descend to ground level for the first time.

It was the long way round. If I'd wanted to make my way along the east side of the park, I could have gotten much nearer my target before I left the shelter of the rooftops, but that would have brought me very close to the secret chapter house maintained by the Crown Elite. Not the sort of risk I wanted to court under any circumstances. Alternatively, I could have stayed concealed by taking to the sewers then, but I preferred to avoid shit's highway if I possibly could, and I didn't see the need here.

Making my quiet way across the parkland to the Marchon estate seemed almost childishly simple, needing little more than the occasional freeze in place when routine patrols passed by. In this one thing, the death of my goddess eased my way, for most believed that the fall of her temple had destroyed or driven into deep exile all of my kind. That meant that certain measures the patrols might once have taken had been much relaxed in recent years.

And why not? Though it hurt me to think it. In the five years since the fall of the temple, I had seen only one other of the Blades of the goddess alive, and Kaman had been nailed to a cross, with his shadow staked to the ground at his feet. When I offered to try to free him, he spat at me and cursed the goddess's name before begging me to make an end of him. I'd used an arrow from a distance and spent the next month playing a game of death tag with the Elite who'd hung him up there.

A ten-foot stone wall surrounded the Marchon estate. The wall was far too long to ward or guard effectively, but the owners had done what they could. It had shards of broken pottery set edge up along the top to deter human intruders, along with sprigs of dried mistletoe to keep out the restless dead. Silver nails would have answered better for that second purpose, but those tended to be stolen faster than they could be replaced, even in this sort of neighborhood. They hadn't bothered with slivers of iron, though I expect I'd have found those at the Marchon country house, where the creatures of wild magic posed a greater threat.

Getting over the top unharmed drained a bit more of my nima away as I had to use a minor sort of spell to protect me from the sharp edges. The baroness had dogs roaming the grounds, big vicious brutes who hunted as much by scent as sight. Triss's enshrouding presence was no help there, but I only met four, and in each case a snoutful of hollowed robin's egg loaded with powdered opium and efik worked the trick nicely. I made a mental note after the last to use some of the funds from this job to buy more of the finely ground and very expensive powders needed for their making. The slender brass case I kept them in was nearly empty.

Like most freestanding great houses, the Marchon place was built more than half as a personal fortress. It had no outward-facing windows on the ground floor, showing the world a blank limestone face. A dense hedge of imperial bush roses grew tight against the building as a further defense, with climbers growing up the wall as far as the second story. That cost me in blood lost to thorns, and I wished I dared use magic to push them aside, but the heavenly smell of fresh blossoms paid for at least some of the pain.

The third-floor balcony was broad and deep, supported by four thick columns faced with slick marble. Had I climbed one of those, I could have avoided the roses but only at the cost of facing an overhang deeper than I was tall—far more trouble than it was worth. Especially since the decorative stonework at the corner of the building was more than half a ladder for my purposes. So I went up the corner and across the top of the second-floor windows to the edge of the balcony, where I froze for several minutes while I checked the current state of things against my memories from earlier visits.

There I found more roses, some on a central trellis that would serve to provide a shaded area for dining outside in the brutal Tien summer, others scattered about in planters of various sizes. These were of more gentle varieties than the vicious imperials of the guardian hedge below. When you combined the roses with a small grove of decorative oranges that topped out just below the level of the balcony, the overall effect was of a floating garden sailing on a sea of blossoms. Quite lovely, even in the dark, and much as I'd remembered it. But I wasn't there for the view, so I soon slipped over the railing and crossed to the small window where I was supposed to meet the recipient of the letter.

I'd just lifted a hand to check the latch when the balcony doors opened behind me spilling light across the marble floor from the chandelier within. Quickly and quietly, I took three long steps and dropped into a crouch within the deeper shadow offered by a large stone planter. I was almost relieved at the interruption. Until then, the job had been far too easy to justify the fee I'd been offered though a jack without Triss's help might have found it a much more difficult task. Combine that ease with the too-expensive magic used on the letter, and it made for a very suspicious package.

As I settled in to wait and find out what might come next, I relaxed my control over Triss so that he could observe as well. Though I maintained a low-level contact with his mind that allowed me to use his senses along with my own, I wanted a more complete picture. So I drew one hand across my face, signaling Triss to thin the shadow veil enough for me to see with my own eyes.

A couple of red-clothed footmen came out through the open door with seat cushions and a cloth for the table and chairs sitting under the shelter of the trellis. Though they maintained the impassive expressions expected of servants to the high nobility, the hesitance of their bearing expressed a certain amount of bewilderment. Who could blame them? It was late and oppressively dark and growing steadily chillier, a strange time indeed for such a one as the baroness to be taking the air.

I didn't recognize her beyond the insignia on her chain of office and the cut and fabric of her clothing. As a noble, she wore the divided skirts and loose shirt that would allow her to instantly defend her seat if duel-challenged by a rival. She had a heavy gold chain around her neck supporting a medallion of office with the Marchon insignia of a jade fox on a gold background. She was not atypical of the breed, tall and broad-shouldered, with the muscles of one who visited the salle daily.

True black hair and an unusually plain face were the only factors that distinguished her from seven-and-seventy other ladies of her standing, though not recognizing her face came as something of a shock to me. There had been a time not all that long ago when I could have identified every major noble in Tien and nine other kingdoms at a glance. But then, she was obviously quite young and probably only recently risen to the peerage.

"Bring the drinks and a small light, then go away," she called in a voice deeper than I'd expected.

The servants did as they were told, adding a tray with two steaming pots and cups to match as well as a dim red magelantern that was only just a hair brighter than a thieves-light. Then they closed the doors, cutting off the brighter light from the room beyond once again. That left only the lantern to fight the darkness and made me much more comfortable. The thin layer of shadow-stuff over my eyes would prevent them from reflecting much light, but not all of it. If I wanted to see, I had to risk being seen.

With her back to the house, the baroness settled in to wait, occasionally sipping at her tea. I could probably have tried for the window again then, but curiosity held me. Who was she waiting for? And how did she expect them to arrive? Even without the second pot, there was no question she was waiting for someone, and very impatiently at that—every line of her body told the same tale.

I wasn't terribly surprised when I heard an almost imperceptibly faint rustling in the roses below a few moments later. I shifted my position slightly to give me a better view of the far corner of the balcony—the same place I had come up and the most logical entrance for a climber.

I don't really know who or what I was expecting, but it was not what I got. For what seemed an awfully long time after the rustling stopped, nothing happened. I was just beginning to think I'd dreamed the whole thing up, when a man appeared in the seat across from the baroness, looking for all the world like he'd been there all along. He nodded casually at the baroness as he picked up a cup and reached toward the second pot.

"Devin, you're very nearly on time," said the baroness, her voice harsh. "However did that happen?"

She probably saved me from betraying myself then, because I'm sure I gasped aloud in the same moment she spoke her piece. That noise was all that prevented Devin from hearing me. Never in my life had I regretted more the way that Triss's assumption of shroud form made it virtually impossible for him to communicate with me. In that shape, he couldn't even give me the sorts of squeezes and prods he indulged in as my shadow, though I could tell by the way he focused his attention on Devin that Triss was every bit as shocked as I was to find him here.

Devin!

I wanted to shout that name aloud, to leap up and hug the man it belonged to, a man the temple had raised me to think of as my brother. Even in the dim light, I couldn't possibly mistake the familiar features, the Blade-trained bearing, the well-worn sword hilts jutting out above his shoulders.

But Devin was dead. Along with so many others, he had died when the temple fell. At least, his name was carved with all the others into a great granite obelisk in front of the ruined temple. The Son of Heaven had ordered the stone erected to commemorate the triumph of the forces of heaven over the "self-declared goddess of justice, rogue of heaven, and her twisted cult of regicides and priest-murderers."

There had been over five hundred names carved in that stone, priest and Blade, novice and master. Of all the servants of the goddess, fewer than two score had escaped the list of the dead, and every one of those names had appeared on the posters that declared the ban and offered a reward for our heads.

That as much as anything was what had convinced me that heaven really had turned against my goddess, that every last name was there. The complete roll of the Blades was a secret known only to full members of the order and to a few of the highest priests, and we were all bound by mighty oaths and deadly magic never to reveal it. But there we all were, our identities exposed to the world by divine fiat.

Devin Urslan was dead, his name set forever in black granite on the tombstone of an entire religion. Yet here he sat, with a high noble of Tien calmly pouring a cup of tea— no. Efik. The rich smoky scent rolled over me as he poured, and I felt a moment of intense longing that I reflexively suppressed. That life was gone forever, murdered by the Son of Heaven and his gods. But then, so was Devin.

I couldn't seem to make my mind deal with the contradiction of Devin both dead and buried and alive and drinking efik. But where thought failed me, temple-taught discipline took over. Aral the jack vanished, and I reverted to Aral the Blade.

The priests and teachers who had molded me into a living weapon for the hand of the goddess had set out to create a tool that could do its job in the most confusing circumstances and under the worst conditions. Routines set as deep as my bones took over.

Stop. Assess the situation. Act decisively.

And so, rather than rushing to embrace the brother I'd believed lost, I listened and I waited. The time to act would identify itself.

3

"**B**aroness Marchon, you're as lovely as ever. And," Devin paused and took a sip of his efik before continuing, "if anything, your manners are more charmingly direct than I remembered."

The baroness looked as though she'd been slapped and, well, she had been. "How dare you! You're nothing more than a filthy peasant with an overdeveloped sense of his own—"

"Do shut up, Baroness, and remember what I am." Devin's voice came out smooth but firm, cutting across her diatribe. "Our contract doesn't cover bowing and scraping, and I don't have the time or the patience to pretend that it does. Your noble blood doesn't impress me a whit. Zass and I have spilled bluer on a number of occasions, and, frankly, it all looks the same when it's leaking into the dirt."

He took another drink, wafting the scent of the efik my way. I drew in a slow, deep breath through my nose—good beans steeped just long enough. How I missed that.

The baroness was snarling, "I . . . You . . . How could—" But she stopped abruptly and straightened her spine before nodding ever so faintly and regally. Her voice when it came again was icy cold and perfectly contained. "I see. Thank you for the reminder of why and for what I hired you, Assassin. In return, you ought to remember that casting no shadow puts you under one. The temple of Namara is a smoking ruin, and your goddess is as dead as you are purported to be. The proscription of Namara's Blades is quite clear about—"

"Ssst," said Devin, raising a hand and cutting her off for a second time. As he spoke, he stood, pulling a short, curved sword from behind his shoulder with his other hand. "We're not alone, Baroness."

I wasn't sure what had betrayed me, probably a sharp breath drawn when the baroness had spoken the name of the goddess. It had been years since I'd heard or said her name aloud. For me it hurt less that way. For others . . . well, what was the point of calling on a dead goddess?

"I know you're here." Devin carefully scanned the area, and I ducked my head to hide my eyes. "Whether you're a simple burglar, an eavesman, or follow some other flavor of the shadow trade, you can't hope to hide from me. You heard what the baroness just said about my shadow, and you know what it means, or you wouldn't have given yourself away then. Will you come out so we can discuss this in an amicable way, or will you declare yourself my enemy by remaining in hiding?"

What to do? It was the hardest question I'd faced in years and one where my training couldn't help me. Part of me still desperately wanted to talk to Devin, to embrace him as a brother returned past all hope and from beyond the grave. But the time that ingrained discipline had given me to think had raised too many questions.

How *had* Devin escaped the fall of the temple when so many others had not? Why, if he had, was his name on the list of the dead and not beside mine with the proscribed? I didn't want to believe that someone I'd trusted might have betrayed the goddess, but what other explanation was there? For that, or for his presence here and in such company for that matter?

The young baroness, with her contempt and her talk of filthy peasants and the hiring of assassins, was exactly the sort of unjust authority Namara had created the order of Blades to address. To find Devin, who'd once killed corrupt generals and deranged duchesses in the name of the goddess, working for such a creature . . .

But was I really so much better? I might not kill for money, but I'd taken my own goddess-trained talents and gone into business as a shadow jack, smuggling goods and letters, playing bodyguard to thugs and jackals, even the occasional bit of contracted theft when I got broke enough. I didn't know what to think or do.

While I crouched there, paralyzed with indecision, Devin drew his second blade. As it came free of the sheath, I looked up and caught a flash of the lapis-inlaid oval of its guard shining like a blue eye forever open—the unblinking eye of justice. It was the message I needed. For me, Devin must remain as dead as if I'd buried him myself, one more part of a past I'd left behind forever.

I might have made a wreck of my life that mirrored the wreck of the temple, but I'd done it without turning the blades of justice into murderer's tools. My swords rested now on the bottom of the sacred lake whence they had come. A weighted bundle that held my every image of the unblinking eye had gone with them. I might ply the shadow trades to keep body and soul together, but I refused to carry any token of the goddess while I did so. I refused to pretend that I was anything other than the petty shadow tradesman I had become or pretend that the goddess would have approved.

Training took over again. Once you have decided to act, act decisively.

I signaled to Triss that we needed to move, and he ceded control back to me. Slipping a black coil of silk line free of my bag, I dropped a loop over the stone planter I'd chosen as my hiding place. Then, as Devin dashed toward us, I took two long steps and leaped over the front of the balcony—putting me clear of the roses. Were it not for a thickened patch of the stuff of shadow acting as a glove, I'd have badly burned my hand on the rope when I used it as a friction brake on the way down.

In the instant my feet touched the ground, I let go the line and started into a gentle lope. I knew that Devin was right behind me. If I wanted to give him the slip, I needed to get as far away as possible as quickly as possible, and I needed to do it without breaking into the kind of hard, noisy run that would allow him to follow me by ear.

Focusing on the task helped me ignore the mad tumble of emotions that kept trying to suck me under. Though I couldn't read specifics from Triss, I could feel weird and wild echoes spilling over from his dreams that suggested an even-more-turbulent state of disorder than my own.

As I hurried along, I made several sharp changes of direction in the hopes of further confusing things, but I always kept moving toward the nearest corner of the estate. At another time, I might have chosen to hide within the grounds and wait for the pursuit to move out and away from the center of things, leaving behind a void I could exploit. But the combination of having a major contingent of the Elite so close and the unknowns represented by Devin's presence decided me against the idea in this case.

The outer wall was in sight, and I'd just started to breathe a little easier when I crashed headlong into another of the baroness's dogs. An opium-and-efik egg smashed across his nose put him out of the game a few seconds later, but not before he'd made noise enough to betray me to someone with Devin's training.

That left me a major dilemma. To get out, I had to get over the wall. Since the estate was properly maintained for security, there were no trees close enough to the wall to jump from unaided by shadow wings, which meant dropping my shroud. If I wanted to maintain my lacuna of shadow I either had to climb out at the corner, where I could brace myself in the angle of the stonework and vault over the pottery shards on top—my original intent—or I had to use the same sort of magic I'd used to get in. If Devin was close by—and I had to assume that he was—I couldn't do either undetected, and we both knew it.

Climbing the corner would make more than enough noise to allow Devin a free shot with dart or blade, and the active use of magic was visible to any practitioner who cared to use his magesight. That was a large part of what made the enveloping darkness Triss and his fellow Shades could offer so valuable. It was passive and innate to the breed, a near invisibility that would baffle even the eyes of a mage.

Moving a few yards away from the place where I'd left the unconscious dog, I put my hands on the hilts of my swords and settled in to listen and wait on Devin's next action. I couldn't afford to give him very long—no more than a couple of minutes—but I didn't want to attack him without giving him the chance to choose another way.

Several seconds slid past. If he hadn't been close before, he certainly was now. More time. Perhaps a minute. I silently slipped the loops that held my swords tight in their sheaths. I needed only to move my hands down a few inches more, and they would drop free.

Devin spoke then, his voice coming from a point some yards off to my left. "I don't know who you are, but I know what you are, Blade of Namara."

No one had called me that in years, and until that instant I'd had no idea how much that hurt me, nor how much more it would hurt to hear it now. I had never in my life felt a stronger desire to kill than I did then. If I'd had the slightest idea who it was I really wanted to kill, I don't think I could have stopped myself from making the attempt. As it was, my knuckles burned from squeezing the hilts of my swords so tight.

"Actually, that's not quite true," said Devin. "I may not *know* who you are, but I bet I can make a very good guess. Let's see, you're no apprentice assassin."

I had to suppress a hiss at that. "Assassin" wasn't normally a word a Blade used when referring to his fellows— however true it might be.

"An apprentice I'd have caught before they made it off the balcony. I don't think you're one of the escaped journey-men either, not having gotten this far running free, though that stumble with the dog was very sloppy tradecraft. There are only four masters that are yet unaccounted for. Jax and Loris both refused the bargain the Son of Heaven offered to those that survived the fall of the temple. They called those of us who took the deal *traitors*."

Deal? What deal? I knew nothing of any deal.

I wanted to shake Devin and make him answer that question, but I knew that moving against him physically would only stop the flow of information. I wondered, too, how the pair could both have been captured and yet remain unaccounted for, and played out what I knew of them in my head. Loris was of the previous generation, and I didn't know him well, but I'd always liked Jax, who was a year or two younger than I. She had a good head on her shoulders.

Devin continued, "Though they later escaped, they both spent a certain amount of . . . time with the Hand of Heaven first. I think either of them would have moved to kill me rather than running."

In that moment, I regretted that I hadn't. The Hand provided the Son of Heaven with his enforcement arm, which included a lot of torture and burning of heretics. I didn't move. Devin knew things that I wanted to, and he was still talking.

If your enemy is doing what you want, don't interfere.

"That leaves Siri and Aral," he said, "the shining stars of my generation. Both in the field at the time of the fall. Which are you, I wonder, my former sister or my lost brother? Mythkiller or Kingslayer? In either case, a potential adornment to the new order of the Assassin-Mage."

This time I did hiss. A mistake.

Devin chuckled in response. "Oh, I didn't like the name much the first time I heard it either, but it's a hell of a lot more honest name for what we are than 'Blade' ever was, and it grows on you if you live long enough. I'm going to make you an offer. If it will make you feel better, you can choose to believe that's because I don't think I can take whichever of you I'm talking to in a fight. And you might be right, or then again, you might be surprised. It makes no difference to me what you believe. What matters to me is what you decide.

"Those of us who took the Son of Heaven's deal have moved on from the ruin of the temple. We had no choice. The goddess really is dead, and there's no bringing her back. The Blades of Namara are gone forever. But that doesn't make us a spent force. We still have the Shades and the skills we learned from the temple. We can take on new apprentices, teach the assassin's arts, summon more Shades from the everdark. We have the potential to be one of the most powerful mage orders this world has ever seen. To rule from behind every throne."

And to betray everything we ever were. I slid my swords free of their sheaths and rolled my shoulders. I didn't want to kill an old friend, but I couldn't see any other way out.

"I know I speak for the order when I say we'd love to have you with us," said Devin. "I won't demand an answer this instant, but we can't afford to leave you running loose for long if you won't side with us. You have forty-eight hours from this moment to decide. If you want to join the future, send a note for me here care of the baroness. If you insist on remaining a part of the past, we'll have no choice but to make sure your name is added to the list of the fallen. Good-bye for now."

The time for words was over.

I started toward the place where I thought Devin's voice was coming from but had only taken a couple of steps when the world came apart with a blinding flash and a tremendous boom. For a good ten seconds, I couldn't see anything but a lavender pattern of branching lines left on my retinas by one of the most violent bursts of magelightning I'd ever encountered. It was well beyond what Devin should have been able to manage without a more formal spell. If he'd wanted to kill me then, there's a good chance he'd have managed it. Instead, he vanished, leaving me alone beside the giant hole he'd blasted in the baroness's wall.

I briefly contemplated looking for him, but I had no doubts that the display was going to draw a lot of the wrong kind of attention, including the Elite. Promising myself that this thing with Devin wasn't over, I slipped out through the hole in the wall and headed back toward the city proper.

I picked up a bottle of Kyle's as I passed through the Gryphon on my way back to my room over the stables. It had been an excruciatingly long and nasty night, and I really needed the drink. I set the bottle carefully beside a borrowed glass on my little table before I started to strip off my gear.

Triss flowed up the wall and into dragon form. "I don't think that's such a good idea."

I yanked off my hood and dropped it on the pallet. "I do. In case you weren't paying attention back there, my old friend Devin's become some kind of fucking assassin for hire along with who knows how many of the others. Not to mention that he wants us to join him in his abomination. If that's not the best reason for getting drunk this side of Namara's murder, I don't know what is."

Triss let out a loud, hissing sound and reared back, but didn't say anything. The purpose of a Blade of Namara was to bring a just death to those who deserved it. Killing was part of our job, and both Triss and I had once been damned good at it; but even the idea of doing it for money seemed the most horrible sort of perversion of what we had once been. I shrugged out of my poncho, throwing it down beside my hood. As I unbuckled my swords, I nodded toward the trunk.

"Open that for me, would you?"

Triss slid down from the wall and briefly covered the trunk in shadow. With a sharp clicking noise, the lid popped open. I flipped the poncho from bed to trunk with the toe of my boot. It landed in a lump guaranteed to leave creases. The hood followed, then my shirt.

"You normally put your swords on the bottom." Triss's voice came out quiet and worried.

"Fuck normal." I grabbed my sword rig off the bed and rebuckled it over my bare shoulders. "In fact, fuck every-thing."

"What are you doing?" Triss sounded more than a little alarmed as I crossed to the door.

I didn't answer, just grabbed the handle and wrenched the door open. Triss dove back into my shadow as the mage-light threw it across the floor of the hayloft. As I strode over to the hay pile, my shadow slid across the trapdoor that led down to the stables. When it did, one dark arm stopped mirroring my own movement long enough to flip the door shut—a sensible precaution on Triss's part though I barely registered it.

I pulled a half dozen of the rough bundles of hay free of the pile, and started leaning them against various of the roof posts. Two fell apart at once when the dried loops of braided grass that held them together for transport to the city gave way under my rude handling. The others held, more or less. I added more, putting a couple along the walls and two against the hay pile itself.

Stepping out into the middle of the big open room, I rolled my shoulders and fixed the positions of the bundles in my mind. A deep breath in, and . . . I let the rage free with my breath. Seemingly of their own accord, my swords dropped into my hands and flicked out, the left taking off the top of a hay bundle in a beheading stroke, the right going home in a heart thrust that sank the tip deep into the post behind it. Pivot and wrench my right blade free while back-cutting with my left to split the beheaded bundle. Stomp and cross swords in a blade-breaking parry. Turn, lunge.

I sliced and chopped and parried and thrust until every bundle was destroyed. Until the sweat rolled down my sides, and the air grew thick with chaff. Until I could barely breathe for coughing. Until my eyes streamed tears from the dust, and I could no longer see Devin's face even in my imagination. It wasn't enough.

With a snap of my wrist, I sent one sword flying down the length of the loft to embed itself in the door of my cubby. Then the other. An utterly useless little trick and suicide in combat, but it felt good, and it freed my hands to collect more bundles. When I was done, there were no more bundles, just a big loose pile of hay and a thick cloud of dust, like smoke. And it still wasn't enough. So I cleaned and resheathed my swords and closed myself up in my little room and reached for the bottle again.

And again, Triss said, "I don't think that's a good idea."

And he was right. So when I twisted the cork stopper free, I only poured two fingers into my glass and sealed the bottle again. Then I knocked back the whiskey and set the glass aside. My poncho came back out of the trunk and got folded properly on the bed. My hood and shirt, too.

I put my swords neatly away beside my knives and laid the trick bag down on top. That's when I remembered the letter and my failed courier's commission. Another in a long string of failures. You'd think I'd be used to them by now, but they never got any easier to face. I reached for the poncho.

"Aren't you going to take another look at the letter?" asked Triss. "There are stronger measures we might try, more destructive perhaps, but—"

"No." I laid the poncho down over the bag.

"You know there might be some clue in there about Devin, don't you?"

"Of course." I didn't for a second believe that the near-simultaneous arrival of Devin and me on that balcony was a coincidence. "Maybe after eight or ten hours of sleep, I'll even care enough to look Maylien up and rake her over the coals about the whole thing, but not tonight."

Or then again, maybe I wouldn't. Maybe I'd just have a drink or six and forget about the whole thing. I added the hood to the pile in the trunk, then my boots. As I changed pants, I could feel Triss glaring at me, so I took extra time and care in putting the grays away—I'd had all I could take of pushing for one night. He made a little hmmphing noise when I closed the lid, but he didn't grouse. I reached for the lock . . . and stopped. I just couldn't do it.

As a Blade, you learn that it's all right to choose not to act. Choosing not to think is another thing entirely. Though I was no longer a Blade, the lesson remained.

With a sigh I opened the trunk again and retrieved the letter. As Triss had noted, there were things we could do now in regard to exposing its secrets that we couldn't have when I'd cared about keeping it intact. I was running through some of those in my head when I took a closer look and discovered it was going to be a simpler task than I'd expected. Since I'd last examined the letter, words had appeared on the previously blank space above the seal.

"For Aral Kingslayer, last Blade of fallen Namara."

Un-fucking-believable. I laughed then, and it was a bitter and black sound like efik left too long a-steeping. I cracked the seal and began to read, with Triss following along over my shoulder. "I seek the redress of Justice," it began.

After the first few lines, I reached for the whiskey bottle. This time Triss didn't try to stop me.

4

My day started with pain. Throbbing pain and cruel light and a truly foul taste in my mouth. Nothing I hadn't experienced before. In fact, I'd been there often enough that I knew better than to open my eyes right away. I groped upward with my left hand, feeling along the top edge of my pallet until I found a plump wineskin.

Keeping my eyes firmly closed, I brought it down and pressed the cool leather against my forehead while I fiddled with the seal. Finally, I very carefully placed the neck in my mouth and took a long pull of small beer. It was bitter and harsh and warm, and it tasted like ambrosia. Good country water would have been better yet, but in a city like Tien, only the crazy and the desperate drank from the wells. Some might have preferred tea, but since I gave up efik, I no longer drink hot drinks. Not if there's any polite way to avoid it.

I didn't try to move or open my eyes till I'd downed half the skin. At that point I still felt like week-old shit, but I knew that just lying there wouldn't help anymore, so I reluctantly cracked an eyelid.

The first thing I saw was the shadow of a dragon. Triss

peered down into my face from a position on the angled ceiling a few feet above my head and gently shook his own. That put my shadow ninety degrees away from where the light would have and announced Triss's unhappiness with me. It wasn't the first time *that* had happened either.

"Morning, Triss," I said. Husked really, since my throat felt like I'd been pouring paint thinner down it. "How are you?"

"It is *not* morning, and I am very angry." His voice came out flat and hard, but quiet enough that it didn't hurt my head. Much. "But you knew the latter and ought to have known the former."

He was right, my one window faced west. Sunlight slipped between the slats of its battered shutters. From the angle it had to be five or six hours past midday. Bad sign. I took another long pull of small beer, then discovered a worse one. When I recapped the skin and tossed it aside it landed with a clink of bottles. Plural.

"What day is it?" I asked.

"Atherasday, the tenth of Seedsdown."

"Oh, thank you." I paused for a moment, hoping for memory to allow me to sidestep the next question. But it failed me, and I had to ask, "What day was it when we saw Devin?"

Triss growled low in his throat and shook his head again. "It was in the last hour of the eighth day of Seedsdown."

"That could be a problem." I sat up and forced myself to stay that way.

I didn't much enjoy it, but it didn't kill me. I had about five hours to make a decision on Devin's offer. No, that's not true. I already knew my answer. There was no way in hell I was going to make common cause with my former brothers and sisters if it wasn't in service to the goddess. Not when any alliance would be made atop her divine corpse. No, what I had to decide was what to do about Devin.

"I need a drink," I said, then felt ashamed of myself. I knew what I had become, but that didn't make me proud of it.

"No," said Triss, "you may want a drink, but it's the last thing in the world that you need."

"Point. What would you suggest instead?"

"That you pack up and we leave this city and never return."

That surprised me. "You don't think we should seek Devin out? Devin and . . . Zass with him?"

"No. I do not want to join anyone who would betray the goddess's memory as they have. I do not want to have to kill them or, more likely considering the way you've let yourself go the last few years, be killed by them." There was a lot of anger in his voice, and I really couldn't blame him.

"So why run?" I asked. "Why not just stay here and ignore them? Them, and that damn girl both." More of my night-before was coming back to me. I found myself glancing into the corner where I'd thrown Maylien's crumpled letter when burning it proved beyond me.

"The girl found you. Do you really think Devin won't if he tries? Or the Elite, should Devin choose to keep his own hands clean? The only reason we have remained safe here for so long is because no one who wanted to find us would have believed we were foolish enough to come back to Tien after we killed its king."

I didn't have an answer for that. Instead, I made a show of dragging myself across the room to retrieve the letter. There were smoke stains along the edges from where I'd held it in the flames of one of Jerik's filthy oil lamps, but no other evidence of my attempts at burning. As I sat down at the table, I glanced at the front again.

For Aral Kingslayer, last Blade of fallen Namara.

I should have torn the letter into shreds. It wasn't for me anyway. The Kingslayer had died with his goddess. All he'd left behind was a broken-down wreck who wore his face. A shadow jack who drank himself unconscious most nights because that was the only way he could get to sleep. I opened the letter again. It beat facing Triss's reproach. Besides, I couldn't remember what was in it.

> *I seek the redress of Justice. My name is Maylien Tal Marchon and I am the true heir to the Barony of Marchon. If you are alive to read this, then I know that you are the Kingslayer and the one person who can help me regain my baronial seat.*

If I'm your only hope, Lady, you might as well walk away from that chair right now.

> *I thought it was you from the moment I first saw you across the common room of the Gryphon's Head several months ago, but I had to make certain. I knew that the baroness's pet assassin—I won't sully the title of Blade by applying it to that Devin-creature—could never hope to stand against you in open combat.*

Against the Kingslayer, maybe not. Against me . . . now those were much shorter odds. I shook my head. Devin. What was I going to do about Devin? That was still the only question that mattered. Triss was almost certainly right. We *should* run. But when I thought about walking away, something deep down in my soul said "no." It wasn't a loud voice, barely a whisper even, but it was very firm. My eyes flicked to the page again.

> *I'll have to lie low for a while after this, but I will look for you in the Gryphon's Head as soon as I am able.*

The rest of the letter babbled on and on about her bona fides and the horrors the current Baroness Marchon was visiting on the heads of her people. Doors broken down in the middle of the night, people disappearing, burned-out crofts, all the usual mayhem and murder and exactly the sort of thing that would once have drawn the attention of the goddess. What Maylien completely failed to mention was anything that I actually cared about at the moment. Like how she knew who Devin was and what he'd been up to these last five years. I crumpled the letter and threw it into the corner again.

"You don't seem to like the contents any more today than you did the first time you read them," said Triss, his voice acid. "I hope that doesn't mean you're about to replay the drunken binge the last reading brought on."

"I don't really have time for that, now do I?"

The shadow of a dragon flicked his wings in a shrug, then flitted down to the table in front of me. "That hasn't stopped you in the past."

"In the past, I didn't know about Devin or any deal my former brethren might have made with the Son of Heaven."

Triss raised his head to stare at me. "That almost sounds like the old Aral, the stubborn one. I take it that we won't be leaving town?"

"Not till we find out a bit more about what happened at the fall of the temple."

"What of Maylien and unseating her wicked baroness?"

"Getting rid of the baroness isn't my problem. My interest in Maylien goes only as far as finding out what she knows about Devin. Oh, and collecting the rest of my fee, of course."

Triss cocked his head to one side skeptically.

"Don't look at me like that," I said. "I delivered her damned letter, didn't I? That's *all* I contracted for—none of this baronial seat bullshit. Come on, let's go have a look around."

I slid from my seat on the trunk to my knees, moving gently to avoid jarring my head. Then, drawing Triss around me, I reached for the lock.

The Spinnerfish was a good tavern in a bad neighborhood. It lay a few streets in from the docks on the Smuggler's Rest end of the harbor. That wasn't what anyone official called the area. Not where they could be heard at any rate. But everyone knew what happened down there.

The shadow port was one-third of what made the Spinnerfish such a successful venue. The second third was Manny Three Fingers, the best seafood cook in the city. Last was Manny's boss, Erk Endfast: a onetime shadow captain and black jack from Oen in the Magelands—he'd left rather quickly as an alternative to making a command performance on the Magearch's gallows. Now he ran the Spinnerfish as neutral territory, a safe place to meet or simply relax for all the players in Tien's shadow trades.

It was also a good place to dig for information. Devin's current company put him well beyond the ken of the sort of dregs and drifters that frequented the Gryphon. Though I didn't normally run in the richer circles of the shadow world, I knew most of the faces, and I knew how the game was played at that level. Perhaps more importantly, I had enough of a rep as a straight-back jack to spring a few locked doors.

I arrived at the Spinnerfish as the sun was setting, which put me ahead of the crowd. So I was able to snag a small table in a corner of the front room. When the waitress came around, I tossed her a silver riel and told her to bring me a tucker of Kyle's with a clean glass and the catch of the day, whatever it happened to be.

The place filled with people at about the same rate as my belly filled with peppered snapper. Things were really hopping by the time I put aside my plate and poured myself a second glass of whiskey from the small bottle. About halfway through sipping it down I noticed Erk himself making his way among the tables, waving at this one, leaning down to have a word with that, asking all and sundry about the fish.

He was tall and very fit and all-over brown, from his hair to his skin to his conservatively expensive outfit. He openly wore a pair of cane knives on his belt, forward curved and heavy—brutally effective weapons and better by far than a sword in a crowded and enclosed space like the Spinnerfish. I was rather surprised when his progress brought him to a halt across from me.

"Aral, how have you been?" he asked, his voice pitched to carry to the nearby tables. "It's been an age. I don't see you

down this close to the docks very often. Mind if I join you?
I've maybe got some jack work for you."

I pasted a smile on my face and waved at the other seat
though I was feeling mighty uneasy. "I always have time for
a man in need of a jack." I knew that Erk knew my jack face,
but we'd never been on a casual basis.

As he sat down, he pulled a small bronze bell from some
inner pocket and set it in the center of the table. "Drum-
ringer."

"Sensitive business then?" I could feel Triss clinging
tightly to my back as he paid extra attention.

The bell was an expensive little piece of permanent
magic. Anyone more than a few feet away who tried to
casually listen in would hear nothing but the distant ringing
of bells. If someone employed magic to stick an ear in, the
ringing would get a whole lot louder. Possibly even deafen-
ingly so if the drum-ringer was a sufficiently powerful one
as the spell-glow of this one suggested.

"Sensitive enough," answered Erk. "I've a favor to ask."

I cocked an eyebrow at that. Favors were not a common
item of trade in the shadow world, and I doubted very much
that he meant that word in the traditional way.

"It's like this; see those three gentlemen at the second
table past the door, the one right by the corner of the bar?
They're planning on causing you some harm, and they're
planning on making their move soon. I really don't like that
sort of thing happening inside the Spinnerfish. So if you'd
do me the favor of stepping outside before you ghost them,
I'd really appreciate it."

I flicked a glance around the room, making sure not to
spend too much eye time on the table in question. I didn't
for a moment doubt what Erk was telling me though I did
idly wonder how he knew. The trio in question looked more
like Kadeshi mercenaries than the bravos I'd have expected.
They sported two swords, an axe, a mail shirt, and couple
of breastplates between them. I'd noticed them when they
came in but hadn't really paid any attention at the time.

Apparently, Devin had decided not to give me the full

two days though why he hadn't come for me himself I didn't know. But that was a puzzle for later. In the meantime, I had a more pressing concern, two really. Erk's request had set a small worm of icy cold to stirring itself in the pit of my stomach.

"Why is it," I asked, keeping my voice as casual as I could, "that you're so certain about *me* ghosting *them*? I'm just a jack, and not exactly dressed for a fight." I tapped one of the long daggers that were my only visible weapons, then adjusted the collar of my light leather jerkin. "And those are hard men armed and armored for war."

One man with knives against a trio of veteran mercenaries doesn't a fight make, more like a massacre. If you bought my jack face, those were fool's odds.

Erk leaned back in his seat. "I was running a skip in the court of the Magearch when Lord Baskin met his much deserved and ever so timely end."

"Oh." Triss squeezed my shoulders hard but didn't make any more obvious moves.

Not that it mattered. Baskin was one of the very few jobs I'd ever been forced to perform in front of witnesses. The first thrust had glanced off a magical chest piece I hadn't known about. He'd managed to get out the door of his rooms and halfway to the great hall before I caught up and finished him.

"Hell of a sprinter, Baskin," said Erk.

"He was that, though I thought all the eyes in that hallway belonged to servants."

"That was certainly how I was faced at the time."

"You do know what my head's worth?"

"Of course," replied Erk. "But that's not my problem. When I left Oen behind, I left all the skips and plays with it. My world is this bar, and as long as nothing bad happens in here, my clients' business is entirely their own."

And that was as nice a threat as anyone had ever made me. Even if Erk didn't choose to sell me directly, he possessed something that a number of people would pay very highly for; a postgoddess view of my face. In the days when

Namara still lived she had prevented the making of any likenesses of her Blades, jostling the elbows of artists who tried to capture images of our features and twisting the tongues and memories of those who might otherwise have described us. Now that she was gone, and Erk had refreshed his memory of me, he could make himself a tidy sum simply by having a good sketch done.

"I'd better see that I take care of my little problem outside then, hadn't I?" I said.

"I *would* appreciate it."

I downed the last of my second glass and looked regretfully at the tucker holding what would have been my third and fourth, then rolled my shoulders to loosen them.

Erk recorked the small bottle. "I'll have this kept aside for the next time you stop in if it comes soon enough."

"Thank you."

"You're welcome." He picked up the bottle, then reached for the drum-ringer, pausing in the instant before he lifted the bell as though just remembering something. "One last thing; going forward I'd also appreciate it if you didn't trail that sort of stupid trash in here in your wake ever again. I don't appreciate having to step in like this."

"I'll see what I can do," I said.

I stood and headed toward the counter, holding my empty glass in front of me as though I wanted a refill. That took me straight toward the trio of Kadeshis, who looked quite pleased and started oh-so-subtly loosening weapons and sliding their chairs back. It also put me on a line to pass within ten feet of the door. As I hit the closest point to the exit, I set my glass on the nearest table and bolted out into the night and a light drizzle.

When I hit the street, they were less than three yards behind me and had already drawn steel though they had to pause briefly to open the small magelantern the leader carried. I could still have lost them if I'd wanted to. Between the dark and the rain, I wouldn't have even needed Triss's help, but I wanted to send Devin a message, written in blood. Besides, I desperately needed a break from running and hiding, even if only for one night. I sprinted just far enough down the street to put a polite distance between me and the Spinnerfish before pivoting to face my attackers and drawing my daggers.

As I did so, Triss gave a questioning squeeze, offering to enshroud me or take a more direct hand in eliminating my attackers. I shook my head. I preferred not to reveal my nature to any third-party watchers if I could avoid it, and vanishing into shadow or having one kill for me would have made for a pretty unmistakable calling card.

Then they were on top of me. They were actually very good, attacking all together in a coordinated rush. The axeman, who also held the lantern, charged me head-on, while the other two slid forward to his left and right so they could come in on my sides. It was smart tactics and a sign of good training and plenty of combat experience.

Someone was going to miss these boys.

I waited for the axeman to make the overhand swing that was his best bet, then slipped forward, moving inside his guard and blocking his descending arm with my own. At the same time, I jammed my right-hand dagger up under his chin and through the roof of his mouth, driving it deep into his brain. I felt something like the sudden electrical shock of magelightning as the coppery smell of blood feathered the air.

That was one.

He dropped the light as he died, but it stayed open, which was too bad since I didn't have time to do anything more direct about it. Using the embedded dagger as a push-off point, I shoved myself downward. Letting go of the hilt as I dropped, I balanced on the ball of my right foot and the knuckles of my left fist and pivoted backward in a sweeping kick. The dead man's left-side swordsman was exactly where I had planned for him to be, and my spinning calf caught him across the shins. He went down in a heap, while the falling corpse of the leader protected me from the right-side swordsman.

Which put me in the clear again.

As I came back upright, I flicked my right wrist, dropping

the much shorter knife I kept in a sheath there into my hand. The right-side swordsman was turning around, but his companion had only gotten back up onto hands and knees, hampered perhaps by the water lightly slicking the cobbles. I sank both my blades deep into his spine, one above his breastplate, one below. Again, I felt a sort of electric charge at the kill.

That was two.

I used the hilts sticking out of his back like the handles of a pommel horse, pivoting and launching myself through the air feetfirst. I hit the last man in the side of the knee, shattering the joint. It was a calculated risk but necessary given our relative positions. He was damned good and had come around faster than I'd hoped.

Two and a half.

He managed one solid swing at me as he went down. I blocked his blade with the inside of my left forearm, where I had a second wrist sheath. His sword broke the knife and tore the sheath loose. The straps burned across my skin, drawing blood. Then I was rolling away, and the second swing of his sword struck the wet cobblestones behind me.

That marked the effective end of the game.

Flipping myself to my feet, I drew my second-to-last blade from the top of my right boot and walked back toward the fallen man. He rolled onto his back, bringing the sword up between the two of us and pointing it at my chest.

"This doesn't have to end this way," he said desperately. "Just tell me what you want. Anything. I'll do it."

I kicked the lantern shut, plunging the street into deep darkness. Then I reversed my grip so that I was holding the dagger by the blade.

"I don't think so," I said.

I snapped my arm down and forward, throwing the knife. Master Kelos would *not* have approved, and he'd probably have been right—throwing a weapon was always a risky bet and usually a dumb move against a better-armed opponent, no matter what the barroom toughs claimed. Of course, that risk was small here. My enemy could move neither far nor fast, and I had another knife. Besides, as the blade's sinking deep into the Kadeshi's throat proved, sometimes a risk paid off nicely.

And sometimes it didn't.

As he died, the dagger flashed blindingly bright—a burst of magelightning arcing from its pommel to my right hand. More lines of lightning shot from there to the other two corpses, centering me in a web of burning light and pain. My view of the world exploded into a wild rainbow cascade of nonsense shapes, and for just a second, I could both taste and hear the colors.

I'd been deathsparked, and I was an idiot.

I slumped to my knees in a filthy puddle. I'd never seen it coming. Because, you see, Blades are immune to death-sparking. The goddess protects us. But the goddess was dead. If I'd ever needed more proof of that, I had it now.

That hurt more than the deathspark, and the pain carried me into darkness.

5

The world tasted of blue, which in turn tasted rather a
lot like badly burned bacon, and it smelled like magelightning. The world also hurt, especially my head. Oh, and
I had a powerful urge to vomit. Sadly, waking up feeling
like I did just then was no more than a strange new variation
on an old, familiar theme. I automatically reached for the
skin of small beer that sat at the top of my pallet. Or, tried
to, actually.

That was when I discovered I couldn't move my arms or
much of anything else. I was bound. Then I remembered
the deathspark, and that explained the pain and my situation
and tasting colors. *Thank you, Devin, you shit-eating bastard.* Rather than fight my bonds, I stopped moving completely as routines that had been carved into my bones came
to the fore. I could almost hear old Master Kelos drilling
me on what to do when captured.

Hide your strength.

I cracked an eye the tiniest margin and found . . . myself
severely disorientated and once more fighting hard against
the impulse to throw up. In part because of the eye-jabbingly

bright magelight hanging a few feet in front of my face. But also because of my sudden mental change of orientation. Rather than lying on my back as I'd initially believed, I was upright and facing a basement room that just screamed dungeon.

Count the opposition, locate the exits, catalog your assets.

I forced down the nausea. In addition to me and whatever I was hanging from, the dungeon contained various implements of torture—many of which I could use as weapons if I could get my hands on them. A quartet of rough-looking men played at dice in a corner. One of them had a few faint glimmers of magic about him—poorly crafted spells probably. Above them was a barred window laced over with some sort of minor spell that blurred what lay beyond. That and a door off to my left provided the only exits I could see without moving.

The place stank of mold and piss and old blood. Especially that last. A lot of blood had been spilled in this room, and not just as a side effect of torture. Not with a bleeding-table standing just a few feet off to my left. The angled marble slab had deep gutters cut into it to direct the blood into the basin at its foot. Though not magical in itself, an exsanguination table was a tool used for some of the darker magics and one more reason to get the hell out of there as quickly as possible.

Test your bindings.

None of the men was currently looking my way, which suggested one of two things. Either they were stupid, or they were very confident about the efficacy of my . . . what *was* I hanging from? It didn't feel like any of the sorts of manacles I'd learned to slip as a child. There were too many fastening points for one thing . . . ankles, knees, chest, throat, elbows, wrists. All snug.

Very carefully and very slowly, I turned my head to the right. The taste of blue came back, but I ignored it. Looking along my bare arm I could see that there was a heavy leather strap buckled just above my elbow and another at my wrist.

The buckles were brass. It was hard to tell given my angle of view and scrambled senses, but they all seemed to be mounted to some sort of magically active wooden framework. I strained weakly at my bonds, but they didn't move, and the effort brought back the nausea, so I stopped and went back to trying to make sense of the framework that held me. Its shape seemed far too complex for its purpose.

"It's a sheuth glyph, Blade," said a rough voice.

I glanced up to find that one of the dice players had turned to look my way. The one with minor bits of magic hanging about him.

"I don't think I know that one," I replied.

"No surprise there." He got up to come closer, approaching me from one side. "It's not anything your kind is supposed to know about. Came straight from Tangara, God of Glyphs, it did." He chuckled then, and it was an evil sound. "He made it special like for the destruction of that bitch Namara's temple."

How could Devin bear to employ such a man? I took a moment then to really fix him in my memory. I wanted to be absolutely sure I would know him anywhere. If I didn't kill him on my way out of here, I was going to make a point of looking him up later.

Middling tall and middling dark, with narrow shoulders and a bit of a paunch, he would have blended into any Tienese crowd without raising an eyebrow. He *was* better dressed than his fellows, wearing bloused pants of rough silk and an embroidered leather vest, where the others wore cotton and badly tanned hide. He also had a slender spit-adder wrapped two or three times around his neck.

It raised its head and hissed at me when they got within a few feet. Its attitude mirrored that of its mage, for that was clearly what the man was, though of a minor enough sort that I didn't recognize the school. Seeing the familiar made me realize that Triss hadn't tried to signal me in any way yet. Though I could feel him lying against my back, he didn't seem to be as present as normal, and that worried me. A lot.

"Sheuth, huh? What's it do?" I asked.

The man smiled, showing uneven teeth. "Can't you guess?" Before I could answer, he went on, "It's got another name; the pillory of light. Working along with the stone there"—the snake's head rose to point at the brilliant mage-light hanging in front of my face—"the sheuths's a binder of shadows. The light makes your pet monster act like a *real* shadow, substanceless and inanimate, and that rack you're on trusses it up even tighter than it does you."

I didn't panic though I felt the first edges of real fear. Quickly I moved my hands through a half dozen of the signals I used with Triss when we couldn't speak aloud. But the device was custom-designed by a god to hold Blades and Shades, and Triss made no response, not even the slightest change of pressure across my back.

Fuck. Fuck, fuck, fuck.

I wanted to bust loose, to kill the bastards who'd messed with my familiar. I couldn't even move my arms though I strained against the straps until the muscles in my chest and shoulders felt raw and shredded. The mage just watched me, smiling all the while, and there was nothing I could do to him. Nothing at all. That was what finally made me stop fighting like an animal and start thinking like a Blade again. And that began with making an honest assessment of my situation, both in terms of my options and how I got there.

If they didn't kill me outright, there might come a moment when I had a chance to act. If I was exhausted, I'd fuck up, and that would be it. I would die, and Triss would die with me, and there'd be nobody to blame but the miserable drunk that had inherited the Kingslayer's skin. But I wasn't going to let that happen.

I didn't much care about me. If I'd had the choice, I would have followed my goddess into the grave when the temple fell. But I didn't have the choice because Triss's life was tied to mine, and I loved him far more than I hated myself. Now, if Triss was going to live, I had to live. That meant I had to get smart, maybe even become the Kingslayer again, if only for a little while—I didn't think I could bear the weight for much longer than that. I took a deep breath and looked my captor in the eye.

"Does it hurt him? Your glyph, I mean."

"Does it hurt the Shade?" He laughed. He. Laughed. Dead man.

"I sure hope so," he said.

Again I wondered how Devin could have let himself get involved with this sort of human filth. Or with the baroness for that matter. What had happened to him in the years since the fall of the temple? I couldn't imagine the Devin I'd grown up with doing any of this.

As I was calculating what I ought to say or do next, the dice game finished up, and two of the other men came over to join the conference. A big rawboned fellow with a deep scar on his forehead and a shorter one who reminded me of a weasel. The fourth man remained by the door.

"Be damned careful you don't block that light," said the mage.

"Don't worry, Lok," said "Scar."

"There's really no need to be careful on my account," I said. "The regular light's more than adequate for anything but reading, and I left my book back at my inn."

Never let them see you sweat. The lessons were still all there. Now, if I could only get back to the place where I lived them without having to think them, I might be able to really call myself a Blade again.

The snake hissed again, and the mage said, "I'm going to enjoy hurting you. Lads, whenever you're ready."

The pair moved to stand close to the wall on either side of me. By tilting my head, I could see one or the other but not both at the same time. I was looking at the one on my left, Scar, when Weasel hit me from the right, striking me just under the front edge of my rib cage on bare skin—they'd stripped me naked. He used a freshly peeled willow branch about as thick around as a dagger's hilt, simultaneously heavy and whippy. Damn! It hurt as bad as any punch or kick would have but wasn't nearly so likely to do lasting damage.

I turned and tried to spit at him, only to catch a shot across my cheekbone from the other side—Scar using a much thinner branch to do the fine work. *Fuck!* It didn't split my cheek, quite. Weasel hit me again, about midway down my thigh. Things got ugly after that as the pair worked me over for a bit. They were very good. They never hit hard enough to break anything, and they kept their blows far enough apart so that I felt each one sharply without any merciful blurring. But the sticks didn't hurt me half as much as my fears for Triss.

Control the pain, don't let it control you.

I forced myself to step outside the pain as I had been taught, to assess what they were doing to me on a tactical level instead of experiencing it viscerally. On the personal level, it was a very professional beating. But what was the point? I couldn't make the bigger picture make any sense at all.

They couldn't be after information. They hadn't asked any questions before they started in with the sticks, and beating was a shitty way to get real information anyway. Most people would tell you whatever they thought you wanted to hear just to make it stop. More importantly, I didn't *know* anything. I hadn't done one thing that really mattered since the temple fell. Devin knew all the same secrets that I did from the days before the goddess died, and even if he didn't, Namara was gone into the grave. None of it mattered anymore.

It didn't make sense as a recruiting tactic, either. If I'd had the least inclination to sign on with Devin and the other traitors to Namara's memory, this would have put a knife in the heart of that plan. Devin knew me well enough to understand that. It was just as bad an idea for sending a message to the other remaining rogue Blades. Jax, Siri, Loris, none of them liked being pushed any more than I did.

The only thing I could think of was that Lok and his boys were freelancing, beating me in a way that wouldn't leave a lot of marks for the sheer joy of kicking the shit out of a Blade. In which case, Devin was an incompetent bastard.

Once again I found myself wishing I hadn't hesitated back at the Marchon estate. If I'd killed Devin as soon as I saw him dishonoring his Namara-given swords, none of this would have happened. But that would have killed Zass as well, and even in the middle of a beating, I knew I didn't want any Shade's death on my conscience if I could possibly avoid it.

Which brought me back to my fears for Triss. I lost control then, maybe went a little mad even, screaming and swearing and wrenching at my bonds again and again for some unknown length of time. An open-handed slap brought me back from that edge, though it was more the different sound of the impact than the sting of the blow driving my lips against my teeth that registered.

"What?" I shook my head in an effort to return the world to proper focus. The part of me that had heard the slap also vaguely remembered there being a question asked or an order given in there somewhere. "Could you pass that one by me again?"

Lok caught me by the chin and turned my head to the right so that I was looking directly at him. With the intense white shock of the magelight only a few feet away, he looked like nothing human. Half of his face lay in such deep shadow that for all purposes it didn't exist, and the other half was washed out, pale as any night-walking undead.

He leaned in so close we were practically kissing, and his breath was foul. "I said, *Blade*, that I want you to tell me everything you know about the man who calls himself Devin Nightblade."

"Wait, what now?" I squeezed my eyes tight shut, then blinked several times while I tried to make sense of the words.

What he'd just said was so far off the page of my read on things that I almost couldn't make sense of the words. Weren't these Devin's trained rats? What possible reason could they have for beating me to get information about Devin?

Lok let go of me and stepped back, speaking very slowly

and clearly. "Devin Nightblade, your onetime comrade in arms, tell us about him, or what you've suffered so far will seem like so many love-caresses from your dead goddess."

I put another mark on Lok's dead-man tally sheet, then opened my mouth to answer. But nothing came out. Nightblade. Nightblade? Really? When had Devin bartered Urslan away for a use-name that all but spat on the grave of the goddess? More importantly, if these boys didn't belong to Devin, my emerging view of the bigger picture had just gone from blurry to spilled paint in a dark studio.

"Hit him again," said Lok.

Scar laid one on the side of my neck, just above the leather collar. It stung like the gods' own bumblebee. It also helped bring me out of my stupor. More because of the threat than the pain. An inch forward, and he would have crushed my larynx. I couldn't afford to die right now, mostly for Triss's sake. But I also very much wanted to have a few steel-edged words with these fellows and with my dear old friend *Nightblade* before I followed my goddess.

"Wait," I said. "Assuming your Devin is the same as mine, I'll happily tell you everything I know." Hell, if it weren't for Zass, I'd have been more than half-tempted to help them string him up in my place here.

Lok looked incredulous. "If they're the same man? You're not seriously suggesting that there's more than one ex-Blade named Devin running around this city, are you?"

"Point." I nodded as firmly as the straps would allow. "What do you want to know?"

"Let's start with his long-term plans for the baroness."

I didn't say, "How the fuck would I know that?" Though it's what I was thinking. "That could be a problem. I haven't seen Devin in five years. I have no idea what he's planning right now."

Lok shook his head sadly. "Are you going to try to tell me you weren't the man that Nightblade talked to on the Marchon estate two nights ago? Because I don't believe you. Think carefully before you answer because I'm starting to think I ought to just let the boys give you another working over before I ask any more questions, this time without playing so gentle."

I wanted to tell Lok I was going to ghost him. I wanted to make him understand what a *really* bad idea all this was, particularly messing with my familiar. But in the short term, that would only put Triss in more danger. And in the long term, Lok was a dead man.

"No," I said. "That was me, but it was my first and only contact with Devin since about a month before the fall of the temple. I didn't even know he was alive until I saw him on the baroness's balcony. Honestly, at the moment I'm wishing he'd stayed as dead as I thought he was."

I don't know whether Lok believed me, but he didn't immediately have his men start in with the sticks again, so I continued, "I can't tell you what Devin's doing right now, or where to find him, or anything like that. I can tell you what his favorite foods were as a kid, and who his first lover was, and a thousand other little details, but you don't want all that. If you could just tell me why you want the information, I could probably narrow it down to the stuff that's actually usefu—ungh!"

Weasel this time, a jab to my floating ribs with the point of the rod.

"I'm not sure you understand the situation here." Lok leaned in close again. "I ask questions. You give answers. Anything else leads to pain. Got it?"

I nodded. I wouldn't do Triss any good if I were a broken bloody mess when the time came to move.

If you control yourself, you control the situation, and your chance to act will come.

As the words slid through my mind, I found myself incredibly sad to realize that I could never thank Master Kelos for his lessons. Without them, I might well have already died here.

"Good," said Lok, "then we can continue. Oh"—and he smiled—"and I think it might help us to get to the point if I explain what I want from you. Yes?"

I painted a smile across my swollen lips and nodded

again. At the same time, I made my three-thousandth attempt at breaking loose. It was just as effective as all the ones that had come before.

Lok grinned at my struggles. "My boss wants to know everything you know about the baroness's little assassin, right down to the color of his underwear. Understand?"

"That's crazy."

Who was Lok working for? A rival to the baroness other than Maylien? Why would anyone care about that level of detail? Everything I learned just made me more confused. These people were the weirdest damn mix of professional and amateur I'd ever met.

"Was that the answer to my question?" asked Lok. "It didn't sound like an answer. It sounded like a comment, and I was pretty sure you weren't supposed to do anything but answer questions."

Before he could do or say anything more, I heard a low thrumming twang and saw a flare of magic at the window. It burned a line across the room from there to the magelight, where it ripped the stone free of its string, then continued to a spot an inch or so to the right of my bleeding ear. At that point, there came a sharp crack, and I felt a spray of pinpricks across my neck and that side of my face.

I didn't know what had just happened, but neither did I care. My chance had arrived, and I wasn't going to fuck up this time.

The tumbling magelight hit me on the chest as it fell, bouncing and rolling away across the room, sending the shadows wild. Against my back, I felt Triss come to life. I snapped the fingers of my right hand to draw his attention to the bindings there. I needed a free hand soonest. An instant later, I felt the first of the straps part: wrist, followed by elbow.

As my arm dropped free of the restraints, the pain of full circulation returning hit. It felt like someone had set fire to the blood in my veins. I blocked out my awareness of the pain while I glanced around, checking to see if I had time to finish cutting myself loose.

I didn't.

Lok was already moving, one hand going for a knife while the other rose to point at my face. I brought my free arm up and across in a blocking motion, signaling my needs to Triss with the positioning of my half-clenched fist.

A stream of magefire burst from Lok's fingers only to vanish into the oval of shadow that suddenly enveloped my arm from elbow to first knuckle, like a buckler carved from the stuff of night. One for me. But only barely, and at the cost of remaining a trussed goose all hung up and ready for the slaughter.

If I couldn't get loose of the rack fast, I was a dead man. Triss had a very limited ability to cope with fire magics—a stronger mage or a true spell would have done him real harm—and even a petty mage like Lok could get through given time.

Scar's stick came in hard then, catching me just above the eye so that bursts of sparkling purple flashed across my vision. At the same time, the spit-adder on Lok's shoulder reared back, ready to send a stream of venom at my eyes. I tilted my shadowy shield to try to catch both that and the inevitable next round of magefire, but I didn't have much hope.

Lok opened his mouth like a man about to laugh. But just then there came a low "thwock" sort of noise. A thin trickle of blood dribbled out of his mouth, and Lok crashed to his knees on the hard flags. I heard bone break with the impact but he just slumped quietly forward, beyond caring. Lok was dead, killed by the crossbow quarrel sticking out of the back of his skull. As his face hit the floor, the snake went into convulsions, dying with its master.

That left Weasel, Scar, and the fourth man.

Scar struck again, but I anticipated the blow this time, blocking it with my Triss-covered forearm. The stick shattered in a burst of white fire as my familiar used the contact to turn the wood into a conduit for a flare of magelightning. Scar screamed and fell to the floor, clutching at his ruined hand. I turned to kill Weasel. But he had already dropped his stick and bolted, heading toward the place where the fourth man was wrenching at the door.

That moved both men from threat to target.

Magefire poured in through the window as the fourth man opened the door, turning him into a human bonfire. The room filled with the scent of charring flesh, and Weasel dropped to his belly, begging for mercy.

He wasn't going to get any from me.

Triss cut me the rest of the way free, and I dropped to the floor. It was all I could do not to go face down like Weasel after the beating and the hours pinned to the glyph. I managed to stay upright, just, but I couldn't walk for shit. I staggered into a big butcher-block table covered with all sorts of sharp and pointy nastiness, much of which cascaded off the back in a little torture-implement avalanche. Iron and steel smacked into stone with a sharp series of clangs and bangs and a couple of deep booongs when bits bounced against a giant copper cauldron.

"Are you all right?" a half-familiar woman's voice called from the window. Even with the spell that had covered it broken, I could see only darkness beyond the bars.

"I will be, thanks to you. What do I owe you for the rescue?"

Triss was going to live because of this woman, whoever she was. She could name her price.

There was a merry laugh and then a smiling face leaned in close to the bars. "Why, a shot at my baronial seat, just as I asked for in my letter . . . Kingslayer."

It was Maylien, my lady of the red dress. The one I'd hoped I'd seen the last of. And now I owed her a barony. At least my life is interesting.

"Damn," Maylien said, suddenly thrusting herself away from the window. "There's someone else out here with me. I—"

There came a faint thud, like a sap catching someone behind the ear, followed by the sound of a body falling, then silence.

6

I dashed to the window, where Maylien had just disappeared from view. Or, I tried to anyway, but my much-abused muscles didn't want to cooperate and I tripped on Weasel instead of stepping over him. As I began to fall, I felt Weasel twist sharply beneath me and heard the scrape of his knife against the floor as he drew it.

Dammit, I don't have time for this.

I did what I could to avoid his thrust, bending awkwardly to my right as the blade came in. Instead of going deep, the knife cut a shallow furrow along the back of my ribs. I rolled farther to my right, trying to get some distance between us as Weasel slithered to his knees and pivoted toward me. Before I'd gotten very far, I slammed into the legs of the bleeding-table, hitting the fresh cut on my ribs and sending little spikes of light across my vision.

Weasel lurched toward me, raising his dagger to sink it into my chest. Under normal circumstances I could have dealt with him easily, even naked and unarmed. But I was still so stiff and sore, I could barely shape a fist, much less hit someone with it. That left magic, but my nima was at least as drained as the rest of me. Not that I had any choice. I signaled Triss for magelightning, but he had his own plans.

The shadow of a dragon rose between Weasel and me, hanging in the air for a moment like a falcon ready to stoop on its prey. Weasel screamed and threw himself back and away, dropping the knife. Triss fell on him anyway, enfolding him with wings of darkness and hiding him from view. Then Triss squeezed, closing into a tight ball of shadow with Weasel hidden at its center. Slowly, the ball contracted, shrinking to the size of a pinhead while I dragged myself upright. I didn't understand what Triss was doing, not initially, but I could feel the tremendous strain of it echoing along the connection between us.

When Triss sprang back to his normal size and shape, Weasel had simply vanished. While I tried to make sense of that, Triss beat his wings sharply and climbed toward the roof. The connection between us attenuated to little more than a slender thread of shadow. His head whipped angrily this way and that as he ranted and raved in the language of the Shades, a sharp, sibilant sound like the swearing of angry snakes. I could make out only a few words, "kill" and "make suffer" and "all"—it's not a tongue they use much with humans.

His attention fell on the injured Scar then, and he stretched across the room, looming above the fallen man like a figure in some mummer's shadow play. Scar screamed when the shadow fell on him, just as Weasel had screamed. Triss squeezed and strained, pushing himself almost to the edge of endurance . . . and then Scar, too, had vanished. That's when I realized what Triss must have done. He had made a gate of himself and sent them to the everdark. I wondered how long they would survive there in the cold and infinite blackness—always falling but never hitting bottom—and I shivered.

I actually shivered.

I'd been trained to kill almost from the day I'd learned to walk, and I *had* killed. Many times. I'd intended to finish both Weasel and Scar myself. I would have done it with a smile on my face and no hesitation. But it would have been quick and clean, an opened vein, a dagger to the heart, a crushed throat. Nothing like what Triss had just done.

The plunge into the everdark was a terrible death, and a rare one. I'd heard whispers of berserk Shades opening the gates of shadow, but I'd never seen it happen nor expected to. It was not something we asked of them. Not ever. Until that moment, it hadn't occurred to me to wonder why. Now I knew the answer. Fear. What Triss had just done to my enemies, he could also do to me if he chose.

Every time I hid myself within his darkness, every time I exercised my magic through him, every time I drew my familiar around me for any reason, I placed myself on the threshold of the everdark with nothing more than a shadow between me and doom. If I didn't trust Triss more than I trusted myself . . .

I shivered again, this time from the subterranean cold of the damp dungeon. Between that and the abuse I'd taken, I was courting shock just by standing there. I needed to get moving. More importantly, I needed to find out what had happened to Maylien. I owed her that and more for helping me to save Triss.

"Triss!" I called as I staggered to the window. "Triss, come here!"

I had to hold on to the bars to stay upright while I looked out into the night. But all I could see was a narrow stretch of empty cobblestones with a blank brick wall beyond and no sign of Maylien.

Shit.

I turned away from the empty night. Triss was still flitting this way and that through the room, looking for something more to kill and still muttering in his own tongue. He'd taken Lok into the shadows, too, though the mage was already dead, and he kept stooping to examine the charred corpse of the fourth man.

I almost wished he'd go ahead and take the bastard. The stink of burned meat had me on the edge of gagging. For a couple of seconds after I called him, I thought Triss wasn't going to come to me. But, after a few more dives at the dead man, he slid back to the place at my feet where the dungeon's lights would have put him.

"Are you all right?" he asked. "They hurt you, and I couldn't stop them." His voice was high and fast, laced with anguish. "I couldn't do anything at all. It felt like one of the nightmares that sometimes take you humans while you sleep, like it had me in its teeth shaking me and shaking me and shaking me, like it would never stop."

"It was pretty nightmarish for me, too," I said.

"I know." My dragon shadow suddenly lifted off the floor and wrapped his wings around me. "I know. I wanted to kill them all, to make them pay for hurting you, and I couldn't. I couldn't! I'm so sorry."

For just an instant, I felt the threat of the everdark in his touch though Triss had not put it there. Then I pushed the feeling aside, relaxing into the embrace of my dearest friend. He was a trained killer and plenty frightening, but then, so was I. We were both of us products of a system designed to create living weapons.

"It's all right, Triss. *I'm* all right. We need to get out of here and find out what happened to the girl."

Of course, by this point, whatever had happened to May-lien was almost certainly over. There had been neither sound nor sign from outside since her first outcry, which suggested she was dead or taken. I couldn't do much about either of those things naked and unarmed, so I figured I'd better take a few seconds more to do something about both conditions.

All the gear I'd had on me when I got deathsparked was lying in a rough pile, but that didn't help much. They'd cut my clothes and boots off me, probably after they hung me on the rack of the glyph, and most of my knives had stayed behind with the dead Kadeshis. I didn't have a lot of other options either. Three of my four captors had gone from the world entirely, taking all their belongings with them. The fourth had burned.

Grabbing the wreckage of my pants, I started to tie myself a breechclout. I'd gotten it just about to the point of addressing Tien's decency laws, when a nervous voice called from somewhere beyond the partially opened door to the dungeon.

"Lok!" it said. "Are you all right? What the hell happened?"

"Shit." I picked up my remaining knife and something that looked like a vicious cross between a fireplace poker and a bone saw and quickly crossed to the doorway.

A hallway lay beyond, with another prison door at the far end. A torch in the passage reflected off a pair of eyes peering through its little barred window at me.

"Lok?"

Triss hissed something in his own language and stretched down the hall, reaching for the far door. Before he could get there, the eyes vanished with a muffled curse and the sound of the viewing panel slamming shut. A moment later, an alarm bell started to clang.

That accelerated the schedule.

I closed and locked the door at my end, then broke the key off in the hole and wedged it before heading for the window. It was narrow, but if we could cut a few of the bars loose, I'd fit through all right, and it was a better bet than fighting our way out through an unknown building. I called to Triss and made my hand into a knife shape to let him know what I wanted, but he kept sliding back and forth along the surface of the door, either not listening or ignoring me again. He wanted more blood.

I did, too, but this wasn't the time.

"Triss!" I snapped. "Do you think you can drop that for a minute and help me with these bars? We'll come back later and we can kill them then. For now, we need to get clear and see what happened to Maylien."

He turned his head my way and hissed something angry and unintelligible.

"Triss, please. Let it go for tonight."

With a sigh, he came back toward me. I made the knife-hand gesture again, but rather than settle around my hands and shoulders, he threw his wings wide, hiding the window and a good bit of the wall around it. For nearly a minute he hung there like a leaf pressed in a book. With a brutal effort I could feel through our bond, he flexed his shoulders and snapped his wings forward, contracting into a pinpoint in an instant. The section of wall vanished into the everdark along with the window it contained. It left behind a hole in the shape of a man-sized dragon. Then Triss collapsed back into my shadow for a moment in exhaustion. This newly revealed talent took a lot out of him.

"That'll work." I climbed up into the hole, using the outline of a hind leg as a step.

About half the hole lay below the surface of the ground. Between that and my still-rocky condition, I ended up slithering my way up and out, smearing myself with dirt and nearly losing my breechclout in the process. I came up in a narrow stone-flagged alley, quiet, dark, completely empty.

No girl. But then, I hadn't expected her to be there. No girl's corpse either, which was a relief.

Though I didn't recognize the alley, I could tell by the paucity of trash in the corners and the lack of sewer smells that I was in one of the city's better neighborhoods. Maybe professional, maybe residential, but still not rich enough for street lighting. Tailor's Wynd or the Underhills or someplace like that. By the stars, it was still a couple of hours short of dawn, which explained the quiet.

Glancing back at the hole I'd just climbed out of, I wondered briefly why anyone would put a dungeon someplace like this. But the very affluence of the neighborhood would provide good cover. And someone who could keep even a petty mage like Lok in their pocket could also afford the spells that would keep the screaming and stink from passing through the window. That reminded me again of the girl, who must have broken the spell to find me. The fact that I needed a reminder said very bad things about my general state.

I took a quick look around for signs of what had happened to her though I didn't hold out much hope on that front. I'm no tracker, and even if I were, deep city is no place to go hunting without a hound. When I didn't find anything in the brief time I figured I had before my new enemies started to be a problem again, I turned to leave. That's when Triss, who had recovered enough to look around the alley behind me, made a noise like a kettle boiling over onto the coals.

"What is it?"

Triss circled an apparently unmarked spot on the cobbles. "Zass was here. He came from above. I can taste him in the stones where he and Devin landed."

I could feel my eyebrows heading for my hairline in surprise. Zass meant Devin, but that wasn't what had startled me. I'd more than half expected his involvement if for no other reason than my current run of luck—all bad. No, what startled me was the fact that Triss could tell Zass had been there. I'd never so much as heard a rumor of any such ability among the Shades.

Before I could ask him about it, a noise from the nearer end of the alley suggested we'd overstayed our safety margin. I glanced briefly up toward the rooftops whence Devin had come and whence he had probably returned. But even with Triss's help I knew I couldn't make it up the smoothly stuccoed wall in my current condition, much less run the rooftops. My nima was overtapped already. If I pushed my magic any further, I'd die and take Triss with me. Even if I'd been up to it, Triss wouldn't have been—I could feel the pain and exhaustion leaking down the link between us though he tried to shield me from it.

Part of being a professional is knowing that sometimes you have to let go, no matter how much you might want to keep trying.

So, instead of going after Devin, I asked Triss to hide me within himself and started walking. We left the alley by its farther mouth and turned left, plodding downslope in what I hoped was the direction of the sea and the docks. After a block or two, I figured out where I was—the Old Mews, which meant I needed to reverse my course and go over the top of the Kanathean Hill to get back home.

I paused a moment to set my position in memory so I could find the alley and dungeon later, after I'd had both rest and food. Then I turned toward the Stumbles and the Gryphon and began my slow walk again, letting Triss relax back into my shadow after a little while to preserve his strength against emergencies. It was a slog, and I desperately needed about fifteen hours of sleep and a triple portion of breakfast.

The few people I encountered along the way gave me a wide berth. Who could blame them? I must have looked like a holy beggar, clad only in a breechclout and covered in scrapes and bruises. When the first of the street vendors started setting up, I was half-tempted to actually try to beg a few coins here and there so I could buy a bit of breakfast. The boiling congee and frying sausages smelled like a little slice of heaven. But I couldn't afford the trouble freelance begging would buy me with the real guttersiders, so I let it go. Gutterside had a most ungentle way of settling quarrels.

I'd just reached the edge of the Stumbles when it finally occurred to me to wonder about how *exactly* I'd ended up in that dungeon. That's when I realized that going back to the Gryphon might not be the best idea I'd ever had since I had no answers for some very important questions. Most notably: How had the parties who put me there known right where to find me and exactly how to take me down? Parties as yet unnamed who might well try to pick me up again. It probably should have struck me earlier, and it might have if I'd been more than half-alive, or less focused on Devin and what he might be doing to Maylien.

Maylien. Dammit!

If Devin killed her, I'd have no choice but to kill him, and probably the baroness as well. Debts owed to the living can be negotiated. The dead can only be paid with absolutes. Justice. Revenge. Redemption.

I shook my head. Worry about it tomorrow. For now, I needed to worry about making sure I had a "tomorrow." So when I passed a certain alley, I turned into it. This one didn't smell nearly as nice as the one up in Old Mews had, and I tried very hard not to think about the stuff squelching over the tops of my bare feet. Triss had sheathed the soles in a toughened layer of shadow stuff to keep me from injuring myself when we got close to the Stumbles, but the muck was ankle-deep here.

About fifty feet in, I found the crumbling stone wall I remembered and used it as a ladder to take me up onto the rooftops. From there I made my slow way to an old brick-faced tenement that had burned two years ago. Most of the place was a dangerous ruin, but one old turret on the south-ern corner had survived mostly intact, and I'd set it up as a fallback.

You always have to have a fallback in case the plan goes bad, even when the plan is as simple as drinking yourself to death.

It was nearly eight stories up, and the stairs were gone. The only way in involved a thirty-foot vertical climb followed by a short diagonal traverse to get to a slightly canted window. Even so, it would have attracted summer squatters had I not spent considerable time and magic making the climb look worse than it was and the floor appear as if it had gone in the fire. In winter, of course, it would have been deathly cold and a complete nightmare to heat, and even I would have been hesitant about making that climb with the bricks iced up.

It took everything I had left to make it up a wall I could normally have managed in my sleep. At the end, I literally fell in through the window of my hidey-hole and crawled to my little straw tick. I barely had the energy to wrap myself in one of the worn woolen horse blankets I'd stashed there before I tumbled into the ocean of sleep and sank into the depths.

I had evil dreams and woke from them both too early and gladly. My everything hurt, and I was as stiff as boiled leather though I'd escaped with no serious injury. Lok's beaters had been very good at their job, and I was glad they were dead though the satisfaction that gave me did nothing for the pain.

Wind woke me, a chilly blow coming in off the sea and whistling through the myriad cracks in the ruined old

building. Fortunately, the warm afternoon sun pouring in
through the shutters I'd forgotten to close offset the worst
of the wind. I'd slept a good ten hours. I could have used ten
more, and I really didn't want to move, but I needed a piss.

As I rolled off the straw mattress, most of my fresh scabs
stayed behind with the blanket they'd stuck to, and I had to
bite back a scream. A couple started bleeding again, though
none badly. Not even the long gash Weasel had left on my
ribs, which looked shallower than I'd expected—though I'd
have to get Triss to double-check it for me.

Getting to my feet made me feel about nine hundred
years old, but I managed it. I staggered my way over to the
open hole where the stairs had once been. I undid my filthy
breechclout and dropped it into the opening, then followed
it with the contents of my bladder. It was only when I was
done that I realized Triss hadn't said a word yet. Turning
back toward my bed, I saw a thin line of shadow stretching
from me to an irregular patch of darkness where I had lain.

If you sketched our connection as a tail, the patch looked
rather like a dragon with its nose tucked under one wing. I
stepped closer, and called Triss's name. The shadow didn't
even twitch. Triss was dead asleep, and that told me just how
awful yesterday had been for him. In the twenty years since
we'd bonded when I was seven, he'd outslept me less than
a dozen times, and only twice had he slept through my getting out of bed.

I left him lying there and crossed the little room to my
supply cache, a big, lidded earthenware amphora sealed with
spelled wax. I'd lifted it special for the purpose from among
an upscale tavern's empties. There wasn't anything better
for keeping the rats and other vermin out of your goods, not
that could be scavenged on the cheap anyway. Inside, I'd left
a worn but still wearable change of clothes, a couple of battered daggers, a smaller jar full of rice, and a bottle of Kyle's.
I set one of the daggers where I could reach it, ignored the
clothes and the rice, opened the whiskey, and took a long
pull—purely medicinal.

At least, that's what I told myself, that the Kyle's was the best way to file the sharpest edges off my collection of aches and pains. I'd just had my third hit off the bottle when Triss made a sort of unhappy clucking noise.

"Don't you think it's a little early for that?" he asked.

"It's medicinal," I said. "And it's midafternoon."

"But the meal you're drinking is breakfast. I think that trumps the actual hour, don't you?" He cocked his head to one side, and I got the distinct impression of a disapproving stare. "Especially considering the day we have ahead of us. Or have you already forgotten about Maylien?"

I hadn't, not quite, but he was still right. With a sigh, I took a last drink, then recorked the bottle and set it aside. Sometimes it's a pain having an external conscience, especially one that won't shut up.

"Better," said Triss. "You're going to need your wits unscrambled if we want to find Devin and stay out of the hands of Lok's crowd." He sounded angry when he mentioned Lok, but the homicidal rage of the previous night seemed to have lightened enough to shift his focus to Devin.

"Lok's crowd." I shook my head. Their behavior didn't make any more sense looking back than it had at the time. "Who do you suppose they are? And what do they want?"

Triss shrugged his wings. "Whoever they are, they know far too much about our kind for my comfort. Once we've recovered the girl, we'll need to find and kill them and their master. The sheuth glyph would be enough to condemn them even without that trick they pulled with the deathspark and those Kadeshi mercenaries. That's all information we don't dare allow to spread."

I shrugged. "With only four Blades left beyond Devin's lot, I don't know that the information matters all that much." Triss froze and gave me a hard look, and I held up a hand. "I'm not saying we shouldn't kill them, just that Blade secrets don't seem to matter that much anymore."

"Do you truly believe that?" asked Triss, and I heard real sadness in his voice.

"I don't know, Triss. If Devin's assassins are the future of the order, maybe it'd be better if more people had ways to take us down. Maybe it would be better if we died out completely."

Triss shook his head wordlessly, then laid his chin on my thigh. I scratched him behind his ears, and we sat like that for a while.

"I'm sorry, Triss," I said finally. "I just get depressed sometimes."

"I know. I'm sorry, too. But that doesn't mean we should give up."

I wanted to say that I gave up a long time ago, but I couldn't do that to Triss. Especially since it wasn't really true. I might have given up on many things, but I'd never give up on him. And now after last night, I was maybe even starting to see some hope for me again. Which meant we probably did need to make some plans for the future.

"You're right about that glyph's being all kinds of bad news for the few of us that remain," I said. "But I'm a lot less worried about the deathspark."

"Why so?"

"A deathspark's a mighty chancy bit of magic under the best of circumstances, even more so when tied to more than one man like that. If your target doesn't take the bait within a day and a night, you've done nothing more than kill the ones you set it on to no good purpose. Beyond that, I doubt it'd even bother any of the other remaining Blades. I didn't see any other swords on the bottom of the sacred lake when I put mine there."

Triss shook his head. "That assumes it was the magic in the goddess's steel that protected you instead of the touch of the goddess herself."

I thought about it for a moment. Some of the powers that resided in the swords of Namara were intrinsic to the weapons themselves, but not all. And a deathspark was damned powerful magic to have to counter. Sacrifice magic always is—not to mention dark as night-spilled blood. It's a sort of necromancy, burning up the life of a person so that their death will rebound on whoever killed them.

"Could be you're right, Triss." Then I shrugged. "Either

way, I'm screwed. I've neither sacred steel nor goddess left to protect me."

"Which means," said Triss, sternly, "that we need to start thinking about how to prepare you for another deathspark."

He had a point. "I assume there are things a person can do to ward against them. I just don't know what since it never mattered to me before. I guess that's one more item to put on the giant list of things we need to know yesterday. Along with who Lok was working for, how they found me, why they wanted to know about Devin, where Devin is, what his plan is, where did he take Maylien, who is Maylien really, and so on."

"None of which can be solved from here," said Triss.

"None of which can be solved from here. Which, I suppose, means that I need to get dressed." I reached for the whiskey again, and Triss stiffened grumpily.

"For external use this time," I said, "much as it pains me to say it. These cuts need cleaning." Triss furled his wings and settled back down. "I need a bath, too, but that's going to have to wait till we're in a better neighborhood."

Half an hour later, I was back on the street dressed as a much poorer and more travel-worn version of myself. Down in the street, the wind wasn't half so cold though it still kicked up a lot of dust and grit. Many of the people I passed had wrapped scarves around their faces or turned up the collars of their vests and jackets. I made a quick stop at a public bath and another at an armorer—the one necessary before I could bear to put my boots on, the other to pick up a hard-used short sword. And that reduced to the brink of starvation the already thin emergency purse that had been tucked into the bottom of my cache.

Half an hour after that, I was making my way through the crowded streets and over the top of the Kanathean Hill toward the Old Mews, hoping desperately that the giant banner of smoke trailing away in front of me wasn't coming from my erstwhile dungeon. Then I got close enough to see the fire.

It wasn't the dungeon.

It was the whole damn neighborhood.

7

The wind off the sea had whipped the flames into an all-devouring madness. The entire neighborhood was lost. I had a damned good idea where and how it had started, and I swore bitterly at the sight. Accidental fires didn't spread this way, not in good neighborhoods, where they could afford to keep the antifire wards in top shape. Not even with these winds.

That made this emberman's work. Lok's mystery boss was covering his tracks and Devin's, too, though I figured that last was an accident. Devin might have fallen a long way, but I simply couldn't imagine him playing emberman. Fire killed wholesale. Using it like this marked you out as someone who couldn't hit the target clean. Incompetent. A temple-trained Blade would sooner cut his own throat.

Though I didn't think it would do me much good, I moved upwind and slipped through the cordon of stingers that were keeping people away from the fire. The line of watchmen, in the black and gold uniforms that gave them their nickname, were fending off a mixed crowd. Gawkers and opportunists mostly, leavened with the occasional concerned resident. I didn't get very deep into the burning neighborhood. Even with the smoke mostly blowing away from me, the heat forced me to turn around before I'd traveled much more than a block.

"Dammit, dammit, dammit!" I turned away from the flames, toward the nearest wall and my shadow. "Triss, what are the chances of us circling around and picking up Devin and Zass's trail somewhere beyond the edge of the fire?"

My shadow leaped and danced in the wild interplay of fire and light-cutting smoke just as you might expect of a normal shadow. The movement cleverly concealed what I recognized as a careful scan for other observers. But we were alone, though whether that was because of the effectiveness of the guards or because no one else was crazy enough to go so deep into the fires, I couldn't say. And my shadow soon slid into the familiar shape of the dragon. He looked nervous and kept a close watch on the closest flames—even normal fire can hurt a Shade if there's enough of it.

"I'm sorry, but it's just not going to happen today," said Triss. "It probably wouldn't have worked even if we were able to start from that trailhead we found last night. Too many hours of spring sunshine have already passed since Zass last touched the stones there." He spread his wings to take in the fires around us. "And now . . ." He shook his head. "Heat and light will have burned the trail completely away."

"I wish you'd told me last night that we'd lose the trail if we waited. We could have—"

"Could have what?" interrupted Triss. "Chased a renegade Blade across the rooftops in the darkness when we were both injured and exhausted? Done so virtually unarmed? Facing who knows what traps Devin might have left on his back trail? With your nima drained to the dregs? And if we *had* caught him, then what? There are simpler and less embarrassing ways to commit suicide than facing Devin under such circumstances."

I wanted to argue, but the heat of the flames was tearing at my back like a fiery scourge. Besides, Triss was right again. There are ways to wield power beyond the ends of your nima, but they require physical reserves I simply hadn't owned the night before.

I sighed and nodded. "I suppose that trying for mage-lightning and bursting your heart instead is probably not the smartest way to end your life."

"Neither is burning alive." Triss looked around worriedly, and I nodded again.

"Point. We'll have to find another angle on Devin and Maylien." A coughing fit prevented my saying anything more. So I threw my arm across my face and started breathing through the fabric of my sleeve as I took us away from the fire.

Once I got out in the clear again, I turned toward the Spinnerfish. I figured I had just enough cash left to cover a meal and a few tongue-loosening drinks. With the shadow trail broken, I needed to find Devin some other way, and the Spinnerfish provided good food, rich information, and a pleasant place out of the wind where I could play bait.

If you want to catch a shark, you spill blood in the water—another thing I'd learned from Master Kelos. And since mine was the blood Devin wanted most . . .

I'd barely put my ass in the chair at the same table I'd had last time when Erk appeared from the back. He was holding my half-finished tucker bottle of Kyle's, two glasses, and the drum-ringer. It saved me the trouble of asking after the bottle but also made me mighty nervous to be singled out like this again.

"Don't you look sour," he said after he poured the two glasses full. "I hope it's not on account of your buying me a drink. I didn't have to save the bottle for you in the first place."

"Nothing on you and the Kyle's," I replied as I picked up my glass, then coughed to cover my jerk when Triss kicked me in the ass. "I'm thinking I should maybe be drinking a bit lighter anyway. Though I do find myself wondering about being graced with your presence at my table two nights in a row."

Erk frowned. "If you're that badly out of count on the

days, maybe you have been tipping the bottle too much. But that's not why I came by and not my business by any means."

"Wait," I said, "what do you mean 'out of count'? What day *is* it?"

Erk raised his eyebrows and took a drink, then said flatly, "Sylvasday."

"Oh." That was four days after Atherasday, which was when I'd been deathsparked. I hadn't realized I'd been out nearly so long. It was my turn to take a drink though, out of deference to Triss, I sipped the whiskey instead of knocking it straight back. Which is what I wanted to do after that news.

"Lose a couple days?" asked Erk.

I nodded. "Though not to drink." I paused then, remembering Erk's reputation as a former black jack. "Actually, you might be able to help me there. Do you know any way to avoid a deathspark?"

"Ouch." He whistled. "That's bad magic, and I can't say I've heard of any way to avoid it except not hitting the target."

"I'd never have thought of that." I couldn't keep the sarcasm out of my voice.

"No, seriously. There's no point in killing a man walking under that mark. He'll burn away from the inside soon enough on his own. Why bloody your dagger? You just need to learn to spot the signs and walk away. Looks a lot like caras-dust addiction actually, bright eyes, lank hair, sweaty, talking too much. The main difference is that your caras snuffler doesn't have an ash-drawn glyph on the back of his neck."

"And if it's him or you?" I asked.

Erk's eyes went far away for a second, then widened. "The Kadeshis, you mean. From the other night. That explains several things." Then he shook his head and seemed to be looking inward. "I'm surprised I didn't notice that. Must have been a very freshly set spark. Well, that, and I'm not really in the business of watching out for that sort of thing anymore." Finally, he shrugged. "Him or you is always a tougher question, but I'd think someone like yourself could have just faded into the shadows and walked away if you'd chosen."

He had me there, but if we started talking about all the mistakes I'd made recently, we'd be there all night, so I moved on. "While I'm asking you questions, I've another. I met a girl recently, and I was wondering if you might know anything about her. That's why I stopped in actually."

"To ask me questions?" He crossed his arms and gave me a very hard look. "If she's a customer, I don't know anything more about her than I know about you when someone asks."

"No, not to ask you questions, but to ask some of your other customers," I said. "You just happened to sit down first. Besides, it's not like that. She's a client of mine, a noble one and she . . . let's just say I owe her one. I'm not looking for anything confidential, just common city gossip. Besides, I doubt she's spent much time in the Spinnerfish. Her name is Maylien and she's related to the Baroness Marchon."

"Sorry," said Erk, his expression closing further. "I'm afraid I can't help you."

Which told me that she *had* eaten at the Spinnerfish often enough for Erk to recognize the name. And that meant someone else there could probably give me something useful. I smiled and took another sip of my whiskey.

"Fair enough. That runs my line out," I said. "What are *you* fishing for tonight? You said the Kadeshis' being tied to a deathspark explained a lot. Is that it?"

"I'm not fishing, and yes, it's the Kadeshis. I wanted to warn you about . . ." He turned in his seat and looked toward the door. A moment later it opened and a tall woman came in. She wore a gold and black uniform with a watch captain's insignia on the shoulders. "Well, that," Erk said as he slipped the drum-ringer into his jacket and headed toward the newcomer.

"Captain Fei," said Erk, "as always, I'm delighted to see you come in. Would you like your usual table?"

Fei nodded absently as she scanned the room. She was

broad across the shoulders and hips, with the heavy muscles of a jindu master. A thick brown braid hung almost to her waist, plaited flat for ease under a helm. She was too pale to be highborn and had freckles on her cheeks and arms as well as light green eyes that marked her as having a foreigner in her ancestral line, and that all too recently. Her face was round, her features plain but pretty, almost soft, an impression belied by the knife scar that ran down and back from her left cheekbone to the point of her jaw.

I hunched my shoulders a bit and looked down at the table when she glanced my way. In other circumstances, I might have made a point of smiling and meeting her eyes to show my innocence, but not in the Spinnerfish. Here and now, not looking like I had something to hide would have marked me out as different from my fellows, suspicious. I didn't play it too big because that would have drawn unwanted attention, too. Especially since Fei knew me. She knew everybody in the shadow trades, having worked with all of the heavy players at one time or another and most of the independents, including me.

Captain Kaelin Fei was something of a Tienese institution, the perfect model of a corrupt cop. She had hooks in every major shadow operation in town, and everyone who mattered knew it, including Fei's boss, the watch commandant, and his boss, the Duchess of Tien. Maybe even King Thauvik himself.

Unlike a regular district captain, Fei had no set area under her watch and no investigatory responsibility. Fei's only job was maintaining stability in the capital city. It was almost surprising that more places hadn't invented a Captain Fei since the role she filled went a long way toward making the locals feel safe and secure. The ones who mattered to government anyway. It was Fei's job to see that shadow wars didn't spill out of places like the Stumbles and Smuggler's Rest to trouble the more upright citizens, and to make sure that what crime there was in the better neighborhoods didn't cause civil unrest. Fei was very good at that job. She was also coming my way.

Fuck.

I ignored her right up until she sat down across from me, at which point I put on a sick smile. "Buy you a drink, Captain?"

"Thank you, Aral, that would be lovely." She raised a hand to signal the waitress and ordered a glass of rice wine. "Been a long time since I last saw you in here."

It was a request for information.

"I like the food well enough, but I'm rarely so much in pocket I can indulge myself."

"And you are now?"

"I'd say that's self-evident."

The captain's sake arrived, and she took a sip before continuing, "S'funny, you don't *look* in pocket." She reached across and touched a stain on my cuff. "Not at all."

Shit. I'd forgotten the clothes. I wanted to blame the dungeon and the deathspark, but too many years of booze and easy jobs made a more likely answer. My heart tried to beat faster, but I forced it to stay slow and steady. The captain might not be able to hear the beat, but she'd see the secondary signs if I let myself get too nervous. For a brief moment I regretted having given up efik—a dose of calm would have gone down very nicely just then.

I darted a look around, then lowered my voice, "Don't tell anyone, but I got rolled last night. In my best clothes no less. Finished up a nice little job and went on a binge. Passed out in the wrong place just like a green fool."

When a tough question comes too close to the truth, the easiest way to throw off the scent is to give an embarrassing confession to something completely different.

"That was a damned stupid move, especially for a jack of your experience and reputation. Even a drunk. Might be time to cut back on the booze."

"It is that," I agreed, and a pressure along my back let me know that Triss thought so, too. When I spoke again, it was as much to him as Fei. "I learned an important lesson last night, and a dangerous one. From here on out I'll be mastering my drinking instead of letting the drink master me. I really am getting my act back together"—I leaned forward—"and I'd take it as a personal favor if you wouldn't pass that story along to anyone, Captain."

She took another sip of her rice wine and gave me a long, considering look. "Your eyes have seen what the bottom looks like. I can see it there, and that didn't used to be the case." She nodded. "You're a smart man, Aral, and a good jack. Every time I've given you a job, it's gotten done without any mess or fuss, which is why you've gotten more than one and will likely see my coin again in the future. Don't let the bottom suck you down again."

"I don't intend to." Triss rubbed my back companionably, and I started to relax.

Mistake.

"Now tell me why you reek of smoke and not from a brazier. The Old Mews is on fire, and you've been up that way today, or I'm a fresh-hatched chick. That's well outside your normal territory. What brought you there?"

"A delivery." How had she smelled that? I hadn't washed my clothes, but I wasn't sitting all that close to her, and there were plenty of stronger scents in the packed tavern. "I can't say more."

"Not even for me?" She batted her long eyelashes at me. On her it looked predatory.

"Not even for the Son of Heaven," I replied. "Where it comes to my hires, I'm a mute, Fei. That's *to* you and . . ." I drew out the pause, "about you."

Fei laughed. "You drive a sharp point there, jack. Fair enough. But if I find out you had anything to do with starting that fire, I'll nail your flayed hide up for display behind the gallows. Nobody does that in my city and lives."

"Then we're fine. Emberman's so far out of my line, you can't even see the shadow from where I stand. That's black-work of the worst sort. I don't kill for money and I'd sooner slit my wrists than take a job that involved fire."

"Glad to hear you so emphatic," said Fei, but her eyes narrowed slightly—curious but not suspicious, though I don't think anyone who hadn't been trained to read faces would have caught it.

I'd slipped somehow, exposed something I oughtn't.

I took a sip of my whiskey and leaned back in my chair and tried to decide how to cover whatever it was I'd given away. But I just didn't know enough. Fei took another drink as well and I could see her weighing things up in her head like a warboard player trying to decide what piece to move next.

"S'funny," she said eventually.

"What?" I asked after a few seconds of silence told me she wanted me to.

"You speak the language so well that I sometimes forget you're not a native, and that despite your looks. Where are you from originally? Your bones are Varyan, but the accent's too faint for me to be sure, and there's enough outbreeding between Varya and Dalridia or the Kvanas to blur things."

"You're very good, Captain. I'm from Emain Wast, right on the edges of the mageburned lands."

Which was half a lie. I was Varyan right enough, but I'd been born in Emain Tarn on the shores of the sacred lake and less than a day's walk from the temple of Namara. Anyone who knew Namara would know that didn't really matter, that her Blades came from every one of the eleven kingdoms that had survived the great burning. But I didn't want Fei putting Namara and me in the same thought even in passing, and Emain Wast lay as far away from the temple as you could get in Varya and still be in a city. I didn't think the captain would buy me as a country boy.

"What were you there, I wonder?"

Fei didn't sound like she was really talking to me, but I answered anyway, "Shadow jack, same as here. Or maybe just a bit shadier." I grinned and flicked my eyebrows up, inviting the captain to share in the joke. "Left the place a half step ahead of one of your counterparts in the law."

"Price on your head?" asked Fei.

I nodded. "Though not big enough to be worth the shipping fee, if you're thinking about trying to collect on it."

"But it *is* big enough that you can't go home."

"Nor anyplace else in Varya or the Kvanas. It taught me a lesson that's stuck, too—that there's good work and bad in the shadows and that I won't touch the latter ever again."

"Once burned . . ." she said.

"I don't think I'll complete the old saw if you don't mind. No burning for me. Not then and not now. Let's just say that I'm cautious about the jobs I'll take and leave it there. But that's more than enough talking about me. What brings you down to this end of town? If the question's not treading on any dangerous ground, that is. If it is, forget I asked."

Fei rolled her glass between her fingers, warming the sake, which had cooled while we talked. "It's not dangerous ground at all. Not for you at any rate, unless you're hiding a mage under those old rags you're wearing. Actually, there might be some coin for you in this job if you're interested and not otherwise engaged."

"Hang on a second." I pulled my shirt out and looked down the collar. "Nope. Nobody in here but one slightly sooty jack." I forced a grin. "Figured I'd best check for mages since the odd spot of nightside delivery *does* fall into my line though not usually so big a package as all that, and I'd rather play honest with you where I can."

Fei snorted, then drank a bit more of her sake. "No. Whoever set this play up runs a couple of cards up from the jack. I'm looking for a king or an ace if it's really a shadowside job and an earl or a baroness if the sunside royalty is playing."

My ears pricked at the word "baroness." "Sounds messy."

"And political. Someone ghosted a couple of Kadeshi mercenaries about a hundred and fifty yards thataway." The captain waved vaguely toward the door. "Which circumstance would normally be grounds for celebration in my office. There's no one like a Kadeshi for making trouble."

"But . . ." I had to fight to keep the interest out of my voice.

"But these bastards all had deathmarks on the backs of their necks of the magelightning variety. A deathspark's a tricky and expensive bit of magery even without tying it to three deaths instead of just the one. And that's saying nothing about how illegal it is. But again, not something I'd normally worry about. My job's making sure things run smooth and quiet, not enforcing the law."

"What happened to the killers? Charcoal? That's how a deathspark works, right?"

"It is and I wish, but no. Whatever party or parties sliced these boys up—a *very* fancy piece of knifework, I might add—has vanished away completely."

"So where *do* you come in? And, more importantly, where do I? I'm always up for a bit more coin, but . . . Bad boys get marked. Bad boys get killed. Killers go completely bye-bye. That sounds about as smooth and quiet as you could ask for things to run. I'd think you'd want to leave it there."

"Nothing would make me happier," said Fei, "but this one's got its very own set of noises and bumps in the person of a baroness of the royal house and her own pet colonel of the Elite, both of whom want to know what happened and why justice has not yet been served on all involved."

Fuck, Elite.

"Okay, I'm still not seeing where I come in," I said.

Meanwhile, Triss started doing the routine where he marches invisible centipedes up and down my back.

"I thought you might want to play ear for me. Outside your normal line, I know, but it's clean, and you're a smart player. The noble pressure means I need to get this one done quick, and that calls for a wide net. If you hear anything I might want to know on this one, I'll make it worth your while."

"Now that sounds like . . . Oh, shit."

The door of the Spinnerfish had just opened.

"What is it?" asked Fei.

"Your Elite colonel, skinny little quink with a bit of a limp?"

"That's him." She wrinkled her nose.

"Well, he's about to join us."

In the moment before Fei turned in her seat and waved

to the colonel, I saw the faintest trace of fear ripple through her eyes. It was erased an instant later by the adamantine nerves that had made her such a power in Tien's shadow trades, but it was there.

Blade training or not, I started to sweat.

8

———◆———

Physically, the colonel did not impress, but he practically burned with magic. Seething light danced around him in wild patterns of oranges and browns for eyes that could see it, a network of active and preset spells that must cost him hours every day to maintain. One thick rope of fiery orange looped around his left wrist and plunged from there into the floor like a fall of molten iron from a blacksmith's crucible or a leash for hell's own hound.

I forced my eyes not to follow its trail down into the earth, not to look for the colonel's buried familiar at the other end of that spell, his stone dog. Because Aral the jack was no mage, and Aral the Blade rated a prominent place on the Elite's death roster. Though the colonel didn't seem to be aware of me in any way, I knew that he had seen who sat with Fei and that he would be watching me too-too close. On my back, Triss's utter lack of movement made a presence of absence as he played at being nothing more than a shadow.

I kept my gaze fixed on the man's feet, expressing deference in expression and posture, and I sweated. The Elite had accounted for more Blades than any other organization in our history. They were nearly as good with the weapons of the body as we were, and much better where it came to magic. But more than that, they had the stone dogs.

Like the statues that guarded Zhan's temples come to life, they stood five feet at the shoulder with thick, strong bodies, and heads like lions. The stone dogs could cut the earth like sharks slicing through clear water. Softer than granite but harder than sandstone, they were fanatically loyal to their Elite companions and to Zhan's rightful ruler. They had killed at least two of the three Blades who died trying for Ashvik VI before my knife spilled royal blood and forever tied me to the name of Kingslayer.

As the colonel made his slow and careful way toward our table, I used the edges of my vision to study his face. Thin and pinched, marked by long pain and the fanaticism endemic to the Elite. An ugly and familiar expression on a stranger's face . . . No, I suddenly realized as he got closer, a familiar face, if you can call a moment's frantic meeting ten years in the past grounds for familiarity.

Fuck, fuck, fuck!

I recognized the colonel though I prayed to lost Namara's memory that he wouldn't recognize me. I had last seen his face on the night I killed a king. Of all the trouble I ran into that night, the worst was a young lieutenant of the Elite.

Dressed and masked in grays and wearing my shadow as a cloak, I had seen him before he saw me. I'd been so proud then, filled with youth's ignorance—for I was younger even than the lieutenant—convinced of the approval of my goddess and flushed with thoughts of success. Certain that I was the best there'd ever been, I'd wanted no dead guards staining my record of a clean kill on the king. I'd tried to slip past him unseen, but the hall was too brightly lit, and the darkness that concealed me also betrayed my presence.

He lunged at me, missing his thrust and leaving himself open to a low return as Triss shifted one way and I the other to confuse his aim. That and his position in the Elite made him a fair target. None of Namara's servants would have faulted me for killing him, but I wanted no other arrows showing on the butt to distract from a perfect bull's-eye on Ashvik. Instead of aiming for an artery, I'd thrust for the big nerve cluster where thigh met groin.

Fool.

The lieutenant went down screaming as my goddess-blessed sword punched through his wards and went deep. I spun away, then used the wall as a backstop and launched myself high over the body in a bit of overfancy and frankly showoffish footwork. That jump was an arrogance that saved my life when his stone dog came up through the floor clawing and biting. The dog shredded my boot and carved bloody furrows in my left calf. I bore the scars to this day and counted it light payment for the lesson driven home.

You can never let your pride trump your professionalism. Not if you want to live.

In combat, you have to sort people into two categories. There are targets, and there's everybody else, and you kill the targets. No exceptions. I'd forgotten that then and it had nearly gotten me killed. Now, as the colonel came closer, moving with a limp I'd given him, I wondered if that "nearly" was about to be removed from the record. If so, it would make for a bitter coincidence though perhaps a not wholly surprising one.

There were never more than a few score of the Elite to start with, the familiar-paired sorcerers who made up the officer and operative class of the Crown Guard. Most of those stayed close to the king's person and the capital, though a few were assigned permanently to Vangzien and the summer palace or Anyang, where special winter courts were sometimes held.

But then the colonel had arrived at our table, and I was out of time for thinking. I moved my gaze from his boots to the tabletop and kept it there. The effort of keeping my shoulders hunched and submissive instead of rolling them into a loosened state of readiness felt like a stone weight pressing down on my mind and back.

"Captain Fei," said the colonel, his tone clipped and contemptuous, more indictment than greeting.

"Colonel Deem." Fei lowered her head in something

halfway between the nod of an equal and the bow of an inferior.

"Any news?"

"Not yet." Fei sniffed and tilted her head my way. "I've just been making inquiries while I waited for you to arrive."

"Is this a person of interest, then?" Deem seemed to really look at me for the first time.

Fei barked a laugh that sounded more than a little false to me. "No, Aral's just a broken-down jack I occasionally employ for odd jobs. I thought he might have heard something that wouldn't have risen to the top of the shadows yet."

"Aral?" Deem stepped even closer, and I could see the network of active spells that enclosed him shift and brighten, ready for action. "That's a very unlucky name."

Breathe, Aral. To keep itchy hands from reaching for a knife or a sword, I rolled my whiskey glass between my palms, breathing deep of the rich smoky aroma released by the heat and motion.

"Tell me about it." I let my very real nerves color my voice. "I was born under an unlucky star, which is why my little brother ended up with the shop in Emain Wast, and I ended up doing shit work a thousand miles from home." I knocked back the last half of my drink in a single swallow, barely tasting it.

"Fell in with the wrong crowd," I continued, babbling intentionally, though I still didn't look up. "Started taking the kind of jobs that don't make a man proud. Got in a fight over a woman. Knives. Won it, too, nearly killed the guy. Turned out he was a noble's son. When the bailiffs came after me, I started running. Didn't stop till I hit the fucking ocean." I waved vaguely toward the docks.

Before I could say more, Deem turned very deliberately back to Fei. "And this is the sort of person you deal with on a regular basis?"

"My job doesn't leave a lot of time for sipping chilled wine with the highborn in the palace," replied Fei, her voice acid. Then she got up and gestured toward the back of the Spinnerfish. "Come on, I've got a private booth where we can talk."

As Deem started to walk away, Fei turned that curious look on me again, and I knew I'd slipped a second time. Maybe by making my sob story a little too smooth and a little too easy to reconcile with what I'd told her earlier. I'd been so focused on Deem, I'd forgotten the quality of my secondary audience. Master Olen would have had very hard words for a cover story that didn't layer properly for *all* my listeners, and the fact that I'd had to cook it up on the spot wouldn't have excused me. I should have remembered that Fei was sharp enough to notice things like how well you lied.

In my line of work, it's much harder to appear bad at things you do well and often more important.

But worrying about it now was like stopping to sharpen your knife *after* you'd already made the sloppy cut. I waited just long enough for the curtain that hid the passage to the private booths to stop moving. Then I made a show of finding my bottle empty and getting up and heading for the door. I'd wanted to learn more about Maylien, but this was no longer the time or the place for it, and I didn't think Erk would miss my business all that much. I had no doubt I was high on his list of least favorite customers at the moment, between the Kadeshis and Fei coming in wearing her city-watch hat instead of the shadow-captain one.

Actually, that made for an interesting study in Erk's ethics. I had no doubt that Erk would have left me hanging without a warning if Fei'd had shadowside reasons for asking after whoever ghosted those Kadeshis. It was only the fact that the captain's attention was official watch business that made Erk give me a shout. Shadowside was us. Sunside was them.

When I hit the street, the sun was already yawning, so I went up a nearby wall and looked around for a place to lie up out of the wind while I waited for full dark. The process made various cuts and bruises sing out for my attention. I found a temporary snug in a steeply slanted niche between two battered dormers on the lee side of a roof. A onetime temple to Calren the Taleteller, first and former Emperor of Heaven, now deceased. It was better built than most of the buildings in the area.

I wedged myself into the gap and settled down to think through my next move. Fish was clearly off my menu for the next couple of days, and I really didn't want to spend any time at the Gryphon, on the off chance that my enemies hadn't marked it yet. There were a couple of other taverns I could try if I wanted to trail a bit more of my blood in the water. But after my chat with Fei and the subsequent dance with Deem, I felt there were way too many sharks swimming around at the moment to make that a good idea.

I needed solid information about Maylien and House Marchon. Especially if the royal baroness who had Deem chewing on Fei's ass turned out to be Marchon. I didn't remember Marchon having any ties to the royal house. Nothing beyond the way the old baron's sister had catered to Ashvik's need to bed girls half his age, that is. But perhaps things had changed. I had to find out what had happened there.

If I could get the information someplace quiet and far enough from my regular haunts, I could use the whole thing as an opportunity for a fadeout and make the trip serve double duty. I knew just the spot, but I couldn't go there without making a brief stop at my main snug in the Gryphon's stable. That was a problem, both because I didn't want to mark the Gryphon and because I didn't want to lead them on to my next destination if they had.

If I really wanted to make a fade, I had to find some way to break my trail to the Gryphon both coming and going, and that was a skip that would run a whole lot smoother if I had any idea how they were trailing me in the first . . . Wait. Could it really be that simple?

I turned to where my shadow lay along the roof slates, almost invisible now in the twilight. "Triss, you can . . . I don't know, is 'smell' the right word for what you did with Zass up in the Old Mews?"

Triss shifted into dragon form and spoke softly, "No. We would say . . ." And here he dropped into his native tongue, making a sort of guttural hiss with liquid undertones. "'Taste' would be closer to the right meaning, but there's really no good word for it in human speech. You just don't have the right senses. It has to do with the interplay between light and shadow and the nature of the everdark." He shrugged his wings. "It's very hard to explain the sensation."

"All right . . . I guess we'll go with taste then. If you can taste where Zass has been, can he do the same for you?"

"Of course."

"Why have I never heard about this before?"

Triss's wings sagged, and he looked ashamed. "The Shade elders and the senior masters instructed us not to speak of it to our companions, said it was a secret of Namara. I never liked that, but I could not disobey the elders, not while . . ." He trailed off and didn't speak of the goddess's death though I knew that was what he meant. "Then, after the fall of the temple, it didn't come up since we never saw any other Shades."

"How does it work?"

"When a shadow falls on something, it leaves a sort of . . ." More hissing. "Call it an *afterflavor* of itself that gets slicked on the surface, at least for a little while. The darker the shadow, the stronger the *flavor*." He spread his wings, then flicked the tips back and forth in a gesture I'd come to recognize as searching after a thought. "Every shadow, no matter how faint or briefly cast, partakes of the everdark. We who are born from the substance of the everdark can sense where shadows have touched—taste the flavor of home in the darkness. If the impressions are strong enough, we can follow them like a trail."

"Could you teach me to do that?" I was grasping after something here, but I still hadn't gotten hold of enough of it to know what its final shape would be. "Or someone else?"

Triss shook his head. "No. You don't have the . . ." He hissed again, sharper this time. "Your mind isn't shaped right."

"What about a spell? Could you help me cook up something that would have the same effect? Magically? Or at least that would let me follow a . . . a taste trail?"

"Maybe." Triss flitted back and forth across the slates

like a pacing cat. "If the spells were set on a spyglass or a dark lantern, it could probably be made to"—long, involved hissing—"the trail so you could follow it, but only for the very"—more hissing—"*Everdarkest*-tasting shadows, like yours where it has been reinforced by my presence."

"Or Devin's because of Zass?"

"Yes, or any Blade's, really. A shadow that holds a Shade is much"—hissing—"realer than a regular shadow, yes, realer. And the more the Shade is present in the shadow at the time, the realer the impression it will leave."

"I'm not sure I followed that one," I said.

"When I am hiding in your shadow, as I did with the colonel a few minutes ago, the shadow would taste stronger than a regular shadow but only to a"—hissing—"truly refined palate. Whereas when I am in my chosen shape"—he flapped his wings for emphasis—"I will leave a much stronger and longer-lasting flavor, easier to track—more real. And the same would happen when I enshroud you."

Now he cocked his head to one side. "Yes, the more I think about it, the more I think it would be possible to set a spell in some item that would allow such a trail to be followed. This is how we are being found, yes?"

"I think so, but it still leaves me confused. Lok's people seemed genuinely to want to know everything I could tell them about Devin. If they're working with or for Devin, why would they need that information? And if they're not, how did they get ahold of such a tracking spell? I seriously doubt there's a third Blade involved. There were never that many of us to start with, and I can't imagine *any* Blade going along with building that rack-thing they had us strapped to."

"Perhaps Devin's allies do not intend to stay his allies."

A little electric thrill danced across my shoulders, like the aftereffects of a big burst of magelightning. Yes. That felt right, a double cross. I nodded.

Don't fight your instincts. A trained mind works on multiple levels, and you have to learn to listen to yourself even when there are no words.

"I think you've got it, Triss. The baroness and Devin

struck me as very uneasy partners. It wouldn't surprise me at all if there's a betrayal on someone's schedule. Or, considering what we know of the new Devin, more than one someone's. We'll use that as our working assumption going forward. Next question, what breaks a shadow trail?"

"Summer sunlight is best, but fire will work, too."

"Like the Old Mews."

"Like the Old Mews," agreed Triss.

"Do you think Devin started . . ." But I couldn't finish the question, still couldn't even imagine the answer being yes. It would be too big a betrayal of what the goddess had expected of us.

"No!" Triss sounded utterly emphatic. "A fire that big in that kind of neighborhood had to involve magic, and Zass would never help in such a thing."

I really hoped Triss was right about that, but I couldn't help imagining the arguments I might make if I were Devin, and I wanted it bad enough. I remembered how angry Triss had gotten at the people who had held us prisoner, how willing, even eager he had been to kill and destroy. Zass hadn't been bound to the rack as we had, but if Devin had wanted to start the burning with that glyph, how much of a push would it have taken?

Evil thoughts. I shook my head and tried to push them aside. We had things that needed doing and . . . hey, maybe I'd just figured out how to manage them.

"Why don't we use our enemies' own tools against them?" I asked.

"What do you mean?"

"The fire in the Old Mews."

"I don't understand," said Triss. "I know you're not suggesting we start a fire to cover our trail."

"Heat and light you said, right?"

"Yes . . ."

Even with the torn-away sleeve of my old shirt tied across my mouth and nose to fend off the worst of the smoke, I couldn't stop coughing as we jumped from one field of coals to another through what had once been a thriving neighborhood. Triss had wrapped himself around me from the knees up to keep away from the fire. I could feel his comforting presence against my skin like cool silk, and I needed all the comfort I could get. The stench from the burning of the Old Mews was horrific.

Wood, of course, a hundred kinds, horsehair that had been used to reinforce plaster and stucco or stuff furniture, straw, cotton, wool, silk. Those were the good smells. The paint and lacquer, lead, copper, the shit from the chamber pots, those were worse. But worst of all was the horrible smell of burned meat. Horse. Dog. Human. Whoever had done this had to die.

"I'm going to find out who started this fire, and I'm going to kill him," I said between coughs. "I owe it to the dead."

And as I said that, I stopped right there. In the middle of a ruined house with smoke rising from the soles of my slowly burning boots and the sweat pouring off me in sheets, I listened to the words coming out of my own mouth, and I really heard them. It froze me where I stood because I had realized a great and terrible truth.

Someone had done real evil here and they needed to die for it. I owed it to the dead. Not just those killed in the fire. I owed it to my goddess and to all my fallen comrades, who would never again have the chance to bring justice to the guilty.

For five years, I had forgotten or chosen to ignore what I was and why I had been given the gifts I had been given. I might not be a Blade of the goddess anymore, or the Kingslayer, or even the kind of man who could consistently tell good from evil—there was too much gray in my world now to ever be sure of the black and white again. But I had no right to ignore wrong when it slapped me in the face. I would stop whoever did this and I would stop them forever. I had to.

I owed it to the dead.

9

The Ismere, a club for gentlemen-merchants, stood only one narrow alley away from the private library of the same name. The former also provided the opportunity for a necessary stop along the way to the latter. My second round of coal-walking through the burned-over Old Mews neighborhood had left me even more committed to tracking down those responsible than the first round had. People were going to die for that. It also left me hot, sweaty, and covered in filth. So when I finally slid into the shadows beneath the club's rooftop water tank, I did so with a rather intense feeling of relief.

After carefully unfastening my heavy pack from the steel rings that attached it to my sword rig, I tucked it into a niche in the tank's supports. Then I stripped off my smoke-stained clothes and briefly contemplated tossing them into the river behind the building. Having recovered the rest of Maylien's silver, I was flush enough to replace my whole wardrobe and use my current best and cleanest to replenish the cache in my fallback. But you never know when a set of old rags might come in handy, so I stowed them beside the pack instead.

Then, naked except for a pair of daggers in wrist sheaths, I climbed the short ladder to the top of the tank, opened the trapdoor, fastened a length of rope to the edge, and lowered myself into darkness. The reservoir was on the low side, less than a quarter full, and a long day in the sun had turned the chest-deep water in the dark-roofed and -sided tank blood-warm. I sank into it with a happy sigh. In the dark, I couldn't see Triss, but I could feel him sliding about on the bottom of the tank, enjoying the water in his own alien way.

Washing the smoke stink out of my hair and skin felt wonderful, despite the extra attention I felt the need to give to my myriad of small cuts and bruises. Unfortunately, I lost my little bar of rough soap when I was still half a leg short of clean. As I made do with even harder scrubbing, I idly wondered if it would survive long enough to slip through the big clay pipes and slide down into one of the large private soaking pools that made club membership so popular with the traveling merchants and wealthier caravaneers. Honestly, I would have liked nothing better than to stay and have an hours-long soak myself, but I had urgent debts to both the living and the dead and couldn't afford to tarry.

Besides, there was always the chance that one of the club's servants might decide to have a quick bath. The exposed rope would make them very suspicious—they always went to such care to hide it from the owners. I could almost certainly fade my way out of any such encounter without having to hurt anyone, but it would be much smarter to avoid the need.

With a regretful sigh I hand-over-handed my way out of the tank. After I'd restowed the rope and changed into clean grays, I sorted my pack into two smaller bundles and carefully hid the larger, smellier one in the top of one of the club's chimneys—cold and dark at this time of year but with enough of a smoke smell of its own to mask the stink of my gear.

Next, six running steps and a Triss-assisted leap carried me across the narrow alley to the Ismere Library. I touched down on the steeply sloping lead roof of the library, then let myself slide down and over the edge to land on a third-floor balcony. The slatted doors were latched but not barred, and the thin strip of copper from my trick bag opened them neatly. The ward of alarm on the door was more tricky, but I'd had plenty of practice at bypassing it over the years.

Inside was a marble-floored reading room with a central table, and several smaller study carrels lined up along the rough mulberry-paper panels that served it for walls. The panels were often used in places where flexibility of floor plan might come in handy or where it was advantageous to let light bleed from room to room. Stopping only long enough to pull out a small leather-wrapped package, I left my swords and pack in one of the carrels. I didn't think I'd missed anything with smoke smell, but caution is always the best strategy when dealing with a librarian, and anything that might harm one of his books. Especially if he's a sorcerer of some repute.

Dealing with a dead king's bodyguard is much less fraught than facing a librarian who thinks you've just taken one of his precious charges through a fire, even a fire as burned-out as the Old Mews. Before slipping out into the main part of the library, I sniffed at the leather I'd wrapped around the book one last time. Clean, or at least, clean enough. Partially hooded magelights mounted on the ends of the shelves cast a dim yellow glow that could easily be brightened by raising the shutters.

I'd once asked Harad, the master librarian, about that and about why there were no actual windows in the stacks. He'd told me that prolonged exposure to direct sunlight was bad for books and that intense magelight was worse. Whatever the reason, I liked the way the shadows lay thick in the library, and Triss liked it even more—it gave him greater freedom. That and the peace and the smell of the books reminded me of the more contemplative parts of Namara's great temple. It wasn't quite like coming home, but it was as close as I was ever likely to get again.

More out of habit than concern, I checked each of the other three reading rooms that occupied the corners of the big square floor plan. It was well past the library's official closing time, but the collection was owned by a private fellowship whose members included the club next door, and merchants sometimes kept weird hours. Catering to that trade was half the reason the Ismere had a built-in apartment for the master librarian.

The other half was so that he could provide security for a lot of valuable property. Thanks to magical techniques borrowed from the inhuman denizens of the Sylvani Empire, the actual production of books was relatively inexpensive; but the materials' costs were high, especially the high-quality paper needed. The Ismere had been started by an extremely successful Kadeshi-born merchant who had paid for the building and provided the bulk of the initial collection. It had been added to steadily over the years by its members—donation of new titles could be used to offset the hefty fees the library charged.

As soon as I'd cleared the third floor, I catwalked down the back stairs to the second floor and gave it a once-over as well. That's where I found Harad, wandering quietly among the rows of books and checking to see that everything had gotten back to its proper place after the departure of the day's visitors. Even in the dim light, the many complex spells that wrapped him round made him easy to spot with magesight. Once I'd made sure we were alone, I got ahead of him and stood quietly in plain view, waiting for him to look up and see me. After a few moments, his eyes lifted and met mine, and he waved.

"You're up late," I said.

"I'm an old man and don't sleep as well as I used to. I like to take the opportunity to check on my charges and see that they are resting better than I am."

"You don't look that old to me." And, in truth, he didn't, no more than fifty, a well-preserved sixty at most, and that in a society where magical healing saw many of the better off into their eighties and nineties.

"But I am old, older by far than anyone most people will ever meet." He waved a hand. "I exclude you, of course, young Aral. You walk strange roads and see much that is hidden from the ordinary run of folk."

I smiled, and, for perhaps the twentieth time, asked, "How old are you, Harad?"

He smiled back and winked, and I waited for the usual coy dodge, but it didn't come. Instead, his smile faded into a thoughtful look.

"Do you really want to know? Truly?"

"Curiosity is one of my besetting sins." Even though I had more pressing questions and duties, Harad hadn't visibly aged in the ten years since I'd first met him, and I really did want to know more about that. This might be my only chance to find out. "That curiosity's what brought me here the first time."

"A decade ago, in the year that butcher Ashvik—may he burn eternally in the deepest of hells—was slain. I remember it like it was yesterday." He smiled again. "And in the long book that is my life, that is not so far from the truth. All right, curious boy, I will answer you . . . in a few minutes. Come back to my kitchen, and I will make us tea."

I wanted to refuse the tea, since it always reminded me of efik, but that might have shut off the potential flow of information, so instead I snorted and grumbled, "Now you're teasing me." Triss's brief squeeze of my shoulders told me that he agreed.

"No, I just prefer to tell things in their right time, and the right time for this tale is still a short way off."

"Have it your way, *old* man."

"For far more years than you've been alive I have done precisely that. I see no reason to change my ways now."

I grinned. After Triss, Harad was the nearest thing I had to a friend these days. Unlike Fei or Jerik or any of my other Tienese associations, there was no flow of debts between us, neither of blood nor of money. Just a mutual interest in books and all that lay between their covers. We'd first met because of that. I had snuck into the library one night because I felt the need to get away from my assignment to kill Ashvik—things hadn't been going well, and I was frustrated. I wanted nothing more than to read some slight volume and let the story lift me out of myself for a while.

Harad had found me at it, sitting in the very reading room where my gear now sat, my nose buried in a particularly lurid sort of adventure novel translated from the original Kanjurese. It was an odd moment really, him knocking very politely on the door frame—the door itself having soundlessly vanished when he approached—and lightly clearing his throat to let me know he was there.

I was mortified, of course, a Blade caught out by a librarian. But as I later learned, he was an exceptionally powerful sort of mage, and that certainly had something to do with it. To this day, I'm not sure why he chose to knock rather than throwing me out or calling in the stingers. Whatever the reason, it put me at my ease in a way I'd never have expected before it happened. Rather than drawing a weapon or some other hostile action, I'd simply set the book aside, and said, "Hello?"

He'd come in then and gently questioned me about my presence in his library and my intent. And, also, by the way, how did I like the book? I'd explained that I liked the story well enough, but that I thought the prose of the translation was pretty awful. That had led to a rather spirited discussion of translation in general, both on the page and in person. Ever since then, I'd had a sort of unofficial library membership and one person in Tien whom I could talk to without the weight of anything beyond mutual interest.

Once the water for the tea had cooled down a bit from its boil, Harad poured it over the powdered tea and carefully stirred with a whisk. An unusual method for Zhan, it spoke of foreign origins in a way much more forceful than Harad's Kadeshi name. It also reminded me of the efik ritual, a thought I pushed aside forcefully.

He'd just finished preparing the second cup—his own—when the timesman at the temple of Shan Starshoulders struck the great bell to signal midnight. Normally, I was too far away to hear it, but here in the wealthiest of the merchant districts, it rang quite clear. It reminded me time was pressing, but somehow I still couldn't bring myself to push Harad.

"There." Harad touched his ear. "That is what I have been waiting for. It signals the right time for this story."

"Which is?" I asked into the silence he left for that purpose.

"My birthday. With the tolling of the midnight bell I enter into my six hundred and eleventh year."

"Your what?"

"Don't give me that look, Aral. You don't feign shock well. The teacher who trained you to it emphasized the open mouth too much, and you have a touch of the ham in you, which pushes the whole thing just a *shade* too far."

The inflection on the word "shade" was so subtle as to be barely there, but it *was* there, and I had to suppress the impulse to twitch when I heard it. Triss, on the other hand, didn't feel any such constraints. He gave me a sharp jab in the ribs.

Harad went on. "Shock's not really a good look on you anyway. It undermines the whole tragic but dangerous image. I'd suggest you stick with the eye twitch and then a quick slide back to the blank stare of the gambler, like now. It plays to your strengths."

I'd recovered by then and also decided he might have a point—Master Kelos had once told me something similar. So I hung on to my closed face. Holding a hot cup in my hands helped there, reminding me as it did of old times and old disciplines at the same time it spiked my desire for a cup of efik.

"But I am shocked," I said, in a tone that belied the words. "Six hundred years old. That's awfully hard to believe."

"No. It's not. We both know that I'm a sorcerer and a powerful one. It's a requirement of the job here. The Ismere holds the largest and most valuable collection of books in all of Zhan—mostly because it is private and thus free of the censoring impulses of generations of Zhani royals." Harad's smile looked more than a trifle smug. "Like any sorcerer, my life is tied to my familiar's. As my companion's is the longer span, we have both measured our threads to his."

Unlike my dead buddy Lok and the spit-adder, where the lengthening of life went the other way—well, right up until Maylien killed him. I wondered what the nature of Harad's familiar was but knew better than to ask. If he'd wanted to tell me, he would have.

He continued, "Don't pretend that you don't know how that bonding works. If nothing else, you've read up on the topic. I know. I lent you the books."

I looked Harad flat in the eyes. "You know what I am, don't you?"

I set my untouched tea aside as Triss pressed himself hard against my back. But Harad simply shrugged and smiled.

"Since you ask, yes, though I would not have raised the issue had you chosen to leave it lie. I have known it from the first moment you snuck into my library a week before you rid the world of King Ashvik, the sixth and hopefully last of that name. It's in the way you walk and the way you hold your head when you lie, techniques passed down through dozens of generations."

"Like this." He shifted subtly in his chair and for just an instant I faced one of the masters of my order. Then he relaxed, and it was gone.

"Oh"—Triss slid out from behind me so that he could see better—"that was Kelos to the life. Very good." Shadow hands applauded.

Harad gave a half bow from his seat, as elegant as any actor's, but said nothing.

"I don't understand," I said after several seconds of silence while I reviewed my options.

They were much constrained by Triss's choosing to expose his presence. Funnily enough, attempting to kill Harad never ranked as a serious choice. Whether that was prudence or curiosity or simply friendship is still an open question.

"Three hundred years ago, servants of your Namara asked me to help out with the training of her Blades. At the time I was running a theater company in Varya and had been for perhaps fifty years before that. The masters wanted to add some refinements to their techniques, and who better to ask than an acting master. I had become bored with the theater at that point and I thought that teaching assassins might make for an entertaining change of scene. I was right, and I stayed a decade or three."

"What happened?" I was fascinated but also a tiny bit horrified at learning about Harad's involvement with my order. It was also funny how the word "assassins" bothered me not at all coming from his lips.

Triss assumed his dragon shape and settled on the floor by my feet. I suppressed an urge to whap him on the nose for exposing our secrets. That pot was already a decade spilled if Harad was being honest with us.

"I got bored and left the temple," said Harad. "It was a bit too much like working with the acting company, really. Then I moved on to another career and another after that. So far, I think that I like librarian the best. I've been here for a hundred and twenty years and might well stay a hundred more. Now that we've dealt with that, what brings you to see me tonight? You can't be done with that necromancer book already." His eyes flicked to my still-full teacup. "You don't read that fast or that steadily—it cuts into your drinking time."

I opened my hands to acknowledge the truth of his dig. "No, I haven't finished it. It's both a little too gruesome and a little too silly for me at the moment though I'd like to try it again someday. I was going to pretend that I had read it and ask you to find me something on what's been happening with the royal family and the succession since the death of Ashvik."

I continued, "I've been going out of my way to avoid as much news of the royal court as I could, but I didn't want to admit that to you as it might give something away. So I was going to make up a cover story about a new client, but somehow that all seems a little ridiculous now. Instead, I'm just going to tell you what I really want to know, why I want to know it, and everything that's happened so far. Then I'll see if you can point me at the right information."

So I did, with helpful pointers from Triss wherever I failed to mention a mistake I'd made—drat him. And when I was done, Harad found me what I needed.

"This is banned in Tien as propaganda." Harad handed over a thick pamphlet written in Kodamian: *Thauvik, the Rise of the Bastard King.* "Which it is, of course, but with a core of truth. The banning means that it's in high demand here at the library. Please don't keep it too long or, if it should come up, let anyone know where you got it. Everything you want to know about the Marchon girls you will find in there."

I nodded and flipped the pamphlet open. The city-state of Kodamia was tucked into the great gap of the Hurnic Mountains just to the west of Zhan. It had fought several bitter wars with its larger neighbor over access to that passage and the kingdoms of the west. Kodamia's strategic position made it the fattest of prizes, and only an astonishingly competent army officered by the dyads—warrior-sorcerer familiar pairings who also served as spies and assassins—and constant vigilance had kept them from succumbing to one of the many invasions they had faced from both sides of the gap. If anyone paid closer attention to the ruling dynasty of Zhan than the Zhani, it was Kodamia.

"Thank you," I said, "but there's no need to worry about my returning it late. I don't have the time to waste. If it's all right with you, I'll just park myself in the third-floor reading room I use as a foyer, and it'll never leave the building."

Harad nodded. "If that's what you want."

"What I want is to go to my fallback and sleep the night and day around, then get so drunk I forget that this whole stupid job ever happened." Triss expressed his disapproval of that suggestion with a grumpy snort. "But what I need to do is make a serious fadeout while I figure out my next move. That means staying away from anyplace that might already have been compromised and minimizing the chance that anyone will pick up my trail again. So, assuming I got here clean, my best bet is to hold still until it's time for the next move, and then to move quickly and decisively."

Harad gestured toward the stairs. "Then, after you."

When we reached the reading room, Harad went straight to the outer doors and opened them. Then he knelt on the threshold and placed one palm on the limestone of the balcony floor.

Looking up, he beckoned to me. "Come here."

I could have asked why, but I figured I'd find out quicker if I just did as I was told. Life is like that sometimes.

"Give me your hand."

I did, and he took it in his free hand. Harad closed his eyes and muttered something under his breath, causing one of the network of spells that wrapped him round to twist and kink slightly. The words sounded like some sort of archaic Kadeshi, but I couldn't make it out well enough to be certain. When he stopped speaking, I felt a shock like a tiny burst of magelightning run from my hand into Harad's.

Triss slid around for a better look then, as the floor of the balcony flared briefly green over most of its surface. The exception being a large black symbol like a circle bounded by crescent wings that ran spiderweb-thin through the stone—some kind of extremely sophisticated ward.

"I've just rekeyed it to you personally," said Harad. "As the most likely entrance for one of your kind, I have long left this door open to anyone companioned by a Shade, but if what you tell me about this Devin and his society of assassins or whatever he wants to call it is true, that's no longer a smart choice."

"Has this ward always been here?" I hadn't ever seen it before, and that was a very neat trick.

"Only for a hundred and twenty years or so. My predecessor used a different system."

I opened my inner eyes as wide as they would go. "How do you hide . . . oh!"

I realized then that the whole of the building was impregnated with just a touch of active magic, barely more than the background noise of the world, and just enough so that the faint lines of the ward were concealed within the greater light. I was impressed: that took a lot of power to set up and maintain. It was far beyond anything I could have managed, both in terms of technique and raw power. But the ward itself looked so weak . . . what could you do with it? Only by looking closely and knowing just where the ward lay could I even make it out now.

"The obvious ward on the door is just another layer of distraction, to keep people from looking for this, isn't it?"

Harad smiled. "Very good. What else can you see?"

"Let me look a little more closely." Again and again, I mentally traced the lines of the spell worked into the balcony, trying to figure out what it did.

"The ward on the balcony floor is just a triggering spell, isn't it? For something much nastier? What does the nasty look like? Is it hidden beneath the surface of the stone?"

Harad shrugged. "Trade secret. Suffice to say that if your friend Devin comes knocking on my door, he will cease to be a problem for you."

"If that happens, let me know. I'll come take care of the body. It's the least I can do."

Harad laughed. "If that happens, there won't be a body." Then he left.

I settled down to read, and Triss took a little nap. He's generally bored by books, and in this case I couldn't blame him. Most of the pamphlet was blah, blah, Thauvic's a vicious bastard, blah. But there were a few things worth knowing. I took a sheet of paper and a quill from a small box by the door—the carrel had its own inkwell—and made notes as I went, just as I had been taught.

—Succession of the Royal House of Tien and the Barony of Marchon.

—When Aral Kingslayer (I really, really hate that name) ended the reign of Ashvik (by sticking a sword through his throat) in 3207, Ashvik's bastard half brother, Thauvik, then Chief Marshal of the army, took the throne with the support of the leading generals and the order of the Elite.

—That he was able to succeed his brother despite his bastardy was due to three factors.

—First and most important, he was very popular with the Elite and the military, where he had risen through the officer ranks based on merit rather than the favor of his brother, who publicly ignored him for most of his career.

—Secondly, though Ashvik had three legitimate children by his queen, he had executed all of them for "treason" to the realm and "attempts against the throne." (All three were innocent, part of why Namara had marked him for death, the rest being the brutal murder of more than ten thousand innocent Kadeshi villagers.)

—Third, though Ashvik's bastard daughters by the Marchon woman (oh, shit) might have had a slightly more legitimate claim on the throne, they were both underage and had been missing and presumed dead for some weeks at the time. The official story was that they'd been sent to the court of the Thane of Aven for finishing, but it was assumed they had been murdered by the late king—their bastard status precluding the need for a trial. (names?)

I hadn't written this much in ages. I stretched my fingers to relieve the cramping and wished whoever had written this book had more sensible priorities, namely the same as mine. I wanted to know what the supposedly murdered girls' names were though I feared one was Maylien. Anything else would have made my life easier, and that didn't seem to be the way the dice were falling. With a sigh, I plunged back in. More blah, consolidation of Thauvik's rule with a little judicious bloodletting including Baron Marchon, blah, enlargement of army and increase of power for the ministry of war, blah. And then something I could use.

—Six years after the disappearance of Ashvik's illegitimate daughters by his last mistress, Juli Dan Marchon (younger sister of the baron), two young women were presented to the court by that same Juli Dan Marchon (now Baroness Marchon) as the long-missing heiresses. At that time, she asked that Maylien, the elder, be confirmed as her successor in the Barony of Marchon. There was no mention of any relationship to the late Ashvik. (I just bet there wasn't).

—Thauvik disinherited Maylien because she had taken mage orders in her exile and settled the succession on Sumey (apparently he was comfortable enough on the throne by then to want to avoid the odium of executing his nieces). A short time later, Juli killed herself, and Sumey became Baroness Marchon. At that point Maylien vanished again, and rumors began to float around that she had murdered her mother, rumors that were hotly (too hotly) denied by her bereaved sister.

There was more about Thauvik and what the author perceived as his ambitions, but nothing that interested me. And that was it. I read my notes aloud both for Triss's benefit and because that made them easier to memorize. Then I asked him to destroy them for me while I tried to think of what to do next. I had neither time nor good options.

I was pledged to help a girl who might have murdered her mother reclaim a baronial seat that the current king had already refused her. Assuming she was still alive, of course. Throw in the fact that I'd assassinated the king's predecessor, who was also Maylien's father and that I was going up against a man who'd once been one of my closest friends and . . . my head was spinning.

"How the hell did I get here?"

"By killing a king," said Triss.

10

I killed a king once upon a time. I was seventeen and armored in the certainty of my faith, completely confident in my purpose in life. I was Aral Kingslayer, Blade of Namara and proud of it. That man was gone now, lost somewhere in the depths of a soul shattered by the murder of his goddess.

I could sense him sometimes, down there in the darkness, showing through in the skills I brought to some shadow-trade task he never would have consented to touch. Or in the momentary outrage I felt at some injustice, a flash of the morals I'd had etched into my bones by the priests and masters. Or, occasionally, in a black sense of humor that had grown somewhat rusty from lack of use over the last five years. I needed him now, to help Aral the jack pay his debts—to Maylien, to Devin, to the dead—but I didn't know how to find him anymore.

I got up from the little desk, leaving the pamphlet for Harad to collect later, and I began to pace and to think. From the very first day I was brought to the temple, I'd been taught how to hunt men and women, how to sneak up and catch them unawares, how to kill them in any of a hundred ways. I was a manhunter to the marrow, trained in the arts of stalking and death by the very best in the world. But that didn't do a damn bit of good when the man you were hunting was yourself.

Or did it? Could I apply the manhunter's skills to myself? If so, where to start?

Then, like it was yesterday, I seemed to hear Master Kelos, "If you don't know how to get at your target, or worse, can't find him, look to his history. If you truly understand a man, if you know his background and habits, you can predict his actions, his location, even the exact moment to strike. Understanding starts from the beginning. What made him the man he is today?"

Where did Aral Kingslayer begin? That gave me my starting point. Because the Kingslayer had not been born with the death of Ashvik; that was merely the moment that made the name. No, the Aral who became the Kingslayer had taken shape at the temple school, where he trained with Siri and Jax and a dozen others, including his good friend Devin.

Some of my earliest memories were of me and Devin together. Our cubicles had sat side by side in one of the hallways of the boys' wing, and since we were of an age, we were often together.

Dalridia, the kingdom in the clouds. I was eleven, Devin twelve. Master Loris had taken us there so that we could train our bodies and our minds to operating in the thin air of the heights. For the first couple of weeks, we did nothing but run and spar and practice combat forms, ending each day with a collapse into the long sleep of exhaustion.

This was the first night where we'd both been able to keep our eyes open past dinner. Loris had gone into the local village for reasons that I no longer remembered, leaving Devin and me alone in the big tent, which gave us extra incentive to stay awake. Truly unsupervised time was rare in the early years at the temple.

Triss and Zass wrestled and chased each other on the canvas walls in a shadow play just for us—the dragon and the tayra. I laughed when my familiar pinned his ferret-wolf opponent. Zass was faster than Triss and more slippery, but not as strong or large—they were well matched.

"That makes it your turn," I said. "Tell me about the mountains of Aven."

"They're much of a height with the mountains of Dalridia, but there's a lot more snow and ice." Devin took a sip of efik.

"Is that why you drink that stuff?" I pointed at his steaming mug and the various implements used to make it. "Because it's so cold where you come from?"

He snorted. "It's a Varyan drink, Aral. I don't think anyone back home even knows the stuff exists. I drink it because I like it and because it calms me down."

"But it's so bitter." I shuddered in mock horror.

Most of the older Blades swore by the calming effects of efik, but among the younger trainees only Devin and Siri had yet acquired a taste for the stuff.

"You're such a puppy," said Devin. "Hey, Zass just won a fall, it's your turn. Tell me about being born in sight of the temple."

Varya, the great temple of Namara, just after the service of mourning. I was seventeen and heartbroken. Alinthide Poisonhand had just been killed in action, the third Blade to die making an attempt on Ashvik VI, the butcher of Kadesh. Mistress Alinthide had been one of my favorite teachers and one of the oldest Blades still in active service at a hundred and fifty-four.

Beautiful and warm, always ready to answer a question about the poisons that were her specialty and looking not a day over twenty-five. I'd had a burning crush on her for almost two years and a completely unrealistic hope that I might be able to do something about it once I'd finished my classes and earned myself a working name.

Once the priestess had returned Alinthide's spirit knife to the goddess—casting the black steel kila into the shaded depths of Namara's pool—we had taken a barge back across the lake from the holy island. When we docked, I had turned away from the temple and into the setting sun, walking blindly along the shores of the great lake, weeping. Triss hung at my back, gently rubbing my shoulders and whispering wordless comfort in my ears.

After perhaps a half mile, I took conscious notice of Devin trailing along at a polite distance—close enough that no one Blade-trained could have missed him but far enough back not to intrude. I waved him forward, and we walked a while in silence, the four of us, Blades-to-be ahead, Shades trailing behind.

When the tears finally stopped, I pulled a couple of roasted efik beans from the little pouch I always kept about me and began to chew. I nearly gagged at the bitterness, but I had neither the time nor the tools to steep and prepare a proper pot. I needed something to calm me down and take the edge off the pounding in my skull right now, and since the priests despised alcohol . . .

"Three!" The word burst out of me, almost against my will, and I felt Triss jerk in startlement as I turned to face Devin. "Three Blades dead in as many seasons. How can the goddess let Ashvik get away with it?"

"Namara is not the only goddess," said Devin, his voice barely above a whisper. "Perhaps in this, she is too strongly opposed."

Zass, who'd been slipping back and forth across our trail, jerked and vanished completely into Devin's shadow at his words.

"Impossible!" I said, and in that moment I believed it utterly. "Namara is unstoppable."

"Then why are there so very many Blades who return to her only as a black steel dagger cast into deep waters?" Devin asked. "So many whose bodies are burned on foreign pyres?"

At first I had no answer. But then, almost as if the

goddess herself were putting it into my mind, I heard a phrase from the book of Namara. The words were spoken in the voice of that high priestess who had died in my first year at the temple, and whether they came from memory or from the goddess, I cannot say.

"The sheath must find the right Blade," I said, and Triss nodded his agreement.

"Sure, and 'those whom Namara would slay are like sheaths for her Blades.'" Devin didn't quite roll his eyes, but I could see that he wanted to. "I'm familiar with that one."

Zass slid back into view, peering up at me from the ground. "Alinthide was one of the very best. If she couldn't do it, then who can?"

"I can." The words came out of my mouth, but it didn't feel like I'd said them, more like they had said me—as if everything I'd done up to this point, all my training, all of what I had become was a prelude to that simple statement. That I could kill a king.

Triss froze, and Devin started to argue with me, to tell me I was crazy and a fool and that I'd never even make it as far as Tien. I could barely hear him. Instead, I looked out over the deep blue waters of the sacred lake and listened to . . . what?

I don't know. At the time, I thought I was listening to the goddess, and things that happened soon thereafter seemed to reinforce that idea. But I'm older now, and not so sure. Not of that, nor really, of anything. The world has become a gray place for me, filled with shadows where once it was all black and white. That inner voice might have been my pride, or folly, or simply a heart filled with anger by the death of someone I loved. Whatever the reason, in that moment I resolved that I would be the Blade who brought down Ashvik.

"I will kill the king," I said, cutting across Devin's argument, while Triss slumped unhappily against my back.

"You can't mean that," said Devin. "You're not even a full Blade yet. You haven't taken your kila. The Elite will tear you to pieces and feed the bits to the stone dogs."

I should probably have felt fear then, but I didn't. All I felt was certainty.

"The goddess has spoken to me."

Perhaps it was the look on my face. Perhaps it was the tone in my voice. Perhaps Zass gave him a nudge. Whatever the reason, Devin stopped arguing.

"You're serious, aren't you?" he finally asked.

I nodded, and his expression changed. The look on his face held something of awe and something of pity, and maybe just the tiniest bit of envy. Yes, envy. I think that it started in that very instant when he finally believed me though I didn't recognize it then, nor for a long time afterward.

"How will you do it?" asked Devin.

"I don't know. I just know that I must." For a brief instant, I felt the enormity of what I had to do pressing down on me like a great weight, could see the barriers ahead—the travel, the expense, the Elite and their stone dogs—but only for an instant.

"We'll have to go to the goddess," said Triss after a moment, "directly. Ask her to give you your kila early and make you a Blade. You have to sheathe the spirit knife in the altar before you leave, and you can't go after Ashvik without an eye and your swords."

He was right, of course. I needed to seek the formal blessing of the goddess. Without it, I would be nothing more than a common assassin.

"I'll go now." I turned on my heel and started back along the shore.

Devin caught my arm. "Don't be a fool, Aral. Even if the goddess approves, the masters won't want to let you go. The easiest way to prevent you is to keep you from ever crossing to the island. If you're seen taking one of the boats, they'll figure it out, and they'll stop you. You'll have to go after dark, and you'll have to swim."

"Point. But how will I get my blades back across?"

I had no worries about swimming out to the island. It was nearly half a mile, and there were things in the lake that devoured the unwary, but I'd swum farther in training, and the creatures would leave me alone because the goddess had called me. But the weight of all that steel would be a problem.

Then I had it. "I can borrow a rush basket from the temple fishermen." They used the floating baskets to keep the fish fresh when they went spearing in the shallows.

Devin nodded. "Good plan."

And Zass asked, "When?"

"I'll wait till an hour past the sun's setting to grab the basket—better not to ask for one, I think—then I'll go. I wish I could leave it till later, but I'm going to want to be well on the road by dawn. It'll take at least another hour just to swim out to the island and back with the basket slowing me down. As to the rest . . ." I shrugged.

I had to petition the goddess. How long it would take for her to decide what to answer, if anything, I wasn't even going to try to guess. I knew that I had been called, but I also knew that the goddess worked when and how she wanted. If I approached her with arrogance in my heart . . .

For perhaps the dozenth time I pressed my forehead against the age-smoothed granite of the flagstones that lay in a ring around the sacred pool, praying silently for permission to deliver the unblinking eye of justice to Ashvik. I was facing outward, toward the heart of the lake where the goddess made her home. A natural stone arch separated the pool from the greater waters while allowing for its continual refreshment.

Triss was with me, but nearly undetectable in the darkness since he chose not to insert himself in the process. Addressing the goddess was my challenge alone.

I tried to push earlier images of this place out of my head, to think only of the mission I wished the goddess to grant me. I tried to banish my memories of Alinthide's kila held high in the hands of the priestess before she cast it into the pool, but I just couldn't do it. Once again, the eyes of my heart followed the ghost of the spirit-dagger as it sailed through the air and landed in the water, watched as it sank with an unnatural slowness into the shaded deeps, stayed focused on the last place it had been visible, a sort of watery window into the darkness of death.

But this time, I found a sort of answer there in the peace of the grave and the stillness of deep water, a place I could lose all thought, even my sense of self. This time the thinking part of me plunged into the deeps, too, following a dead love into darkness and oblivion.

Time passed like a stream flowing through my mind. It could have been hours or minutes or days. Eventually, I raised my head. Now I faced Namara. An idol of polished granite, she seemed, risen from the deeps, cold and unmoving and yet somehow more alive than I could ever hope to be. No words passed her gray lips, nor expression touched the stone of her beautiful face, but I felt myself summoned. Without thinking or wondering, I stepped out onto the surface of the water, walking across it to meet my goddess.

From the waist down she was submerged, her lower half hidden in the darkness. Above, she was naked, her bared stone breasts hanging a few feet above my head, her six arms extended in front of her. Namara had come, risen from the deeps to accept me into her service.

I . . . how can I express it? Find a place on the side of a hill on a perfect summer evening. Lie back on the heather and look up. As the blue turns to red and then fades to black velvet, the stars spring out one by one. Imagine what it feels like to be the sky filling up with starlight and moonlight and liquid midnight and to know this is why you exist—to hold the beauty of the night. That's how I felt when I bowed before my goddess and accepted her blessing.

Namara's uppermost pair of hands held two daggers. The black kila that signified my service to the goddess was extended on the open palm of her right. Normally such magical blades would have glowed in magesight, but because this magic was divine, their light was hidden. The eye of my mission was gripped firmly in her left. Her middle pair

of hands cradled twin swords, short and curved, unbreak-
able, unrusting, and forever sharp. With her lowest pair of
hands she extended a tray that held the harness and sheaths
of the three greater blades as well as many lesser knives and
tokens, the hunting gear of the Blade.

First I took up the harness, sliding it over my shoulders
and fastening the straps as I had been taught. It should have
been wet, slippery, smelling of lake. It was dry and smooth
and utterly devoid of any scent, even the faintest hint of
fresh-cut leather. Then I took my swords, seating them
firmly in their shoulder-draw rig and fastening the catches
that would hold them in place.

Next I reached for the black steel of the kila. For the first
time since the goddess had risen, I became aware of Triss
as he flowed outward silkily along my arms so that we
touched the spirit knife together. Clad now in shadow, I
picked up the heavy black dagger with its tripled blade,
clutching it in both hands.

"Wind and wave." I raised its point to the sky, then lowered it to touch the water. "Stone and heart's blood." I pressed
the tip between the breasts of the goddess, then reversed it to
prick the left side of my chest. "I bind myself to the will of
Namara, her Blade forevermore." It flared brightly in magesight, then faded back to a normal dull black.

I lowered the kila to my side then, for there were only
two possible sheaths for the spirit knife, and neither of them
was a part of the Blade's gear. Going to one knee before the
goddess, I lowered my head and closed my eyes.

"Command me."

*Ashvik must die for the horror he wrought in Kadesh and
for his crimes against his own blood and people in Zhan.
Will you show the tyrant that Justice never sleeps?* The
voice seemed to come from everywhere and nowhere.

"I will," I said, though I did not yet lift my head.

Then take him the unblinking eye.

Now I looked up. The stone hand that held the short
straight dagger we called an eye was now open, though no
sound had betrayed its movement.

I stood and took the eye. Pressing it to my lips, I whispered, "For Ashvik," then slipped it into a downward-facing sheath fastened to one of the chest straps of my harness.

I looked one last time into the cool gray face of my goddess—beautiful and utterly still, a form carved in stone and yet so very, very alive. Then I turned and walked back across the waters to shore.

I see her like that sometimes, in my nightmares, just for an instant. Then she becomes nothing more than a statue on the bottom of the lake, dead granite bereft of all presence, the way she was the last time I saw her. I start drinking early on the days that follow such dreams.

Devin and Zass were waiting for us when we swam back from the island. "That was fast," Devin said, when I stood up in the shallows. "I'm surprised you were even able to swim out and back. Did Namara refuse you?"

I was too surprised by his words to speak, so I reached into the basket and lifted out my kila by way of an answer. A sharply indrawn breath was his only response. Once I'd waded ashore, I set the spirit knife aside while I pulled out the harness. This time the collection of leather straps and sheaths dripped vigorously, and I caught the faint scent of lake water as I started to buckle it into place.

"How long was I gone?"

"A bit more than an hour," replied Devin. "You're a faster swimmer with that basket than I would be. And that must have been the shortest investiture vigil in the history of the order. Did you sprint from shore to pool?"

"No. It felt like I was there for ages and ages, much longer than I was gone, even without the swimming." I snapped my last buckle into place and rolled my shoulders to make sure everything was hanging properly. "Are you certain it's only been an hour?"

Devin nodded, and I thought I saw Zass do so as well though he was nearly invisible in that light. "Perhaps the goddess bent time for you," said the Shade. "Triss?"

My familiar poked his head over my shoulder, and I felt his shadowy scales rub my cheek. "I don't know. Whatever happened, I was inside it and felt nothing. But time is running now, and we have to be quick if we want to avoid days wasted in arguing with the masters."

As usual, Triss was right. I scooped up the kila again and turned to Devin. "Will you come with me to witness the ceremony?"

His teeth shone white in the dark, marking a brief smile. "Of course."

It was easy enough for two Shade-cloaked boys to slip past the priest attendants at the door to the inner temple and move on from there to the Sanctuary of the Blades undetected. We paused there at the entrance to draw aside the shadows over our eyes and look for any senior Blades within. I couldn't see anyone, but that meant less than it might in any other place. Blades often paid Namara their respects or made prayers while hidden in shadow.

Still, as a new-forged Blade, I had both the right and the duty. Signaling my intent to Triss with a gesture, I stepped across the threshold and out of his shadow. The sanctuary was a large, domed oval with tapered ends, perhaps thirty feet across at its narrowest and entered by doors at either end.

Over the very center of the room was a circular skylight open to the weather. Underneath the opening lay a wide circle of lapis lazuli with a great sphere of obsidian sunk in its center. From above and in concert with the white oval of the dome, it presented the aspect of a great unblinking eye with the globe as its pupil.

Walking quickly but silently as I had been taught, I crossed from the door to the edge of the lapis band, where I knelt briefly and bowed my head to the orb. I couldn't tell whether Devin had accompanied me in shadow or if he hung back a bit, somewhere behind me, and I realized that it didn't really matter. Not that or the presence of any other Blade. This was between me and my goddess.

Rising, I approached the chest-high sphere. The obsidian was smooth and polished. I could see my own face in a reflection clearer than the lake on the calmest day. The only thing marring the perfection of the stone was the hilts of the kila standing out from the surface here and there. Unlike pitons hammered into rock, they looked as though they'd been simply slid into the orb as cleanly as the sharpest stiletto going into an unprotected back.

I looked for the place where the high priestess had withdrawn Alinthide's spirit knife, but there was no hole to mark its passing and I could only make a rough guess. Bending forward, I kissed the stone where I thought it had been and whispered a prayer for her soul. Then I lifted my own kila high over my head and drove it down toward that same spot with all the strength in my body.

I had seen the investiture of other Blades several times in the past. But some part of me still expected the black steel to glance away from the black stone with a ringing sound and a shower of sparks, braced for the shock of that impact to transmit itself up my hand and arm to my shoulder, anticipated numbness and pain and the shame of failure.

None of that happened. The kila went into the sphere as neatly and smoothly as a practice thrust going into the throat of a hog or goat—when the cooks needed an animal slaughtered, it was always done by a trainee. It slid in until the guard touched stone, then stopped smoothly. But when I tugged at the hilt briefly before releasing my grip, the blade felt as firmly planted as if it had been welded in place. There it would remain until I died, and some future priest or priestess came to return it to Namara. Or so I believed at the time.

I was wrong.

11

It's funny how two disparate moments in time can become forever tied together by memory and pain. I can't look back on the transcendent joy of the night of my investiture as a Blade without also seeing what came later. It's part of why I try never to think about something that was once one of my most important memories.

When I do let the memories loose, it's impossible for me to revisit the moment when my kila joined me to the goddess through her great orb without also returning to the day five years later, when I came home from a mission and found the temple in ruins and my goddess murdered. In one memory, the orb sits in the heart of the temple, whole and symbolically wedding the goddess to her Blades through the marriage of stone and steel. In the other, the orb is cracked and ruined, a broken stone promise lying just outside the temple gate. The kila were pried loose and carried off to lie at the feet of the Son of Heaven.

I've been told that the knives of the last few living Blades are sunk in the back wall of the Son of Heaven's privy, where the man can piss on them each morning. I don't know if that's true, but I do know that several of the surviving masters died trying to recover the lost kila over the last five years. I wonder if the Son pulled their blades out when they died and let them splash into the depths below. It would have a certain sort of obscene symmetry, wouldn't it?

Pain from the cramping of clenched muscles drew my attention back to the now. I pushed even the thought of memory aside for a moment, forced myself to see only the library and the present. It was that or go and find a bottle of Kyle's, knowing I wouldn't stop drinking till I hit the bottom. I wanted that drink, I wanted it so very badly, and I might have gone looking for it if not for my debts to the living and dead. That, and my unspoken promise to Triss, not to give up drinking—I hadn't the strength for that—just to stop being a drunk.

I went to the balcony and looked out over the city. It was dark and still, almost quiet here at the nadir of the day in a wealthy part of town. It was a few hours yet before the delivery people and the house servants responsible for feeding the well-to-do would start to make their scurrying prebreakfast rounds. A sharp contrast with the Stumbles or Smuggler's Rest, neighborhoods where things never quieted down completely.

Places like the Gryphon and the Spinnerfish never closed. The night traders needed havens where they could meet and eat. The whores and their clients wanted dark corners and beds by the hour. And always, always, always in those neighborhoods there were damned souls in need of a drink. That last was half of why *I'd* taken a room there once upon a time.

Turning away from the balcony and its doorway on the night, I pried my hands loose from the death grip they'd taken on my shoulders and prepared to dive back into the deeps of my own past once again. I didn't want to go there, but I still hadn't gotten what I needed, and I didn't know where else I could find it.

Turn back the years and find . . .

After I'd placed my kila in the great orb, a voice came out of the darkness, and it hadn't belonged to Devin.

"Ashvik?" Master Kelos had asked.

"Ashvik," I'd answered, ready to argue with him. "For the goddess and for Alinthide."

"Good hunting," was all he'd said.

I'd nodded and turned back toward the door. I saw neither Kelos, nor Devin, though as I went out into the hall, a hand had briefly squeezed my shoulder. Another had placed a small fat purse in my hand. Devin and Kelos? That's what I'd believed at the time, but things that came later make me wonder if both weren't Kelos.

But that wasn't the memory I needed right now. Perhaps I could find it in my first visit to Tien, in the months leading up to the night I killed a king. During the first few weeks, I'd tried to catch him away from the palace, twice at the Marchon place when he went to bed his mistress, once on a progress through the Duchy of Jenua, and another time when he met with his brother Thauvik at military headquarters. Each time I'd been thwarted by the Elite and their stone dogs, unable to get within even a long bowshot of the king.

Ashvik was guarded too well. I began to understand why Alinthide and the others had died. It should have been frightening, or, at the very least, sobering. Instead, I found it the reverse. The challenge intoxicated me. *I* was going to succeed where the great had failed. I was going to deliver justice to the tyrant. I was going to prove the power of Namara to the world. All that because only I could, and because she had chosen *me*, and most of all because I was the best there was.

I was an arrogant fool. I was lucky. I was also right.

At that time and for that situation, I really was the best in the world, and that was why the goddess had chosen me for the mission. I won't lie to myself and deny it, but neither will I lie to myself about my sins of arrogance and ignorance. Being one of the world's best at anything is a funny sort of situation. It's a bit like walking along a fence top between two very deep pits. On the one side is overconfidence, on the other self-doubt. A misstep in either direction can set you up for a fall into ruin. And lying to yourself is one of the easiest missteps to make.

That's part of why I say that I was the best, because it's the truth. I was, for a year or two. I'm not anymore, not with what I've become. For that matter, I wouldn't be even if I were the Kingslayer still, not if Siri the Mythkiller is alive at any rate. She took the honors from me when I was at my best and held the title for a little less than half a decade before the temple fell, which isn't a quarter so long as Kelos held it fifty years ago when he was in his prime.

But back then, I was so very, very good. I watched and I waited and I worked my way ever closer to the king. First, I learned the guard routines in the grounds, penetrating a little closer to the castle every night, slipping past dogs and guards, groundskeepers, and courtiers out for clandestine fucks in the gardens.

When I could come and go as easily as any shadow in the night, I moved in closer, entering the castle proper, moving through the halls, burrowing my way steadily deeper. It took a month and a half from when I started to sniff out the palace's secrets to finding my doorway into the Grand Tower where the royal apartments lay.

The details don't really matter except in the broadest sense. I could enter the grounds any of a dozen ways, up through a culvert, over the walls in five places, through the main gates with the nonresident courtiers, in by the postern with the deliveries . . .

From there my path narrowed. Only three routes into the castle proper left me in a good position to approach the Grand Tower. Via the kitchens and up the shaft of the dumbwaiter to the monarch's informal dining chamber, hanging in wait in the rafters of the audience hall after the court had retired, or trailing behind the shift change of the Crown Guard as they made their way from the barracks to their positions around the outer perimeter of the Tower.

All had their problems. The route from the audience hall was long and heavily guarded. The dumbwaiter was a rat trap, hard to climb undetected and easy to seal if they spotted us. Trailing the guards meant treading very close behind the soldiers and the pair of Elite who officered them for close to ten minutes, plenty of time for the stone dogs to hear an extra pair of feet.

Unfortunately, that last was also the best route because of timing. The Crown Guard's officers checked in with the Elite providing internal security for the Grand Tower while their own men took up position. Likewise, the exiting troop's Elite checked in then. It gave everyone an important chance to compare notes. It also gave Triss and me a brief window when there was no exterior Elite presence covering the wall where the gate from the pleasure gardens entered the Tower.

The gate itself was hopeless, but a fast climber with the right equipment could make it up the outside of the wall to a small overhung niche between the supports of a fifth-floor balcony, and he could do it before the Elite lieutenant who supervised the gate finished his conference with his fellows.

The first time we'd made the climb, I'd bored two small holes in the mortar where the stone corbels met the wall—completely invisible from the ground level—so that I could set a pair of anchors whenever I wanted. Of course, by the time I was done, the lieutenant had arrived, so Triss and I had to wait for the next shift change to descend. But that was the whole point of the anchors, they allowed me to hang a narrow rope sling between the corbels like a sailor's hammock. There we could lie safe while I observed the security arrangements.

An awful lot of a Blade's job involves sitting and waiting.

Killing someone is relatively easy if you don't care about who sees it happen or about getting away. No security is so good that it can keep out a determined professional assassin willing to die to reach his target. Fortunately for the people who guard kings, there are very few professionals interested in dying for the job. Even among the Blades.

I know that the stories paint us as fanatical assassins totally devoted to the goddess and ready to martyr ourselves at Namara's whim. That's true enough, but it's also beside the point. If Namara had ever asked one of her Blades to go on a suicide mission, I don't think any of us would have refused the goddess, or even resented the order. But the goddess never asked. If you'd questioned me about that back in the day, I'd have told you it was because she loved her Blades and would never allow unnecessary harm to come to us.

Again, that would be true but largely beside the point, because it's only one truth. Another is that children with the right sort of mind-set to become a Blade are few and far between. Those with the mind-set and both the familiar and the mage gifts are even rarer. The Shades are quite picky about who they will bond with—probably two-thirds of the children presented to them are turned away. Finally, it takes more than a decade of training to make even a novice Blade. The goddess can't afford to throw a single one away.

Which is why Triss and I spent four hours hanging in a scrap of silk over a multistory drop, chewing carefully measured-out efik beans while I watched and listened. If we were going to get away clean after I killed the king, we needed to get in clean. That meant watching and waiting and thinking and planning. It also meant dealing with the permanent ward built into the tile mosaic of the balcony.

Permanent wards come in two types, keyed and unkeyed. Keyed wards react only to people who haven't been spelled into their memories. Unkeyed wards react to everybody. In both cases, it's basically impossible for a person to cross the ward without triggering it. That's why people generally don't bother to hide them; they're as much a warning as a barrier. When people do try to cross them, what happens when the ward is triggered is limited only by the power and imagination of the wardcaster.

Permanent wards are very dangerous. They're also stupid. They can't be adapted to changing conditions without a lot of work on the part of the wardcaster. Even just adding a new person to the key takes time and a good deal of power. Beyond that, if they're someplace like the balcony, where they're exposed to wind and weather, they can't be too sensitive.

You don't want a fifty-foot column of magical fire shoot-ing into the air every time a passing pigeon lands for a min-ute or a couple of leaves blow across the balcony. That's hard on the nerves and trains guards not to pay attention to the wards when they trigger. If you do it enough, it drains the ward. At the same time, you don't want some clever mage with a pigeon for a familiar landing his companion safely on the ward to spy on you. So you make compromises. You set the ward to have a nasty but not flashy reaction if some-thing living and smaller than a cat lands on it. You also set it to ignore leaves and other wholly dead stuff.

Say, for example, a piece of silk with weights sewn in all around the edges so it can be cast like a net. If you're really cautious, you'll build some sort of magic detection into the ward so that something with an active spell on it like an eyespy or hearsay will get the pillar-of-fire treatment. But say your piece of silk doesn't have an active spell on it, say it's just been prepared to be magically sensitive itself, and say that it works slowly. Now, that is *very* hard to detect.

So, for the last hour we were hanging under the balcony, a silken net lay atop it soaking up a perfect mirror image of the ward. When we got back to our snug, I took that sheet of silk, attached it to a prespelled mat of felt with Triss's help, and created a custom wardblack that would render the ward effectively blind.

That's how you penetrate really good security without getting caught: slowly, carefully, one custom-built piece at a time.

The second time we climbed the tower, I spent a good half hour lying flat on the wardblack with a tiny ear trumpet pressed to the iron-bound oak door before pulling a corner-bright out of my trick bag and slipping the end under the door so that I could peer inside. Like every aspect of this job, it was a risk, but a calculated one.

Take a strip of silver an inch wide and a bit thicker than a sheet of parchment. Tarnish it dead black, then polish the two ends up into tiny mirrors. Enchant it so that what one mirror sees the other shows. Now you have a way to see around corners and under doors. The magic involved is small, passive, and inherent to the device, which means it barely glows to the sorcerer's eye. The bigger problem comes from the mirrors. You can't do it without them, and mirrors shine, but a cornerbright's less risky than the alternatives.

Once the cornerbright revealed a dark and empty room, we slipped inside, where I pulled a tiny magelantern from my trick bag. I opened the directional shutters just enough to illuminate a narrow band in front of me. The stone was a dim one and dark red, so the light wouldn't be visible from any distance—a thieveslamp.

The beam revealed a small council room with a heavy wooden table, a half dozen chairs—including one meant to evoke the throne—and a small side desk where a secretary could stand. A floor below the king's apartments, the room provided a private venue to meet with a few trusted advisors. There were no windows, only the two heavy doors. The one leading into the tower was flanked by a pair of shallow alcoves for guards.

Not a good place for an ambush. I might, barely, have contrived to sling myself under the table and wait there for the king to arrive. But even on the incredibly tiny chance that I succeeded in hiding out till he arrived and killing him with a dagger to the groin, I'd never make it out alive.

It would have been tempting to try something fancy with the royal chair and poison if I didn't know that Alinthide had been killed after trying a similar trick. There was no way the council room wasn't being checked for poison on a daily basis.

I might, if I were very lucky and very stupid, be able to get Ashvik with a poisoned dart from the edge of the balcony, if the door happened to open at the right time, and I wasn't spotted from below, and there was no one sitting in the nearer chair to block the shot. I couldn't make my move here. So I spent another long span with my ear to the inner door.

This time I had something to listen to. Every few minutes someone, or rather two someones, passed the door. First one

way, then the other. One of the few real disadvantages the
Elite had was that the stone dogs made a lot of noise once
they came up out of the earth. No matter how graceful and
gentle-footed you are, when you weigh a thousand-plus
pounds, and your feet are made of stone, sneaking is not
your forte.

The noises from the guard rounds suggested a short hall
lay beyond the door, one with stairs at either end and a few
doors the Elite had to check. The latter probably magically,
or they'd have rattled the handles. After an hour or so of the
routine, I decided I'd have to risk the cornerbright if I wanted
to learn anything more. I waited until the stone dog had just
passed, then slipped the tiniest edge of the device under the
door.

I could see a narrow band of hallway and another door
as well as the retreating backs of a young Elite lieutenant
and his familiar. By tilting the strip as much as the narrow
crack under the door would allow, I was able to follow their
progress as far as the base of a set of stairs, where they
waved upward—probably at a second Elite on the landing
above. Then I pulled back the cornerbright before they could
turn around and spy it.

I rolled onto my back beside the door and waited for the
pair to pass again. The heavy, grating footsteps of the stone
dog got closer and closer. Even though I knew it couldn't
have sniffed me out, I had to work to keep my heart from
speeding up.

Everything had gone fine so far. Everything was going
fine. Everything would be fine. I repeated that to myself
again and again. I even believed it.

Right up until the moment the stone dog's head came
through the wall two feet above my face. My skin burned
with cold as shock rolled over me like a powder-snow avalanche in Dalridia's mountains. Every muscle in my body
went rigid—bone-deep reflexes that wanted me to jump and
shriek warring with a lifetime's training in stealth.

The training saved me. Mine and Triss's. Rather than
jerk away from those great stone jaws or reach for a knife

to defend myself, I held my breath and froze. In that very same instant Triss burst outward from my skin, covering us both in his enshrouding darkness. The next few moments seemed to take as long as my entire life up to that point. I could hear the stone dog snuffling around a foot or two above my face, feel his cold, dank breath through the shadows that shrouded me every time he breathed out. I turned my head to the side so that he could not feel mine in return.

Moving as quietly as I possibly could, I slid a hand to the hilt of the eye of the goddess and slowly slipped it from the sheath on my chest, holding it ready. If I moved before it sensed me, I could probably drive the knife into the stone dog's neck. The eye was a magical blade like my swords, and the only weapon I could reach that had any hope of killing a stone dog.

In my mind's eye I pictured the positioning of the beast's head, lower now than when I had first seen it sliding through the rough stone surface of the wall like a seal surfacing in Tien's bay. My best chance for living out the night involved striking now, before it spotted me. But if I did that, my chance of completing the mission and killing Ashvik dropped to nothing, both because the Elite would be forewarned and because I would have profaned the eye of the goddess.

The snuffling grew louder as the dog's head dropped lower. I squeezed the hilt of the eye tight. Tighter. Stopped. Relaxed my grip. Both on the knife and my fear. The goddess had sent me on a mission. If I killed the stone dog now, I might live, but I would also fail in my charge. If I held still and left things in Namara's hands, she might see fit to allow me life and success both. More time slid by in heart-tearing slowness. The dog did not find me. Neither did it leave. Years seemed to pass. Then, with a noise like splashing mud, it was gone.

I slid the eye back into its sheath, drew my swords, and placed them at my sides. Then I reached a hand up and ran it across the stones of the wall where the dog's head had come through. They were unmarked. The shakes took me, and Triss returned to dragon form.

"Are you all right?" he asked, his voice anxious.

I nodded though I couldn't stop shaking.

"You'd better chew another bean," he said. "Efik'll help."

"It's too soon after my last one."

You had to be careful with straight efik. Too much, and it'd level you instead of leveling your nerves. Do that too often, and you might get to like it. Maybe you'd end up sitting in a back alley with the rest of the sleepwalkers, cutting stripes in your arms and rubbing powdered efik into the gashes. Maybe it'd kill you. But even after I stopped shaking I couldn't get my heartbeat to stop rabbiting. Finally, Triss opened my pouch and pulled out a bean. Holding it between claws of shadow, he offered it to me.

"Really, I think you need it."

I nodded and took the bean. Dropped it into my mouth, chewed slowly. In moments I could feel my calm returning, my heart's pace slowing. The stone dog and its master passed by on their rounds several more times, each without looking in. On the fourth round I rolled over again and slipped my cornerbright under the door though I did not resheathe my swords.

This time they were going the other way, down the stairs. They were gone for perhaps five minutes. Leaving the cornerbright exposed as I waited for the top of the returning Elite's head to appear coming up the stairs almost had me shaking again, but I needed to know exactly how long the hall would remain open. On his next trek downstairs I examined the ward of alarm that hung in front of the door across the hall—a simple temporary spell.

There are a lot of reasons to avoid the hassle of using a permanent ward. There's duration—you have a space you want warded only at night or only for a few hours each day. Creating a moving target—you want to keep changing things around so no one can make a wardblack. Adaptability—you want different results at different times, silent alert instead of immolation, or whatever. Timing out—you're using it as part of a system that involves guards, and you want it to make all kinds of noise if they don't check in with the spell every so often.

Whatever the reason, they're much harder to deceive than permanent wards. Take the one on the door. It would probably trigger if the Elite took ten minutes instead of five downstairs. It would certainly trigger if I opened the door, and it was inaccessible if I didn't. There were ways I could deal with that, but not without leaving signs of tampering.

That meant I couldn't go beyond this point until I was ready to go all the way. So I turned away and went looking for a better route in. But three more rounds of spying over the following week proved what I'd already guessed—it was the balcony and the council room or nothing, and I wasn't going to walk away without taking a shot. So, on a quiet afternoon in Harvestide I made my decision. It would be tomorrow.

I would kill the king or die trying.

12

Even though I'd managed to successfully slip into the Grand Tower previously, this trip felt different. Every noise was louder, every check and pause longer, every surprise more startling. Various techniques I'd learned to slow my heart and quiet my breathing helped. So did a carefully gauged series of efik beans chewed on the run. But I still felt as tight as an overdrawn bowstring by the time I reached the little council chamber.

After I'd shut the outer door, I laid my length on the floor and pressed my tiny ear trumpet against the crack of the inner door. I stayed there for nearly half an hour listening to the patrolling Elite, making sure the routine remained unchanged and working myself up to the next step. Once I felt sure of both the guard and the steadiness of my hands, I slipped the cornerbright under the door and did a final check on the hall and the door wards.

Everything looked the same, so I quickly fixed a pair of long leather straps across the width of the door and slid two thin wedges underneath it. The straps had been prepared using a simple spell of binding and stiffening that would keep them in place and rigid for some hours. One went just above the floor, and the other about a foot above that and an inch or so below the bottommost of the heavy iron bands that bound the thick oak planks together.

Next I drew a slim dagger and gestured Triss to action—unless something went wrong, there would be no speech between us until the end of the mission. At my sign, Triss slid down my arm and enveloped my hand and the dagger in a dense layer of shadow. Concentrating his presence most heavily along the blade's leading edge, he exerted himself and created a knife-thin gate into the everdark—not that I realized it at the time.

Placing the shadowed edge against the wood of the door a hairsbreadth below that bottommost iron band, I began to saw silently away at the planks. I had to stop and wait out the passing of the guard twice in that time. The seam, lying in the shadow of the iron band, was nearly invisible, but the knife's tip was another story. When I was done, I had converted the bottom foot of the door into a free-floating horizontal plank held tightly in place by the wedges. Next, I reattached it to the main body of the door with a second pair of leather straps mounted vertically. These were shorter and more flexible, serving as hinges.

When the guard next went down the stairs, I quickly pulled out the wedges, flipped my impromptu trapdoor open, and slid most of my body out into the narrow hallway. Above me, the door ward glowed peacefully away, untriggered because the door itself remained shut. I was really working against time now; the pass-through I'd just cut simply couldn't be repaired without leaving traces any mage could see.

Cracking the door across the way took much longer because I had to duck back into the council room every time the guard came back, and I couldn't rig it with straps until I was inside the second room, out of sight of the guard. But eventually I had a second pass-through rigged. This one opened into the sitting room of a large and apparently vacant suite, probably belonging to the recently executed crown prince.

Using my dim red thieveslamp, I quietly explored the apartment. Beyond the sitting room lay a withdrawing room and a sleeping chamber, all beginning to develop the empty smell that even the best-kept vacant rooms start to acquire after a while. Most importantly, I found the garderobe. It was hidden behind a small door off the withdrawing room.

In a less secure castle, such a privy would have been situated on an outside wall and simply voided its contents into empty space. Not in Tien Palace. Here, the broad ceramic pipe that angled back from the hole in the marble bench disgorged itself into a central shaft that led down through the building into the sewers below the castle. For ease of cleaning—it wouldn't do to stink up the royal quarters—the central shaft was big enough to easily accommodate a man.

Were that shaft less carefully secured, it would have provided a perfect route into the royal apartments. But it was simply too heavily guarded down in the deeps at the sewer level. Master Urayal had demonstrated that by his death, and I had further verified it with my own extensive explorations of Tien's undercity. But it wasn't the shaft or the sewers I was interested in.

Working quickly, I levered up the marble bench with its central hole and set it aside. Then, more tricky and more messy, I pulled out the pipe. The former I left leaning against the garderobe wall. The latter I tucked into the late prince's wardrobe. That opened a path to the central shaft that a fleeing assassin could quickly and easily take.

Next, I opened my trick bag and pulled out a good-sized smudge candle, attaching it to the wall of the shaft as far down as I could reach. Looking at it from above, I could just see the faint glow of the spells that had been cooked into the wax and its half dozen wicks. I was just pulling back when the glow was partially occluded as a ragged and rotting hand reached up from below to catch at my wrist.

That momentary silhouette gave me a critical instant to set the grip of my other hand on the lip of the privy above. Without that, the sharp yank the reaching hand delivered would have tipped me over the edge and sent me plunging headfirst down the long stone shaft. Even so, it was a close-run thing. Pain hammered up my arm as the bones of my wrist ground together in the inhumanly strong grip of the thing lurking below. Then it started pulling.

I had to clench my jaw to keep from screaming as my right shoulder tried to come out of its socket. It hurt even more when I twisted my hand, grabbed its wrist in turn, and started to pull back.

"Triss!" I hissed. "Help me with this thing!"

Shadow surged down along my right arm to enclose both my wrist and the hand gripping it in liquid night. Immediately, there was an easing of the pressure. At the same time, tendrils of darkness wrapped themselves around my upper back and shoulders, adding Triss's strength to my own as I fought to bring the thing up into the garderobe. It fought back hard though it made no sound other than a sort of dreadful scrabbling and scratching on the stones of the shaft as I dragged it slowly up into the light.

"Ware!" said Triss, his voice soft but urgent. "It's going to—"

The thing suddenly stopped resisting, somehow managing to launch itself up out of the throat of the garderobe, lunging for my neck with its free hand. It met a shield of night and slid off without finding its target and together we fell back against the door of the garderobe and on out into the room beyond, knocking over my thieveslight in the process. That caused the shutter to snap shut—it was designed to do so at the slightest impact—and plunged the room into complete darkness.

We landed hard with my attacker on top, its bony knees pressing into my ribs as it started to squeeze with its legs, but I was ready. Even as we'd gone through the door I had flicked my left arm, sending the knife in my wrist sheath sliding into my hand. Now I drove the slender blade up into the soft flesh in the hollow of the monster's right armpit.

It didn't even flinch as the steel went in to the hilt. Instead, it brought that hand back around for another grab at my throat. This time Triss couldn't keep it off, though he did manage to form a thick layer of himself into a sort of shadow gorget that kept the thing from crushing my throat outright. Between that and the band that was protecting my right wrist, there wasn't much Triss left to do anything else.

If the thing had been one-tenth as smart as it was strong, Ashvik's defenses would have accounted for their fourth Blade that night. But once it had a grip on my throat, it seemed to forget entirely that that left me a free arm. Reaching back over my shoulder, I drew one of my swords—the guard dragged along the floor as I did so, making a grating noise that seemed horribly loud by comparison to the near silence of our fight so far.

With purple starting to flash around the edges of my vision as its scissoring legs slowly squeezed my lungs empty, I brought the sword around and lopped its head off. For three long beats of my heart, I thought it was going to keep right on squeezing, but then the pressure eased, and it slumped forward onto my chest. Whether it was the beheading or the virtue of the goddess's sword that did for it, I couldn't say.

What I really wanted to do just then, more than anything, was collapse in a heap for a few minutes and then go home to the temple. Instead, I put an arm on a dead shoulder and shoved. The thing came apart like a child's straw doll gone rotten.

"Triss, light," I husked.

A moment later, I had the thieveslight in my hand. I flicked it briefly over the corpse of my attacker—some variety of restless dead by the look of it. The people of the Kvanas dispose of their fallen by exposing them on tall platforms. What the crows don't take quickly stiffens and dries into the consistency of jerky.

This thing looked liked six months on the drying rack. The general state of decay marked it as one of the risen—mistakenly called zombies by some—and a devilishly clever move on Ashvik's part. Not only dangerous on its own, but also for the curse it carried. Without the protections the goddess wove around her Blades, I might already be on my way to becoming this thing's replacement. I shuddered and said a quick prayer of thanks to Namara.

I still see it in my nightmares occasionally, but at the time I put the horror aside in a little box, as I had been taught. *It is acceptable to feel fear, it is folly to hold on to it.* Then I went to listen at the door to the withdrawing room to see whether the fight had attracted the attention of the patrolling Elite. But it had been fast and it had been quiet and I got lucky. No one came.

I looked back over at the corpse and noticed that it now looked like ten months a-drying. I put a heel on the exposed end of a thighbone and started to shift my weight. It gave off a distinct sewer smell as it powdered, and I decided that maybe I'd leave the shit-soaked risen out of the story if I ever got to tell it to anyone. Class it with magical defenses and call it an animate ward maybe.

But that was getting ahead of myself. I had a job to do, so five minutes later I was back in the damn garderobe. After making sure the smudge candle remained in place—thank Namara for small favors, it did—I made quick use of the hole. The encounter had rather forcefully reminded me of my bladder—fear will do that. Then I stepped up onto the lip of the privy. That put me high enough to rub a potion into the plaster of the ceiling over an area a couple of feet across.

It made more noise than I'd have liked as it liquefied and slowly dropped onto the rug, but there was no avoiding it, and at least it was quieter than the damned risen had been. When enough plaster had dissolved away, I attached another set of trapdoor straps to the planks of the floor above, this time making sure to set a latch.

Time pressed ever more heavily on my shoulders. Like the pass-throughs I'd cut into the outer doors, the dissolved plaster left a trail that couldn't be erased. Still, I listened carefully for several minutes before I started cutting into the planks above. This time I used one of my swords so I could cut faster. As soon as I had a big enough opening, I blacked out my thieveslamp and unspelled the latch, easing the trapdoor open. There was a gentle fluttering noise and a light thud as the rug dropped through from above. I was in.

Thankfully, it was as dark above as below. I reopened my lamp then and affixed a sheet of paper with a ward of fire to the hanging edge of the trapdoor. Then I leaped and caught the lip, pulling myself up into the king's garderobe. Even with the hole in the floor, the space felt stuffy because of the tightness of the door's seal. That was one of the many reasons I'd taken the risk with the pass-throughs rather than just cutting through the ceiling of the council room.

Garderobes had thick, well-set doors intended to spare noble noses. Those same features meant they also spared noble ears from the noises of my entry. They also stacked. There was no way of knowing what lay above the council room, but because of the placement of that central sewer shaft, the garderobes had to be built one above the other, and the suite above my original entry point belonged to King Ashvik.

With my feet straddling the hole in the floor, I pressed my ear trumpet against the door. I wanted nothing more than to act fast, but I had to know if there was an Elite bodyguard stationed in the withdrawing room. I thought the sitting room a much more likely choice, and a niche in the hall just outside the royal suite most likely of all, but I wasn't going to let incaution ruin me at this point. Only after I felt sure of the room beyond did I ease the door open.

The withdrawing room was dark save for a thin line of light coming under the door that corresponded to the bed-chamber in the room below. I was at the most dangerous stage of my mission, with the king likely sleeping behind one door and Elite bodyguards and stone dogs possibly behind the other. The temptation to go for the king as quickly and quietly as possible was almost overwhelming. Instead, I drew my left-hand sword and forced myself to listen at the door to the sitting room. There I heard . . .

Nothing.

It was empty. I checked the eye the goddess had given me for the king. It was loose in its sheath, ready to find a home in a royal heart. I crossed to check the door to the bedchamber. Faint noises of habitation came from within, little creaks of the sort furniture made when you shifted position, the occasional deep breath . . . the king was in, and likely awake. The door opened away from me and was hinged on the left side, so I switched to my right-hand sword.

Now!

I turned the handle and quickly pushed the door open. Ashvik was sitting on the edge of a chaise, facing a window that looked out over the palace, his back to me.

"I told you I was *not* to be bothered," he growled without even turning my way. "If you're here for anything less than an invasion from Kodamia, I'll have you boiled alive. Maybe in the bath right here." He pointed at a big red marble tub in the corner.

I slipped my second sword free of its sheath.

"Well," he demanded, "spit it out. Why have you come?"

"To bring you justice."

"What!" Ashvik spun in his seat. "I—"

His words ended in a rasping gurgle as I plunged one sword into his chest and the other into his throat. For a couple of heartbeats his eyes blazed hate at me, but then, as easily as a sheep slaughtered for the table, he died. I don't know what I had expected to happen at that point, a suddenly hammering alarm, a great cloud of evil smoke rising from the corpse, wild cries of celebration? Whatever the answer, I didn't get it.

Ashvik VI, King of Zhan, Butcher of Kadesh, and murderer of his own royal sons simply slumped gently backward and slid off my blades, and I felt nothing.

As I had been taught, I flicked the swords to clear the blood, then resheathed them at my back. Next I arranged the dead king on the chaise as though he were sleeping. I took the Eye of Namara from its sheath and sank it deep into Ashvik's chest, making sure that the blue lapis eye on its pommel stared straight at the door. And still, I felt nothing, not even satisfaction at a task well done.

With a lesser villain, the goddess might have given me a scroll detailing the man's wrongdoing to leave at the scene of the execution. But Ashvik's crimes were great and known to all. His next life would not be a good one.

Turning away from the body, I left the room and closed the door behind me, never looking back. In the withdrawing room, I used magic to lock the king's bedroom door. Then I took a second paper ward from my bag and put it in place across the outer door. This one would howl like the wolf of the underworld when the paper tore. Then into the garderobe, shut the door, drop down, seal the trap with the fire ward, and on through the dead prince's apartments. Five minutes after the death of the king, I was back in the small council chamber, sealing the door to the hall with the last of my spelled straps. They wouldn't stop the Elite and their stone dogs, but they'd buy me a few precious seconds each.

Taking a small risk, I slipped out onto the balcony and tucked myself up against the railing in a shadowy corner. Now I just needed the body to go undiscovered for the hour or so until the next shift change gave me a chance to slip out without being spotted by the Elite in the courtyard below. It was hard to fight the impulse to just go now, but my chances of getting away clean would go up dramatically if I was patient.

Haste kills.

After about ten minutes, the enormity of what I'd just done started to sink in. Not the part about killing my first man, that particular horror wouldn't hit me until months later, when I first had to kill a guard. No, for me on the balcony that night, Ashvik wasn't yet human. He was simply evil.

What I started feeling then was another thing entirely, religious ecstasy riding atop a golden wave of triumph. My goddess had set me a task, and I had succeeded where three older and more experienced Blades had failed. Namara had put her faith in me, just as I put my faith in her, and for her I had removed a monster from the world. More, I had done it clean without being spotted or harming a living soul other than my target. The risen, being neither alive nor possessing a soul, I felt I could discount.

Though it took months for the name to attach itself to me, I was in that moment more Kingslayer than I would ever

be again. I really and truly believed in myself as some kind
of invincible weapon of justice in the hand of Namara. I
knew I was going to rid the world of evil. The feeling lasted
about thirty seconds.

That's how long it took before my alarm ward got triggered. A single hellish howl from above alerted me that
someone had just entered the royal withdrawing room.
Which meant I needed to go, middle of the guard shift or
not. I rose into a crouch and peered down through the rails
of the balcony, waiting for the general alarm to go up and
counting seconds in my head. The call would bring chaos
in its wake, brief but exploitable, and I wanted to wait until
that happened if I had the time, hence the count.

One. Two. At three, the Elite who had set off the ward
would have crossed the room and tried the king's door. He
wouldn't bother knocking, not with my ward howling away.
Four. At five he would break the door in. *Eight. Nine.* By
ten he would have checked the body and found it still warm
though not warm enough. After that, things got fuzzier.
Eleven.

If I was lucky, the Elite would make a quick search and
find the trapdoor I'd cut in the garderobe floor before sounding the alarm. *Seventeen.* Opening it would trigger my fire
ward and light the smudge candle I'd left in the waste shaft.
Nineteen. The logical conclusion then would—My thoughts
were interrupted at *twenty* by the sound of a door crashing
open a floor above me and halfway round the tower.

A magically augmented voice cried out, "Assassins in
the sewers!"

A half second later, alarm trumpets started blaring out
all over the palace—more magic. The Crown Guards below
me had begun looking around anxiously in the first seconds
after the howl of my ward. But their Elite commander, a
young lieutenant, had held his ground with complete professionalism, keeping his area under tight watch. Now he
started barking orders though he didn't move otherwise.

There was no way he'd miss me blotting out the stars as
I sail-jumped across the courtyard above him nor fail to see

me when he looked up, but I couldn't wait for a better opportunity. I stood, took two running steps, jumped, and launched myself from the rail of the balcony, spreading my arms wide and commanding Triss to spin us wings of shadow.

I traded a two-story drop for about seventy feet of horizontal glide to land on the curtain wall that separated the Grand Tower from the main palace. At that point, I had to make a sudden change of plans when what looked like half the Zhani army stampeded out of their barracks and into the middle of my exit strategy. I'd intended to make another sail-jump down to the grounds and leg it for the outer wall, but I didn't think gliding into a seething mass of armed soldiers would do much for my long-term survival prospects.

Instead, I turned and ran along the top of the wall to the farther of the two towers it connected, the one that housed the royal kitchens. From there, I started working my way toward the formal ballroom. That's when I ran into an Elite lieutenant named Deem and his stone dog—name unknown. I won the pass but almost lost a leg in the process.

The rest of my trip out of the palace went by in a sort of nightmare blur. At Triss's insistence, I took a couple of extra efik beans to help ward off shock while he clamped a bandage of shadows over the gashes on my calf and heel. Of course, he had to thin himself out everywhere else to do so, and that made me a whole lot less invisible. Combine that with the attention summoned by the wild grating howls of the fallen lieutenant's stone dog and the deep tearing pain in my leg at every step, and I honestly can't tell you how I managed to come out the other end in one piece.

I don't even remember how I got from there to the snug I'd set up as my fallback in case I couldn't get out of Tien immediately after the execution. I'd like to say that Namara guided and guarded me, and I know I thought so at the time. But these days I've come to doubt that the gods intervene so directly. If Namara were that powerful, why did she need us to act as her hands? No, the answer is probably Triss, whispering in my ear and guiding my steps in the right direction, just as he so often has.

My snug was an attic storeroom in a great house not too far from the palace. It belonged to an out-of-favor viscount who had removed himself to his country estates for "health reasons." In other words, he thought it healthier to stay far away from the king, whose displeasure he'd incurred. The place had only a skeleton staff for the duration, and the room I'd adopted as my own chiefly held storm shutters and other winter necessities.

I spent the next several days wandering the edges of delirium, waking only now and then to chew a few efik beans handed me by Triss and wash them down with tepid water out of a skin I'd cached the week before—I didn't have the energy to brew up a proper pot. I would have recovered a lot faster if I could have put my teeth to the dried fruit and jerky I'd left with the skin instead of all that efik, but for the first time in my life, I simply had no appetite.

I felt terribly weak and shaky when I finally decided to venture out on the fourth day, but I'd run out of beans the night before, and I needed efik then more than I've ever needed alcohol since. Wrapping bandages around my torn calf made the flesh feel like I'd poured boiling water over it. Up to that point, Triss had kept my wounds bound in his own shadow-stuff, providing another of the many benefits to partnering a Shade. For reasons we didn't understand, that proximity to the everdark cooled and soothed as well as any snowpack while simultaneously warding against wound rot.

When I felt up to moving, I slipped downstairs to the master's quarters. There I borrowed a beautifully made but long-out-of-fashion suit of court clothes from the depths of a wardrobe that looked like it might not have been opened in the last century. Green and gold silk patterned with water tigers and twining vines, cut loose for ease of dueling. It was part of a set with a beautiful, if antiquated, matching court dress that had no doubt belonged to the lady of the house. I also found a pair of overlarge riding boots that accommodated my bandages though I had to pack the other boot with rags to make it fit.

Sandals or light court shoes would have been more appropriate considering the weather and my attire, but I didn't want to advertise the fact that I had a badly ripped-up leg right at the moment. Not after leaving so much blood and a boot behind in the palace. Besides, if I stole a shabby enough horse, the boots and the unfashionable clothes would blend right into a cover identity as some noble's down-at-the-heels rural cousin. Though I'd also need to do some careful work with cosmetics if I wanted anyone to believe I was a Zhani noble from anything closer than a few yards away.

Getting one of the cart horses saddled and out of the stables was easy enough once I'd set the mulch pile on the far side of the house afire. Everything but my swords packed down into the saddlebags with room to spare. After I removed the guards, the swords slid easily into a pair of thick bamboo tool handles I'd prepared for the purpose.

As I rode out onto the road in front of the estate and turned left toward the palace, Triss hissed quietly in my ear.

"Where are we going?" he asked.

"Little Varya," I whispered back.

"That's on the wrong side of Tien!" His voice rose, and I made a quelling gesture.

"That's what they'll be thinking, too, if the search hasn't already moved out of the city. If the lieutenant lived, he'll have told them it was a Blade. They'll be watching the roads to Kodamia, so I'm going to go south along the coast into the Magelands. Then I can cross the mountains through the high passes at Dalridia. It'll take longer, but it's less risky."

"Except for the part where we have to ride so close to the palace."

"I need efik for the trip home, Triss, and Little Varya's the only place in Tien I can get it. My leg's still pretty bad."

Triss hissed. "True, though I wish it wasn't. All right. But we'll have to be quick about it."

I nodded. "Really, Triss, it'll be fine. I'll be fine." But if I didn't get another bag of beans soon, I was going to shake myself to pieces. "I know what I'm doing."

13

Maybe the past did hold the keys to the present. I hadn't found my lost self in my memories—though the quivering efik addict who'd just killed a king had all too much in common with the drunk wearing that same skin today. But I did know exactly where to look for Devin now, and for that I could thank the efik. It was funny, really, that when I'd been a Blade, it had never occurred to me to think of efik as anything other than a tool of my trade. A dangerous one, to be certain, but just another tool I used.

Even when I'd given up efik after I came back to Tien, I hadn't seen it as more than that. I'd quit because the old Aral, Aral the Kingslayer, drank efik when he could get it and chewed the beans when he couldn't, just like all the other Blades. And every damned bean provided another reminder of the life the Son of Heaven had stolen from me. At the same time, Aral the Kingslayer had never touched alcohol.

So, when it came time to let the Kingslayer go, to really become Aral the jack, I drank myself unconscious every day for a week. It was the best method I could see for making a break between the two lives. It had honestly never occurred to me that I was just swapping one drug for another. Looking back now with the eyes of a drunk, I could see that back then I wasn't all that different from the sleepwalkers with their razors and efik-crusted scabs. Still wasn't in some ways, no matter that Triss had approved of my efik habit and hated my drinking.

I hadn't touched efik since then, but I remembered exactly how it tasted and how it made me feel, and I knew exactly where to find it. I knew how much it sold for by the mug and the ounce, and when the shipments came in from Varya, and which smugglers made the deliveries. Because efik was moderately illegal in Tien, there were only three alley-knockers where you could find a proper cup or pick up a bag of roasted beans.

All three of the illegal taverns were in Little Varya. If Devin wanted efik, that's where he'd have to go to find it, and that's where I'd find him. It's a good thing that most of the world had known so little about the habits and workings of the Blades back in the day, or people like the Elite would have known right where to look to find us. But the Blades had always been rare—a few hundred in a continental population that ran into many tens of millions—and more a matter of legend and speculation than anything real for most people. Beyond that, the power of Namara had blurred the memories of those few who did encounter one of us.

Figuring I'd have better luck traveling light and fast, I left my larger pack behind in the chimney of the Ismere Club. It'd be safe enough there, and none of the stuff in it would matter to me this side of setting up a new snug. As I stepped out onto the library's little balcony, I turned and looked over the river flowing by on my left. A thought occurred to me.

"Triss, could you follow a shadow across running water?"

"I don't think so. Not for long, anyway. Water *will* hold the—" He hissed something in his own language. "When we used to play tag on the lake's surface on a very still night, Zass and I and the other Shades could follow each other easily enough across the surface. But in a wind or on a river,

the movement of the water would break up the"—hissing—
"too quickly."

"I was hoping you'd say that."

The Zien River bisected Tien, entering between two of
the hills that held the wealthier neighborhoods and exiting
by way of the harbor. In the lower parts of the city, several
long canals extended the reach of boat traffic outward from
the hub where river met bay. By stealing a dinghy, I was
able to slip from the river into the Channary Canal, which
took me right to Little Varya's doorstep. A slower route than
the chimney road, but not by much, and the advantages of
leaving no trail more than made up for the lost time.

"It feels strange to be looking for efik again after all these
years," Triss said in a very quiet voice. "It's almost like the
old days."

"We're not looking for efik. We're looking for Devin.
Now hush. We don't want anyone noticing me talking to
myself and answering back in another voice."

I stretched then and rolled my shoulders before reluctantly reaching for the oars again. It was unusual exercise
for me, and every pull reminded me forcefully of the cut
Weasel had made across the back of my ribs. None of my
other injuries liked it much either, but it was the ribs that
made me sweat.

Even at this hour, the river and canals carried a lot of
traffic. Farmers bringing in early vegetables and greens from
the southwest—bok choy, pea pods, baby daikon . . . Fishermen hauling the late catch upriver to restaurants and great
houses. Shippers moving loads they didn't trust to the crush
of the day traffic. And, of course, the smugglers pretending
to be one or another of the other sorts of traffic. The rain
had stopped, but it was still cloudy and dark as the inside
of a miser's wallet—perfect smuggling weather.

Twice as I made my way toward Little Varya, customs
cutters slid in close and played their big magelanterns over
my boat. But there was nothing to see except for me, my

shadow, and a tiny pack tucked under the thwart. That last might possibly have gotten me stopped and briefly searched on a slow night, but not now. Not with so much bigger game on the prowl. Still, it was a relief to slip into the quiet waters at the foot of the Channary Canal.

The canal ended at the base of the Channary Hill, in an artificial bay where the nobles living at the top of the slope kept a small but fancy marina. A narrow brick lane ran along the western shore, marking the edge of Little Varya, and it was there that the first alley-knocker lay. From the water's surface, the whole area looked almost empty in the small hours of the morning, almost bleak, much quieter than the open waters behind me.

I rowed us in to shore on the west side of the canal a few yards short of the marina gates, where things looked considerably less fancy. I didn't bother to tie up because the last thing I did before hopping onto the dock was to rake a shadow-edged sword blade along the bottom of my little boat, scuttling it. I didn't want to leave any ideas for Devin to pick up on if he hadn't already figured out the running-water trick.

Behind me, sewage-laced canal water fountained up through the great rent I'd made in the planks, raising a truly delightful smell. You could get a pretty serious fine for dumping shit in the water, but that didn't stop some people, and unlike the main river, the canals didn't have a steady flow to keep it all moving out to sea. Before I'd made it the length of the dock, my little rowboat had already sunk to the gunnels. I'd have felt worse about that if I hadn't made sure to steal my dinghy from an ostentatiously rich yacht anchored in the river between the Ismere and the Palace Hill. The owners could afford the loss.

I paused at the foot of the dock and took a second look around, borrowing Triss's senses for a moment so that I could see beyond the end of my nose. I didn't spot anyone other than the dozing guard at the marina gate and a couple of day-working drunks staggering their way home from the taverns to catch a too-short sleep. It was just past four bells now, and the casual drinkers had gone home hours ago, while the night workers, both shadowsiders and sunsiders, had only just settled in to drink. That left the streets mostly empty. It was a marked change from the tens of thousands of people who would pour into the streets with the rising of the sun.

Normally, the relative emptiness would have made keeping an eye open for threats easier, but if Devin was around and enshrouded, I'd never know it until I stumbled into him or he struck. If he got it right, I'd never know another thing at all. With that in mind, I flipped my sword to an underhand grip and tucked it back against my shoulder rather than resheathing it. The darkened steel of the blade would blend well enough with the gray of my overshirt in this light. Both derived their shading from the juice of the oris.

As long as no one got very close or produced a too-bright magelight to shine on me, I could keep the sword in hand without alarming any potential passersby. Somehow that didn't make it any easier for me to climb up to the lane. I'd never had to worry about being stalked by a Blade before, and I didn't much like the idea. I did have the grace to wonder whether my own targets had felt that same little lead ball sitting in the bottom of their stomachs at the thought of an invisible assassin stalking them that I did now.

Probably. With a roll of my shoulders, I started forward, soft-footing my way up the half dozen stone steps that led from dock to lane. At the top, I turned right and headed for a narrow unmarked door wedged into an improbably short wall between a tailor's and a cobbler's. The door headed a steep stair that led down to the Cat's Gratitude. The illicit tavern occupied a low cellar filled with dim light, tiny tables, and people who'd rather not be recognized.

I didn't bother going inside, just walked past about six inches from the door while Triss had a bit of a sniff around. When he didn't signal me, I knew that we'd missed the mark, so I continued along my way till I hit a slim gap between two of the buildings fronting the lane.

When I turned in, the scuttling flight of a startled rat

allowed me a moment's relaxation, signaling as it did an otherwise empty darkness. Not even a Shade could hide you from a rat's nose. A pass down the clogged and stinking snicket behind the alley-knocker yielded another miss. As I headed for the next alley-knocker—two blocks in from the canal and a couple farther north—the tension slowly returned to my back and shoulders. The only other soul I saw was the driver of a cart making the run from the Coast Road to the canal end with a dim oil lantern bobbing along just above his head to light the way.

The Manticore's Smile topped an old tannery. The bar and tables were hidden from curious eyes on the hill above by a bunch of tattered old sails dipped in oris and strung up awning fashion over the whole area. Because it was open to the air on all sides, I actually had to climb up and circle around the whole perimeter to let Triss check for Zass's spoor.

When I ordered a tucker bottle of Kyle's and a clean glass to give me an excuse to mingle with the other patrons, Triss gave me sharp pinch on the heel. I stumbled at that and had to bite back a snarl. What did he want me to do? Wander around empty-handed? Because that'd go down great with the management of an illegal club. Ask for a pot of tea?

The Manticore didn't sell anything but alcohol and things that made alcohol seem as tame as candy. I didn't really have a lot of options if I wanted something with an intact seal from a reputable distiller. So I silently promised Triss that I'd just have the one glass, and myself that I'd tell him about that promise as soon as I got to someplace we could speak again. Then I walked to the edge of the roof and pretended to look out over the city as I drifted along.

Twenty minutes later, I'd made the full circuit and drunk a glass and a half—I had a brief talk with Ashelia, an old smuggling acquaintance who thought she might have some business for me. Again, I didn't have much choice but to play friendly. Getting loose of her cost another half glass and a promise to look her up as soon as I finished my present job.

"Well?" I asked Triss as soon as I'd gotten clear of the rickety stairs that led back to the ground.

"Nothing," Triss said, his tone falling somewhere between depressed and angry. "No Zass. No Devin. Nothing to make it worth the . . . effort involved."

I winced at the obvious message. "Look, Triss, I'm sorry about the Kyle's. I needed to be drinking something for cover purposes."

"So you bought a whole bottle?"

"In a place like the Manticore, you want to see the seal. Besides, it's a small bottle. And I was only going to have one drink."

"I counted two."

"That was because of Ashelia. If I hadn't kept drinking, she might have gotten suspicious."

"That *would* be out of character, now wouldn't it?"

I yanked the bottle out of the pocket I'd tucked it into and threw it over my shoulder to shatter on the cobbles.

"Happy?" I growled.

"Delighted," he snapped back.

"Good."

Without another word, I turned up the street and headed for the western edge of Little Varya where it butted up against the Downunders as the Coast Road entered Tien. The Downunders had started out as a shantytown catering to the drovers and traders who dealt in goods and animals that were too cheap or otherwise unsuited for ship travel, and it had never really recovered from its squalid beginnings. The streets got narrower and dirtier as I got closer and closer to the Dead Man's Pouch, offering a thousand hiding places for a Blade waiting to strike. Once again, I slipped my left-hand sword free of its sheath to carry against my shoulder.

The Dead Man stood between a more reputable sort of tavern on its right and a flophouse on its left. A signpost without a sign hung over the front door in a subtle nod to the alley-knocker's name. In Tien, a dead man's pouch was usually gone before the body hit the ground.

The building leaned to the left, as though it wanted to have a lie down at the flophouse, or perhaps feared catching an incurable case of legitimacy from its other neighbor. The windows were boarded over, and several big planks appeared to have been nailed across the door as well, though the latter were just for show. You *couldn't* open the door from this side, but that was because of a huge iron latch that opened easily enough from the inside. Quite a few patrons left by the "front" door, though most entered by knocking on the alley-side door. Which was the origin of the term alley-knockers, also occasionally called three-knocks.

I'd just turned toward the pitch-black gap on the flop-house side when Triss slapped me sharply in the soles of both feet to let me know he'd tasted Devin's trail. I kept walking as if nothing had happened, though it took a huge effort of will not to look around or reach for my second sword. The narrow gap ahead suddenly seemed twice as dark, a perfect place for an ambush. As I walked, I edged to my left, steadily shifting my practically invisible shadow so that it reached out toward the gap ahead of me.

As soon as my shadow's head touched the near-absolute darkness of the space between the buildings I felt Triss flowing out and away from me, extending himself to invisibly check the whole of the narrow passage. A moment later, I got a reassuring squeeze on my left foot. The way was empty, both of Devin and his traces, but I didn't relax. He could still have set up with a crossbow in the courtyard that backed the Dead Man. The open area outside the main entrance provided a secluded place to park extra tables in the stifling heat of Midsummer and Sunshammer.

"We're clear," Triss whispered, when I stepped into the deeper shadows.

"The trace in the street out front, coming or going?" I asked.

"Going, and quite recently. It got stronger as it moved away from the Dead Man's Pouch, but I couldn't sense any hint of his arrival here."

"Let's circle round the main door then and see if Devin came in that way before we decide whether to follow him or see where his back trail leads."

A quick slide around the courtyard revealed that Devin

had arrived by coming north across the roofs from the direction of the nastiest part of the Downunders. Looping back to the front of the alley-knocker, we checked Devin's departure trail, which headed north and west toward the Palace Hill and the bulk of the city.

So, follow Devin? Or see if we could find out what brought him to the Downunders? I didn't have time to do both, not with dawn less than two hours away. It was the hint of a double cross that decided me. If Maylien had told me the truth about being the true heir, then she represented a major threat to Baroness Marchon. That was a card that might come in damned handy for Devin in the event of a falling-out. The Downunders were very nearly as far away from the Marchon estate as it was possible to get without leaving Tien, well outside the baroness's easy reach. It was a perfect place to stash a backup plan.

Over the next hour, Triss and I painstakingly backtracked Devin two-thirds of the way across the rooftops of the Downunders looking for where he'd come from. It was slow, frustrating work. Between the many breaks in the trail made as Devin jumped across lanes, the various aches and twinges coming from my cuts and bruises, and the dilapidated nature of the buildings, I spent a lot of time swearing.

I must have put my foot through a half dozen roofs, and only just avoided doing so at least twice that many times more. Maybe the most annoying part of the whole thing came from knowing that Devin had probably made the trip in about ten minutes. At this point he could easily have finished his errand to the north and gotten back around in front of us again.

We'd come to a temporary halt atop a tiny temple tucked in tight against the base of the western bluff of the Channary Hill. Dedicated to Govana, goddess of the herds, the temple was built of sandstone blocks and much sturdier than the buildings around it. Devin's trail had come to an unexpected dead end on top of its small tower. We'd checked every roof within sail-jumping distance and found nothing but the trail we'd followed to get there.

"It's like he came up through the roof of the tower." Triss was flitting back and forth across the close-set stones, sniffing and tasting with his tongue. He'd shifted back to dragon form when we returned to the tower after our fruitless search of the surrounding buildings, and I didn't have the energy to argue with him about the wisdom of that. "That, or he simply dropped out of the sky."

"Now there's an unhappy thought." I glanced up at the bluff. "And one that should have occurred to me before you said something."

Seven or eight aging and out-of-fashion great houses hugged the cliff edge a hundred and fifty feet overhead, and that only counted the visible ones in easy sailing distance given the height. There were probably a dozen more out of sight that would have allowed Devin to make the jump to the temple. Unlike the houses around the palace or the Marchon estate, where the nobles and merchant princes kept the neighborhood exclusive, the Channary Hill great houses could belong to practically anybody.

All four of the hills of Tien had been colonized by the nobility over the thousand-plus years of the city's existence. The Palace Hill held the bulk of those still in use, with the Sovann Hill, where House Marchon stood, coming in a distant second. The abandoned great houses on the equally abandoned Kanathean Hill had long since been torn down, and their stones incorporated into the streets and homes of the Old Mews, Dyers Slope, and a half dozen other neighborhoods.

The Channary Hill was much more of a mixed bag. On the eastern slopes overlooking the ocean and the harbor, you could find quite a number of country nobles who didn't want to venture too deep into the evil city, intermixed with bankrupt city nobles clinging to these cheapest of Tien's great houses by their fingernails. While on the western bluff the remaining houses had a dusty popularity among social climbers who wanted to claim a palace view or shadow captains who needed a whiff of legitimacy for portions of their business.

In short, the place provided a perfect environment for a renegade Blade looking for a snug, as long as he had the funds. Knowing the money I could have made as a black jack, I had no doubt that the freelance-assassin business kept Devin solidly in funds. Time to start looking for the fastest way up the bluff.

"Come on, Triss, we'd better climb up and have a look."

"We don't have enough time to check even half of the houses before the morning sun burns off Zass's trail." Triss sounded gloomy.

"So we'll do what we can and hope we get lucky."

We didn't get lucky, at least not in terms of tracing Devin's trail back to its source. There were just too many jumping-off spots on too many great houses for us to have any reasonable chance of checking them all. Every third-story window on the bluff side provided a potential point of departure. It would have taken hours to search any single house and days to search them all, possibly longer. No, finding Devin's snug that way would have been virtually impossible. Finding the Crown Guard watching Devin's snug on the other hand . . .

Them, I practically tripped over. The first pair lay hidden in a hollow carefully excavated under the thickest part of a huge patch of imperial roses gone feral. I'd never have seen them if first light hadn't started me nosing around for someplace I could lie up for the coming day. I'd wanted to stay close and keep an eye on several of the better candidates for Devin's base of operations.

The dense rose thicket provided a good vantage on three of the five best choices, and I'd actually started to crawl into its depths when a small noise ahead warned me to freeze. The Crown Guards wore mottled green from head to toe, and green and brown paint on their faces. The only way I could even tell they were Crown Guard was by the dragon-crown insignia engraved on the deliberately verdigrised guard of the sword strapped across the nearer of the pair's back. It was clearly visible even in the predawn light, so close had I come before I saw them.

If not for Triss's enshrouding presence and the fact that I'd approached them from behind and with a good deal of stealth, they would certainly have seen me well before I spotted them. Even just crossing in front of them might have given me away if they were there waiting for Devin—and I had to assume they were. Trained soldiers actively lying in wait for a Blade would certainly have picked out light-colored sight points, and would be watching for any telltale obscuring darkness to pass between them and their marks.

They'd be just as happy to nail up my skin as Devin's—might not even know they'd gotten the wrong man. That made for a very cautious exit on my part. It took me fully three times as long to back my way oh-so-carefully and even more stealthily out of the rose thicket than it had to sneak in. Which, I suppose, gave me plenty of time to admire the fragrance.

As soon as I'd retreated to a safe distance, I set out just as cautiously to look for other likely hiding places around the area. I wanted to see how many of them held similar surprises. Their placement and numbers could tell me a lot about what the target was.

I found a round dozen, including a command post a fair distance back from the main perimeter on the upslope side. It held a captain of the Elite and his stone dog along with three more Crown Guards. Cold sweat started all over my body when I spotted them. I found it all too easy to imagine the consequences if I'd tripped over the stone dog and his master instead of the pair of guards in the rose thicket.

The smart thing to do at that point would have been to go home. Better yet, I could follow Triss's original advice and leave town entirely and permanently. Trying to slip past a cordon of watchers set up for the express purpose of spotting a shadow-shrouded Blade was a lousy recipe for even short-term survival. On the other hand, if this *was* Devin's snug—and the presence of a surrounding troop of Crown Guards commanded by an Elite captain sure as hell suggested it was—then Maylien might be in there somewhere. I really hated decisions like this.

14

Devin had co-opted a decaying great house of ducal size and state, a massive pile of badly pitted sandstone leaking rotted mortar from a thousand joints in need of repointing. It still looked sturdier than most of its neighbors, perhaps because it had further to fall before it finally hit bottom.

The tallest tower stood a bit over five stories, which gave it between one and two floors on the other four. A virtual maze of steeply angled roofways connected the five towers into a figure with several more sides than it had any right to.

I couldn't see any lights or other evidence of anyone's moving around the house or grounds. That was one benefit of a house run on assassin's hours. In a normal great house, the kitchen and pantry staff would certainly be preparing breakfast at this time of day. They might be doing the same here—impossible to tell since great houses never had windows below the second floor—but the odds were much lower.

I could only see two doors, both clearly in view of several of the watching posts, which observation pointed up my primary dilemma. Go in or walk away? The problem was that I didn't *know* Maylien was inside. If she wasn't, breaking into an unknown great house under these conditions was profoundly stupid. Maybe even borderline suicidal. If she *was* in there, I could at least cross off the stupid part. I didn't see any way around suicidal.

The funny thing was that if this were a mission for the goddess, I'd have walked away right then. That might sound counterintuitive, but really it's just part of the job.

Mind before heart.

Namara taught her Blades to treat assignments professionally, not emotionally. That meant balancing risks and rewards honestly and walking away more often than you might think.

On the walking away side of the table there lay the Elite and his stone dog, a heavy argument even without the Crown Guard. Add to that the admittedly slim possibility that they were here after someone other than Devin. Alternatively, if they *were* hunting for him—as I believed—there was a decent chance they'd solve my Devin problem for me. Conceivably my Maylien problem, too, if they chose to release any prisoners their target might be holding.

Balance that against the argument for going in. Maylien might be there. She might be alive. And it was barely possible that if both those things were true, I could sneak her out in one piece past the Crown Guard and the Elite.

That's the point where you walk away if you're looking at things professionally. Emotionally, on the other hand . . . Maylien had saved my life. More importantly, she'd saved Triss's life. I owed her whatever I had the power to give. I also kept coming back to the fact that Colonel Deem had been under pressure from a royal baroness. A baroness whose name seemed all too likely to be Sumey Marchon, who would certainly prefer that Maylien died in the coming crossfire.

But who did I think I was kidding? Of course I was going in. The real question was how. The Elite captain had placed his teams very well. The only thing that made it even remotely possible was the combination of knowing they were there and the fact that they'd had to choose their positions more in terms of concealing themselves than for perfect surveillance. They couldn't afford to scare off the target. With a target who could make himself invisible, that meant playing things very conservatively.

Half an hour after I'd admitted to myself that I had to try, I was sliding down the leaded roof into an oddly shaped little valley made by the nearby intersections of several roof segments. As long as I stayed low, the various bits of steeply slanting lead would hide me from the watchers on the ground.

The sun was up by then, but not yet so high I could see it over the rooftops. The thought of making noise still made me nervous, but I really needed to let my familiar know where we stood. I also needed to give him the option of talking me out of my insane little plan since I hadn't been able to drop my shroud and consult with him before. Now I released my hold on Triss, and, an instant later, a small dragon's shadow lay beside me on the leads. I spilled the story to date in the ghost of a whisper.

"What do you think?" I asked finally. "This is our last chance to give this up and slip away clean."

"I owe Maylien as much as you do. She saved you for me as much as she saved me for you."

I suppressed an urge to tell him that balance didn't come out even, not with the current Aral on one side of the scales anyway. I didn't think he'd appreciate the sentiment, not even in jest.

Instead, I drew a knife and placed its edge against the lead of the roof, and said, "Then we go in."

Triss nodded, and the familiar cold-silk feeling of his presence slid up my body and down my arm to the knife's edge. It took less than a minute to slice open three sides of a square, allowing me to pry up a flap of lead and expose the underlying planks. I didn't want them tumbling noisily to the floor of the attic below, so I was more careful now, working between two joists and lifting the boards out as

I cut them free. Another few minutes, and I was able to poke my head through the narrow gap and take a quick look around.

The attic ranged in height from next to nothing at the edges to over twelve feet at the nearest visible peak. It was also a maze, mirroring the tangled structure of the roofs above. The detritus of generations of owners lay strewn around, all of it covered in dust and the various leavings of the house's less official residents. Without moving, I could see clear evidence of slinks, pigeons, rats, and nipperkins.

The roof hung within a few feet of the attic floor here, which allowed me to collect the planks and, with Triss's aid, lever the flap shut behind me. The whole process was quiet and fast but not silent. There was nothing I could do about that except tuck the fresh-cut planks as far back under the eaves as possible and move fast. That, plus the size and cluttered nature of the attic and the closing of the flap, would conceal my point of entrance even from a dedicated searcher. Hopefully for long enough.

"Triss, can you scout around and see what options we have for getting downstairs?"

"Of course." The near-total darkness of the attic allowed Triss the freedom to thin himself out and expand to many times his normal area, sliding along the floor's surface and encompassing the space within himself.

"There are two small trapdoors," he said, when he returned a few seconds later. "There's also a main stair down to what's probably the servants' wing, and a second, narrower stair going who knows where. More importantly, I found a good-sized gap that opens into the top of one of the interior walls. It's covered by a trunk that's nailed to the floor."

"False bottom in the trunk."

"Almost certainly."

"Nice! I haven't seen that trick in ages."

A lot of great houses had secret passages or rooms. Some provided hidey-holes for goods or people. Many opened into escape routes or provided access to nearby chambers for clandestine affairs. Others had been put in for purposes of spying on the guests, or murdering them in their beds. All of them were an assassin's friend.

"Guide me to the trunk."

Triss shifted so that I could feel his presence as a pair of invisible hands on my shoulders. He steered me swiftly through the darkness to the trunk. It was a huge thing of oak and rusted iron, with a couple of giant splits at the corners. The no-doubt carefully-thought-out combination made it look too heavy to bother moving and too ruined to sell. Opening the lid revealed a mess of moth-eaten old wool that seemed to cry out for mice and rats to come and make a nest of it.

"Triss?"

Shadow gloved my hands as I reached into the tangle, groping for . . . there! A few inches under the surface, I found an iron loop. Pulling on it pivoted the shallow tray full of wool up and out of the way, revealing a dark opening.

Sliding a leg over the lip of the trunk, I felt around with my foot until I found the top of a wooden ladder leading down into the wall. Another iron loop pulled the tray back into place above me, while a long rod connected to the trunk's hinges quietly closed the lid. The ladder descended perhaps twelve feet to a wide plank set loosely across the deep floor joists. Pulling my tiny thieveslight from the trick bag, I shined the dull red beam around. I was in a narrow space between the walls, with a dead end a few feet to my left and a narrow passage heading away on my right.

Every couple of yards a gap between planks opened down into the joists, where more boards had been mounted just above the ceilings of the rooms below, allowing a person to crawl down and into those ceilings. At a guess, some of those would cross-connect to other passages in the walls. It made for a pretty typical network of the spying and murdering sort.

"Triss, can you slip around through the walls and see if there's any light or sound coming from anywhere close at hand?"

The shadow of a dragon appeared on the wall, and Triss

nodded once before extending himself like a snake, slithering down into the depths of one of the floor gaps. Almost as soon as Triss had gone, he returned. Shaking his head, he tried another. On the fourth attempt I felt a sudden tug along the thread of shadow linking us. He'd found something. Closing up my lamp, I bent and slipped into the gap, scraping my still-healing back against the bottom of the wall as I did so.

Fuck, but that hurt! Clenching my jaw to keep from swearing aloud, I started crawling. It was hard on my much-abused body, harder than all the climbing and roof jumping had been earlier. Maybe because climbing and roof jumping were a part of my regular routine even as a jack.

I passed under a second overhead passage and into another ceiling before I saw daylight shining up through a gap just beyond the next wall. It was coming around the edges of a tiny wooden slide affixed to the floor. When I moved it, I could see about three-quarters of a large room that might once have been an audience chamber of some sort. Judging by the angle and the restrictions on my view, the peephole was hidden in the crown molding, an observation the professional side of my brain made and filed away independently of the emotional side, which had an entirely different and more intense focus.

Maylien! She sported a number of minor cuts and a really spectacular black eye, but she was alive. She sat sullenly against the far wall, not far from the filthy eastern windows that provided the light. She wore a loose shirt and something midway between a split skirt and pair of bloused pants, similar to a noble's dueling clothes, but in coarse peasant fabrics. It was not all that different from what I was wearing, actually.

She had chains on her wrists and ankles. And she wore the most murderous expression I'd seen on any woman's face since Siri had missed her shot at the High Khan of Avars after we'd gone through a week of maneuvering to set up the kill. The khan had died old and in his sleep— bastard.

Maybe ten feet to Maylien's left a man sat with his feet up

on a scarred oak table. He had one hand hooked through the loop on the end of a rope pull. The rope, in turn, ran across the table, connecting to the release on a very heavy steel blade suspended between two wooden tracks. I recognized the design as having been stolen from the Sylvani Empire's latest device for making beheading more efficient.

Underneath the blade sat a small wicker cage holding something gray and fluffy. I couldn't tell what it was from that angle, but judging by the way it kept pacing and growling, it was very, very angry.

"They're threatening her familiar to keep her under control!" Triss hissed in my ear, his voice aseethe with rage. "We've got to do something!"

"Sst!" I made an angry chopping motion, signaling him to shut up.

He did because it was the smart thing to do. But the way he kept sliding back and forth across my back like an agitated snake told me everything I needed to know about his continued fury. I felt the exact same way. Threatening a familiar was the usual way you controlled a mage. We'd both seen it dozens of times in the past, but after our own recent imprisonment, it struck a lot closer to home. The man with the rope didn't know it yet, but he was about to meet the lords of judgment.

The cleanest way to come at the problem would have been to back up about two rooms and find a quiet way down to the lower floor. Then sneak around to nail him with a shadow-sharp thrust through the wall he was leaning against. Done properly, it would kill him so quickly he'd never have a chance to even think about tugging on that rope. But clean took time we really didn't have.

Not when Devin might come back at any moment. Not with a small army waiting to attack the house, likewise at any moment. And especially not with that bastard holding a rope he could pull at any moment. No, I needed to do this quick and dirty and I needed to find some way to pin that rope down for a bit.

A spell-guided throwing knife might have served, but

there was no way to get that to work through the peephole. Likewise an arrow if I'd had a bow and room to draw it. I had a few blowdarts in my pouch, but the broken-down blowgun was stowed with the bulk of my gear in a chimney on top of the Ismere Club.

Come on, Aral. Think! There must be something. But my mind kept going around in the same circle: knife, arrow, dart, knife, arrow . . . Wait a moment. Could I . . . ?

"Triss," I breathed in a voice lighter than any whisper. "Do you think you could make yourself into a tube for a blowdart? I need to pin that rope."

Triss froze on my back, digging his claws in lightly.

After a moment he replied just as quietly, "Maybe." Then, more confidently, "Yes. Yes, I could."

The rest of the plan fell together in my head. Quick and dirty to be sure, but also reasonably likely to succeed. I slid the peephole closed and neatly laid my tools out on the planks around me. First, my swords, about a handspan behind the peephole with the hilts toward the hole. Next, a long steel blowdart, one of six in my trick bag. After that, I very carefully reversed my position so that the bulk of my body lay above the audience chamber. Finally, I told Triss what I wanted him to do. As soon as he nodded in agreement, we began.

Opening the peephole once again, I took a quick look to make sure nothing had changed. Then I rose as high as the constricted space would allow and set the blowdart between my teeth. It was instantly surrounded by a hollow tube of night that ran from my lips down and through the peephole. Without looking—it was Triss's job to make sure it hit the target—I blew as hard as I could. As soon as the dart left the gun, I reached for my swords.

In that same instant, Triss shifted back to dragon form and pressed himself flat along the boards beneath me, pushing hard. Just as he had when he freed me from Lok's dungeon, he slowly forced his wings forward while contracting down to a pinpoint. Then I was falling through a dragon-shaped hole in the ceiling, my swords in my hands. I landed on my feet and let myself tumble backward into a roll. Spinning as I came upright again, I leaped forward to chop the guard's hand off at the wrist before he could free the rope from the dart temporarily pinning it to the table.

The guard clutched at his hand and started screaming, but not for long. I silenced him with a thrust of my second sword. As I started to tug the chopping blade free of the table, Maylien shrieked an unfamiliar word in a voice both louder and more frightened than the guard's.

I turned to find her pointing back over my shoulder toward the hanging blade, and I knew without looking there must have been a second guard concealed in the peephole's blind spot. I left one sword stuck in the table as I pivoted on the ball of my foot and dove, sliding on my belly across the floor toward the falling blade. The distance was short, but so was time.

All I could do was punch the little wicker cage hard with my empty hand and hope I'd gotten there fast enough. The cage bounced away in the instant before the falling blade dropped into the space it had just occupied. I should have lost a hand then. Would have, too, if Triss hadn't managed to catch the blade in the inches before it could hit the floor.

That took all his strength and focus, at least for a few seconds. But even with Triss intervening, the blade pinned my wrist, leaving me dreadfully exposed. Trying hard not to imagine the feeling of the guard's weapon driving deep into my back, I slid my sword under the edge of the bigger blade and used it as a lever.

As soon as I freed my hand, I started rolling, aiming toward the place I'd last seen the guard who had, very obligingly, not yet stabbed me in the back. That probably had something to do with his shrieks and the squalling and hissing of Maylien's familiar, all of which came from the same direction. But I really hadn't had time to look.

Reflex or chance guided me into the guard's shins, and he went down in a heap. I didn't bother to get up, just flipped my sword from overhand to under and sank it deep in his side, twisting and levering in search of something vital.

Somewhere in there the man stopped moving, Maylien stopped yelling, and her familiar stopped snarling. For a few brief seconds, all was bliss and silence, and I had leisure to figure out that the cage must have come apart when I hit it, freeing the familiar to save my life.

Then came the applause.

"Very nicely done, Aral. Oh, very nice. If you'd managed it even a few minutes earlier, you'd be out the door and gone by now."

It was Devin's voice.

Fuck.

I rolled over onto my back, bringing my sword up defensively. It wasn't much of a shield, but it was all I had.

"There's no need to be so dramatic," he said. "If I'd wanted to kill you, I wouldn't have spoken. I'd just have pulled the trigger."

Devin stood in the doorway holding a small crossbow, its quarrel aimed directly at my left eye. I had no doubt that a moment before it had been pointing at the spot where my spine connected to my skull. I also had no doubt that the dark smear of stuff on the head would kill me in a matter of minutes, whether it hit a vital spot or not. I couldn't tell what the poison was from here, but none of the options made me want to try my luck.

"Maylien," said Devin. "Tell your pet to land next to Aral, or I will be forced to kill it and, tragically, you."

Maylien didn't say a word, but the gray and black cloud of fury that had been hovering a few feet from Devin and hissing angrily, turned in the air and came to land beside me. It wasn't until then that I finally got a good look at it.

Miniature gryphon, or gryphinx. Which meant that Maylien had spent those missing years with the Rovers, a seminomadic order of mages that spent much of their time clearing the roads and hunting bandits and highwaymen. Maylien's partnering of a gryphinx meant she'd taken mage orders with them, or at least started along that path, and that spoke well of her. The Rovers had always had good relations with Namara's priesthood and shared many of the same values.

"There's a nice pet," said Devin. "That wasn't so hard, was it?"

The little gryphinx hissed and mantled at that, which pretty much mirrored my feelings.

"Gently, Bontrang," said Maylien, and I recognized in his name the word she'd cried out earlier.

Bontrang let out another angry squall, then dropped back onto his haunches and flicked his tail around to cover his front feet. He *looked* calm that way, but I could hear the very faint scraping as he repeatedly flexed and released his talons under the tail. The gryphinx was about the size of a large house cat, with the head, wings, and front legs of a hawk and the body and coloring of a gray tabby.

"Very good," said Devin. "Aral, I'm going to ask you to stay right where you are. Flat on your back in the middle of the room is about as safe as I can make you this side of dead. Triss, please don't try anything clever. I don't want to have to kill Aral, but I will if you force me to it. So I'd like you in plain sight."

Triss slid out from under me, assuming his dragon form as he did so. "How's this?" His voice burned with anger.

"Perfect. That puts everyone where I want them. Now we're going to have a little talk."

"Don't you want to move me over with the others?" asked Maylien. "It's going to be hard to keep an eye on me way over here."

"Not at all. I like you in chains. If anything, I'd prefer to lock Aral up next to you. *That* would simplify things, but I can't think of a safe way to arrange it at the moment, so we'll just leave him there. Besides, with your pet sitting next to Aral like that, I've got all the leverage over you that I need."

"Bontrang's not a pet," snapped Maylien. "He's my familiar, and a damned good one."

"Call him whatever you wish, child. He's still a glorified house cat. Now, do shut up, or I'll have to shoot him. The adults have things we need to discus."

Maylien shut up though I could read rage in the angle of her chin and the tension in her neck and shoulders. I felt the same way but made a conscious effort not to show it.

"Aren't you going to ask me to throw my sword aside?" I asked, keeping my voice casual.

"No, I think you'll feel safer with a weapon in hand, and that'll make you easier to deal with, more rational. It also keeps you from getting any ridiculous ideas like throwing it at me. That's a reasonable trade-off for the risk. I take it from your arrival here that you've chosen not to accept the deal I offered you at Marchon House?"

I nodded and tried not to look over Devin's shoulder into the hallway. I wanted the Crown Guard to have one clean shot at his back when they finally got here.

"Pity that. You'd be a real asset for the new Order of the Assassin Mage. It would make our path much easier if I could just get you to come in with the rest of us." Possibly in response to some unintentional cue from me, Devin stepped deeper into the room then, moving to the side so that he had a wall at his back. "Hell, you wouldn't even have to participate in any of our funding activities if you didn't want to."

"Contract murder, you mean?" I asked. "Not interested."

Triss hissed his agreement.

"I prefer 'paid assassination' if it's all the same to you." Devin moved again, stepping to the side and resting a hip on the table where his henchman's hand still lay beside the sword I'd used to chop it off—the crossbow never wavered from its aim at my left eye. "But that's not all we do. We hire out for a lot of freelance work these days. Some not so different from your jack work here in Tien. But you wouldn't have to play that game.

"After our last encounter, I checked in with the ruling council, and we've agreed you're an important enough catch to offer you a new deal. You and Triss can join us in an advisory capacity, teaching the next generation the skills that you know so well. You wouldn't be allowed a vote on the council, of course, but your hands would be completely free of blood."

"This council you keep mentioning. Who are we talking about?" And where the hell were the Crown Guard? Had they missed Devin's arrival?

"Sorry, but until you're on the inside, you don't need to know any of the involved names but mine. For that matter, if you didn't already know about me, we wouldn't give you that much." Then he shook his head sadly. "You're not going to see reason, are you?"

"Reason? Really? It's not like you're asking me to train a new generation of Blades. Namara's dead. No, you want me to help you create an army of assassins unbound by any ethical restriction. An order of murderers that would answer to no one but itself in the shape of this council of yours. Then you tell me that if I do this, I won't have blood on my hands? Secondhand blood is still blood."

"You're sure you won't reconsider? No, I can see that you won't. I guess—"

Devin's voice cut off abruptly as he spun in place and fired the crossbow at an angle back through the door. There was a choked gurgling noise in response—the distinctive sound of someone taking a quarrel in the throat.

The Crown Guard had arrived. Now I just had to survive long enough to get Maylien free and make a break for it.

15

Devin vanished into a pool of shadow. As the first
Crown Guards burst through the doorway, the shadow
licked out, and the guard lost his head. I was already moving
by then, rolling back up onto my shoulders, then flipping
myself forward onto my feet.

"Catch!" The shadow shifted again, and the sword I'd
left embedded in the table came spinning my way. The
enemy of my enemy, and all that.

I put out my right hand and the hilt slapped into it, a
perfect toss on Devin's part. I lunged toward Maylien as two
more Crown Guards died in the doorway. Before I could do
anything about the chains that held her, the back wall of the
room exploded inward, propelled by magic. A dozen more
Crown Guards charged in through the choking cloud of
wood and plaster dust.

The nearest tried to skewer me with her woldo, a pole-
mounted short sword, and I had to turn away from Maylien
to parry the blow. Dust began to fill my nose and throat, and
I coughed violently but kept moving. Before the guard could

recover from her thrust, I stepped in and opened her throat with a backhanded cut.

As I fended off another attack, I croaked back over my shoulder to Maylien, "Hang on, I'll get you loose in a second."

"Screw that," said Maylien, between her own coughs. "I'll get myself loose. You deal with the Crown Guards. Bontrang!"

The little gryphinx shot past my head as I slid between two of the guards, killing one with a thrust up and under the ribs and breaking the knee of the other with a spinning back kick. Triss tore out that one's throat when my shadow fell across him. As I moved past the dead guard, an arrow passed just behind my head. I turned to look for the archer, but Devin's shadow abruptly hid him from sight, and I stopped worrying about him.

I killed three more guards in quick succession and had moved to go after a fourth when Triss's voice suddenly yelled "Down!" and I dropped to the floor. All the hair along the back of my body stood on end as a sheet of magelightning sizzled through the place I had just been. I rolled sharply to my left, just dodging a thrown axe, then spun myself back up onto my feet in time to bat another axe away with my sword.

Then the captain of the Elite was on me, a short axe in each hand, and I found myself backing up fast as he pressed me. The next few seconds passed in a blur as we exchanged a dozen blows and counters at a pace I hadn't had to sustain in years. He was better than I, at least as I was now, and I couldn't touch him. I kept him from scoring on me, but only barely and with the constant worry that his stone dog might take me from behind at any moment.

Then Triss came to my rescue, enfolding me in shadow all in an instant and surrendering me his senses. The captain very nearly had me in the moment of transition before I'd fully submerged Triss's consciousness in my own. The tip of his left axe tore away a huge strip of my shirt between armpit and waist, while the back of its head slid bruisingly along my ribs.

I countered with a thrust straight toward the captain's groin. He leaped backward just in time, wisely moving away from the sword he couldn't see within the moving shadow he could. I followed, pressing him back and back again. Triss's presence gave me other advantages beyond the invisible attack, including the ability to "see" all around me in three dimensions through his unvision.

It revealed why the stone dog hadn't taken my life earlier. The dog and a half dozen Crown Guards were engaged with the shadow that hid Devin—they had not been prepared to meet two Blades. The unvision also showed me Maylien and Bontrang working together to free her by repeatedly directing some sort of low-magic force burst against the locks of her shackles. Slow work that. Much slower than a pick if you didn't want to accidentally rip your hand off. Most importantly, my unvision spied subtle movement in the hall beyond the door where the first guards had entered. More archers probably.

"Devin! Ware the door, we've company coming!" For a moment it almost felt like old times, and I had to remind myself we were at best temporary allies.

"Busy here! Deal with it!"

But four more guards had also arrived from the other direction, backing up their captain and putting me once more on the defensive. This group all had woldos, and they were using the sword-spears to blindly thrust again and again into my lacuna of shadow. Easy enough to avoid on an individual basis, but much harder coming from multiple directions and with the captain and his axes and possible spells to keep an eye on as well. That was the situation when the first arrow sank into the floor at my heels.

The archers couldn't go for a straight shot with the captain and his spear-wielders in the line of fire but they *could* plink away in the general vicinity of my feet and hope they got lucky. I was just trying to decide if I could afford to turn and rush the archers when Maylien let loose on them with a truly hellacious burst of magefire.

At which point, the world came apart. The magefire ignited the cloud of dust still hanging in the air in a massive explosion. The blast took out what was left of the wall between the audience chamber and the hallway, at which point the ceiling fell in.

At least, that's the way I thought it happened, looking backward at the results. In the moment, I heard a huge noise like thunder experienced from the inside and found myself thrown toward the captain and his companions. Somehow I managed to avoid a skewering as we all tumbled together into the large dining room that had backed the audience chamber.

I'd balled up by then, dropping my swords and rolling with the force of the blast as I'd been taught. It took me halfway across the room, throwing me into and through the legs of the nearer rows of chairs with bone-jarring force. As I bounced to a halt under the table, I thought sure my luck had run out. I was badly tangled up with the remains of two or three shattered chairs, disarmed, and easy meat for anyone still standing. That's when the ceiling came down, bringing with it various bits of junk from the attic and a goodly piece of the roof above that, reversing the direction of my fortunes.

Instead of a trap, the huge oak table had suddenly become a refuge. Oh, I still had to free myself from the wreckage of the chairs, but I did that quickly enough. I had a new collection of cuts and bruises layered over the old, of course, but none too severe, and nothing like what I'd have had if the ceiling had landed on me. As soon as I could manage it, I slithered stiffly out from under the table and surveyed the damage.

Various cries and faint stirrings in the rubble marked other survivors of the battle and collapse, by implication if not immediately by position or persuasion, though nobody else seemed to have mastered the trick of digging themselves out yet. It seemed a perfect time to make a quick exit, so I started toward where I'd last seen Maylien in hopes of finding her alive and ready to travel.

That's when Devin called out, "Aral, help! The dog's got me!" His voice was gasping, laced with pain and panic.

With his cry to orient me, I spotted the stone dog, a massive presence near what had once been an outside wall, its paw pressing down into a low-lying pool of shadow. The huge beast was covered in dust and debris, which is why I hadn't seen it earlier, but it seemed otherwise unharmed. I started to turn back toward Maylien, but I couldn't help picturing Devin—my onetime friend—lying there under the great weight of that stone paw, his ribs creaking as it slowly pressed down.

I couldn't leave him to die like that. Damn me, but I couldn't do it. Even knowing that he'd betrayed the memory of our goddess, I couldn't leave a fellow Blade in the hands of the Elite.

The funny thing is that the old Aral would have done it in a heartbeat. Aral Kingslayer would have looked at what Devin had done and seen only the black and white, and he'd have condemned Devin to death without a qualm. But the new Aral had lost that clarity of purpose. He understood too much about bending to circumstance.

I didn't know what pressures had been brought to bear on Devin. I didn't know what I might have done in the same situation. Oh, I wanted to believe that I'd have chosen to die by torture rather than betray my goddess, and I really think that I would have. But I didn't *know* I'd have done it, especially if they'd threatened Triss. Because of that and because of Zass, I couldn't just let an old enemy kill the new one who had once been my friend. With a snarl of frustration, I released my hold on Triss.

"Find the Elite," I said, "quickly!" Triss dove into the wreckage near where I'd come out.

"Here!" he called a moment later, raising a shadowy tail above a heap of broken lath and shattered plaster. Then he started digging.

Within moments, Triss had exposed the Elite captain's head and right arm. I flicked a wrist, releasing the dagger there into my hand, then knelt to press it against the captain's chin. There was a time when I'd simply have cut his throat, but I wanted to give him a chance.

"Call off your dog," I said.

"Fuck you." He had dark blood on his lips, and he spat some of it into my face.

"Aral!" Devin's voice was weaker now. More desperate.

"Do it now, or die," I said.

"I'm already dead," said the captain. "We both know you're going to kill me."

"Only if I have to."

He spat at me a second time, and I drove the dagger up, through the soft place behind his chin and the roof of his mouth, into his brain. Behind me the stone dog gave one great howl, then fell over with a crash that shook the floor.

"Devin?" I called. "Are you dead?"

"I don't think so."

"Then you owe me. Get the fuck out of my city."

I'd taken a life to save a life. And somehow the fact that the life I'd ended belonged to someone who'd cheerfully have killed me if our circumstances were reversed didn't make me feel any better about the whole thing. But sometimes that's just how it is. So I wiped the blood off my face and went to see if I could find Maylien.

We still needed to get out of there, and I didn't think we had a whole lot of time to manage it. A big and more or less intact chunk of the roof had fallen atop the place where I thought she ought to be, so I sent Triss into the wreckage.

He emerged a few moments later and gave me a shadowy grin. "She's fine, trapped in a little pocket between the wall and a big piece of ceiling, but essentially unharmed. I didn't want her to attempt anything drastic with magic from where she is, for fear she'd make it worse, so I told her we'd get her out soon."

"Great, any idea how do we do that?"

"You don't," said Devin from somewhere behind me. "At least not right away. We weren't done talking. You know I can't let you leave until we come to an arrangement."

"You're not serious." I turned around to find Devin aiming an arrow at me from somewhere near the place the door used to be. He'd apparently salvaged one of the fallen guard's bows. "For fuck's sake, man, I just saved your life."

"That's why I didn't shoot you in the back. I wanted to give you one last chance to change your mind. We need your expertise, Aral. You could do so much for us. Don't make me throw a treasure like you away."

"Zass," said Triss. "My master just saved your master's life. You will *not* let him do this."

Zass said nothing, but the string of the bow suddenly broke with a sharp twanging noise, momentarily disarming Devin. Somehow, it felt like a loss.

"I won't say it again, Devin. Get out of my city and don't come back. Don't force me to kill you." There was a time where I might have been able to make that threat stick. Now . . . I just had to hope he wouldn't make me try.

I turned my back on Devin. "Triss, what if we went out what's left of this window and you cut a hole through the wall behind Maylien. Can you make that work?"

"Yes, I think I can. I'm tired but not impossibly so."

"Then, let's do it." I put one foot up on the twisted frame.

Behind me, I heard Devin's swords slide out of their sheaths, a deliberate threat on his part, since we both knew he could have drawn them silently. I kept going, climbing out through the window. Either he would kill me or he wouldn't. At this point, there was very little I could do to stop him except run away, and I wasn't leaving Maylien behind. I'd lost my own swords in the blast and cave-in, and there was no possible way for me to defeat another ex-Blade knives against swords. Not on this ground at any rate.

As I slid around to hang on the wall just outside where Maylien lay trapped, I heard Devin swearing behind me. Then he put his swords away just as noisily as he'd drawn them.

"This isn't over, Aral. If it wouldn't have upset Zass, I'd have killed you just now."

"Fuck you, Devin. I—oh, shit." Out of the corner of my eye I'd seen movement on the road in front of the great house. More Crown Guards on the way, along with at least a half dozen Elite judging by the stone dogs. "We need to speed things up, Triss, the next wave's going to be here in a couple of minutes."

He spread himself out on the old masonry of the wall for a time, focusing his strength, then flapped his wings and sent the stones to the everdark. It was still as creepy as all hell to watch him do that, but I was beginning to believe that I might someday get used to it. Bontrang exploded outward through the hole, with Maylien sticking her head out a moment later.

"Thank you," she said. "I knew you wouldn't let me down, Kingslayer." I looked away from the admiration in her eyes.

"Look, we don't have a lot of time here, and I don't have a rope. Can you climb onto my back?"

"Of course."

Maylien slid farther out of the hole, putting her arms around my neck and shoulder, then pivoting to hang free for a moment before she wrapped her legs around my waist. As I took the strain of her full weight, I had to suppress a groan. She was a tall woman and sword-trained, and I was a bruised and battered wreck. Without Triss's help, we'd have fallen off the wall.

"Ready?" I asked through gritted teeth.

"Ready."

I started down, moving as fast as I could. When I got about eight feet from the bottom, Maylien let go and dropped, touching down only lightly with her feet before dropping into a backward roll to soak up the force of her fall. Apparently, she'd taken me at my word about needing to get out of there fast. A moment after she dropped, I kicked off and followed her. By the time I'd rolled to my feet, she was beside me. That was good because the deep baying of one of the stone dogs started then—we'd been spotted.

"Take my hand," I said, "and run."

She did, and Triss widened himself out into a broad curtain of shadow between us and our pursuers while I aimed us straight toward the edge of the bluff. In this light, Triss's intervention wouldn't allow us to slip away, but it would make it much harder for any archers to hit us, especially since they'd have to shoot on the run. If any of them tried, they shot wide enough of the mark that I didn't know about it.

We had to slow a bit when we crossed from the ruined gardens into the wall of overgrown shrubs that had colonized the broken ground along the top of the bluff. Branches slapped at my face and chest, and weeds clutched at my boots, while Bontrang flitted in and out above us.

Maylien went up several points in my estimation over the next minute or two. Both because she kept her mouth shut to save her breath for running and because she would have soon pulled ahead of me if she'd let go of my hand. When it came to running, she was in decidedly better shape than I was. Not having to worry about Maylien gave me more leisure to worry whether Triss would be able to manage the task ahead.

If not, we were all going to die. As fast as we ran, the stone dogs were faster still. The three following us had started out less than a quarter mile behind and they'd gained ground fast as we sprinted toward the edge of the bluff. The brush and trees that so hampered us barely registered for the dogs, who left a swath of crushed and shattered greenery in their wake. The only good thing about the dogs' speed was that they'd left their masters behind, temporarily saving us the necessity of dodging magefire and -lightning and other nastier sorts of magic. They'd closed to within twenty feet when we abruptly ran out of running room.

"Trust me," I said to Maylien, as we broke through the last of the brush before the cliff's edge.

Then I scooped her into my arms and leaped into space. As I did so, Triss caught hold of my shoulders and spread himself out above us like a great black wing. I frantically fed Triss nima as we moved lurchingly out and away from the bluff, filling that wing from the well of my soul. Somehow, we stayed aloft.

It was more of a slow and loosely guided fall with a lot of wild swings and random turns in one direction or another than a true sail-jump, but we didn't just fall. That felt like a miracle, really, since we normally used my arms as supports for Triss's shadow wings and they carried half the weight. Even the massive quantities of magic I was pouring into the effort were barely enough to keep us aloft under the circumstances. I desperately hoped we could hold it together long enough for something roughly resembling a successful landing, and wished I still had a goddess to pray to on the subject.

Behind us the stone dogs bayed wildly and briefly, then dove down through the ground into the rocky bones of the Channary Hill, heading for the base of the bluff. We hadn't gotten away yet, not by anyone's count.

"I love this," Maylien said suddenly, reminding me that she was more than just deadweight.

"You what?" With all the nima it was taking to fight the twisting and bobbing, I didn't really have the spare energy or breath for conversation, but I was simply too shocked not to ask.

"I've always wanted to fly," she said. "Bontrang makes it seem like such fun. Look at all the people down below." She pointed toward the Downunders, where the morning crowd had filled the streets. "Don't they look surprised?" Quite a few had noticed us, and they started pointing and calling out to their fellows. "Oh, this is glorious!"

Crazy woman.

We lurched abruptly left at that moment, nearly flipping over. I was still trying to think of some way to respond to Maylien that didn't involve a lot of swearing when a bright whip of magic like a giant chain forged from links of green fire slashed past a few feet to my right.

Triss screamed, and we jolted sharply to the right, dropping a dozen feet as he jerked in his wing on that side. The spell, whatever it was, had grazed him, and magic was one of the few things that could really harm a Shade. Below us, the people in the streets started running and shouting.

I ignored them in favor of feeding Triss even more of my rapidly failing magic. I took a risk by taking my eyes off

our landing zone to glance back over my shoulder. I wanted
to get a mark on the bastard who'd hurt my familiar. I
couldn't do much about the attack right now, but I promised
myself a reckoning later. I'd just spotted a mounted figure
on the slope now far above and behind us, when a second
glowing chain of power lashed down toward us from his
raised hands like some giant magical whip.

The spell missed by a much wider margin than the previous burst—Triss's injury had transformed an already frighteningly erratic descent into something completely unpredictable
and terrifying. The burst of light that accompanied the spell
also gave me one instant's bright and perfect view of the
caster, burning his image into my mind. Colonel Deem,
mounted atop his massive stone dog as if it were a horse.
I had a brief moment to hope he hadn't gotten an equally clear
look at me. Then Maylien screamed, Triss screeched a warning, and I turned back frontward in time to see a thatch roof
coming up to meet us.

The perfect, soft landing place. There was only one little
problem. Deem's spell had landed first. The roof was on fire.

16

─━─◆─━─

We missed the worst of the flames, crashing through the roof in a cascade of smoldering thatch and shattered bamboo poles. There was a sharp jerk up and back on my shoulders as Triss caught at the edges of the rotten bamboo roof supports in an attempt to slow us even further. Then they gave way like the rest, and we fell the last couple of feet with burning thatch raining down all around us. I'm not sure who was more surprised, the occupants of the little leather shop at the sudden fire and the manner of our entrance, or me at our having survived it.

But there was no time to worry about that or do more than marvel briefly at the fortune that had kept us from hitting a more solid roof. It was a good thing for us that the Downunders was one of the few parts of Tien where the odds of hitting a rotten roof were better than even. My feet had barely touched the floor when Maylien slipped from my arms and started for the door. Much as I needed to follow her, I paused a moment longer.

"Triss, are you all right?" I asked.

"Yesss," he said, but I knew from the hiss in his speech

that he was in pain. "Go! I will recover sssoon enough if I resst. Fire and sun, but that hurts." Then he let go of his dragon form and collapsed into my shadow.

I wanted to do more for him, but the smoke was getting thicker by the second, and somewhere nearby the stone dogs were swimming through the earth in pursuit. I did take a moment to open my trick bag and pull out one of the half dozen heavy gold riels I kept there for direst emergency.

"Sorry," I said, tossing it to the old man standing in open-mouthed shock behind the counter. "Now, run."

Then I took off after Maylien. As I crashed through the door and out onto the street, I was glad to see that a bucket brigade had already started to form. I couldn't bear the thought of a second neighborhood burning in my wake. Better to let the Elite kill me than that—curse them! If I'd known they were going to do this, I'd have . . . what?

I honestly didn't know the answer. I'd never succumbed to the particular cynicism endemic among the Blades that painted abusive rule as a thing of uttermost routine. No matter how many times I'd seen corrupt officials abuse their powers, it always shocked me when someone like an officer of the Elite casually harmed the people under his protection.

Even as that thought crossed my mind, another lash of the great magical chain fell from above. It struck across the street, about a half dozen buildings up, and ignited another fire. Two really, one in the just-blasted building and another within my heart. There was no way Colonel Deem could possibly have picked us out from the rest of the milling crowd at this distance. No, he was just blasting away and hoping to eliminate us in the general destruction. As I looked around at the flaming ruin authored by one of Zhan's "authorities," I swore that this would not go unanswered. I half turned back toward the bluff, though what I intended to do I couldn't say.

Then Maylien caught my arm. "Do you have any of the money I paid you? Devin's people stole what coin I had on me."

"Sure," I reached for my pouch, "how much do you need?"

"Five silver riels should do it."

I handed them over, and Maylien darted away. "Wait, what do you need it for?"

"Come on," she called back over her shoulder. "Hurry! There's a man over here who'll lend us his cart horses for a fee, and we need to ride."

I shook myself free of the anger that had taken me, forcing it back down into the depths for later use, and followed Maylien across the street to where she was cutting a couple of horses loose from their traces. She was right, we needed to be gone, and I shouldn't have lost sight of that. Nor let the weight of arranging our escape fall on her. I was the one who was supposed to be rescuing Maylien, wasn't I?

Just who was rescuing whom became even more debatable when Maylien practically had to push me onto the back of one of the horses a few moments later. I'd stopped moving after catching up to her, lost track of everything for a moment, really. And not for the first time. Odd batches of seconds seemed to be slipping away from me and leaving no memory of their passing. It wasn't until Maylien gave me a shove toward the horse and ordered me to mount up that I did so.

It was a damned good thing the two horses had been harness mates, because it meant that mine followed Maylien's without any prompting on my part. Bits of the world kept vanishing into white nothingness around the edges of my vision as we rode, and it took most of my attention just to stay ahorse. The white blots rang old alarm bells in the back of my head, but I couldn't make my mind work well enough to think of why.

Then, without any sense of transition at all, I found myself sitting in a thick bed of ferns beside a fire, with a tin cup in my hand, and that seemed very strange. Especially since the sun had gone away somewhere along the line, replaced by the moon and a slice of starry sky bounded by overhanging branches.

What the hell . . . ?

"I said that you should try to take another drink." It was Maylien's voice, coming from somewhere off on the other side of the fire though I couldn't see her. She sounded concerned.

That didn't make any more sense than the darkness or the bed of ferns, but she seemed pretty sure about drinking. Almost absently, I raised the cup to my lips and took a big mouthful of some incredibly raw alcohol. It burned gloriously as it went down.

"What the hell is this stuff?" I asked, in something halfway between a cough and a croak.

"You'd have to ask the very sketchy-looking fellow I bought it from back at the crossroads for the details, but it probably started out as rice, and it's certainly not legal." Maylien laughed then, a wry, earthy sort of sound. "But I've told you that twice already. What are the chances it's going to stick this time?"

"I don't know. I don't remember asking before. Actually, I don't remember anything much after we got on the horses. Where are we? What happened?"

One of the shadows on the left side of the fire moved, resolving itself into Maylien's face as she pushed back the hood that had covered her until then. Beside her, Bontrang stirred, fixing me with one bright eye and making a small, inquisitive, trilling noise.

"You sounded almost coherent there," she said to me. "And Bontrang's paying attention to you for the first time in hours. Are you really back?" She got up and came to kneel beside me, looking into my eyes for several long beats. "I think you are." She produced a rough clay bottle from somewhere and poured a clear liquid into my cup. "You'd better have some more of that."

"I don't think Triss would approve of . . . Wait, Triss!"

"Shh." Maylien put a finger to my lips. "He's sleeping, and he needs it even more than you do if I am any judge. Now have another drink. It's the nastiest rotgut I've ever tasted, but it'll do you a world of good to get more inside you."

She eyed me sternly, and I sniffed at my cup—hellfire

but it smelled raw—then took another drink. It tasted awful but somehow wonderful at the same time. And again I could feel it burning as it headed down my throat. At least at first. When it hit my stomach, the feeling simply went away.

"That's really strange," I said.

"What?" asked Maylien.

"Normally with liquor this strong I'd expect it to light a fire in my belly, but it's just going away."

Maylien laughed again, still earthy, but lighter this time. "Then it's working. 'Spirits for the drained spirit.' That's what the Rovers used to say, though *you've* probably never heard the phrase, what with the way Namara's priests were down on booze."

She cocked her head to one side. "Someday you'll have to tell me how you ended up pretending to be a drunk. That was inspired, you know. The way you put away your whiskey at the Gryphon is why it took me six months to decide you really were Aral Kingslayer."

My head started to spin, and I took another drink. Surprisingly, that seemed to bring things back into focus again, so I drained off the rest of the cup. Maylien topped me up again before I could argue.

"You need all you can get right now," she said.

"Can we back up to the part where I asked you what happened and where we are? Only this time with you answering?"

Again the laugh. "All right. Where should I start?"

"How about what happened after we got on the horses? The world started to flash white around the edges about then, and I don't really remember much between then and waking up here a couple of minutes ago." I felt a sudden twinge. "You're sure Triss is all right?"

"Yes, and stop saying his name. You'll wake him." Maylien settled back beside the little gryphinx. "Those white flashes are what happens when you overtap your nima. Which is why I've been feeding you the strongest moonshine I could find every chance I could get since we left the city shortly after sunrise."

"'Spirits for the spirit' . . ." I said.

"Exactly. There's nothing like strong drink to carry you over until you can get some sleep if you're an overextended mage. It's useless or even counterproductive under normal circumstances, but when you've pushed yourself beyond your limits, it can save your life. Of course, you didn't know that, what with Namara's followers being so notoriously down on alcohol. The thing that really surprised me was how very much of it you kept putting away without ever coming back to full consciousness.

"Well, that and the fact that you managed to stay on that horse even when you were nine-tenths unconscious. The first was your Shade's fault, of course, though *I* didn't know it till he explained it to me an hour or two ago, but I still don't know how you can hang on to something as tight as you did that horse when no one's at home in your skull."

I took another drink from my cup, hoping to calm the head-spinning effect Maylien's conversational style seemed to induce. "Well, if you spend much time climbing buildings while under fire or exhausted, you tend to develop a serious reflex for hanging on to things. But even so, you've lost me again. Twice. What did Triss tell you that explained my continued problems?"

"Nima, of course. Shades need to eat, the same as anyone. That's what your Shade said, anyway. Now, during the night they can draw strength from the darkness itself, but in daytime, if they overextend themselves, they have nothing to feed on but the nima of their human companions. Your Shade got pretty badly clipped by that fire-chain spell. So, the only way he could keep it together was by tapping your nima. But you were *already* pretty much overtapped before that happened. Without that moonshine I've been feeding you, I think you'd probably both be dead. With it, I was able to get you through till nightfall, when your Shade could rest and soak up the dark."

I took another drink while I let all of that settle in. It was frighteningly bad stuff, and yet I found myself wanting

more, which meant it was probably time to put it down even
if it had saved my life. I set my cup aside.

"All right, I think that answers the 'what happened' part
of my question, but I'd still like to know where we are."

Maylien smiled, her teeth shining bright in the firelight.
"We're a bit less than a half day's slow ride south and west
of Tien by the shortest road. We took a much longer and more
roundabout way, so it took us from dawn to dusk to get here."

"And *here* is?"

"Nowhere really, a little dell on crown lands about a
quarter mile back from the smuggler's track we took to get
here. Between the trees and the hills, the campsite's invisible
to anyone not right on top of it. It's frequented mostly by
poachers. They're going to be a little bit grumpy about my
using up a bunch of their woodpile without replacing it, but
I'll square it with them later."

"You sound like you know the area well, and the
poachers."

"Well enough," said Maylien. "I've spent a good part of
the past four years traveling in this part of the country. The
smuggler's way"—she gestured off behind her—"is one of
the three best routes from the Barony of Marchon to Tien
proper if you don't want to meet up with either the Crown
or Baronial Guards. The Rovers taught me how to survive
in the wilderness while the crown and my dear sister taught
me to avoid the various guards."

Maylien leaned back against a log and stretched her feet
toward the fire. "As for the poachers, and the smugglers,
too. Well . . ." She shrugged. "We all get along well enough.
We live much the same lifestyle, and the same people would
see us all hanged if they could."

"But you were raised by the Rovers." I nodded at Bontrang. "Don't they frown on your shadowside acquaintances?
They hunt bandits and other wilderness criminals as a part
of their holy mission, don't they?"

Maylien laughed. "Bandits, yes. Bandits prey on travelers
and pilgrims, and the Rovers kill them wherever they find

them. But as long as the poachers and smugglers leave the people on the roads alone, the Rovers leave them alone. The order was established to protect travelers, they don't give a damn about protecting taxes and tariffs."

"I didn't realize that."

"They don't advertise the fact. Otherwise, people like the various Barons of Marchon might decide that they didn't want to dedicate house lands to Rover chapter houses."

Something struck me then. "You talk about the Rovers like you're not really one of them, but the nature of your familiar says otherwise. I know that you and your sister spent six years off the edge of the map of official history, but I don't know what happened beyond that or how you came to join the Rovers' order."

"I didn't. Not really, though I desperately wanted to once upon a time. My mother gave Sumey and me to the Rovers at the Marchon chapter house when we were thirteen and fourteen to protect us from our father. They handed us over to one of their traveling bands, which happened to be spending a few weeks at the chapter house, and the band whisked us right out of the kingdom.

"Between fourteen and twenty I spent more nights under the stars than under a roof. I've walked or ridden over most of the kingdoms of the east, from the northern marches of the Sylvani Empire in the south to Kadesh in the north and from the eastern ocean to the western mage wastes. I think those were the happiest years of my life . . . and the worst of Sumey's."

"How so?"

"Sumey hated every minute of the road. She complained constantly. After a couple of months of that, the Rovers parked her in a chapter house in Aven. But I'd fallen in love with the road, so I stayed with my traveling band. I learned to hunt and ride and fight as well as any Zhani warrior-noble. I even fell in love with a Rover, Serak, and I took Bontrang as my familiar when it turned out I had both gifts. I even went so far as to ask to take the Rover's oath."

"And then what happened?" I asked.

"What makes you think something happened?"

"The fact that you're here with me and fighting for a baronial seat instead of off on the road with the Rovers maybe?"

Maylien looked into the fire. "We were in the Kvanas. A lesser khan took a fancy to me, knocked me on the head, and carried me off. It was a really stupid move on his part. I'm a decent mage and a better swordswoman. When I woke up, I killed him and slipped away, but not before the other Rovers of our band came after me. There was a big fight, and Serak was killed along with about half our band."

She got up and walked away from the fire, turning her back to me. "We went to the High Khan for redress, but the khan I'd killed was a nephew of his. He threatened to sell the lot of us into slavery in the Sylvani Empire if we didn't get the hell out of his lands. So we went. We didn't have any choice. I had been supposed to take my Rover's oath a few weeks after that, but I was devastated and angry and terribly bitter. The senior members of our band told me that I needed to wait, that vows should never be said in anger.

"While I was waiting, I got to thinking about what makes a good ruler and what makes a bad one, and the fact that I had fallen heir to Marchon when my uncle died without issue. I hadn't been back to the barony proper in years, but the chapter house there made sure that the news made it to me. And then I started thinking about how I would feel if someone else took the seat when my mother died and did something horrible like what had happened to me and Serak. It would be my responsibility, you see. So I left the Rovers, and collected my sister, and we came back to Tien so that I could take up my seat . . ."

"And then it all went to hell," I said. Having read some of it, I could make guesses as to how, but I wanted to hear it from Maylien.

Maylien nodded. "And then it all went to hell. Thauvik advanced my sister's claim over mine. Which was all right. It meant that I could go back to the Rovers once things settled down. Except they didn't settle down. My mother died within a few months, almost certainly by poison. At first I believed Sumey when she said that Mother had committed suicide. But then, bit by bit, I came to believe that she'd been murdered and that it had to be my sister who'd done it. I'd already started to hate Sumey more than a little by then."

"Why?" If I was going to put Maylien in her sister's place—and my debts bound me to do just that—I wanted to know as much as I could about both of them.

"As soon as Sumey took the seat, she started to do . . . things to our people, treat them like animals and worse than animals. I don't know if she was always that way, and I'd just never seen it before, or if something happened to her during her years in Aven, and that changed her, or what. Whatever the reason, my nightmares about someone else doing horrible things from the baronial seat that I ought to have inherited started to come true. And it was made a thousand times worse by the fact that the person doing horrible things was my sister. How could someone so close to me turn into something so awful?"

I looked away from Maylien, into the fire. I didn't have an answer for her question. If I had, Devin's betrayals of the goddess and her ideals might have hurt less. Or then again, they might not. It would all depend on the nature of that answer.

If Devin and Sumey were simply bad people waiting for the right moment to go rotten, then we could bask in the armor of righteousness. But if they were just people like Maylien and I were just people, and the only reason that it was the two of us here and the two of them there was a matter of circumstance . . .

One of the things I'd learned over the years since the temple fell was that nothing was ever simple. Maylien hadn't moved since she stopped talking. She just kept staring out into the darkness. I was still pretty weak, so I rolled onto my hands and knees before I tried to get up.

When that didn't kill me, I slowly and carefully pushed myself to my feet. It wouldn't do to fall into the fire and make her rescue me again. I walked over to stand behind Maylien, making plenty of noise so she'd know I was there. She didn't turn around, so I put a hand on her shoulder. I could feel her crying, though the tears made no sound.

"Maylien, what your sister has done belongs on her conscience, not yours."

She shrugged my hand off. "I *am* Marchon, or should be. Sumey has tortured and murdered people . . . my people, and done it under the banner of the Marchon. What Marchon does is my responsibility. Those deaths are on my head."

"Did you make your sister Baroness Marchon?"

"No, of course not! That was Thauvik's doing. And my sister's . . . when she murdered my mother to take the seat."

"And you've been trying to fix it ever since?"

"Yes, but that's not enough." Maylien turned to face me. "Don't you see? It can never be enough. My sister is a monster. She's already done things at least as bad as what happened to me and Serak. I should have seen it coming, done something about it earlier, prevented it somehow."

"You want to make it never have happened, right?" I asked, and my voice sounded to me like it was bubbling up through bitter waters—an aftereffect of my nima loss, maybe.

"Yes!"

I shook my head. "That's not how it works. You can't change the past . . . No matter how much you might want to, no matter how awful it was. Not even gods can change the past. You can't let the weight of might-have-been fall on your shoulders, or it will crush you."

"You're not just talking about me and Sumey anymore, are you?"

I looked through Maylien, into the past, and saw deep water with the sun shining dimly down from above. Beneath me a broken stone goddess lay sprawled on the floor of the lake, weeds starting to grow in her hair. Though my lungs burned already, I swam deeper so that I could place my swords in one cracked stone hand.

"No," I said, "I'm not. But that doesn't make what I'm

saying any less true for you and Sumey. When the temple fell, I took the weight of a dead goddess onto my shoulders, and the guilt destroyed me."

"I don't understand." Maylien canted her head to the side. "You're here now, talking to me. How can you say the guilt destroyed you?"

"Because I'm not the man I was then, not the man you were looking for to help you with your sister, really. Aral Kingslayer, the Blade of Namara, didn't get the opportunity to die in defense of his goddess, and the guilt of that drove him so deep into the bottle that he never came back out again. I might wear the same face, and I might have shared the same bottle, but I'm not really him."

I laughed, and it sounded harsh in my ears but also strangely hopeful. "Maybe that's why I've actually managed to poke my head out into the light again, because I'm finally beginning to understand that."

Maylien stepped in close and kissed me gently on the lips.

"What was that for?" I asked after a long moment.

"For understanding."

She kissed me again, longer this time.

"And that?"

"For caring." She smiled then, in the dark. "And this next is simply because I want to."

I kissed her back this time and didn't have to bend down to do it. For a little while we simply held each other there in the night. It was the first time in more than five years that I'd held a woman like that, and it felt good. Maylien felt good. She was strong and athletic, like Jax or Siri or one of the other female Blades I'd shared a bed with, but softer somehow. She smelled of the road and hard riding, but also of woman, and she brought back memories long lost. Of camaraderie and shared purpose and nights spent together out of simple companionship. I found that I wanted her badly.

But it had been a very long day on top of a very long night, and I soon felt the world slowly tilting to my left.

When I lurched rightward to compensate, Maylien slipped from my arms and half dragged–half led me back to my bed of ferns.

"Finish your drink," she said, handing me the cup, and I did.

Then she pushed me gently back into the ferns and tucked a rough blanket over me. "Now get some sleep."

I reached up and ran a hand along her side from ribs to hip. "And in the morning . . ."

"We'll see." She smiled at me, then got up to deal with the fire.

17

I jarred awake once in the night when I sensed someone leaning over me. Reflexes put a dagger in my left hand with a flick of the wrist, but vaulting to my feet proved beyond me. I was far too weak and dazed to do much more than sit up.

"It's just me, put that away and go back to sleep." Maylien put her hand gently on my chest and pushed me flat. Then she dropped a second blanket over me, and tucked herself in against my side. "It's going to be a cold night, and we'll be warmer if we share."

I was out before I had time to respond.

I woke when the dawnlight reached over the treetops and touched my eyelids, though I didn't look around right away. Sometime in the night, I'd turned and curled myself around Maylien, and I pressed my face gently against the back of her head, trying to put the day off a little bit longer. I wanted to prolong the pleasure of holding a woman while she slept. I hadn't done that in years, not since Jax and I had last traveled together.

As I woke further, I did a quick assessment of my general state of being. Where our bodies touched, I felt warm and wonderful. Every other part of me was sore and stiff and cold, especially the arm that pillowed Maylien's head. My right hand was three-quarters asleep as well as half-frozen where it stuck out from under the blankets in front of her face. All too soon, the aches and pains started to outweigh my resolve to hold still, and I was forced to shift around.

"Mmm." Maylien grumbled sleepily. "Stop moving around." But then she sighed and stretched. "Too late. I'm awake." She turned her head to look at me over her shoulder and smiled. "Good morning."

"Good morning yourself," I said, speaking into her shoulder. I wanted to kiss her, but after all the raw rice alcohol I'd drunk the night before, I figured my mouth probably tasted like one of the more decayed varieties of restless dead. "Any thoughts on where we might find breakfast?"

"I can offer you yesterday's cold bacon and last week's stale black bread," said a disgustingly chipper male voice from somewhere on the far side of last night's campfire.

I jerked in surprise and looked up, but that was all I did. The voice didn't sound like it belonged to someone with dire intent. More importantly, by getting so close without waking us, its owner had proven that if he'd wanted to kill us, we would have already died.

The stranger was sitting cross-legged on a thick pad on the ground about fifteen feet away with the sunrise behind him. I couldn't make out a lot of detail against the sun, but I could tell that he had on a large, round, peasant hat and dark clothes, and no visibly exposed weapons. Instead, his hands were in his lap, where he was quietly scratching Bontrang's head.

The little gryphinx's presence reminded me to worry about Triss—who would normally have warned me about any stranger's approach. Reaching out through our bond, I could feel Triss's presence but only dimly. He was still very deeply asleep, and I decided to leave him that way for now.

"It's not much of a breakfast, I know," said the stranger, "but it's all I've got to hand."

Maylien had stiffened in my arms at the newcomer's first words and slid half out of the blanket. Now she relaxed and shivered before sliding back down to snuggle against me.

"That sounds pretty dreadful actually. Why don't you go find something better and wake us when you get back." When our unexpected guest showed no sign of moving, she sighed. "Yeah, I didn't think that was going to happen." Then she glanced over her shoulder at me. "But where are my manners? This is Heyin, one of my oldest friends, and—as you will no doubt soon agree—the world's worst cook."

"Don't be like that," said Heyin. "I'm offering you the same food I was planning on having for *my* breakfast."

"Doesn't matter," said Maylien. "Your digestive system is made of old leather and leftover bits of yak intestine. Whether or not you can eat something has no bearing on its relationship to actual food." Maylien shrugged then. "On the other hand, I doubt we'll get a better offer. So, what do you think, Aral? Should we take him up on his revolting breakfast?"

"Aral." Heyin whistled low and soft before I could answer. "Then you *have* found your famous Blade."

"Actually, this time, he found me." Maylien squeezed my arm under the blanket. "He saved my life yesterday. Aral, Heyin. Heyin, Aral."

Heyin clambered to his feet—startling Bontrang, who squawked loudly and flapped over to complain at Maylien. Then Heyin gave me a deep bow.

"For saving my baroness, I owe you whatever is in my power to give. Sadly, for the moment, that mostly consists of a rather inadequate breakfast. However, if the baroness will consent to get herself out of bed and on the road, I will be happy to promise a better meal later, when we get back to Marchon's house-in-exile."

"All right," Maylien mock-grumbled, "all right. I'm getting up. See, this is me getting up."

Maylien rolled out from under the blankets. When I started to follow, she put a hand on my chest and gently pushed me back down again. "You stay. You're nowhere near recovered, no matter what you think."

I wanted to argue, but the fact that she'd hardly had to exert herself to keep me from rising lent weight to her case, so I let myself be convinced. She started poking at the coals, then added wood from the pile.

"Might as well toast the bread and make sandwiches." She looked up at Heyin. "I don't suppose you thought to bring along a teapot?"

"No, though I've got a tin pan and a couple of moderately fresh cakes of Kadesh Jade I can shave into the pot."

"Ooh, that changes things. For good tea I can forgive the food." She pointed over the hill. "There's a little stream just over that way. Why don't you go fill your pan while I get the fire built back up."

"As my baroness knows, I live only to serve."

Heyin nodded at me and sketched a little bow to Maylien, then started off in the indicated direction. As he moved out of the direct sunlight, I saw that he was much older than I'd have guessed from his voice, with streaks of white in his long ponytail and mustache and several old scars visible on his hands and arms.

I waited a few more minutes, until Maylien had the fire built up, then slowly pushed myself into a sitting position. It was a lot more work than it should have been. I felt like a heap of ground-up mystery meat ready for the sausage maker. Admittedly, I felt like a significantly better cut of mystery meat than I had last night, but that wasn't saying much. I gently poked at the fresh bruise on my ribs, sliding my fingers though the giant hole in my shirt where the axe had nearly opened me up.

"I think I'm going to need some new clothes."

"You and me both." Maylien tugged ruefully at the torn-out left knee of her divided skirts. "We'll have to fix that when we get to Exile House. These have moved from the category of convenient disguise to polishing cloths, and yours are worse."

She was right. Between the dust, the dirt, and the travel stains, it was hard to even tell what color my clothes had once been. Add in the rips and tears and the stink, and the only practical use I could imagine for anything I was wearing was lining the nest of a not-very-picky rat.

I decided it was time to wake Triss then and gently poked my shadow. "Triss, are you all right?"

My shadow stirred sluggishly and slowly reshaped itself into a small dragon. "Whazzat?"

"I asked if you were all right."

"Oh, sure. I've never felt better in my life." He reached back and licked his right wing at the shoulder joint, then growled before going off into an extended string of Shade-talk. It sounded like someone shaking a sackful of angry snakes, and I was pretty sure a translation would have come out all kinds of obscene.

Finally, he shifted back to Zhani, "Still, I think I'll live." Then his voice dropped lower, filling with concern. "How are you?"

"Likewise, thanks to Maylien." I decided to omit any reference to the rummer's overproofed rice-whiskey—or whatever you wanted to call it—on the grounds that if Triss didn't remember it, he'd be happier not knowing. "She got us out of Tien and clear of the Elite without much help from me. And now . . ." I looked at Maylien as I realized I didn't know what happened next. "Well, better ask her that, I guess."

Maylien frowned. "Back to Exile House to clean up and resupply, though I suspect we won't be able to stay long. I sent Bontrang there yesterday afternoon with a message for Heyin, to let him know where we were then and that we were coming. I'd expected him to wait there, not come out and meet us on the road. The fact that he's here suggests all is not well in Marchon."

"Who is Heyin?" I asked.

"A foolish old man who refused to die when he was supposed to," Heyin replied as he came back over the hill.

Beside me, Triss started to shift his shape, but I patted him and shook my head. "He knows what we are, Triss. There's no need to hide."

Triss nodded at that, then curled up on my shady side,

tucking his nose under his tail and going straight back to sleep. That worried me rather a lot, but there was nothing I could do about it. I rested my hand lightly between his wings, trying to reassure myself with the contact of fingers against invisible scales that felt strangely insubstantial.

Maylien gave Heyin a stern look. "That's not true. Heyin was the captain of my mother's guard before my sister had him stripped of his position and thrown into the street for failing to prevent the old baroness's death."

"Which may be the only thing in the whole world that your sister and I ever agreed on." Heyin set the pan down on a rock Maylien had laid among the coals for that purpose. "Though she really ought to have had me flogged and beheaded as well." Heyin's voice was casual, but his eyes seethed with rage and shame. "I would not have resisted."

"She couldn't very well do that," said Maylien. "Not when your failure was to stop a *suicide*."

"Not without admitting it was murder, no." Heyin opened a small paper package, pulling out a slab of smoked bacon, which he proceeded to slice up. "And if she'd done that, then someone might have thought to investigate just who it was that had murdered the old baroness. Which is why I would not have resisted. I did fail to protect your mother in life; if my death could bring your sister to justice for that murder, I would quite happily commit formal suicide in the market square of Marchon tomorrow."

"That wouldn't do anything but provide my sister with a great deal of satisfaction." Maylien admonished him.

"Which argument is how you talked me out of it the first time." Heyin finished with the bacon and started cutting a loaf of black bread into thick slices, handing them off to Maylien to arrange on another rock for rough toasting. "What I still don't understand is how you convinced me to become the captain of your guard-in-exile. Or why you chose to do so, when you would have been fully justified in spitting on me and sending me into the wilderness to die." He leaned his head to one side as he started in on making the tea. "You still could, you know. You have but to say the word."

Maylien rolled her eyes theatrically. "How many times do I have to tell you that I need you, old man? Without you I could never have set up Exile House or even begun to oppose my sister properly. I was a stranger to my people and far more Rover than baronial heir; you were one of them and respected. Without you to vouch for me, I would have had to choose between fleeing Zhan and remaining to die by my sister's hand. Now, finally, because you paved the way for me among my people, we may have a chance to see my sister pay for her crimes." She turned then, and they both looked at me.

I shrugged. "I'll have to get some fresh clothes and rest up for a few days, but if you want me to kill your sister for you, I can certainly manage that. Even with Devin protecting her, it shouldn't be impossible. She just doesn't have the resources to keep a"—but I couldn't bring myself to say "Blade"—"to keep me and Triss out." I ran a finger along the spinal ridge of my dragon's shadow, but he was too deeply asleep to respond—very worrying.

"I wish that were all I had to ask of you," said Maylien. "But it wouldn't do the trick. If I am to take the baronial seat and not have Thauvik simply assign it to some unknown cousin, I have to kill Sumey myself in a proper duel and seize the coronet. I need you to get me to Sumey in a setting where she will have no choice but to accept my challenge."

"You need me to do what?" I blinked. "I think I missed a step there. You're a mage." I nodded at Bontrang, who had settled down where he could keep a sharp eye on the bacon. "You don't even have standing to issue a challenge. Do you? I thought Zhani law forbade the mageborn from dueling for peerages."

"Not quite. The crown despises the practice because it is believed that a mage has an unfair advantage in combat. But the Right of Challenge is much older than Crown Law. It's a survivor of the Code Martial of the ancient kingdom. If I can get to Sumey in front of proper witnesses and forswear the use of magic for the duration of our duel, she cannot deny my challenge—we are too close in blood."

Bontrang made a little growling noise though whether

he was responding more to Maylien's words or to her angry tone was impossible to tell.

Maylien continued, "The trick will be getting there. Crown Law can't deny Right of Challenge, even from a mage such as myself. What it can do is make it *very* hard for any mage to live to issue such a challenge."

I was still flailing. "Could you elaborate on that? Obscure dueling codes weren't really a major topic of study at the temple. Namara issued sentences of death, not challenges."

Maylien nodded. "If I weren't a mage and I wanted to challenge my sister, all I would have to do is walk up to the entrance of wherever she was and demand that I be taken to her to issue my challenge. Whoever met me at the door would then have to take me to her at once. She wouldn't be allowed to use guards or other direct measures to prevent me from entering her presence, and we would duel on the spot. But Crown Law has put all sorts of barriers up around the conditions of challenge in the case of the mageborn."

"Such as?"

"To start with, I have to send a formal announcement of my intention to challenge. Both to my sister and to the crown. In it, I have to name a day and a place, and that place must be on Marchon lands. The crown then sends a pair of witnesses to the event, and if I don't show up, the challenge is considered forfeit. At which point, they declare me an outlaw and under sentence of death throughout Zhan." Bontrang growled again.

"I think I'm starting to see how this works now," I said. "I take it all those rules about not using guards or other direct measures to stop you from reaching your sister go out the window, too."

"Exactly. She may use any means that were available to her at the time of the announcement of intent to challenge, though she may not increase the size of her guard or beg help of the crown."

"Do you have to tie both your arms behind your back, too?" I asked.

"No. The Code Martial describes the conditions of the

duel itself and those they have not been able to alter though
I have little doubt they would like to do just as you suggest.
That or simply have anyone with both the mage gifts and
noble blood killed outright."

"As much as I hate to interrupt," said Heyin, "the toast
will all too soon go from done to burnt if I don't, and the
tea is almost ready as well."

Heyin handed out rough sandwiches then. As soon as I
took a bite I realized just how hungry I was after two nights
and a day of putting nothing in my stomach but alcohol. I
took the tea when it was ready, too, since there was no graceful way to refuse, and drank a token sip before quietly setting
it aside. As always, it reminded me too much of efik and
what I had lost. Heyin finished eating quickly, then immediately started to clean up the campsite and pack away our
small stock of gear.

"So, how bad is it?" Maylien asked Heyin as he reached
for our blankets.

He shrugged. "Honestly, I don't know."

"How bad is what?" I asked.

"Whatever it is that's making my captain very politely
but very firmly push us to get moving."

"I'm not pushing. I'm easing the way." Maylien gave him
a hard look, and Heyin held up a hand before she could say
anything. "No, really. What I know doesn't justify pushing.
Reports of the place were both vague and unreliable, and
we haven't been able to get inside. But something about it
nags at me."

"The place?" prompted Maylien.

"A little keep not far from the Marchon seat," said Heyin.
"There's been talk of your sister going there in secret, but
no one knows why, and we haven't been able to get inside.
And we won't without magic or a major assault."

"Which needs either me or my orders."

"More or less," said Heyin. "But really, it would be better
to show you. Tomorrow. After both of you have rested and
eaten and bathed." Heyin sniffed. "Especially that last."

"Heyin!" Maylien glared at him, but he was impervious.

"It's more than a day's ride from here, and Exile House is almost on the way. We won't lose much time by stopping, and I think it would be better if you arrived looking more like a baroness and less like a rag-seller. Your people expect you to look the part."

Maylien tossed the last bits of bacon from her sandwich to Bontrang, then started helping Heyin with the packing. I got up to help, but Triss continued sleeping and wouldn't be moved. As soon as I got more than a few feet away from Triss, though, I became aware of just how much of my nima was steadily draining away down the link between us—much as pulling a bandage off a seeping wound will make you aware of all the blood you're losing. The feeling made me go all dizzy and staggery. That's when Maylien ordered me to sit down again and poured me out the last of the rummer's moonshine. That took the edge off my growing worry and made me feel a false sort of cheer, but only for a little while.

When it was time to go, I managed to wake Triss long enough to get him in the saddle with me, where he hid himself in my shadow, but then he went right back to sleep. Within an hour, I'd started seeing white blots again and lost track of everything but staying on the horse. Somewhere close to lunchtime, we stopped at the house of a prosperous farmer who hailed Maylien as his baroness. He cheerfully supplied us with a meal and a large jar of something almost painfully alcoholic that he called rice-white. It was basically a more polished cousin of the rummer's stuff, and I spent the rest of the day teetering back and forth between keeling over from overtapped exhaustion and keeling over from the booze.

I got a bit of my strength back at sunset, shortly before we arrived at Exile House. So I was alert enough to register a sort of blurry impression of lots of ruined stone walls and collapsed structures wrapped around a tight core of carefully renovated and camouflaged buildings. There were a few dozen men and women around, most in rough martial attire with bands bearing an inverted emblem of House Marchon on their sword arms—upside down, the jade fox sitting in its gold field looked subtly wrong. Maylien and Heyin had put together a substantial counterforce. Unfortunately, getting down off my horse and into the bathhouse soaked up most of my reserves, so I didn't find out any more then.

I dozed off twice in the soaking tub and had to be prodded awake by Chul, the young soldier Heyin had assigned to make sure I didn't drown. He also found me a robe, and after I'd dragged myself to the privy and back, he led me to a tiny stone-walled room where a thick feather bed lay atop a low platform and some quite beautiful and obviously hastily-thrown-down rugs. It smelled strongly of last summer's apples.

"I'm very sorry about the state of your . . . bedroom," he said, sounding both deeply embarrassed and confused. "The baroness has told us to treat you as the most honored of guests, and we would normally have given you one of the tower rooms, but she also asked that we put you in a place where the sun doesn't shine. She specified no windows and as many feet of wood and stone between you and the sky as we could manage. That made things . . . difficult."

"It's perfect," I said. "Mayl—your baroness is a very wise young woman." I lowered myself gladly onto the bed. It felt wonderful.

"We had to take the latch off the door because it wasn't really designed to be opened from this side. So just give it a shove when you want to get out. There's no privy down here, but I can bring you a piss-pot if you'd like."

I tried to answer, but all I managed was a mumble before sleep reached up and pulled me under.

Something cool and wet touched my forehead, and I blinked my eyes open. A shadow crossed through the dim lanternlight that came in through the door of my little sleeping chamber. My eyes flicked upward. Triss hung on the wall above and to my left, his paw extended toward my face, where a wet cloth lay just above my eyes.

"How do you feel?" he asked quietly.

I stretched. Tentatively at first, then with more enthusiasm. I was stiff and a little weak but not really sore anywhere except my throat, which, for reasons unknown, felt awfully hashed. I was also *seriously* hungry.

"I feel pretty good, Triss. Apparently a solid night's sleep in a nice bed was just what I needed."

A wry chuckle drew my attention to the foot of the bed. Maylien stood just inside the doorway, with Bontrang perched on a leather pad on her shoulder.

"What's so funny?" I asked.

"Try a week's sleep interspersed with bits of delirium," said Maylien.

I looked at Triss. "Really?"

He shrugged his wings. "That's what they tell me, but I couldn't really say. I've only been up and around since sunset yesterday myself."

"What happened?"

Triss contracted briefly in embarrassment. "Apparently, I did. The magelightning hurt me much worse than I let on—"

"Triss . . ."

He looked off to the side. "At first I didn't want to worry you because you were in rough shape, too. You needed to stay focused on getting us clear of the Elite. After, I knew you'd be mad that I hadn't told you, and I was so busy just holding myself together that I could barely string two words together. It just seemed easier not to have to argue about it." He shrank again. "I'm feeling much better now . . ."

"You should have told me, you muttonhead." I reached up and ran a fingertip along the underside of his jaw, reveling in his scaly solidity.

"I know. I'm sorry. When we couldn't get you to wake up after I did yesterday night, I was really worried."

I glanced a question at Maylien.

She shrugged, but only with the shoulder opposite Bontrang. "I don't know. You'd need to talk to a healer who specializes in mage care to figure out what happened there. If I had to guess, I'd say that for most of the week, Triss was draining your magical reserves away faster than you could replenish them, and it took you some time to recover after he stopped. Call it soul-exhaustion maybe, since nima rises from the well of the soul."

"That sounds ugly," I said.

Maylien nodded. "We weren't entirely sure either of you was going to make it. If the healers hadn't been able to get you to drink some clear soup and rice-white in your brief rounds of waking delirium, I don't think you would have."

"That'd explain the throat then. That rice-white stuff tastes like it runs three parts paint thinner to one part water."

Triss gave me the hairy eyeball but didn't say anything. I pushed myself up and back to lean against the wall in a half-sitting position—the longer I was awake the better I felt . . . and the hungrier. Like a monster that had been wakened by hearing its name, my stomach let out a quite audible growl.

"So, if it suddenly occurred to me that I was ravenous, what would be the chances of my getting something to eat?"

"Well, if you're up to moving, I can take you to the kitchens and see what's available. Otherwise, I'll send someone to get you something."

"Let's go then!" I flicked the blankets off, then hurriedly recaptured them when I realized I was naked.

Maylien blushed prettily and looked away. "I forgot about that. Let me arrange some clothes for you." She backed into the hall.

"You weren't so shy on the road," I teased.

"Uh, about that . . . just a moment." She turned and said over her shoulder into the hall, "Chul, could you find a pair of pants and a shirt for our guest?"

"Of course, Baroness." From the tone of his voice, Chul didn't much like the idea of leaving his baroness alone with me, but he didn't argue either.

Once the sounds of Chul's moving away had grown faint enough to indicate some real distance, Maylien looked back at me, her expression carefully blank. "I have to apologize for my conduct on the road, Aral. As Heyin has been at pains to remind me, the duties and conduct demanded of a baroness are not at all the same as those of the Rover's apprentice I used to be. When we were alone together on the way here, I treated you as I might have treated a fellow Rover in my traveling days. I said and did things that were not in keeping with my present obligations. I'm very sorry if I gave you an impression I shouldn't have."

I felt like all the air had abruptly left the room, or like I'd caught a solid kick just under the ribs. In either case, I found it very hard to draw the breath I needed to reply as I should. It wasn't about sex, though it could have been nice if things had gone that way. It was about the sudden severing of a connection that had only begun to form, the first such connection I'd tried to make in years.

"I'm sorry, too," I said quietly. "I should have remembered why you sought me out and treated you like the baroness I intend to help you become and . . ." I trailed off lamely, unable to say "not like Jax or one of the other Blade women"— that wouldn't be appropriate either. Finally, after the silence had gone on too long, I forced out, "I should have treated you like a baroness and not an old friend."

Bontrang hissed sharply, and the look on Maylien's face shifted from blank to tightly closed. I felt even worse. But before I could do anything to repair the situation, Chul returned, and Maylien stepped aside to let him into the room.

"Thank you, Chul. Could you make sure that . . . my guest is dressed properly, then bring him up to the kitchens for food? Aral, I'll see you later. I've got things to attend to."

And then she left me.

18

"I guess the real question is whether you want to try to shut the place down cold now or just have someone nip in and take a quick look around," I said.

With sunset a half hour off, Maylien, Heyin, and I sat high up in a massive old oak tree on a heavily forested slope. Across the deep narrow valley below us, a small stone-walled keep stood on the edge of a fast-moving little river. Bontrang had chosen a perch above us, up where the branches wouldn't support a human's weight, while Triss opted to stay hidden within my shadow as he did most of the time I was in company.

The keep sat well down under the shoulder of the opposite ridge, centering the open scar of the cut where they'd quarried the limestone for the outer walls. The setting of the tiny stone-and-timber fort felt more than a little off to me, as though the builders had been more interested in keeping the place out of sight than making it truly defensible.

Oh, it had most of the usual defensive accoutrements, high outer walls of smooth-cut stone, a narrow moat fed by the stream that ran through the valley, corner towers with light catapults . . . But big ancient trees stood all around it within easy bowshot of the walls, and a ballista or other siege engine on the ridge would be able to hammer the central tower almost unimpeded. An attacker using burning pitch could set the place alight in minutes.

It might be strong enough to repel a casual assault by unskilled rabble, but it would never hold against a determined assault from even a moderately well-armed force. On the other hand, its tiny size made it a damned hard problem in terms of infiltration. That was why Maylien had asked me to have a look at it now that I was up and around again. She didn't want to pay the blood tithe of a frontal assault for an unknown return, especially since Sumey might be able to use such an attack against her at court. And Heyin had flat refused to let his baroness go in there herself when they "had a damned sneaking specialist sleeping off a bender in the basement!"

I'm pretty sure I wasn't supposed to have heard that particular debate, but then, I *am* a sneaking specialist.

"I think we should start with a quick look around, Aral. If you'd be willing to oblige me." Maylien's tone sounded just as stiff and formal as it had every time we'd talked since I shoved my foot down my throat two nights before. "We might need to make a major assault at some later point, but I'd like to know what my sister is using the keep for first. She's got a habit of tucking her dirty work away where it's hard to find, like that dungeon she had you locked up in back in Zhan."

I nodded. As I'd found out yesterday, Maylien had tracked me down by the simple expedient of having a spy in her sister's house who'd gotten her a list of Sumey's city properties. The Old Mews dungeon had been in the basement of the fourth building on the list. Knowing that told us that it had probably been Sumey who started the fire as well rather than Devin. I was frankly relieved by the thought—it felt better to believe that my onetime friend hadn't sunk so low.

"Whatever she's doing here, she's kept it awfully quiet," said Heyin. "And I don't like the feel of the place. We're only about an hour's hard ride from the Marchon seat at

Shaisin, but the countryside's as empty as if we had a nest
of petty dragons living in the forest, and that's just not right.
The ground's lousy for farming and technically baronial
land, but the timber's damn good. There ought to be illicit
loggers and charcoal-men about, or poachers at the very
least. It's not natural."

"Has Sumey declared the area off-limits in any formal
way?" I asked.

"No," replied Heyin. "There aren't even the usual dire
warnings posted at the bounds. Everyone knows it's baronial
land and legally off-limits, of course. But most times and
places that only makes sure the poachers stay extra quiet. It
doesn't scare them away."

Maylien spoke. "When Heyin and I came out here last
week, I asked a couple of the smallholders around the edges
of the land what they knew about it. These are people who
aren't afraid to defy my sister's rule. If they were, they
wouldn't be talking to me or I to them. But not one of them
is willing to trespass here, nor talk much about why that is.
I got a few bleats about the haunted castle and a few more
about the night-walking dead, but that was it."

"Seems like awfully fresh construction for a haunted
castle," I said.

Heyin nodded. "I checked into the rumors of night-
walkers as well—I'd heard from those same folk before ever
I brought Maylien to see them. But there don't seem to be
any more disappearances or unexplained corpses turning
up around the edges of the wood than you'd normally expect
to see in this kind of country."

"The forest proper is completely empty of people?" I
asked.

"It is," said Heyin. "But you can't confine ghouls and
ghasts to one area like that. Especially not when there's
potential prey to be had by crossing the boundaries."

Triss flickered into dragon shape, showing himself. "You
and I can't, maybe. But a powerful enough necromancer
could."

"Is that what *you* think is in the keep, Triss?" I asked.

"No." Triss's tongue flicked out. "The deeper shadows in the forest on the way here didn't taste as I would expect them to if there were someone like that around, not enough rough magic. But it can be done, and the shadows don't taste quite right either . . ." He shook his head in frustration. "There's something almost familiar there though I haven't been able to place it."

"Well, the sun's nearly down," I said. "So, why don't I just slide over there, have a look around, and save us further speculation?"

"I agree that's our best course of action," said Maylien. "Shall we go?"

"I don't think that 'we' should go anywhere," I said.

Heyin spoke at the same time, saying, "Baroness, we discussed this already. Surely you're not planning on going with him?"

"Of course I'm going," replied Maylien. "The whole reason for bringing Aral into our plans was so that he could get me through my sister's defenses come the day of the challenge. If that's going to happen, we need to practice working together against the nastiest security my sister can put together. If either one of you can think of a better way to do that than to have me go with Aral here and now, you're welcome to tell me about it."

"I'm convinced," I said, though I didn't much like the impersonal sound of "bringing Aral into our plans." It made me feel like a piece on a game board instead of a human being. "Let's go."

Heyin said something unintelligible under his breath, but he didn't elaborate or make any other argument, just sighed loudly when Maylien and I started down the tree.

I pointed across the moat to the guard slowly walking back and forth atop the nearest of the keep's little towers. All of the towers had guards, but this one was farthest from the front gate and the weakest link in the defense.

"That's our first hurdle, right there. We can't get over the outer wall without doing something about him. You can't anyway. I could probably get past him on my own, but if I'm going to carve a hole big enough for you to follow me through, he's got to either die or take a convenient nap. This is your domain and your mission, so it's your choice as to which."

Maylien grimaced. "Which would you recommend under the circumstances?"

"There are pluses and minuses to both choices. Dead is easier, and it's permanent. There's no chance of the guard waking up and sounding the alarm. It's also not something we'll be able to conceal later. Leave a corpse, and they *know* someone ghosted a guard. Get rid of the body, and they'll still be pretty sure that someone killed the guy. Perhaps most importantly, if I do ghost him there's no bringing him back. Right now all that we know he's guilty of is working for your sister. He could be every bit as bad as those torturers who had me strung up in Tien, but he could just be a local kid who needs to make a living."

"What about putting him to sleep?"

"That's significantly harder to manage without using magic, which would light us up if your sister's got another petty mage like Lok around. I have to get in close and dose him with opium and efik or cut off his air for a bit. Either way is imprecise. He could die, or he could wake up too early, or not all there. Best way to deal with too early's to tie him up, but that's as good a calling card as ghosting him would be if he's found or wakes up. There's no way to pretend we weren't here if he's discovered gagged and bound. Even if he's not, there'll be rope burns and other signs. Knocking him out and tying him up's still my first choice, though. I'd rather not ghost anyone who might not deserve it."

Maylien frowned. "My sister's kept this place even quieter than she did that nasty little dungeon in Tien. Considering the kinds of things that was set up for, and the unholy . . . pursuits my sister has taken a liking to in the last few years, I really doubt that anyone here is an innocent lamb. But you're right that we can't know that without investigating first."

She closed her eyes for a moment, then opened them and

straightened her spine. "I'm the rightful Baroness of Marchon. That man over there is one of my people, even if he does work for my sister. He deserves the benefit of the doubt. If you can put him to sleep without too great a risk to yourself, do it. If you can't . . . if there's any real chance that he'll give us away or harm you, kill him."

"Wait here. I'll throw a rope down when I've taken care of him." I slipped down to the edge of the moat and eyed the water.

It looked cold and smelled wrong somehow, swampy and rank where it appeared clean and clear. I didn't really want to swim, but the heights of the walls relative to the surrounding trees made for an impossible sail-jump. Also, if I swam, I'd be much harder to see coming. So I edged my way out onto a root in order to ease myself into the moat quietly. Dim moonlight cast my shadow on the surface of the water, and Triss let out a hiss, then quickly changed shape and spread dragon wings wide between me and the water.

"Back up," he whispered urgently.

"Why?" I asked, but I was already moving.

"Faster."

Up on the tower the guard turned and looked our way, raising his lantern as he did so. I flattened myself in the leaf litter under the trees, and Triss flowed over me, covering me in shadow. Together, we waited for the guard to turn away.

"What's wrong?" I asked once Triss finally signaled that the guard had moved back to his normal pattern.

"Something in the water," said Triss. "I don't know what, but when I touched the surface, I could feel things moving around down in the deeps. It tasted like the shadows under the trees. I don't think swimming would be wise."

"And I don't think we can make the tower's deck with a sail-jump," I replied. "It's simply too far above the nearer trees."

"So we don't jump for the top. There's a little ridge in the bedrock just below the base of the wall, a few inches above the water. If you aim for that, I don't think we'll have any trouble."

"Except for the part where I smash face-first into the wall and fall into the water if we come in too fast. Oh, and the bit where you have to shift from wings to claws in the instant between hitting the wall and falling into the water."

"We've done harder jumps in the past," said Triss.

"We were a lot younger then, and in better training, and you hadn't been recently injured."

"Are you saying you're too old and out of shape to manage your end of things? Because I'll understand if you are. I know I can do my part, but I'm sure we can find some other way for an old man like you to get in if we need to."

"Listen here you lizard-brained excuse for a shadow-puppet . . ." I trailed off as I realized I was grinning.

For the first time in I couldn't remember how long, Triss had simply teased me for teasing's sake. For years now every one of his pokes or prods had a hidden nag underneath—worries about my drinking, or my choices in the jobs I took to keep us off the streets, or simply how dangerous it was for us to be living in Tien with a price on our heads.

Triss grinned back at me. "Does that sudden silence mean you've decided you're not quite too decrepit to pull off a trick you could have done in your sleep a few years ago? Or, to put a finer point on it, that I'm right? . . . as usual."

"Let's just say that we'll make the attempt. The worst that happens is we blow it and die horribly, and my last words will be 'I told you so.'"

"I can live with that."

"Why doesn't that surprise me? We'd better fill Maylien in on the new plan before we go."

After all the discussion, the jump itself was almost anti-climactic. I did hit the wall quite a bit harder than I'd have liked—hard enough to knock the wind out of me and make a noise that drew the guard's attention. But I managed not to slip off into the water, and Triss kept us hidden in shadow until the guard gave up and went back to his slow march again. Climbing up the tower wasn't much fun. The stone-work was all fresh-cut and very clean and straight. And the mortar had been applied with care and an eye to eliminating fingerholds.

Without Triss's ability to cling to cracks finer than any sheet of paper, I'd have had to swim back across the moat or spend the night balanced on the three-inch ridge we'd used as our landing point. Add in the need to do things very quietly, and it took close to half an hour to make it up a tiny little forty-foot wall.

As I waited under the edge of the parapet for the guard to pass by on his rounds, I reached into my trick bag for the case holding the last of my opium-and-efik-packed eggs. What I got when I opened it was a handful of eggshell shards and drug-dusted fingers. Dammit! It was all right before the sail-jump, so it must have shattered when we smacked into the base of the wall despite the special packaging. One of the hazards of working with eggs.

I'd lost the easiest way of dealing with the guard, which meant I had to revisit whether it wouldn't be better simply to ghost him. It was much easier to kill a man silently than it was to knock him out without making a lot of noise or seriously hurting him. But I found that making the right decision about when to kill had become the hardest task of all, and I froze.

A younger me wouldn't have hesitated for an instant if a man's life had lain between me and the most efficient execution of my charge. But that version of me had the certainty of the goddess as the bedrock underneath his feet. My definition of justice had been no more and no less than whatever my goddess desired. If she chose to order a person killed and another stood in the way, then killing that other was a necessary expedient. You couldn't let sentiment, or pride, or any other emotion get in the way of duty and professionalism.

But the goddess was dead, and I had only the shifting sands of my own conscience to stand on. Here and now, the choice was mine, no matter what I told Maylien. If I spilled this young guard's blood, the stain would be on my hands. Long seconds slid past as I hung there dithering.

"What's wrong?" Triss whispered in the faintest ghost of a voice.

I just shook my head because I needed to work it through on my own. I'd been avoiding this choice for five years though I hadn't realized it until now. This was really why I'd chosen to lose myself in minor sorts of shadow work instead of trying to hunt down the Son of Heaven or looking for some other real purpose for my life.

I was a trained killer, one of the half dozen best in the world. In the five years I had served the goddess as a full Blade, I had taken at least a hundred lives. I had been a human weapon, honed to the finest edge possible by the training of the temple. The Blade of Justice made flesh. I knew my purpose then: to bring death to those who deserved it. I was so very, very good at the job, and I loved my work and my goddess.

More than efik, or alcohol, I had been hooked on the feeling that came with being the living embodiment of Namara's will. Not the killing—that had brought me no pleasure—but the certainty. Knowing that I was born to destroy the enemies of justice was the sweetest feeling in the world. When the other gods killed Namara, I'd lost that along with everything else.

That was the problem with relying on gods instead of thinking for yourself. When you base your morality on what heaven tells you to do, heaven can always cut you off at the knees by changing its mind.

Oh, I'd killed since the temple fell. Mostly it had been in self-defense, though I would cheerfully have killed Lok and his men for what they did to Triss. But until this moment, I hadn't had to face the choice whether or not to kill someone in pursuit of some other goal. The temptation, really, as I now realized. That was the real reason I'd tried to put the decision off on Maylien, to make it her mission instead of mine. More than anything, I'd wanted to give my will over into another's hand again, to do what I did best without having to take the weight of decision on my own shoulders.

It would be so easy to do, to kill this faceless guard and

believe that I'd done it because Maylien had ordered me to. That I owed her Triss's life and mine and that paying that debt meant doing whatever she asked of me. It would be so easy to let her become my new goddess, if only for a little while. And I wanted it. I wanted it so badly, the luxury of turning off my mind and simply being what my training and aptitude had shaped me into. A weapon for another's hand.

A scuffing sound from above told me that the guard had come close again. If he followed his pattern, he would look out over the woods behind me for a count of five, then turn around and walk to the other side of the tower. *One.* Through Triss's unvision I watched as he leaned out above me craning his neck and exposing the pale skin under his chin.

Two. All I had to do was flick a dagger into my hand, bring my arm up, straighten my legs . . . he'd die without a sound. *Three.* So easy to let my reflexes decide for me. *Four.* I pressed my face into the limestone, drawing its dusty smell deep into my lungs. *Five.* He started to turn away, but I could still just manage it . . . if I let myself. *Six.* And he was gone, stepping back from the edge in the same moment that I did.

Seven. A hand up onto the lip of the parapet. *Eight.* Another. *Nine.* Pull myself up and over. *Ten.* Drop down and grab. I hit him fast and from behind, wrapping my left arm tight around his neck, cutting off air and blood flow at the same time that I pinned his right arm to his side with my own. I lifted him back off his feet as Triss wrapped around his legs and his other arm, holding him immobile.

It would have been simpler to break his neck. Much simpler. Even then. I fought the temptation, keeping the pressure on until he went limp. Counted carefully. Cut off the blood too long, and something happened to the mind. Too short, and he'd wake up within minutes. Finally, I let off and eased him to the ground, hoping I'd gotten it right. A gag, bindings at wrists and ankles, a couple of loops of cord tying him tight against the base of the catapult, and done. He still might die—bound and unconscious people did sometimes— but I had made my own decision, taken the hard road and done what I could to preserve his life within the constraints of my assignment.

I signaled Maylien, and she sent Bontrang over to take the end of a rope back to her. We pulled it tight between the nearest tree and one of the crenellations and she hand-over-handed her way up the slightly inclined rope.

Maylien peered through a low, barred window in the back of the central keep. "That looks familiar."

"All too," I agreed. The dimly magelit room was a much-expanded version of the torture chamber where I'd been held.

"Except here she hasn't bothered hiring out an illusion to keep the neighbors from seeing what goes on down there. Maybe you *should* have killed that guard. He had to know what happens here. As soon as I can get a big enough force together, I'm going to destroy this place."

"Why wait?" I asked. The sight of the glyph rack and memories of what its twin had done to Triss had my blood burning.

"You can't be serious. A keep this size must hold at least thirty of my sister's guards. I know Blades are good, but there's just the two of us."

I opened my mouth to point out that two mages, one a former Blade, with the element of surprise to help ought to be more than adequate to the job. Before I could say a word, several drops of cold rank water fell on my face and Triss slapped my shoulder, hard. I caught Maylien around the waist, dragging her with me as I dove to the left.

"What are you doing!" she demanded as she landed atop me.

"Moving!" I started us rolling across the cobbles.

Something that smelled like it ought to have been buried a long time ago landed with a soggy thump in front of the window where we had been kneeling only a moment before. Chalk one up for those rumors of the night-walking dead and another for Triss's concern about things in the moat.

19

The undead moved fast. Rising from where it had just missed its pounce, the creature threw itself after us within seconds. Because we were already rolling onward, it missed again, this time ending up flat on its belly.

I threw Maylien a few yards beyond where the roll had carried us, then flipped back to my feet before it came at me again. I went right back down a moment later when I couldn't get my new swords clear of their sheaths in time to prevent the creature's clawing hands from striking me full in the chest. Maylien had given me a beautiful pair to replace the ones I'd lost at Devin's, but they were a tiny bit too wide for my old hip-draw rig—a problem I thought I'd fixed already.

Triss briefly shaped himself into a shadowy breastplate then, or the thing would have torn my heart out. As filthy fingernails skittered across hardened shadow, I had a moment to desperately hope Triss's efforts would also suffice to keep the creature from passing its horrible curse along to me. With the death of the goddess, I'd almost certainly lost my magical immunity to the restless dead.

Then I went ass over ears and had to let go of my still-sheathed swords as I turned the fall into a clumsy backward roll. I expected to have to fend off another attack as I came to my feet again, but Maylien had entered the fray by then, scything in with a crouching spin-kick that knocked the legs out from under the risen. Or whatever it was—it was hard to get enough of a fix on it in the moonlit courtyard to make more than a guess.

Maylien's maneuver finally gave me time to free my swords. As the monster started to push itself to its feet, I stepped in and swung simultaneous cuts from both sides. Aiming to take the damned thing's arms off just above the elbows, I struck with maximum force. Instead, of shearing neatly through rotted flesh and decaying bone, as I'd expected, I felt more like I'd chopped into wet oak. And, where the magical swords of my goddess might have done the trick anyway, I had only ordinary steel.

It wasn't enough, and my swords stuck fast as undead muscles bunched and twisted, pinching tight like a half-sawn branch nipping a saw blade. I had to leave them behind a moment later as I threw myself backward into another roll when the risen lunged toward my groin, its mouth gaping wide to tear and rend.

Bontrang tried to claw the monster's eyes out then, but it batted him aside. Even with my swords stuck deep in its biceps hampering its movements, the thing moved scary fast. Maylien snarled something incoherent as Bontrang fluttered weakly back to land on her shoulder, then she sent a wave of magefire washing over the creature.

The flames momentarily filled the narrow courtyard between the keep and the outer wall with light and heat, wiping out my night vision in the process. The risen screamed as the horrible smell of burning rotted flesh filled the air. Bits of cracked and blackened skin fall away, but the risen was far too soggy from its time in the moat to actually catch fire. Still screaming, it turned and lurched toward Maylien.

She'd drawn her own sword by then, a slender double-edged dueling blade of the sort favored by the Zhani nobility. She swung a backhanded cut as she dodged out of the way of the creature's charge. Several of its fingers fell to the ground with a noise like demented hail. I had a perfect opportunity then to sink a dagger in the back of its neck, but didn't bother. This was a chopping job if I'd ever seen one.

What it really wanted was an axe. Failing that, I needed to get at least one of my swords back. Short and broad, they'd do a much better job on the risen than Maylien's dueling blade. So I lunged forward, catching hold of the sword sunk in the creature's left arm. Putting one hand on the hilt and the other on the crosspiece, I applied my whole weight, twisting and torquing the blade out and down.

The blade bent alarmingly, then came free with a wrench and a ringing sound, as it sprang back straight. Somewhere in there, I caught a sharp knock on the side of the head. It sent me spinning away, with red sparks dancing across my vision and the taste of blood in my mouth from a cheek torn by my own teeth. If Triss hadn't taken the worst of the blow, I'd have lost my ear. I whispered a quick thanks, then the risen was coming at me again.

I wasn't in a good position for an effective shot with my sword, so I turned side on and kicked the thing full in the chest. A knee to the groin would have been easier and a more effective target on a living man, but I didn't think it'd help much here. What I really wanted was to shove it back and away long enough to let me think. I managed that, knocking it onto its ass, but only at the cost of filthy hands and undead fingers digging painfully at my shin and calf. Triss was there again, sheathing my leg in shadow, and again I hoped it would be enough to spare me the risen curse.

As the creature clambered back to its feet, Bontrang dove at its head from the side, slapping the creature with his wings, then shearing off before it could make any move to catch him. An instant later, Maylien hit it with more magefire. It snarled and turned toward her, and I finally saw my chance.

"Triss, I need an edge!" Then I stepped in, set my feet, and swung a double-handed blow right at the base of the thing's neck.

It was like hitting a tree trunk. The shock of the impact numbed my hands and nearly sprained my wrists as the sword tried to tear itself free of my grip, but Triss came through. With the essence of the everdark transforming my sword's edge into a sliver of deadly night, the blade slowed but never quite stopped, plowing through undead flesh and bone to behead the monster.

Not that that killed it. The head was still angrily snapping its jaws as it rolled away, while the body kept right on going in a straight line. It would take a long and hot fire or powerful and properly tailored magic to fully destroy the thing. We had time for neither, as a crossbow quarrel struck the cobbles near my feet and shattered just then. One of the other guards had gotten into firing position.

"We have to get under cover!" I yelled.

Maylien had ended up back by the low window into the dungeon, and she turned to it now. Calling Bontrang to her, she moved her hands through a quick and intricate pattern that left lines of magical light behind in a beautiful cat's cradle for those that had the eyes to see it. Then she touched the palms of her hands to the two closest bars and spoke a word of opening.

Blue light erupted from the point of contact with a tremendous shattering boom like someone had broken a bottle filled with thunder. Maylien flew back and away from the window at the same time that the bars ripped free of their moorings and fell inward. A second quarrel struck the place she'd just been crouching even as Maylien—who had landed neatly on her feet—started back in my direction.

"Go!" she shouted, and I went, diving to slide headfirst through the gap she'd opened in the bars.

She followed a moment later, dropping down beside me out of the line of fire. She had a satisfied smile on her face and gave Bontrang an appreciative scritch on the top of the head.

"Pretty fancy spellwork for such short notice," I said as I started to check over the places the risen had touched me—if it had drawn blood, the wound would need to be cleansed with fire.

"Thanks." Maylien's breathing sounded ragged. "Bontrang and I practiced, though I wish it took less out me—I need to sit for a moment."

"Gotta check for risen contamination anyway," I responded.

Maylien spoke again as she checked herself over. "That spell's what I'd intended to use when I came to get you out of that dungeon in Tien. But then Devin dropped a net over Bontrang, bopped me on the head, and carried us both off as easily as a couple of sleeping children."

I looked away for a moment. "I'm sorry I didn't come after you right then. I wanted to, but I just didn't have anything left to do it with."

"I wouldn't have let you if you'd tried," interjected Triss before turning to Maylien. "Aral was overtapped, inches from dying."

"It's all right." Maylien put a hand on my shoulder and squeezed. "Best thing you could have done, truly. Devin had a bunch of traps laid for you. He really wanted to capture you for something though he wouldn't say what, and he was furious when you didn't come after him right away. It threw his plans off."

"Do you know that those plans were?" I asked, feeling a little sick—what else had my old friend intended to do to me?

"No. He ranted a little about how you and Sumey were both making things hard for him, but he wasn't dumb enough to spell anything out for me. Sorry."

By then we'd both finished checking for cursed wounds, and I noticed how very sad she looked though I didn't know why, so I reached up to cover her hand with my own. For a moment we sat silently like that, then she pulled gently away. Before I could do or say anything in response, we were interrupted.

"I don't know where they went." The voice was outside

but close by. "That big flash blinded me, and they were gone when I could see again."

"Just get out of the courtyard, you idiot!" someone yelled back from somewhere above. "Another of the baroness's pets is on the way in from the moat, and you don't want to be there when it arrives."

"Oh shit! I—" The other voice rose into a scream, then cut off suddenly.

Fuck.

"I think it's time we got moving again." I climbed to my feet. "Too bad we can't put the bars back."

Maylien nodded and followed as I started quietly across the room. In addition to duplicating the equipment of the other torture chamber, this one had a large rack, an iron maiden, and a cauldron full of oil atop a fire grate. And just inside the door we found a huge, red marble tub and a large copper for heating water.

"What the hell is that for?" asked Maylien.

"I don't know." After glancing into the empty hallway beyond the door's narrow barred window, I bent to work on the lock with Triss's help. "Maybe your sister likes to lounge in a hot bath while she watches people have their fingernails pulled out."

"I wish I could put it past her. Or pretend she wasn't my full sister." Maylien shuddered and hugged herself. "But blood-madness runs in my family. First my father, then my sister, and lately my uncle. Sometimes I wonder when it will take me."

I felt the lock give and stood up. "You seem to be doing all right so far." It was an inadequate response, but I was too horrifyingly aware of the possibility that she was right to make a better one.

As I started to open the door, something smacked into it from the other side and slammed it back shut. Before I could force it open again a solid thunk announced someone's dropping a heavy bar into place. I glanced through the tiny window again, but couldn't see anything.

"Triss," I said, my mind racing ahead to try to anticipate

the kind of resistance we'd face after he took the bar off for us—crossbows certainly, maybe woldos or other pole arms, possibly attack from two sides . . . "You're going to have to—"

Maylien tugged on my sleeve. "I hate to interrupt but another one of those things just came in through the window."

"Always wondered what it'd be like to see someone ripped to pieces by the pets." A man's face appeared in the window, leering evilly through the bars as he spoke. "Give us a good show, won't you, love?"

"Watch *this*." Maylien slapped her hand against the bars and sent a blast of magefire through the narrow opening.

The man on the other side shrieked horribly and fell away, which gave me an idea for the risen. I started back across the torture chamber toward the window.

"Follow my lead," I called over my shoulder as I raced to get into the right position.

The monster met me halfway, charging forward in the same eager and powerful but uncoordinated manner as its predecessor. That was just what I'd hoped for. As its bony hands reached for my chest, I caught it by the wrists, dropping onto my back and pulling. It lost its balance, falling toward me, and I planted both feet in its stomach, lifting and thrusting so that it passed over me and went sailing through the air. It landed headfirst in the big cauldron with a splash. For a moment, only its lower legs stuck out above the surface.

"Maylien!" I yelled but she had already anticipated my request, blasting the oil-filled cauldron with magefire.

The oil ignited with a whumpfing sound, and further trails of fire radiated out around the cauldron from the risen-spattered oil. Burning undead hands rose from beneath the oil's surface and clutched at the edge of the cauldron. Maylien grabbed a heavy cleaver from a nearby table and brought it down with a sharp whack that severed the thing's left hand. Unbalanced, the risen fell back into the flaming oil. When it tried to get out again a moment later, Maylien removed the right hand as well.

The burning hands started to crawl away. Since I wanted

a closer look, I skewered them on the end of one of my swords instead of just flicking them back into the cauldron. This risen—and a close look showed it was definitely one of the risen—seemed further gone than its predecessor. What little flesh was left on its bones stretched out in narrow ribbons of muscle and tendon. The fingernails were gone completely though it looked like someone had filed the finger bones themselves to ragged points. It was harder to get a fix on the thing's head, as we didn't dare let it get out of the cauldron, but in the brief moments it was above the surface it, too, seemed more stripped down and skull-like.

After a couple of minutes of our shoving it repeatedly back into the fire, the body seemed to lose the coordination necessary to make a serious attempt at escaping the cauldron, though it continued to thrash and flail feebly. That was right about the time a badly aimed crossbow quarrel came sailing in through the window of the inner door and gonged off the cauldron. Maylien sent a burst of magefire at the door while I scraped the hands off my sword and back into the cauldron.

I would have liked to let the risen cook a little bit longer, but the guards had just become the bigger threat, so I slid my swords under the edge of the cauldron and levered it over. A cascade of burning oil washed across the floor, quickly lighting the door and every bit of wood near it on fire. Since that included a couple of major support posts, I figured it would make for a hell of a distraction. I hated to use fire under most circumstances, but I figured the people guarding this chamber of horrors had earned it.

Rather than attempt the rapidly growing inferno around the door, we reversed course and went back out the window. Between the smoke pouring out of all the lower windows and the distraction of the angry headless risen that was still staggering around the courtyard, nobody noticed us at first. We made it back to the rope we'd left on our way in and most of the way up the wall before the first crossbow was fired our way.

"Do you think there are any more of those risen in the

moat?" Maylien asked as she dropped down on the roof of the little tower.

"Why?"

"Because if we stay here, someone's going to think to use one of the catapults on the other towers to lob something a lot more lethal than a few quarrels at us, and if we try to climb down that line I crawled up, we'll be easy targets." She shrugged. "I guess there's only one to find out." Then she vaulted over the parapet.

"Crazy woman!"

"But you're going after her, aren't you?" Triss sounded resigned.

"Of course I am. What if there *are* more risen? She'll need help." I followed Maylien over the parapet and into the water.

Before I'd taken three strokes, Triss made a little relieved sound. "I can't taste them in the water anymore. I think we're clear."

Maylien was already out of the water when I reached the shore, and she offered me a hand up.

"That was insane, you do know that, right?" I asked as she pulled me up.

"A little, maybe." She grinned and her teeth shone white in the darkness. "But then, so's this." She stepped in very close and put her arms around my neck. "Don't you think?" Then she gave me a kiss that just about melted my knees—enough so that Triss had to steady me.

"I dunno. Seems like a great idea to me. But I thought the future baroness wasn't supposed to do things like that." I'd intended it as a joke, but it came out sharper than I'd intended—I guess I was still stinging from her earlier rejection.

Maylien's cheeks flushed. "I'm sorry about that but . . . well, I'm *not* supposed to be doing things like this. Heyin would tear his hair out if he could see us here, but I'm not going to worry about that right now if you won't. Just for tonight, I'm going back to being the Rover I spent most of my life as and letting the future baroness take a well-earned break. We could easily have been killed back there, and confronting my sister's going to be even more dangerous. So the chances are pretty good I'm going to die rather than become a baroness anyway, aren't they?"

I nodded because she was right, though it hurt me to acknowledge it. I was quite certain I could kill Maylien's sister if I needed to. Getting Maylien into position to do it herself after sending a formal warning to Sumey that she was coming and when? Not so much. For that matter, even if I got her there safely, Sumey might simply turn out to be the better swordswoman.

"If I don't die," continued Maylien, "I'm going to have plenty of time to wear the shackles of baronial etiquette later on. So, right here, right now, I intend to do something just because I want to do it and not because I'm supposed to do it, maybe for the last time."

I glanced over my shoulder to the place where flames were starting to crawl up the side of the keep. "What about the keep?"

Maylien nipped my earlobe. "The way its going up? It'll just add to the afterglow."

"Crazy woman . . ."

"Uh-huh. Does that mean you're turning me down?"

"No, but let's get a little farther away first."

"Fair enough."

When we'd put some distance between us and the fire, I pulled her in under the shadow of a pine and gave her a kiss. She returned it in a way that left me breathless.

"It's been an awfully long time for me," I husked. More than five years.

"Me, too." And she sounded more than a little breathless herself. "Since I returned to Zhan, actually. All right for the future baroness perhaps, but not easy for the Rover I used to be." We kissed again.

"Oh, how I've missed this." She drew her fingers across the base of her belly then, setting the simple spell that prevented pregnancy.

A wasted effort that, since I had long since chosen to give

up my ability to have children. Most of the Blades of Namara did so rather than run the risk of creating divided loyalties.

A worried-looking Heyin was waiting in the woods across the river when we turned up some time later.

"I thought you said you were only going to take a quiet look around." He pointed accusingly back the way we'd just come, to where a huge column of smoke stretched toward the moon, and flames were pouring out of what remained of the keep's upper stories.

"Things got complicated." Maylien sounded contrite but gave me a wicked wink when Heyin glanced back at the fire.

Heyin sighed. "Tell me about it."

So, we did, or most of it at least.

"You're damned lucky there weren't any more of those things in the moat, Maylien," he said when we came to the end of our tale. "What madness possesses you that you do such damn-fool things?"

"Aral keeps calling me a crazy woman," she replied. "Does that answer work for you? If not, call it a calculated risk. I figured if there were more, they'd have shown up by then."

Heyin shook his head and sighed, but didn't argue. "What were they, anyway? I thought the risen were supposed to be slow, shambling sorts of creatures. The thing you described sounds more like what you'd get if you could somehow hype a ghoul up on caras dust."

I nodded. "As far as the way they moved, yes. But they definitely weren't ghouls. No fangs and no real claws for starters, just ragged nails on the one that still had the flesh to hold them. They were stronger and tougher than ghouls, too. No, they were risen all right, but someone had done something special with them. I want to say I've heard or read something like it somewhere before, but I can't pin down when or where."

"Speaking of pinned down," said Heyin. "We should be

going. That fire's likely to draw the attention of any patrols that Sumey has out in the area, and I'd rather not run into one of them."

"Baroness Marchon!" a young woman ran in and knelt before Maylien's chair.

Two weeks had passed since the destruction of the keep—the fire had burned it to the foundations, robbing us of any opportunity for learning anything further from the site. We still hadn't settled on the details for a plan to get Maylien through to her sister for a duel though we had the broad outlines down. It pretty much had to happen at Marchon House in Tien, for example. We were sitting in Exile House's formal dining room going over a map of the Sovann Hill for about the forty-seventh time.

"What is it?" asked Maylien.

"A carrier pigeon just came in with a spell-sealed message for you," said the woman.

Maylien took the tiny scrap of paper and started reading. Within moments, her expression turned dark.

"What is it?" asked Heyin.

"It's from our *friend* in Sumey's household. My sister is going to move to have me impeached before the king. She's planning on using the loss of the keep we torched as cause to have me declared outlaw though how she can prove I had anything to do with that, I don't know. This says she will bring the charges when the king next holds formal court in five days' time. If she succeeds, I will no longer be eligible to issue challenge. We have to move now, before that can happen."

"I'll draft the letter for you," said Heyin. "When should I say you will be coming for her?"

20

Down! I tapped Maylien on the shoulder, giving her the prearranged signal. She dropped flat on the wet roof, and I dropped on top of her, while Triss settled over both of us. We stayed there in the dark and the cold spring rain, getting steadily damper and more frustrated for about a quarter of an hour before Triss finally whispered that we could move again. Then we crawled backward toward the narrow street that ran behind the large and expensive apartment house we'd only just ascended.

Above and ahead of us on the Temple of Athera, one of the Elite hunkered down on the lee side of the bell tower, resting his forehead against the shoulder of the stone dog staring off to the northwest. The dog stood atop a thick limestone buttress that made for one of the few rooftop positions that could both support its weight and provide a way for it to get up there. Between the night and the rain, they'd have been nearly invisible to normal eyes. But in magesight, the glow of the Elite's many active spells illuminated them from within.

When we'd first slipped up over the edge of the roof, the

man had been hidden by the bell tower, and his unspelled stone dog had all but vanished against the stone and slate of the rooftop. But then the Elite came around the corner, all aglow with his spells, and started scanning the southern rooftops. Triss and I could still have gotten past him and his familiar unnoticed on our own, but there simply wasn't enough of Triss to cover both Maylien and me fully if we tried to move. So we'd had to wait until the Elite took his little break for an opportunity to move back off the roof.

Now we dropped over the roof's edge onto a third-floor balcony, putting the building between us and the watchers. From there it was easy enough to climb down a floor and drop the rest of the way to the street below unseen. We retraced our steps further, moving back into a dark and stinking alley that provided some shelter from the rain as well as from the eyes of our foes. Bontrang briefly stuck his head out of Maylien's bag then and made a piteous little squawking noise. It sounded to me like a complaint about the awful weather.

I couldn't help but agree with him. Both because I sympathized about the misery factor and because it would have been awfully nice to have his eyes in the sky to warn us about things like all the damned Elite on the rooftops. On the other hand, at least the storm was keeping everyone who didn't have to be there off the streets.

"That's the third roadblock we've run into in the hour since sundown," I said, "and that smells bad. One member of the Elite blocking a chimney road route up onto the Sovann Hill could easily be there on some business unrelated to ours. Maybe even two. But make it three, and add in the Crown Guards who are crawling all over the fucking place, and it means that the king or someone close to him is trying to cordon off the area. Now, there might be some reason for that other than your challenge tomorrow morning, but I'm having trouble believing in that much coincidence."

"It's no coincidence, I'm sure of it." Maylien's eyes were downcast, her voice discouraged. "My sister seems to have enlisted crown support."

"I thought the crown was specifically forbidden from interfering in this sort of challenge," Triss said from within my shadow, "that your sister could only use her own resources."

Maylien sighed and shook her head. "Against *me* yes. Against an unidentified renegade Blade? Or, depending on what she's told them, Aral the Kingslayer? I don't think she'd have any trouble enlisting crown support in that case. Hell, if she's really got Deem in her pocket, she might not even need to talk to Uncle Thauvik."

"When did you come up with all that?" I asked. I didn't like it one little bit, but it fit the circumstances.

"A few minutes ago, as we were climbing back down the third wall that we'd just climbed up."

"That's a major problem," said Triss. His voice seemed to be coming from somewhere near the entrance of the alley then—he'd spread himself out to keep an eye on things as soon as we ducked into the deeper dark. "We can't do a big sail-jump with Maylien riding along. That plus all the royal attention severely limits our number of possible routes up the hill."

"So you two can't get to Marchon House *with me*, and I can't get into Marchon House *without you*," said Maylien. "Basically, we're dead in the water."

"There's got to be some way around this," I said. "Maybe we can split up and meet on the hill somewhere. If we didn't have to cover you, Triss and I could get past the cordon easily enough. If the crown's really not allowed to interfere with your challenge, you *should* be able to pass through without any problems, right?"

"In theory," said Maylien. "But I've got a nasty feeling it's not going to work that way in practice. You're right about this whole thing stinking. I don't know whether that's because Thauvik has decided to support my sister's claim against me as actively as he dares, or if it's just antimage prejudice. Either way, I'm afraid there'll be trouble with the guards."

"I'd love to say something reassuring at this point," I replied, "but I suspect you're right. The question is do we try it anyway? If we do, then how do we do it without blowing the whole game if you turn out to be right?"

"Well," said Triss, "there are a couple of Crown Guards coming along the street at the far end of the alley—I can see their lantern. How about we have Maylien step out that way and see what they do when they spot her? We should be far enough from the Elite on the temple there to keep things quiet if we have to take them down."

I didn't like the idea much, but I couldn't think of anything better, so I just shrugged and said, "Maylien?"

"Let's do it."

As we hurried toward the farther street, we put together our basic plan. When we reached the end of the alley, Maylien set Bontrang on my shoulder and touched his forehead lightly, giving him mental orders. He squawked complainingly again but bobbed his head. Then Maylien stepped out into the street and turned away from the oncoming guards without ever looking their way, heading toward the hill. I pulled Triss around me and stayed in the shadows, waiting for the guards to go past.

The pair were tall and professional, the picture of crack troopers and much of a size, though the woman didn't have quite the same breadth of shoulder. After they went by, I launched Bontrang into the air and slipped in behind them. Maylien, who'd been walking slowly to start with, slowed even more as she approached the intersection ahead, as though unsure about where she was. It was really intended to keep down the number of potential witnesses. The guards obliged us by catching her up just short of the crossing street—a wider artery leading up onto the Sovann and important enough to have a scattering of streetlights.

"My lady? Could you answer a few questions for us?" asked the man, his voice extremely polite—as it ought to be when dealing with an obvious noble.

Maylien had put on an elaborate and expensive dueling blade that had belonged to her mother. It marked her as a member of the high nobility, as did the rich silk of the clothes she'd chosen to wear. Now she played the part as well, turning to give the soldier a sharp, annoyed look.

"Why?" she demanded. "What do you want to know?"

"We're looking for a serious criminal," he answered, keeping his voice polite. "One of those Namara cultists that the true gods proscribed a few years ago. The assassins."

There was a time those comments would have sent me into a rage that I'd have had a hard time restraining. But after five years on the run, I'd gotten very good at controlling my responses to nasty things said about me and mine. If I hadn't, I'd have died. Now I just tightened my jaw and moved in closer.

"I thought the Blades were all supposed to be dead," said Maylien.

"We're working on it," answered the guard. "But there are a few left around, and one of them's in the area right now . . ."

He had more to say, but I stopped listening as his partner's actions suddenly drew my full attention. She'd very quietly opened her pouch, using her partner and the wet darkness to hide her movement from Maylien. As she reached inside, I decided I had to take a risk, and so, hoping there were no mages about to see me, I summoned a charge of magelightning, focusing it in my right hand.

When she pulled out a small piece of paper with a line drawing of Maylien and a tiny dimly glowing rune on it, I extended the shadow that surrounded me to touch the back of her neck and released the lightning with a brilliant flare. I didn't know what the rune was for, but I knew I couldn't let her activate it.

She went down in a heap, dead or unconscious. Her partner whirled around in surprise at the flash, half-drawing his sword. I summoned a second charge and touched his chest, and he went down, too, dropping the lantern, which shattered, spilling its lightstone into the street. Then I released Triss and knelt to check the nearer guard's pulse.

Maylien kicked the light into a nearby sewer grate, where

it vanished, plunging us back into near-total darkness. No one opened any shutters to see what was going on, so I had to assume that we'd been quiet and fast enough to avoid any attention. Not a huge surprise given the hours and the noise of the storm, even with the flash and the sizzle of the mage-lightning, but not something to take for granted, either.

"I take it they were about to cause us some trouble?" Maylien asked.

I nodded. The man was unconscious but not dead. I moved on to the woman, scooping up the soggy sheet of paper and handing it to Maylien to look at, while I checked the guard's pulse. She was out but not gone, too—a pleasant surprise. I'd expected to kill at least one of them. It probably had something to do with the rain and the wet street. I'd noticed that seemed to drain off some of the strength of lightning magic, dispersing it into the surrounding area somehow. Actually, now that I thought about it, that might well have been what kept the Kadeshi deathspark from killing me.

Maylien whistled. "This is a summoning rune. Touch it, and it'll alert whoever's at the other end and give them a trace to follow. What do you want to bet that if I tap this with my finger, a whole swarm of Elite will be along shortly."

"Do you want to call this off?" I asked.

She tore the sheet in half, breaking the rune, then dropped it after the magelight. "No. If I walk away now, I'll be outlawed. I'll have to leave Zhan forever and surrender Marchon to my sister. If I can get through to her and challenge successfully, Thauvik won't have any choice but to acknowledge my claim to the barony. He might try to have me declared outlaw anyway, but the other peers won't like that, and I'll have a damn good chance of fighting it off."

She glanced at the fallen guards. "Are they . . ."

"Down but not dead." I caught the man's arm and pulled him into a sitting position, then up onto my shoulder. "We'd better get them out of the street."

Maylien let out a little sigh of relief, then bent to lift the woman. "I'm glad of that, even if it is inconvenient for me.

It's not their fault my sister's a monster, and the king is supporting her." She got the woman onto her shoulders, and we headed back toward the alley. "I just wish we could erase their memories of the past few minutes, but that's magic far beyond my skill. When they wake, and the last thing they remember is my face, it's going to make it that much harder to fight any charges the king might bring."

"I could . . ." I drew a thumb across my throat. I didn't particularly want to kill them, but I'd do it if I had to.

"No. I'll deal with it when and if I need to. There are way too many ifs between here and there to justify killing anyone we don't have to. We might not even make it up the hill. If we do, we might not get past Sumey's guards or Devin. If we manage that, I might be killed in the duel. If I win, Thauvik might choose not to try to have me removed. We'll leave them as they are."

"Good." I turned into the alley and dumped my load in the shadows. "I hate when I have to kill people for being in the wrong place at the wrong time."

Maylien dropped her guard beside mine, opening up a space on her shoulder that was quickly occupied by the return of a sopping-wet and very grumpy Bontrang. She soothed him a bit and quickly dried him off with a rag before coaxing him back into the bag. While she was doing that, I arranged the guards so that neither one of them was going to keel over and drown in a puddle before they woke up.

"So now what do we do?" Maylien edged back to look out the end of the alley. "It's not getting any earlier, we're still miles away from our goal, and I'm not seeing any way to make it up that hill. Not with the Elite blocking the high road and the Crown Guard blocking the low road."

"Actually," I said, "the guards are blocking the *middle* road."

Maylien whipped around to face me, her face a pale blur in the darkness. "You're not suggesting the sewers, are you? In the middle of a rainstorm? That's insane."

"It is. Which is exactly why I think we might able to make it work. Only three sewer lines coming down off the

Sovann Hill are big enough to pass a person walking upright. In dry weather I'd bet money on all of them being covered by the Elite and the stone dogs, but with all this rain, no one sane is going into the sewers."

"How do you know that much about the system?"

"Back when I was working out a plan to kill Ashvik, I had to learn enough about the basic layout of Tien's main sewers to know whether they were a good option or not. There've been miles and miles of the things built over the last five hundred years."

"Did you go in through the sewers then? I've never heard anyone talk about the details."

"No. The sewers that lead to the palace are a nightmare for anyone trying to use them to get at the king. Full of dead ends and traps—many of Durkoth design—plus all kinds of patrols and checkpoints."

Triss nodded from my shadow. "Which is why Master Urayal and Patiss died down there. Nasty place."

"All right, but the palace is on the other side of the river. Why would you know the ones over here so well?"

"Because we've been living over here, and that's what I was taught to do. But I really only know the mains. I'm sure there are at least another dozen lines coming down off the hill that would pass someone willing to crawl through sewage on their belly in the dark. Depending on how they're connected to the storm drains, one of them might well provide us a better and safer route, but I couldn't tell you where those were if my life depended on it."

"Oh, how sad. Here I was thinking how much fun it would be to crawl through sewage on my belly, and now you've dashed my hopes. I guess we get to drown instead."

"If you've got a better idea, I'm all for it," I replied. I decided not to mention the possibility of restless dead in the tunnels.

Maylien just shook her head.

It took us two miserable hours underground to travel the five short blocks I felt we needed to get past the cordon. We nearly drowned half a dozen times, but with ropes and magic and Triss's help, we did finally make it. The only positive things I can say about the trip were: One, the rushing storm waters had cleared out the worst of the stench and all of the shit that wasn't permanently glued to the bricks. And two, we didn't run into any of the restless dead, risen or otherwise.

We came up out of the sewers in a narrow street lined with the walled homes of the lesser well-to-do. From there we dragged ourselves into an even narrower alley, where we collapsed against some wealthy merchant's or minor noble's back wall. Unspeakable muck coated the bricks beneath us, but it couldn't be significantly worse than the unspeakable muck we'd had to wallow through to get there, so it probably all equaled out.

Beside me, Maylien poked at her ruined clothes and sighed ruefully. "So much for going into the duel looking like the rightful baroness."

"Don't worry about it. We can always stop by your sister's rooms on the way in and steal you something more appropriate."

"I wish we could, but someone might recognize the outfit. As much as I hate it, the manner of my defeat of Sumey is going to have almost as much to do with whether I can hold the barony successfully as the fact of the defeat itself. Which means we *will* have to do something about my clothes, I'm just not sure what or when yet. Maybe I can find something of my mother's at Marchon House, though that doesn't solve the immediate problem."

Before I could respond, an utterly soggy Bontrang dropped out of the sky and into Maylien's lap. He didn't bother to complain about the weather this time. When she scooped him up, he just tucked his beak under her chin and started purring frantically. The little fellow had practically gone berserk when Maylien insisted he stay aboveground while we went into the sewers, but it was safer for both of them that way.

In the darkness of the alley, I couldn't see Triss, but he must have felt some of the same sympathy for Bontrang and Maylien that I did. He shifted into dragon shape and draped his head across my lap affectionately. I scratched him behind his invisible ears and wished we could just stay like that for the next four or five hundred years. Unfortunately, that wasn't an option. I could already feel the warmth of exertion losing the fight to the cold and wet.

"Maylien?" I dragged myself up out of the muck.

"Yes."

"Why don't you and Bontrang stay here while I hunt us up that change of clothes. I can do it quicker alone." I stripped off my sodden woolen hood and vest and draped them over Maylien and Bontrang. It wasn't much, but it was all I had to offer.

Maylien pulled them around her gratefully. "Thank you. Bontrang's freezing, and I'm starting to get cold, too."

I nodded. "I noticed the way he's shivering between the purrs. We all need to get dry and get moving, and that starts with clothes. You'll need something to carry Bontrang in, too. That bag's no good anymore."

I'm not, in general, a big fan of theft, though I'll do it when I absolutely have to. So, I promised myself to leave a couple of Maylien's silver riels in the bottom of whatever petty noble's wardrobe I ended up raiding for our clothes. I also prefer not to scare the life out anyone who hasn't earned it. Which is why I intended to pick a wardrobe in an empty bedroom.

Here on the lower slopes of the Sovann Hill, people couldn't afford the extensive magical protections and alarms that I'd have found up closer to Marchon House. It was relatively simple to pick a large house that felt mostly empty and use Triss and a bit of minor spellwork to open the delivery door that led into the dark kitchen.

From there it was a short jaunt up the servants' stairs to the upper floors, where Triss found me an empty guest room. Of course, it being an old house, there was a certain inevitable amount of creaking and squeaking as I moved around, no matter how careful I tried to be. But the wind and the storm seemed more than adequate to cover it, and since no one showed up right away to disabuse me of the notion, I went about my business.

As was often the case in the smaller noble houses during spring and the switchover from winter wardrobe to summer wardrobe, a guest room had been pressed into service for temporary storage. It held the winter clothes that had to be kept handy for a few more weeks yet in case of cold snaps as well as little sachets of fleabane and worrymoth.

As I dug around through the clothes spread across the bed, I found a moment to be thankful I was in Tien. Here loose silks and cottons provided the outfit of choice for the upper class, a marked contrast to someplace like Aven, where everyone favored tailored wool and fitted leather and lots of boning and laces. It meant that I could manage with stuff that was merely near my size, and also that if it worked for me, it'd probably work for Maylien. I did make sure to pick out women's clothes of the best fabrics for her given that she might have to use them for the duel. The divided skirts were fuller than the pants I nicked for myself, but only a little.

After changing my own clothes, I wrapped up a bundle for her, using the bed's top blanket as my sack. I was just finishing that up when Triss gave me a sharp poke in the ribs. I'd had him watching the hall, and that was the signal that someone was out there now. I doused my thieveslight.

"Window," hissed Triss, and I started moving. "Now! It's the steward, and he's got an axe. I think he must have heard something."

That was when the door to the guest room burst open. Damn all old houses with their creaky floors, and damn efficient servants, too, the bane of the housebreaker's existence. I'd intended to at least open the window first, but I didn't have the time, so I just put Maylien's bundle of clothes in front of my face and crashed right through the shutters. I suppose the fact that they were light summer shutters and not the heavy winter storm shutters counted as a point in the favor of efficient staff, but I didn't feel it really balanced out.

I hit the ground running. With Triss providing a shroud of darkness to hide me, I knew the man would never be able to spot or follow me. On the other hand, the way he started screaming for the watch was going to present a real problem in fairly short order. The window was on the front side of the house, and Maylien was out back and a few houses down. So I doubled back around the house as soon as I had shed the impetus provided by the drop.

When I vaulted over the back wall, I found Maylien already waiting for me, with Bontrang hissing angrily on her shoulder. "What the hell went wrong?"

"I picked the only house in the neighborhood where they pay the servants well enough to care, apparently. Now, come on!" I turned and started running, and Maylien fell in behind me. "We have to get out of here."

Normally, I wouldn't have been that fussed about it. Put a couple of blocks between us and the break-in, and we'd be set. But normally the neighborhood wasn't crawling with Crown Guards and—a deep grating howl went up from somewhere behind us, punctuating my thought—stone dogs.

21

Maylien threw herself down on the muddy ground and rolled under the low canopy of a golden willow, following Bontrang into the natural tent. I entered more cautiously, duck-walking to preserve the knees of my stolen pants. They were already the worse for twenty minutes of climbing walls and running through backyards with the forces of the crown in howling pursuit.

We'd shaken them loose somewhere on the outskirts of the royal preserve by slipping in and out across the borders between crown land and various private estates. Our current hiding place lay on a tiny island centering the miniature man-made lake on the Earl of Anaryun's city estate—a spot I'd scouted for just such a temporary refuge years ago when I was nosing Marchon House as a venue for killing Ashvik. Luckily, nothing seemed to have changed since then. We'd been able to follow a narrow calf-deep track built for the use of the gardeners and concealed among the lily pads out to the island.

I had no doubt the Crown Guard was still out there looking for us, but they'd gotten much more circumspect about it now that they'd completely lost sight of us. That quiet might also have something to do with the fact that we were getting close to Marchon House and a much greater potential for charges of crown interference with a scheduled challenge.

I'd brought us to the island because we needed to hole up for an hour or two, and the shelter of the willow was perfect for the purpose. Not even crack troops like the Elite and Crown Guard can maintain maximum alertness for very long without dulling their edge. Our chances would look much better if we vanished for a bit before making our next move. It also gave Maylien a chance to finally change into clean dry clothes.

"Sorry about all the running and hiding," I said. "I really didn't expect I'd get pinched by an elderly steward for stealing clothes." I handed them over. "Do you want me to hold anything for you?"

Maylien grinned, her teeth shining briefly in the darkness. then shivered. "I bet you say that to all the girls when you're trying to get them out of their clothes. Here, take Bontrang. He's half-frozen. Oh, and you'd actually better hang on to the clothes, too. I can't strip and keep them off the ground at the same time."

I took the little shivering gryphinx and stuffed him into the front of my shirt against my skin. He was cold and wet and smelled of soggy cat, and was very, very happy to be out of the elements. He started purring at once, and I rubbed his neck affectionately. Triss, who had come to quite like the little fellow, wrapped himself protectively around the gryphinx as well.

Meanwhile, Maylien skinned out of her ruined shirt and pants, leaving me wishing for better light. She was a beautiful woman, and we hadn't gotten another chance to be alone together since the keep fire. Heyin had gone out of his way to prevent us. I couldn't fault him for that, however much it might have frustrated me. Protecting Maylien *was* his job.

"Hand me that shirt." Maylien took it and slipped it on. "Skirt next. Ahh, much better. Now, what's our next move?"

"We stay right here for at least an hour. We've still got

four hours till daybreak and we need to let the heat die down a bit."

"Well, damn," said Maylien, and she gave a throaty chuckle.

"What?"

"If we've got an hour to kill in here, and we want to have any hope of staying warm and limber while we do it, I'm going to end up taking these clothes right off again."

Triss let out a derisive snort. "You'd better let me hold Bontrang since he's still half-frozen, and we can keep watch. Humans would be so much easier to deal with if they had mating seasons like everybody else does."

Even the richest neighborhoods have cheap taverns. Little hidden hole-in-the-wall-type places that cater to servants of the high-and-mighty. The Footman's Step was one such, marked out only by the coach step nailed to a narrow door in the middle of an otherwise blank wall. It was tucked into a little wedge of property between two wealthy estates and had matched its façade to the walls of its well-to-do neighbors in an effort not to offend anyone's delicate sensibilities.

Normally, it would have been closed here in the brief hours before dawn, but a well-paying private party had rented the front room. So, when I knocked lightly on the door, it was quickly opened. Inside, Heyin and a dozen of his best people waited for us. They wore heavy canvas work clothing of the sort favored by masons and carpenters and had appropriate tools and equipment neatly piled in one corner.

The only thing remotely suspicious about them was that they were carrying more in the way of ladders, rope, and bamboo poles for scaffolding than such a group might normally have. A fact explained by the very real-looking work order they had for cornice repair on the notoriously tall great house of the Duke of Jenua.

"You're late," said Heyin. "We were worried. Especially with all the noise and fuss. What happened?"

So we filled him in, minus any description of how exactly

we'd killed time under the willow though I'm sure he had his suspicions. One unexpected plus from said time killing was it had warmed both of us up enough to take a quick bath in the lake, leaving us something approaching clean.

"What about you?" I asked Heyin after we'd finished bringing him up to date. "Were you stopped?"

"Twice. Both times they checked faces against a drawing of Maylien with a rune at the bottom."

"We saw one of those," I said. "Did they do anything else?"

Heyin nodded and lowered his voice. "It was subtle, and I doubt any of the others noticed since they wouldn't know to look for that kind of thing, but one of the guards made sure to step on every single one of our shadows. I thought I saw another rune scribed on the sole of his boot."

Triss squeezed my shoulders and hissed very quietly. I felt more than a little like hissing myself. Instead, I asked, "Is everything ready?"

"Whenever you are," said Heyin.

"Then let's go."

I led the way through the edge of the royal preserve, where we had to move in a series of short dashes and long pauses. Triss and I would scout ahead, then slide back to lead the others forward. This close to Marchon House, the royal patrols were actually significantly lighter than normal though I couldn't say if that was more to avoid the charge of interference or simply because the outer cordon had soaked up all the available troops.

When we got to the place where the Marchon estate met the royal preserve, we split up. Triss and I led the bulk of Maylien's guard one way while Maylien took Heyin and a couple of others in the opposite direction. The estate was a large one, and I left the men and women of the guard spaced out along the wall at fifty-pace intervals, each with a length of rope with a metal tool tied to one end. I kept going after I ran out of guards, speeded up even, though I had to climb into another estate to do so. I wanted to put as much distance between me and them as possible before the timesman at the temple of Shan struck the fourth hour.

When the bell rang, I started counting to a thousand. I needed to give our planned distraction time to work. With the ringing of the bell, each of the guards I'd left behind would be noisily throwing their tool-weighted ropes over the wall, then dragging them back to the top, which would make a sound like so many grappling hooks being pulled tight.

After that, they were supposed to scatter and meet back at the Footman. Some of them were bound to be picked up by the Crown Guard, but that was a price they'd all agreed to pay if necessary. Since none of them was carrying anything illegal, the worst they'd get was a light beating and a couple of weeks in jail for trespassing. And, if Maylien won her duel, she could bail them all out as soon as she was confirmed as Baroness Marchon.

At the end of my count, I silently placed a light ladder against the wall—a single bamboo pole with shorter lengths driven through it to form rungs. I went up and over the wall, carrying a second ladder, which I placed on the other side. I left them both in place since we wanted them to be found.

We also wanted to leave the thickest possible shadow trail for Devin, so instead of my taking control, Triss covered me as I dashed a couple of hundred feet into the grounds. That presence would strengthen the spoor he left behind. At the end of the dash, we dodged left and right as though we'd encountered a couple of patrols. Then we turned and ran back along a slightly different path to my ladders. The goal was to make Devin think Maylien and I hadn't been able to get past the guards and had backed off to come in from another angle.

Maylien was actually on the far side of the estate, coming in by a completely different route. If all had gone according to plan, she was already over the wall and in the company of her spy within the house—the chief cook. The cook was going slip her into the house with the morning deliveries. Easy enough to do since they'd already been thoroughly checked at the main gate of the estate. Then she would take Maylien to a hiding place in the kitchens to wait for the dawn.

Heyin would get rid of Maylien's ladder and take care of Bontrang for the duration. No familiar could be trusted to stay out of a fight if his companion's life was in imminent danger, so Bontrang had to be kept away from the duel.

After our run-ins with the Elite and Crown Guard, we'd argued about my part in the next bit of the plan. Maylien wanted me to get clear so that I wouldn't encounter whomever the king chose to send as his witnesses to the duel. She suspected Deem and possibly a second officer of the Elite—people who would happily try to kill me given any chance. She'd already made me swear not to interfere with the duel as long as it was conducted honorably, and now she figured I was better off out of it completely.

I'd insisted we stick to the original plan, with me providing a backup in case of treachery, and I'd refused to be budged. So, after using the neighbor's decorative trout stream to break my shadow trail, Triss and I doubled back to the estate and made a second climb onto the wall, this time using a rope and a leather-wrapped grappling hook.

Then we made our slow and painstaking way to the house by moving from tree to tree and touching the ground as little as possible. Since the whole estate was crawling with Sumey's guards, it took Triss and me the better part of two hours and three major backtracks to get within sail-jumping distance of the house, which had its compensations. The spring was starting to fade, but many of the trees were still in bloom. The smell of the myrtle and flowering pears was particularly lovely and made doubly sweet by the very real chance that this was the last time I'd ever smell them.

I ended up about thirty feet up a grand old katsura, perched on a branch a bit bigger around than my thigh. The leaves chattered quietly away in the predawn breeze, a lovely but dangerous sound, as it masked the noises made by the patrolling guards below. After half an hour of waiting for a good gap, I concluded that the timing was never going to come out right for a clean jump.

That left two choices. Jump anyway. With the rain still coming down, there were no stars to blot out, and I was all in gray and black—not easily visible against the backdrop of Triss and the darkness above. Or, remain fully enshrouded and drop to the ground to slip between patrols on foot, which would leave a trail for Devin. Either way, I needed to make my move. Dawn was coming on fast. If not for the clouds, the sky would already have begun to lighten. For about the millionth time, I wished that Triss and I had a good way of communicating under these sorts of circumstances. Then I jumped.

I landed on the narrow ledge of a second-floor window and stayed there for a few seconds while I checked to see whether anyone had noticed. If so, they were playing things mighty casual, so I headed for the most difficult of the possible routes up this side of the house. I felt pretty sure that at this late hour, Devin would already be in place for the duel, but I wanted to confuse my shadow trail just in case.

At the top I perched myself on the narrow strip of lead roofing that lay between one of the house's many chimneys and the wall I'd just climbed. I wanted to give Devin a little more time to get in place if he hadn't already. The duel was supposed to take place in the hour after dawn in the receiving garden out front, between the main house and the forward-thrusting wings. I knew it well from my attempts to catch a king there once upon a time.

Devin's problem now was quite similar to the one I'd had then. If he intended to provide a backstop for Sumey's sword-handling skills, he needed a place to hide. Somewhere from which he could both watch and act if the duel started to go wrong. He had four major constraints. First, he had to stay hidden from any Elite witnesses. I didn't think that any deal Sumey had cut with Deem would extend to ignoring the presence of a former Blade—the enmity between Blade and Elite just ran too deep.

Which led to Devin's second problem. He needed to not get caught. There are a very limited number of ways to affect a witnessed sword duel from a distance. The constraints get even tighter if you can't use magic because the witnesses are also mages. He couldn't just nail Maylien with an arrow in the back or push her onto Sumey's sword with a spell. The scandal would finish Sumey as thoroughly as losing the duel would. And that would be true even if she were able to convince people she hadn't ordered her sister's death herself.

That left Devin an extremely short list of options, all of them small and inaccurate over any distance. I was figuring a blowgun loaded with tiny pebbles from the carriageway. Delivered with the right timing and to the right target—an ear, say—the distraction could easily prove fatal, and the pebble would effectively vanish among its mates.

Third, deniability. If Deem—or whoever the witnesses turned out to be—did spot Devin, he needed to be someplace where the baroness could reasonably claim to have had nothing to do with his presence. It probably wouldn't save her if Devin was caught in the act; but if he was spotted beforehand or couldn't be linked to any obvious tampering afterward, it might keep her neck off the block. That put any position within the house off-limits to Devin, leaving him on the roof or somewhere on the ground.

Finally, he had to know he couldn't trust the baroness. Especially if he'd seen the glyph rack in the torture chamber Maylien had rescued me from. He'd want a quick way out in case the baroness decided to sell him to the Elite.

All of which meant Devin only had one really good option for his sniper's nest, a particularly deep niche between the end pair of dormers on the west-facing wing of the house. There *were* other choices but none as good: a similar perch atop the east-facing wing, but at that hour it would be in full sun, which would make him easier to spot as well as putting the sun in his eyes. There was also a second-floor balcony on the main house that would provide a cleaner shot and better concealment, but it would make escape virtually impossible if the Elite did spot him.

It would be the dormer. Of course, that all assumed the baroness really had set Devin up as a backstop, but I had no doubts. People who hired the sort of person Devin had become never played fair.

Over the next three-quarters of an hour, the rain tapered off, and the clouds started to break up, exposing the dawn sun as a half disk lying on the crest of the Kanathean Hill. If everything had gone right with Maylien—and I felt sure there'd have been a serious commotion if it hadn't—she would be issuing her challenge in short order. Time to move. I ducked around the chimney and crept along the back of the wing. I wanted to come down on Devin's position from above and behind.

When I finally poked my head over the peak of the roof I spotted a pool of too-deep shadow exactly where I'd expected to find Devin. He really didn't have another good choice. Ducking down, I moved back far enough to put the nearer of the two dormers between us. Then I slipped over the ridgeline and moved silently out onto the dormer, a process made much easier by the thick lead of the roof. One of the things I loved about working great houses was that they never went for the cheaper and noisier options like slate or terra-cotta tiles.

It took a while, but eventually I was lying along the roof of the dormer directly above and out of sight of the dark blot that concealed Devin. I wanted to wait until events below provided a distraction before making my move. Obligingly enough, I'd only just come to rest when a small coach pulled up beside the arched stone gate at the foot of the garden. It was pulled by a stone dog. As I lifted the curtain of shadow from in front of my eyes so that I could see better, the coach's door opened, and Colonel Deem climbed down from the cab.

He was followed a moment later by another familiar face, a stiff-backed Captain Fei of the watch. Though it was hard to tell from this distance, the combination of her posture and demeanor suggested Fei was mighty unhappy about something. As Deem passed the stone dog on his limping way to the house, he waved his hand and triggered a small spell that released the creature from the traces so it could join him. At no time did he or his familiar so much as glance back at Fei.

A noise from the main doors drew my attention away from Deem then. Sumey was descending the front stairs, followed by a virtual explosion of servants and guards. She wore both the baronial coronet and her chain of office. While she continued down the path toward Deem, most of her retinue peeled off at the base of the steps. Some started setting out chairs, tables, and all the other accoutrements of a formal audience while others took a length of rope and began staking out a large dueling ring.

"Colonel Deem," the baroness called as they closed. "So nice to see you." She offered him her hand to tuck into his elbow. "Come sit with me while I wait for this charade to be over."

She nodded vaguely at Fei as she turned back toward the house, but that was the only acknowledgment she made of the other woman. Clearly she was no more happy with the second crown witness than Deem was. Not happy, but also not surprised. I wondered what that meant but had no way of finding out, so I pushed it aside for later thought. Fei didn't look happy either, wrinkling her nose at the retreating back of the baroness.

Soon Sumey and the colonel were seated side by side at the center of the furniture arrangement, with the colonel's stone dog at their feet. Fei was shunted off to a slightly smaller but still comfortable seat on one side. Servants continued to dash back and forth from the house, bringing tea and cakes and other dainties. As the minutes slid past I began to worry about Maylien.

Then, the baroness leaped to her feet and pointed at a young maid in an ill-fitting red dress, demanding loudly, "You there, girl, what's that you're carrying?" The girl had a long slender bundle of fabric tucked under one arm, which she now raised in both hands.

"Your death, Sumey," she declared in ringing tones, and I recognized her voice as Maylien's.

"What!" yelled Sumey. "Wait, guards, stop her!"

But Maylien was already too close for anyone to interfere with the challenge, and, with many a sidelong glance at Deem and Fei, the guards did nothing.

When she saw that, the baroness turned a sneering gaze on her sister. "You come to challenge me in the clothes of a maid? How humiliating for you." As she had all along, she pitched her voice high and clear, a noble used to playing for her court.

Maylien didn't say anything, just reached inside the bundle and withdrew her sword. Then she slipped the tip of the blade into the front of her bodice and, in a surprisingly graceful move, slit the dress completely down the front. It fell away to reveal a loose divided skirt and a shirt, all in a rich jade silk. For reasons not readily apparent, the baroness stiffened angrily.

Maylien shrugged off the remnants of the dress. "I come to challenge you in the clothes of the woman you murdered, our mother, Juli Dan Marchon, last true ruler of Marchon. I am Maylien Dan Marchon Tal Pridu and I claim my right under the Code Martial of Zhan to offer blood challenge to Sumey Dan Marchon Tal Pridu. I challenge for the rule of the Barony of Marchon and I call on the representatives of the crown here present at my request to witness the duel." She, too, spoke for the audience.

Deem rose from his chair, a tightly closed look on his face, and addressed the baroness, "I am honor-bound to point out that I know this woman to be a mage." He turned to Maylien. "As a duly sworn representative of the crown, I may recognize your right to challenge under the Code Martial if and only if you forswear the use of any magic for the duration of the duel. Do you so forswear the use of magic?"

"By my honor and my blood, I do so forswear it."

"Then I will witness your challenge for the crown."

Captain Fei now rose from her chair. "Likewise, I'm sure." Deem turned a glare on the captain, and Fei shrugged, but then nodded. "As a duly sworn representative of the crown, I will witness the challenge here issued. That make you happy, Colonel?"

Deem turned to the baroness. "Baroness Marchon, the challenger has forsworn magic and her blood claim is valid. Will you accept the challenge and duel to the death? Or will you refuse it and concede the baronial coronet, going into voluntary exile forthwith?"

"I accept. Captain," she called to the head of her guard, "bring me my sword." She turned to Maylien. "This is going to end with me bathing in your blood." Then she laughed. "Oh, I'm going to enjoy spilling your life away as I've enjoyed nothing else in years, sister mine."

"Then you've become a true child of our father the butcher, Sumey." Maylien shook her head sadly. "I loved you once. You know that, don't you? Somewhere down in the hell that has come to fill your head, you have to remember what it meant to be sisters."

Sumey didn't answer, just smiled and drew the sword her guard captain offered her. I used the noise to cover the drawing of a long dagger of my own. When Sumey gestured for her sister to proceed her into the ring, I noted that her sword was unusually broad and heavy for a dueling blade—an odd choice.

Maylien stepped over the rope, crossing to the far side of the ring and turning back to her sister. "Having recently seen evidence of the depravity you take pleasure in these days, I've no doubt spilled blood brings you joy. I only hope you can still smile when the blood on the ground is yours. Then at least one of us will be happy with what has to happen here today." She raised her sword. "Whenever you're ready."

Sumey took off her coronet and the formal chain of baronial office with its insignia of a jade fox on a golden background, handing them both over to Deem to be presented to the winner. Next she took off her formal jacket and other outer garments, stripping down to her own shirt and divided skirt for the duel. Then she entered the ring and likewise raised her sword.

The two sisters faced each other now across a distance of perhaps twenty-five feet. They were much of a size, though Sumey was slightly broader across the shoulders. Both wore loose silk, Sumey's a golden brown that complemented her sister's green. As the two began to slowly circle and move together, I edged closer to the lip of the roof and Devin below. Soon.

Sumey suddenly lunged at her sister, swinging a low cut at Maylien's right knee. Maylien parried while simultaneously hopping back. There was a bright clash of steel and Maylien's sword bent sharply, slowing Sumey's just enough to allow her jump to carry her clear, before springing back straight as she brought it up and around.

What the hell? I'd fenced with Maylien only a few days previously, helping her train for the fight, and not even my heaviest strokes had that kind of effect on her sword. Unless Sumey was a good bit stronger than I was, that shouldn't have happened.

If Maylien was surprised, she didn't show it, using the impetus of her sister's blow to flip her blade around into a neat backhanded slice at Sumey's throat. Without showing any sign of effort, Sumey brought her much heavier sword up in a hard parry that slapped Maylien's blade aside. Again, Maylien flowed with the movement, eeling her blade down and around in a corkscrew to slash at Sumey's thigh.

Rather than parry, Sumey moved forward so that Maylien's hilt caught her rather than the blade, though she didn't stop there. She bulled forward and crashed chest first into her sister. Maylien flew back and away, losing her footing. Though she managed to turn the fall into a backward roll, it almost took her clear of the ring, which would have been very bad form.

I lost track of the duel over the next few seconds because whatever happened to Maylien, I needed to settle with Devin, and Maylien's fall offered the perfect distraction. I rolled over the edge of the dormer, dropping about five feet to land on Devin. I'd intended to use my dagger and the weight of my body to nail him to the roof—you don't let a target live. Especially one as dangerous as Devin.

Deem's presence in the garden below should have been more than reminder enough for that. But when the moment actually came, I found that I just couldn't kill a man who'd once been a brother to me. Not like this. Not stabbing from behind in cold blood. As I fell, I shifted the dagger out from between us, smacking him behind the ear with the pommel as soon as contact allowed me to judge that target instead. Devin grunted noisily, and I hoped that the sounds of the duel below would cover it. I moved my dagger to lie against the right side of his neck, just above the big artery.

"Hello, Devin," I whispered into his ear. It was just him and me at the moment, since Zass and Triss were both in cloud shape and submerged by our respective wills. "We need to have a little talk."

"Why not just kill me and get it over with?" he asked after a moment, and I could hear strain and pain in his voice. "It's what I'd do to you."

I really didn't have an answer for that, not one I was willing to tell Devin anyway. Telling him that he still mattered to me would be like handing him a dagger with my name on it. Instead, I looked back down at the duel. I couldn't say why, but I wanted to know the results there before I made any final decisions about Devin.

There had clearly been several more passes to the fight, though none conclusive. Maylien was orbiting her sister now, moving in fast for tiny cuts at wrist or foot and refusing to fully engage. From what I could see over the next minute or two, it was her best strategy. She was clearly a better swordswoman than her sister, and she should have been able to parlay that into a quick victory, but she had two major disadvantages.

Sumey's much heavier sword and seemingly unnatural strength and stamina. Normally, the weight of that sword would have worked against Sumey in anything longer than the briefest of matches. Whipping it around as wildly as Maylien was forcing her to should already have tired her out, but the weight didn't seem to bother Sumey at all. That strength allowed her to use the heavier blade as a hammer on her sister's more conventional dueling sword, smashing it repeatedly in a clear attempt at breaking Maylien's blade.

"What the hell is happening down there?" I asked, though I didn't expect any answers.

Devin let out a cruel little snort. "What's happening is that Sumey is going to carve her precious older sister into cutlets while you watch from the sidelines. Of course, it could never have ended any other way."

"If you're so sure of Sumey's victory, why are you here?" I felt around in the shadows with my free hand until I found the blowgun I'd expected. "And what's this for?"

"You really don't know what's going on, do you?" Devin's tone fell somewhere between incredulous and bitter. "You've never in your whole fucking life known the real score, Aral. You've always just charged in and trusted to the old King-slayer magic to carry the day. And do you know what the funniest joke of all is? It always fucking works. No matter what the odds, Aral the gods-be-damned Kingslayer always comes out on top."

"I don't understand."

"How do you do it, Aral? How do you always manage to fail upward? No matter how half-assed your plan. No matter how much others who've worked harder and actually thought things through try. No matter what you actually deserve. The dice always come up crowns for you. Well, this time, buddy, the dice are loaded, and you're rolling nothing but skulls. This time you're going to lose, and I'm going to be here to watch."

Below, Sumey executed a particularly quick turn and counter, smashing Maylien's blade so hard that I fully expected it to snap on the spot. But somehow Maylien managed to flow with the blow, throwing herself sideways into a cartwheel and saving her sword.

"What in the world are you talking about, Devin? You're here with this and . . ." As I shook the blowgun, a long steel dart fell out of the end.

It hit the lead roof with a dull tinkle then started to roll away. Its end was heavily coated with something dark and sticky, manticore venom by the green undertones. What the hell . . . ?

"That's not for Maylien," I said. "You'd never be able to hide something that blatant from the witnesses. Who are you here to kill? And why?"

"Just watch the duel, Aral. If your Maylien is good enough, maybe you'll get to find out."

"Sumey? Deem? Fei?"

"Just watch."

Another minute went past, and I could see that Maylien was tiring. If she didn't pull a trick out of her bag, she was going to die soon. And there was nothing I could do about it without breaking my promise and throwing away everything she was fighting for. Another pass, and another. She had to—Oh, beautiful!

Rather than parrying her sister's blow, Maylien had thrown herself flat on the ground, feet toward Sumey. It wasn't the first time that she'd dodged rather than parry, but it was the first time since the earliest moments of the duel that she'd moved in tight with her sister instead of out and away. When Sumey shifted to follow the expected move back and away, she stepped right into a scissors kick that took her at knee and shin.

Sumey landed flat on her belly at right angles to her sister, with her sword momentarily trapped on the wrong side of her body. She was wide open to Maylien's slithering thrust. It was a beautiful blow, driving deep between Sumey's ribs, up and in, straight into the heart. Sumey died instantly. You could tell by the lack of blood flowing out of the wound that her heart had stopped pumping. I relaxed, though I didn't remove my blade from Devin's neck.

Below, Fei rose and started toward the fallen sisters. "I think that about does it."

"So much for your mind games, Devin," I said. "Now let's . . ."

Sumey moved. It was impossible. Maylien's blade transfixed her heart, but she was getting up anyway. And still the blood didn't flow.

"I told you to watch." Devin's voice sounded smug.

"What's the hell is going on here!" Captain Fei reared back and away from Sumey.

"I'm killing my sister." Sumey rose onto hands and knees. "And you're going to witness it for the crown like a good little pet if you know what's good for you."

And now I had a pretty good idea who the dart had been for.

Reaching back with her left hand, Sumey caught Maylien's sword between her fingers and casually snapped it off where it emerged from her rib cage.

22

I couldn't force what was happening below to make sense. Sumey Dan Marchon had taken a thrust to the heart and simply shrugged it off. Even now, she was calmly rising to her feet despite the length of Zhani steel sticking out of her side. I was totally unprepared for the current turn of events.

I didn't realize Devin had been counting on it and the distraction it would provide until I felt him smack my dagger away from his neck. Before I could do anything to regain my advantage, Devin gave a hard kick that sent us both spilling over the edge of the roof and tumbling into space some five stories above the ground. Through my connection to Triss, I tried desperately to form a shadow sail. He was less than halfway through the transition when we slammed into a narrow fourth-floor balcony.

I landed on my back, with Devin on top of me, both of us having shed our enshrouding shadows along the way. He took advantage of the shock and the impact to smash my wrist against the marble railing. Pain ripped through my arm, and my dagger tumbled away into the air beyond the balcony.

Devin popped up into a crouch, drawing a long knife as he pivoted to face me. "And now, I'm going to kill you."

If he'd acted immediately, he might well have managed it. I was still stunned, and though I had released Triss to his own recognizance, he hadn't yet manifested himself in any significant way. But whether Devin had the same problem killing an old friend that I'd had, or he wanted to gloat first, or was prevented by Zass, or whatever, I couldn't say. All I know is he hesitated and lost the moment.

"Assassins! Assassins on the balcony!" It was Sumey's voice as clear and strong as ever. "Deem, Blades, kill them!"

Her cry was answered by the deep grating howl of a stone dog and a great chain of green fire lashing along the marble posts of the railing. Heat licked through the gaps, chewing at the right side of my body. I felt pain shock through Triss as parts of my shirt started to smolder, but Devin caught it much worse. The top of his head was above the protection of the railing. He screamed wildly and dropped his knife to slap at his scalp when his hair burst into sudden flame.

I kicked him in the chest, sending him backward into the side railing. It saved his life as a second chain of fire lashed vertically through the place he'd just been, wrapping over the edge of the railing and burning across my shins. It hurt like nobody's business, but my boots took the worst of it, and I wasn't badly crisped. I scooted back into the corner of the balcony, where there was more cover, while Devin did the same opposite me.

Our swords came out in the same instant, his left, my right. Before either of us could make a move toward the other, his shadow shifted, twisting into the shape of a tayra and sliding onto the floor between us.

"Truce!" cried the ferret-wolf. "Truce until the Elite is dead. It's our only chance."

"Done," said the dragon that suddenly appeared to sniff noses with the tayra. "The stone dog will be here in seconds."

Then both shadows flowed to the railing side of the balcony, weaving a shining curtain of magic between them that deflected the next fall of Deem's lash. Devin clenched his jaw so tight I thought his teeth might shatter, and he glared at me as if daring me to argue.

Since I figured it would piss him off even more, I smiled, mustered my cheeriest voice, and said, "It's always good to know who's the boss. So, what's the plan?"

We weren't exactly in the best tactical position I'd ever occupied. The wooden doors and window that led from our balcony into the house were burning madly, as was the room beyond. That only left down or up. Both directions posed problems.

"I got the damned dog last time," said Devin. "It's your turn." Then, as the stone dog's head came up through the floor of the balcony, Devin did a neat backflip over the railing behind him.

I shouted, "You're the one with the magic swords, asshole!"

But he was already gone, and the stone dog seemed to agree with him as to who got to fight whom, turning a snarling glare on me as its front legs emerged from the stone. But terror is a wonderful driver of inspiration, and I jumped straight out of my crouch and up onto the railing.

That left me exposed to another blast from Deem, but I figured he wouldn't take the risk of hitting his familiar. It was only as I leaped from there to catch the edge of the roof above that it occurred to me that the damn dog might be proof against its master's magical fire. But Deem didn't fry me just then, and my plan moved to phase two.

The dog was fully up and through the balcony now. It leaped after me, which was actually what I'd counted on. As a great stone paw swiped at my legs, I pulled my feet up bare inches above the swing. Long claws sank deep into the stone wall below me, and I planted both boots on the back of its paw before it could move again, using that momentary footing to launch myself the rest of the way onto the roof.

The dog came after me, charging up the limestone wall as easily as a squirrel might run up a tree. I took three long steps. Then, just as the stone dog came up over the lip of the roof, I let myself fall forward as if I'd tripped. Landing on palms and toe tips, I could feel the roof already starting to warm from the magically generated fire below.

"Triss, joist!" I slid my right hand over a seam in the lead roof to guide him.

The dog pounced, and I pushed off with my right hand, rolling madly away. In that same moment, Triss released a blast of pure magical force focused on the thick joist running beneath the seam in the lead. It shattered one of the main supports for the patch of roof where I'd just been. Combine that with the fire beneath, and there was never a chance it would stand up to the incredible impact of a thousand-pound dog trying to crush a man.

The stone dog went straight through into the fire below while I reversed course, spreading my arms as I leaped off the roof. Time to join Devin in going after Deem. The colonel was by far the more fragile link in the Elite partnership. Triss made wings of my arms, though much narrower than usual, and we went down *fast*! After our last experience sail-jumping around the colonel, I couldn't blame him for the caution.

I used our abbreviated hang time to take quick stock of the situation below. The garden was in total pandemonium. The guards and servants had scattered, variously running for the house, the hills, or the koi pond—presumably to get buckets of water to throw on the rapidly spreading fire. Maylien, who only had about two-thirds of a sword left, was dodging in and out between the hedges and larger bits of sculpture to avoid closing with her sister again. She didn't look happy, but I was pretty sure she'd be all right on her own for a few more minutes.

Devin, on the other hand, was in real trouble. He was unshrouded and fighting against both Fei and Deem. The latter was using his free hand to hurl short bursts of mage-lightning at Devin every few seconds. That forced Zass to focus all his energy on magical defense and explained why Devin hadn't shadowed up.

I lost track of things for a few moments then as I hit

bottom and had to go straight into a series of diving rolls to bleed off the extra speed from our precipitous descent. As soon as I was up, I drew my second sword and dashed toward the whirling knot of steel and magic that was the Deem-Fei-Devin fight.

"Aral!" Maylien yelled from somewhere off to my left. "I could use some help here! Call Bontrang, dammit!"

I mentally kicked myself. We'd prearranged a signal with Heyin to release the gryphinx in case of treachery, and I'd forgotten all about it until then.

I made a half turn to orient myself properly and pointed my swords skyward. "Triss, now!"

He flowed over the blades, momentarily masking them in shadow, and together we sent a great V of magelightning up into the clear morning air, brilliant green so there would be no mistaking the intent. Then I turned back toward the more urgent problem. I'd taken barely two steps before I heard a tremendous crash from above and behind me.

I glanced up in time to see a huge horizontal pillar of flame extend itself from a gaping hole in the Marchon House. The stone dog led the fire like the head of a comet, dropping out and down from the doors it had just shattered. It didn't look any the worse for wear and was already bunching its legs for landing. While the few remaining servants finally bolted, I mentally calculated angles and distances. The dog was going to land in front of me and much closer to Devin and Deem. There was no way I could get to them before it did.

I still had to try. But before I'd gone two steps, Zass let out a horrible hissing screech and Devin went down hard, falling flat on his back. The stone dog landed with a noise like a building coming down, plunging deep into the ground and vanishing under the surface. Fei and Deem both moved in on Devin.

They were going to kill him, and then me. Sumey would kill Maylien. It would all be over, and there was nothing I could do about it because I was too damn far away at the critical moment. But then a mad idea occurred to me.

With a rolling snap of elbows and shoulders I disarmed myself, throwing both of my swords at Deem's back as I continued to run forward. Magic never would have worked; the colonel was too wrapped around with spells of protection for me to unravel them all in the time I had, and I simply didn't have anything else to try. Master Kelos was probably rolling in his grave at the very idea—he'd given us enough lectures about the uncertainty involved in throwing even a knife in anything but a distraction tactic. A sword thrown to kill was the ultimate fool's bet. Doubly so in this case since I hadn't ever practiced the trick with these blades.

But sometimes even fools win. My left-hand sword hit Deem high in the side, but it had underrotated, coming in more like a slice than a stab and it bounced off without seriously hurting him. The right-hand blade, on the other hand, sank a foot and a half into the colonel's back, right at kidney height, and he fell forward, fouling Fei's thrust at Devin.

A moment later, Fei was leaping backward, with blood sheeting down over her sword hand from a nasty slash on her forearm. Deem was lying flat on his belly, unmoving. And Devin had rolled over and up onto his feet, though his left leg was also covered in blood, and he had to move by hopping. The stone dog hadn't yet resurfaced, and now Devin made sure it never would by beheading its fallen master. I crossed the last of the distance to Deem's corpse in a mad dash and retrieved my swords. I was exhausted, but I still had Devin, Fei, and Sumey to manage and no idea what to do about any of them.

I pointed one sword each at Devin and Fei. "All right, we need to stop—"

I was interrupted by a piercing scream from the direction I'd last seen Maylien heading. But then she let out a wild string of profanity, and I knew she was still in the fight. In fact, it sounded like she was coming back our way.

"I think your girlfriend's about to die, Aral," said Devin. "Don't you think you should go do something about that?"

"What *is* Sumey?" I demanded. "Tell me right now, or I'll kill you, right now."

The shadow of a dragon fell on the ground between us. "I'll help."

"Killing me won't save her. You know that, right?" Devin smiled, though I could see it cost him. "You can probably beat me right now, but it'll take time you don't have." In addition to the deep gash in his left thigh, he had numerous minor cuts and a truly ugly band of blisters running across his brow and up into the charred remnants of his hair. "But I might be willing to cut a deal. I want to walk away from this."

I glanced from Devin to Fei, wondering what she thought of all this. I really didn't want to kill her, but I wasn't sure I was going to have any other options. When my eyes met hers, her nostrils flared, and she gave a faint shake of her head, opening her wounded hand—she'd shifted her sword to her uninjured side.

"I've got nothing, Aral." Then, as if she couldn't help herself Fei asked, "You're the Kingslayer, aren't you?"

"He is that, honey," Devin said with a sneer. "Pride of fucking Namara."

I moved without thinking, lunging at Devin, one sword going for an eye, the other for his groin. His double parry was slow and wouldn't have saved him, if he hadn't leaped backward at the same time. But he'd forgotten his wounded leg, and he went down on his back when it folded under him.

"Here's the only fucking deal you're going to get, Devin. You tell me what Sumey is in the next ten seconds, and I don't kill you for the next ten seconds."

"Fuck you." He raised his swords, and I wanted to cry because he was right.

I *didn't* have time for this. I could kill Devin, but not easily and certainly not quickly. Even wounded and on his back, he could cost me minutes I didn't dare waste.

"I'll help," said Fei, raising her sword to point at Devin. "We can work out our own deal later."

Maylien suddenly came into view, emerging from behind a bit of hedge maybe a score of yards beyond Devin. She was limping badly, and covered in blood and mud from the ring and garden. She'd lost her sword somewhere along the line and she had an unconscious Bontrang clutched against her side. She saw us and started in our direction.

Sumey followed her out from behind the hedge. She was walking slow and steady, her sword held casually in front of her. If it weren't for the gleaming steel stub sticking out from between her ribs, I'd never have known she'd been stabbed. Where the hell was the blood? She should be covered in the stuff. And then I had it.

"She's one of the risen, isn't she?"

I didn't realize I'd spoken aloud until Devin answered me. "She is that. Give the man his prize. Not that knowing it is going to do you a damn bit of good. You can't kill her—"

But I was already ahead of him, and I interrupted. "Not with these swords maybe, but with one of Namara's . . ." I pointed one of mine at one of his. "Looks like you get to live, Devin. I'll trade you one of my swords and your life for one of yours if you hand it over right now. I'll even give it back to you once I'm done. Oath to Namara."

"Deal." He flipped his left-hand sword around to offer me the hilt.

I dropped one of mine at his side and took it. Sumey and Maylien were barely twenty feet away, and I started toward them. Devin laughed.

"What's so funny?" I asked.

"It won't work. I was about to tell you that when you cut me off. I've already stabbed her through the heart with that very same blade. I did it right after the bitch burned the Old Mews down to hide her plans to eventually betray me. She just smiled and asked if we still had a deal. What could I say? Namara's dead, Aral, and her magic with her."

"She may be as dead as your soul, Devin. But I'm not." I dashed forward, putting myself between Maylien and her sister. "Sumey!"

The risen looked up at me, a cold dead smile curling her lips. "Yes?"

"This ends here and now."

"Yes," she said. "It does. Take your best shot." She dropped her sword to her side and laughed. "Then I'll take mine."

I lunged forward and drove Devin's goddess-made sword straight between Sumey's breasts. It was a futile gesture, and I knew it was a futile gesture. But Sumey, with her torture chambers and her cruelty and her contempt, was everything the goddess had ever stood against, everything I had ever stood against. I couldn't not try.

The sword went home to the hilt and Sumey smiled at me. She opened her mouth to speak, but all that came out was a sort of sigh that might have contained the word "Namara." For an instant, I thought I felt something like fingers touching my forehead in the ghost of a benediction. Sumey's expression twisted from contempt to hatred as her body went limp, and she slumped slowly to the ground. For a few long seconds she glared hate at me. Then the animating will left her body, and she died.

"I don't understand," Devin said, as I withdrew the sword from Sumey's chest. "That's the same damn thrust I made."

I turned and walked over to where he lay. "Here's your sword."

Only it wasn't his. It hadn't been his in years. It was ever and always Namara's. And maybe, just for a few seconds, it had been mine.

"How did you do that?" Devin demanded, without taking the offered hilt.

"*I* didn't."

"Namara's dead, Aral. Dead. Dead. Dead."

And suddenly I pitied him. "Somewhere along the line you lost sight of the one thing that really mattered, didn't you, Devin? The Emperor of Heaven may have killed Namara, but no one can ever kill Justice."

I dropped the sword at his feet. I didn't need it, and maybe, just maybe, it would help him find his way. It was all I could do for him, or to him, for that matter. Then I turned my attention to Maylien and Fei. The latter was binding a strip of clean red fabric around a deep burn in the former's arm. Triss put himself between me and Devin in dragon shape, guarding my back.

"What happened?" I asked Maylien.

"Sumey clawed my arm, and I burned the wound clean because I'd realized what she was by then. The backlash of the pain is what knocked Bontrang out."

I put an arm around Maylien's waist and gave her a squeeze. "You all right?" She squeezed me back and nodded.

"I will be once Bontrang comes around. It hit him pretty hard, but I can feel him starting to wake up now. What are we going to do about . . ." She indicated Captain Fei with her chin.

"The simplest answer would be for me to kill you, Captain. You know that, right?"

Fei shook her head and put away her sword. "I don't think so, Aral. If you really wanted me dead, we wouldn't be talking. No, the way I see it, you need at least one live official witness prepared to swear that Maylien here delivered the duel's killing blow in a completely legal and magic-free manner."

"That would certainly make things easier," I said. "Maybe we need to make an arrangement."

"Arrangement is practically my middle name," said Fei. "Tell me what you want, and we'll talk."

"Two things. Maylien takes Marchon."

"Of course."

"Aral Kingslayer was never here."

Fei smiled. "As far as I know, Aral Kingslayer hasn't been seen or heard from since the fall of Namara's temple."

"And in exchange?" I asked.

"Oh, all kinds of things. For starters, Marchon's a rich barony, and I'm a poor civil servant."

Maylien nodded. "I'm sure we can manage a big donation to Captain Fei's fund for the betterment of Captain Fei. What else?"

"Well," Fei said to me, "you know the kinds of things I get up to. I'm sure you'll be very helpful with all sorts of jobs in the future. Take for example the matter of . . . no." She glanced meaningfully at Devin, who'd just gotten to his feet and shook her head. "Let's talk about this later, in private. Suffice it to say that you owe me nine-and-ninety kinds of favors, and we've got a deal." She sniffed, then turned her head toward the burning wing of the house. "Smoky. Shouldn't you two be doing something about that fire?"

"Yes," said Maylien, "probably, though I have no idea what. I suspect we'll lose the whole wing though I can hope the fire wards will protect the main building."

That's when Heyin and his people came running up the carriageway. Maylien hurried to meet them while Devin began to limp away. I started after Maylien.

Out of the corner of my eye I caught the shadow of a tayra touching noses with the shadow of a dragon. Then the tayra sadly bowed its shoulders, and the dragon fell in behind me.

Epilogue

I paused at the edge of the orange grove and drew aside the curtain of shadow that covered my face. I wanted a better look at the third-floor balcony and my goal. The moon was high and near to full, providing a clear view. The climb was easy enough, but the dense thicket of imperial roses I had to pass through to get to the wall made for a painful obstacle. Sadly, in the first clutches of fall, they were long past their blooming season, which would have provided some small recompense for the blood I'd lose slipping through them.

I crossed the open ground to the roses fast and low, staying hidden within Triss's enshrouding presence. Then I worked my way quietly through the wall of thorns to the corner of the building. From there it was easy enough to climb to the level of the second-floor windows and use them to make my way across to the balcony. A short jump got me from there to the railing. Over and down into the shadow of a planter, and I was in position. Now it was just a matter of waiting.

And not long either. I couldn't have been there more than

a quarter of an hour when the door from the house opened.
Two footmen came out carrying a tray and some cushions,
quickly moving to the small marble table that sat within the
shadow of the arbor. They put two glasses and two plates
on the table along with a lamp and a variety of decanters
and small covered dishes. They arranged cushions on three
of the four chairs. They wore red shirts and pants, as was
the current fashion for servants, as well as slightly baffled
expressions, which were always in fashion for anyone who
had to deal with the whims of the nobility.

Once the table was set, they withdrew into the house,
leaving the door open behind them. The Baroness Marchon
came out a moment later. She was tall and athletic, with long
dark hair drawn back in a braid and a wicked smile I knew
well. She had a little gryphinx perched on her shoulder.

"Aral"—she sat down at the table—"come, sit down. Talk
to me."

I let the shadow covering Triss had provided fall away,
then crossed the marble tiles to take the second seat. A
dragon's shadow curled up in the third and was soon joined
by Bontrang. Maylien poured me a small glass of Kyle's, an
eighteen and cask-strength. Triss made a tsking noise but
didn't insert himself any further into the conversation. He
approved of Maylien if not the drink.

"It's good to see you," I said.

"You, too; I'm glad you agreed to come this time. You
haven't answered my last couple of invites."

"I've been out of town, trying to find out more about the
risen and when your sister might have succumbed to the
curse. That satisfies curiosity and necessity both since I'm
trying to lie low at the moment. I'm going to have trouble
with Fei sooner or later, and I figure if I keep myself out of
her sight as much as possible, that will help. Besides, Heyin
was here, and I know it gives him hives when you see me,
so waiting for him to return to Marchon seemed prudent."

"You might have a point there." Maylien nodded. "Speaking of Fei and curiosity, there's something I've been wondering about the good captain."

"What's that?"

"Why was she so willing to cut a deal? She works for the king, and you're pretty much at the top of his most-wanted list."

"She doesn't actually," I said.

"What?"

"Work for Thauvik. Fei works for Fei first and Tien second. The king and the law don't even enter into it. Besides, she owed me one."

"You just lost me again."

"That poison dart Devin had prepped. It was for Fei, in case Sumey was revealed and Sumey and Deem couldn't get Fei to play ball. At least I'm pretty sure that's what it was for."

"But Fei didn't know about the dart, not when we first started talking deal anyway."

"No, but she knew by then what Sumey was and that she had owned both Deem and Devin. It's not a long jump from there to realizing that Fei's own survival odds went way up when things came out as they did. Even if Fei'd agreed to a deal with Sumey, she'd have had a target on her back afterward, and she knew that. Also, you'll note, I made a point to mention the dart later."

"Well, maybe." She shrugged. "While you were away, did you find out anything more about Sumey's plans?"

"Her plans, no. But I've learned more about the risen than I ever wanted to, and I know how she managed to keep herself looking healthy and normal all this time. Remember that big marble tub in that torture chamber in Marchon?"

"That was really creepy."

"More than you know. She used it for bathing. In blood. Apparently, the blood of the living can keep the risen from decaying if it's good and fresh and they soak in it often enough. It's how she kept her looks and her mind."

"That's horrible."

I nodded. "What about you? Have you found anything here at the house?"

Maylien nodded and lifted the cover on one of the larger plates. There was a narrow scroll on it.

"This was in a stone casket inside a hidden vault in the wine cellar. It was behind a rack of my mother's favorite reds. There were some other things in there that made it pretty clear Sumey has been using it in the years since my mother died, so she knew about it."

"What is it?"

Maylien looked away from me. "It's a proclamation legitimizing Sumey and me. Ashvik made the two of us his legal heirs. Now that I've reclaimed my birthright by taking Marchon, that document means that the throne ought to have gone to me. It's dated a few days before you killed Ashvik, and I suspect that its existence is why my mother sent us into hiding. She didn't want us to follow our half brothers to the headsman's block. I think the real reason Sumey hired Devin was to help her kill Thauvik and make her Queen of Zhan."

I whistled. "That would certainly explain a few things."

Maylien didn't say anything, and I realized there were tears on her cheeks.

"What's wrong?" I put a hand on her shoulder.

"Do you remember that first night we spent together, sleeping by the campfire? When Heyin interrupted us in the morning."

"Of course. What about it?"

"Do you remember all those things I said about why I had to oust Sumey? About how every horrible thing Sumey did was my responsibility because the barony was mine by right?"

"I do."

She was crying openly now. "It's all still true with Thauvik. My uncle is a bad man and a bad king. Not as awful as my sister or my father, to be sure, but not good, and he's getting worse all the time. And every damned evil thing he does is being done from a throne that was supposed to go to me."

"What are you saying?"

"That I have to take the throne or accept all the evil my uncle does as my own." Now she looked up and met my eyes and there was steel in her gaze. "I don't want to have to do this, but I have no choice. Will you help me remove Thauvik from the throne?"

I have to admit that I thought about it. The temptation I'd experienced at Sumey's keep was still there. The temptation to let Maylien take the place of Namara as my personal goddess, to become an instrument for someone else's hand and let her make all the hard decisions. But I'd only just started to find out who Aral the jack could be. Who *I* could be if I let the Kingslayer go and became my own man once and for all.

I couldn't let myself be drawn into Maylien's sphere. Not yet. Maybe not ever. It'd be almost as bad for me as crawling into the bottle of Kyle's sitting there on the table and pulling the cork in behind me once again.

"No," I said. "I won't. I just . . . can't. Not as I am now." I was Aral the jack now; Aral Kingslayer was as dead as the goddess that made him, and I needed to finally bury my dead. "I'm sorry. Triss, come on. We're going."

Maylien didn't say another word. Not until I'd reached the edge of the balcony.

"Aral?" Her voice was low, quiet, hurting.

"Yes." I didn't turn back, but I did stop. I owed her that for helping me put my feet on the right path once again.

"I'm sorry, too. I thought that would be your answer, but I had to ask." Her voice dropped even lower. "You do understand, don't you?"

I nodded. "I know you did."

"I have one more thing I have to ask you."

"What is it?" I said through a throat gone suddenly tight. I didn't know what she wanted, but I knew from the sound of her voice that I wasn't going to like it.

"I know you won't kill my uncle for me, and I don't blame you. Truly, I don't. This isn't your fight. But I *will* be queen someday." She said that hard and fast, and I knew she meant it. "I have no other choice, but it terrifies me, too. What if it's the power that does this to my family? What if I'm going to become my sister all over again, or worse, my father? Not the risen part—there's been no evidence of the curse since I burned out the wound—but the slow slide into evil." She paused, and I could tell that she was crying again. "I think you love me, at least a little."

"I do." That's more than half of the reason I had to leave her now, because loving her would make it that much easier to give myself into her keeping. To surrender the chance to find out what I could be on my own.

"Good. Because I want you to do something for me." Her voice changed again, becoming firm, almost cold. The voice of the queen to come. "If I become a monster, I want you to kill me. I won't live like that, and you're the only one who can stop me. Will you promise to do that for me?"

"Yes." And now I was the one who was crying.

"Thank you."

I didn't say "you're welcome," and I didn't look back, just jumped over the railing and glided to the ground. Then I walked home to the Gryphon and asked Jerik to get me a glass of Kyle's. A glass. Not a bottle. I couldn't kill another king for Maylien. That was still beyond me. But maybe, just maybe, I could do a little good here and there, save a life, rescue a hostage, stop a robbery. Bring a little justice to the world. Find out who Aral the jack really was. And if I wanted to do any of that, I had to be sober.

It wasn't much, but it was a start.

Terms and Characters

Alinthide Poisonhand—A master Blade, the third to die making an attempt on Ashvik VI.

Alley-Knocker—An illegal bar or cafe.

Anaryan, Earl of—A Zhani noble.

Anyang—Zhani city on the southern coast. Home of the winter palace.

Aral Kingslayer—Ex-Blade turned jack of the shadow trades.

Ashelia—A smuggler.

Ashvik VI or *Ashvik Dan Pridu*—Late King of Zhan, executed by Aral. Also known as the Butcher of Kadesh.

Athera Trinity—The three-faced goddess of fate.

Balor Lifending—God of the dead and the next Emperor of Heaven.

Black Jack—A professional killer or assassin.

Blade—Temple assassin of the goddess Namara.

Bontrang—A miniature gryphon.

Calren the Taleteller—God of beginnings and first Emperor of Heaven.

Caras Dust—Powerful magically bred stimulant.

Caras Snuffler—A caras addict.

Cat's Gratitude—An alley-knocker in Little Varya.

Channary Canal—Canal running from the base of the Channary Hill to the Zien River in Tien.

Channary Hill—One of the four great hills of Tien.

Chimney Forest—The city above, rooftops, etc.

Chimney Road—A path across the rooftops of a city. "Running the chimney road."

Coals—Particularly hot stolen goods.

Code Martial—Ancient system of Zhani law predating the conquerors who make up the current noble class of Zhan.

Cornerbright—Magical device for seeing around corners.

Crown Law—Zhan's modern legal system.

Dalridia—Kingdom in the southern Hurnic Mountains.

Dead Man's Purse, the—An alley-knocker in Little Varya.

Deathspark—A piece of magic that turns a human being into a trap triggered by his own death.

Deem, Colonel—An officer of the Elite.

Devin Urslan—A former Blade.

Downunders—A bad neighborhood in Tien.

Dragon Crown—The royal crown of Zhan, often replicated in insignia of Zhani crown agents.

Drum-Ringer—A bell enchanted to prevent eavesdropping.

Dustmen—Dealers in caras dust.

Eavesman—A spy or eavesdropper.

Elite, the—Zhani mages. They fulfill the roles of secret police and spy corps among other functions.

Emberman—A professional arsonist.

Erk Endfast—Owner of the Spinnerfish, ex–black jack, ex–shadow captain.

Everdark, the—The home dimension of the Shades.

Eyespy—A type of eavesdropping spell.

Face, Facing—Identity. "I'd faced myself as an Aveni bravo."

Fallback—A safe house.

Familiar Gift—The ability to soul-bond with another being, providing the focus half of the power/focus dichotomy necessary to become a mage.

Fire and sun!—A Shade curse.

Ghost, Ghosting—To kill.

Govana—Goddess of the herds.

Gryphon's Head—A tavern in Tien, the capital city of Zhan. Informal office for Aral.

Guttersiders—Slang for the professional beggars and their allies.

Hand of Heaven—The Son of Heaven's office of the inquisition.

Harad—Head librarian at the Ismere Library.

Hearsay—A type of eavesdropping spell.

Heyin—Lieutenant of the exiled Baroness Marchon.

Howler—Slang name for the Elite.

Imperial Bush Roses—Living security fencing.

Ismere Club—A private club for merchants.

Ismere Library—A private lending library in Tien, founded by a wealthy merchant from Kadesh.

Jack—A slang term for an unofficial or extragovernmental problem solver, see also "shadow jack," "black jack," "sunside jack."

Jax—A former Blade and onetime lover of Aral's.

Jenua, Duchy of—A duchy in Zhan.

Jerik—The bartender/owner of the Gryphon's Head tavern.

Jindu—Tienese martial art heavily weighted toward punches and kicks.

Kaelin Fei, Captain—Watch officer in charge of Tien's Silent Branch. Also known as the Mufflers.

Kaman—A former Blade, crucified by the Elite, then killed by Aral at his own request.

Kanathean Hill—One of the four great hills of Tien.

Kelos Deathwalker—A master Blade who taught Aral.

Kila—The spirit-dagger of the Blade, symbolizing the bond to Namara.

Kodamia—City-state to the west of Tien, controlling the only good pass through the Hurnic Mountains.

Kvanas, the Four—Group of interrelated kingdoms just north of Varya. Sometimes referred to as the Khanates.

Kyle's—An expensive Aveni whiskey.

Liess—A Shade, familiar of Sharl.

Little Varya—An immigrant neighborhood in Tien.

Lok—A hedge wizard with a spit-adder familiar, works for the Countess Marchon.

Loris—A former Blade.

Magearch—Title for the mage governor of the cities in the Magelands.

Mage gift—The ability to perform magic, providing the power half of the power/focus dichotomy necessary to become a mage.

Magelands—A loose confederation of city-states governed by the faculty of the mage colleges that center them.

Magelights—Relatively expensive permanent light globes made with magic.

Magesight—The ability to see magic, part of the mage gift.

Mage Wastes—Huge area of magically created wasteland on the western edge of the civilized lands.

Malthiss—A Shade, familiar of Kelos Deathwalker.

Manny Three Fingers—The cook at the Spinnerfish.

Manticore's Smile, the—An alley-knocker in Little Varya.

Marchon—A barony in the kingdom of Zhan. The house emblem is a seated jade fox on a gold background.

Maylien Dan Marchon Tal Pridu—A client of Aral's.

Mufflers—Captain Fei's organization, so known because they keep things quiet.

Namara—The now-deceased goddess of justice and the downtrodden, patroness of the Blades. Her symbol is an unblinking eye.

Nightghast—One of the restless dead, known to eat humans.

Night Market—The black market.

Nima—Mana, the stuff of magic.

Nipperkins—Magical vermin.

Noble Dragons—Elemental beings that usually take the form of giant lizardlike creatures.

Old Mews—An upscale neighborhood in Tien.

Olen—A master Blade who taught Aral.

Oris Plant—A common weed that can be used to produce a cheap gray dye or an expensive black one.

Others—The various nonhuman races.

Palace Hill—One of the four great hills of Tien.

Patiss—A Shade, familiar of Master Urayal.

Petty Dragons—Giant acid-spitting lizards, not to be confused with noble dragons.

Quink—Slang word, roughly: freak.

Rabbit Run—An emergency escape route.

Restless Dead—Catchall term for the undead.

Riel—Currency of Zhan, issued in both silver and gold.

Right of Challenge—Part of Zhan's old Code Martial.

Risen, the—A type of restless dead, similar to a zombie.

Sellcinders—A fence or dealer in hot merchandise.

Serak—A Rover, deceased lover of the young Maylien.

Serass—A Shade, familiar of Alinthide.

Shade—Familiar of the Blades, a living shadow.

Shadow Captain—A mob boss.

Shadow Jack—A jack who earns his living as a problem solver in the shadow trades.

Shadowside—The underworld or demimonde.

Shadow Trades—The various flavors of illegal activity.

Shadow World—The demimonde or underworld.

Shaisin—Small town in Zhan, baronial seat of Marchon.

Shan Starshoulders—The god who holds up the sky, current Emperor of Heaven.

Sheuth Glyph—A glyph for the binding of shadows.

Shrouding—When a Shade encloses his blade in shadow.

Siri Mythkiller—A former Blade.

Skip—A con game or other illegal job, also a "play."

Sleepwalker—An efik addict.

Slink—Magical vermin.

Smuggler's Rest—The unofficial name of the docks near the Spinnerfish.

Snug—A resting place or residence.

Son or Daughter of Heaven—The title of the chief priest or priestess who leads the combined religions of the eleven kingdoms.

Sovann Hill—One of the four great hills of Tien.

Spinnerfish, the—A shadowside tavern by the docks.

Stingers—Slang term for Tienese City Watch.

Stone Dog—A living statue, roughly the size of a small horse. The familiar of the Elite.

Straight-Back Jack—A shadow jack who gets the job done and keeps his promises.

Stumbles, the—Neighborhood of Tien that houses the Gryphon's Head tavern.

Sumey Dan Marchon Tal Pridu—Baroness Marchon and sister of Maylien.

Sunside—The shadowside term for more legitimate operations.

Sunside Jack—A jack who works aboveboard, similar to a modern detective.

Sylvani Empire—Sometimes called the Sylvain, a huge empire covering much of the southern half of the continent. Ruled by a nonhuman race, it is ancient, and hostile to the human lands of the north.

Tailor's Wynd—An upscale neighborhood in Tien.

Tangara—God of glyphs and runes and other magical writing.

Thauvik IV or *Thauvik Tal Pridu, the Bastard King*—King of Zhan and bastard half brother of the late Ashvik.

Thieveslamp/Thieveslight—A dim red magelight in a tiny bull's-eye lantern.

Tien—A coastal city, the thousand-year-old capital of Zhan.

Timesman—The keeper of the hours at the temple of Shan, Emperor of Heaven.

Travelers—A seminomadic order of mages dedicated to making the roads safe for all.

Triss—Aral's familiar. A Shade that inhabits Aral's shadow.

Tuckaside—A place to stash goods, usually stolen.

Tucker—Tucker bottle, a quarter-sized liquor bottle, suitable for two or for one heavy drinker.

Underhills—An upscale neighborhood in Tien.

Urayal—A Master Blade.

Vangzien—Zhani city at the confluence where the Vang River flows into the Zien River in the foothills of the Hurnic Mountains. Home of the summer palace.

Warboard—Chesslike game.

Wardblack—A custom-built magical rug that blocks the function of a specific ward.

Westbridge—A bridge over the Zien upriver from the palace, and the neighborhood around it.

Worrymoth—An herb believed to drive away moths.

Zass—A Shade, familiar of Devin.

Zhan—One of the eleven human kingdoms of the east. Home to the city of Tien.

Currency

Bronze Sixth Kip (sixer)
Bronze Kip
Bronze Shen
Silver Half Riel
Silver Riel
Gold Half Riel
Gold Riel
Gold Oriel

Value in Bronze Kips

~0.15 = Bronze Sixth Kip
1 = Bronze Kip
10 = Bronze Shen
60 = Silver Half Riel
120 = Silver Riel

Value in Silver Riels

0.5 = Silver Half Riel
1 = Silver Riel
5 = Gold Half Riel
10 = Gold Riel
50 = Gold Oriel

Calendar

———•———

(370 days in 11 months of 32 days each, plus two extra 9-day holiday weeks: Summer-Round in the middle of Midsummer, and Winter-Round between Darktide and Coldfast)

 1 *Coldfast*
 2 *Meltentide*
 3 *Greening*
 4 *Seedsdown*
 5 *Opening*
 6 *Midsummer*
 7 *Sunshammer*
 8 *Firstgrain*
 9 *Harvestide*
10 *Talewynd*
11 *Darktide*

Days of the Week

1. *Calrensday*—In the beginning.
2. *Atherasday*—Hearth and home.
3. *Durkothsday*—Holdover from the prehuman tale of days.
4. *Shansday*—The middle time.
5. *Namarsday*—Traditional day for nobles to sit in judgment.
6. *Sylvasday*—Holdover from the prehuman tale of days.
7. *Balorsday*—Day of the dead.
8. *Madensday*—The day of madness when no work is done.

Look for the next thrilling book
in the Fallen Blade series

BARED BLADE

by Kelly McCullough

Former temple assassin Aral Kingslayer is a man with a price on his head and a mark on his soul. After his goddess was murdered, Aral found refuge in the shadow jack business, fixing problems for those on the fringes of Tien's underworld. It's a long step down from working for the goddess of justice, but it gives Aral and Triss— the living shadow who is his secret partner—a reason to get up in the morning.

Unfortunately, it's not a very noble reason. So when two women hit a rough spot in the tavern Aral uses for an office, he and Triss decide to lend a helping hand. But soon their good deed lands them in the middle of a three-way battle to find an artifact that just might be the key to preventing a war. And with so many factions on their trail, Aral and Triss are attracting a lot more attention than anyone featured on ten thousand wanted posters can afford . . .

Now available from Ace Books